Critical Acclaim for

Northern Frights

"Don Hutchison is an editor who inspires writers to climb higher and reach farther. His *Northern Frights* series is bringing us some of the finest imaginative fiction being written today."

—Hugh B. Cave
World Fantasy Award winning author of *The Dawning*

"*Northern Frights* is Canada's best anthology series of any type..."

—Robert J. Sawyer
Nebula Award winning author of *Calculating God*

"What's notable about the books is editor Hutchison's shrewd eye and keen sense of taste. No story is included purely for the cheap thrill or its power to raise goosebumps. Rather, horror is handled like a finely honed scalpel to slice to the heart of our misgivings and fears about the ironies, mysteries and tragedies that worm their way into our lives."

—*The Toronto Star*

"Any self-respecting writer should be glad to appear in *Northern Frights* and every self-respecting reader should make sure he or she reads it."

—Edward Bryant in *Locus* magazine

Wild Things Live There

The Best of Northern Frights

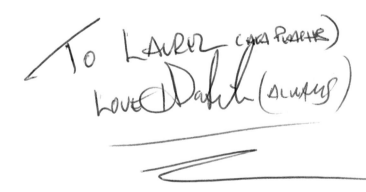

To LAUREL (aka PIRATER)
Love Don... (ALWAYS)

Wild Things Live There

The Best of Northern Frights

edited by Don Hutchison

mosaic press

National Library of Canada Cataloguing in Publication Data

Wild things live there: the best of Northern frights
A collection of 16 stories which were previously published in Northern
frights v. 1-5.

ISBN 0-88962-765-7
1. Horror tales, Canadian (English) 2. Canadian fiction (English) — 20th
century. I. Hutchison, Don

PS8323.S3W54 2001   C813'.0873808054   C2001-902923-3
PR9197.35.F35W54 2001

Published by MOSAIC PRESS, 1252 Speers Rd., Units 1 & 2, Oakville,
ON L6L 5N(, Canada and Mosaic Press, 4500 Witmer Industrial Estates,
PMB 145, Niagara Falls, NY 14305-1386

Mosaic Press acknowledges the assistance of the Canada Council and
the Department of Canadian Heritage, Government of Canada, for their
support of our publishing programme.

MOSAIC PRESS, in Canada:
1252 Speers Road, Units 1 & 2,
Oakville, Ontario
L6L 5N9
Phone/Fax: 905-825-2130
mosaicpress@on.aibn.com

MOSAIC PRESS, in U.S.A.:
4500 Witmer Industrial Estates
PMB 145, Niagara Falls, NY
14305-1386
Phone/Fax: 1-800-387-8992
mosaicpress@on.aibn.com

Le Conseil des Arts   The Canada Council
du Canada   for the Arts

Contents

photo by Michael Rowe

Don Hutchison, Toronto, Ontario.

Foreword

*W*ild Things Live There: The Best of Northern Frights is a tribute to the many authors who honored all five of the *Northern Frights* books with outstanding work. The idea behind the series was to present a showcase for dark fantasy stories either written by Canadians or set in Canada. As an antidote to cultural specialization, we challenged would-be contributors to produce fiction of exceptional merit regardless of geographic background. Were they able to meet those standards? You bet! Proof of their accomplishment lies in the fact that many of our previously unpublished authors have "graduated" to major short story markets, won prestigious awards, sold novels, and even edited their own anthologies. They have seen their *Northern Frights* stories reprinted in magazines and other anthologies, recorded as audio books, and optioned for motion pictures and television. Thanks to their efforts, the series itself has earned glowing reviews, numerous awards and award nominations, and gratifying recognition beyond our borders.

I would like to thank Howard Aster at Mosaic Press for undertaking the series and for his enthusiastic support over the years. Thanks also to artists Henry Van Der Linde, James Kroesen and Dale Sproule for their evocative cover illustrations. Many friends helped with their advice and encouragement, especially Bob Knowlton, Peter Halasz, Larry Hancock, and Kathy Johnson.

As we said last time out, you never know where a good story will take you. Although there's no substitute for actually getting away from it all, you can go a long way with a good book, a comfortable chair and a little imagination. Thanks for letting us be your tour guides through some scary and even challenging landscapes. We hope you enjoyed the trip.

Don Hutchison
Toronto, Ontario
September, 2001

Northern Frights
Award Winning Short Fiction

The Northern Frights Series, six volumes,
edited by Don Hutchison
published by Mosaic Press:

Northern Frights
ISBN 0-88962-514-X HC
Mosaic Press, 1992

Northern Frights 2
ISBN 0-88962-564-6 PB
Mosaic Press, 1994

Northern Frights 3
ISBN 0-88962-589-1 PB
Mosaic Press, 1995

Northern Frights 4
ISBN 0-88962-639-1 PB
Mosaic Press, 1997

Northern Frights 5
ISBN 0-88962-676-6 PB
Mosaic Press, 1999

Wild Things Live There:
The Best of Northern Frights
ISBN 0-88962-765-7
Mosaic Press, 2001

Introduction:
Last Walk on the
Night Side
by Michael Rowe

T he book you are holding in your hand represents more than just a collection of very fine horror stories, though most readers will be more than satisfied with that. For horror purists, who, like highly discerning oenophiles for whom the experience of drinking the best wine includes far more than a passing knowledge of the wine's vintage and provenance, the identifiably Canadian bouquet of these stories carries with it more than a hint of frozen black nights, more than a few oaken notes of vast, dim forests, or coffins, all shot through with shattering flashes of auroral blood-red and arctic white, the whole of it blazing against the velvet black expanse of the imagination. In spite (or perhaps because of) two dueling biases: the first, that horror fiction is not enhanced by a regional perspective, and the second, that Canadians by their very nature are too prissy for what could colloquially be called a "homegrown horror sensibility," Don Hutchison has wrested from the writers in this book an important cultural contribution to the Canadian literary body politic, opening a tributary from which a uniquely Canadian point of view on what makes the night move will flow into the bottomless, always shifting, ocean of horror literature, to be absorbed there among the best of the best.

MICHAEL ROWE

Some years back, in an essay on Canadian horror films in *The Scream Factory*, Robert Thomson and I described Canada as being "like vichyssoise: a familiar-looking food presented as oddly foreign, a little French, very cold, and very difficult to stir." We posited that the Canadian psyche is often constitutionally less well able to create — and enjoy — literature that isn't, well, *literature*, tending to pride itself on something it interprets as great art, or at least of significant cultural reach. Though I think that in many ways this description still holds water, at the dawn of the new century I think this is somewhat changed, especially when it comes to horror fiction and films. Canadian authors now compete for face-out shelf space with hot American and British horror authors; they win the Bram Stoker Award and the International Horror Guild Award, their stories and scripts are made into successful films, both in the cinema and on television. It would be difficult to overstate that the reason for this, the reason we have a "dark side" is Don Hutchison and the *Northern Frights* series of Canadian horror anthologies.

Ask yourself this, as I have on numerous occasions prior to meeting Don Hutchison, and afterwards: What kind of imagination, not to mention moxie, would it have taken in 1992 to approach a publisher with an idea for a horror anthology featuring stories that were exclusively Canadian, either in content or nationality of the author? And there would be no quarter or concession given to (nudge, nudge, wink, wink) "spoof" horror stories, the kind of ironic *belles lettres* that stiffs write when they can't quite bring themselves to get down and dirty with the horror, to write stories that *scare* people. Hutchison collected an inaugural volume of jewel-like tales from some very fine writers, ranging from newcomers to some of the finest practitioners of the art. For the first time in the history of speculative fiction, Canada — geographically and culturally — was forefront in the sightlines of serious readers and critics in the genre. Established writers like Garfield Reeves-Stevens, Rick Hautala, and superstar Charles L. Grant, settled comfortably next to relative newcomers like Edo van Belkom and David Nickle, (who would go on to win the Bram Stoker Award for a later collaboration), and Gemma Files (who won the International Horror Guild Award for her story, "The Emperor's Old Bones," which appeared in *Northern Frights 5*). Most significantly, from a marketing point of view, the series smashed the established publishing truism that setting a story in *Canada* (ancestral seat of Anne of Green Gables and Farley Mowatt's adventures in Saskatchewan and various other tundras) was the kiss of death for horror fiction. *Northern Frights* proved that, under the pen of a skilled writer, the moonswept wilderness of the Canadian subconscious was as wolf-haunted and blasted as that of any other. Many fine horror writers since then (some of them *Northern Frights* alumni) have gone on to publish mainstream horror novels and short story collections set squarely in Canada, something that would have been unlikely in the days prior to the series, when there would have been consequential pressure placed upon writers to mask the streets of our cities and provinces with American flags, taxi cabs, locations, and dialects.

The series was — and remains — a testament to the power of talent and uncompromising commitment to excellence, and a skilled and seamless collaboration between editor and writer. After having been nominated for both the World Fantasy Award and the Aurora Award (which Hutchison won, twice), any Editor would have been well within his rights to bypass the dreaded "slush pile," electing to work on a by-invitation-only basis. Fortunately for many previously unpublished writers, Hutchison continued to determinedly sift through an impressive pile of cold-call submissions, dedicated to the notion that there was gold in these hills of paper and nightmares. The fact of the matter is simple and incontestable: the existence of horror fiction in Canada, and its acceptance on the world's stage, is owed to Don Hutchison and the *Northern Frights* series

Horror is personal, and so are the beginnings of friendships and collaborations between writers and editors. In the summer of 1992, I studied writing at Harvard under the aegis of several writers and editors. One of them was Kathryn Cramer, who taught a course in horror and fantasy writing. My story, "Wild Things Live There," was written that summer as part of the course work. Although I was already a widely published working writer at that point, I had never thought of horror writing even though horror was (and always has been) my first literary love. The story lay in my files for a couple of years until I was writing my first book, a collection of interviews with erotica writers. During the course of the interviews, I met and made friends with Nancy Kilpatrick, a horror writer who was also an erotica writer. She had appeared in two volumes of the *Northern Frights* series and I casually asked her if there was to be a third volume. She said there was, but she wasn't sure Hutchison was reading for it any longer. She offered to call him and find out, an offer I readily accepted. When the word came through that he was still looking at submissions, I immediately dug out "Wild Things Live There," dusted it off, and took a cab up to Hutchison's house to deliver it in person. His wife, Jean, met me at the door and promised to see that he would get it. I thanked her and returned home. The phone was ringing as I walked through the door, with the news that he liked the story, and wanted to publish it in *Northern Frights 3*. I was ecstatic. We met for lunch a few weeks later, and that was the beginning of a mutually rewarding and exceptionally close friendship. The rest, as we say, is history. "Wild Things Live There" was eventually given an Honourable Mention in *The Year's Best Fantasy and Horror*, and was optioned for the movies. More importantly, though, to me as a writer, seeing *Northern Frights 3* face-out of the bookshelf at The World's Biggest Bookstore, opening the book, with its vivid Henry Van Der Linde cover illustration of a vampire rising from its grave, all dark green and black, and turning to my first published horror story there on page one, remains one of the seminal moments of my entire career, right up there with my first publication, my first book contract, my first National Magazine Award nomination, and my first great review.

Horror *is* personal, and as one of the writers whose first horror story was published in the *Northern Frights* series, it is a daunting and humbling honour to have been asked to write the Introduction to this last book in the series, and one which I approach with a profound and bittersweet sense of graduation. When a series comes to the "best of" stage, that means that it has run its course, and the time is at hand to celebrate the good times we've all had together, the joy of having been part of something important (although occasionally imitated) and final. The years bracketing the appearance of *Northern Frights* and *The Best of Northern Frights* were special for all of us associated with the series. Many of the writers you will read here launched their careers in *Northern Frights*, and the luckiest of us will remember what it felt like to work with an editor as deft and elegant as Don Hutchison. Let other, lesser talents stand on soapboxes, shrilly proclaiming their importance to anyone they can seduce into listening. Hutchison hasn't ever been about that, and neither has this anthology series. The stories here all stand on their own merits, and have been judged and rewarded accordingly.

There is a word used to describe editors like Don Hutchison that has sadly gone out of fashion in this brash age of websites and writers-as-rock-stars, where celebrity for its own sake overrides anything as pedestrian as *quality*, or the ability to move a reader through any number of emotions, from joy to terror. The word is *gentleman*. It connotes grace, quiet, courtesy, without self-aggrandizement or hubris, with no compromise permitted when it comes to the quality of the work. To have worked with Don on the *Northern Frights* series is to have seen this first hand, and for those of use who have elected to pursue editing our own anthologies, it provided a template for how to treat writers, and how to coax from those writers the kind of stories that readers would respect, and thrill to. As writers, working with him allowed us to shine, secure in the knowledge that none of us would be allowed to do anything but our best for this series.

Daunting, but satisfying? Hell, yes. Bring it on.

The work, for its part, speaks for itself. Here is the best of it. Enjoy our walk on the night side, and remember that wild things live here, so watch yourselves.

Michael Rowe
Toronto and Chandos Lake, Ontario
Summer, 2001

The Eddies

by Garfield Reeves-Stevens

As a team, ex-Torontonians Garfield Reeves-Stevens and his wife Judith are Emmy-nominated scriptwriters, New York Times *best-selling novelists, and the popular authors of numerous Star Trek books. On his own, Garfield Reeves-Stevens is the author of five thriller novels combining elements of science fiction and dark fantasy, leading him to be dubbed "the Tom Clancy of horror" by no less an authority than Stephen King.*

Gar's melding of scientific extrapolation with supernatural terror has seldom been as impressive as in this high-voltage ghost story written for Northern Frights 2. *"The Eddies" was one of three stories chosen from that volume to be reprinted in Karl Wagner's* Year's Best Horror Stories *for DAW Books. Sadly, the series was terminated before this story could be so honored. We are pleased to draw your attention to it now.*

Billy jumped back as if he thought the clown were trying to kill him. Billy had never seen the clown before, but I had. She's been a fixture of the city for more than twenty years, ever since they broke ground for the CN Tower. Maybe even longer than that, now that I think about it.

If you've been to Toronto, downtown, around the SkyDome, the Convention Centre, any of the roads or walkways that lead to the Tower, then you've seen her, too. Think hard. She's a short, round woman with gray curls flattened under an old Toronto Blue Jays baseball cap, always in a bright yellow waistcoat that looks green with grime when you get up close. Then there's the tattered toy monkey with the long arms wrapped around her neck. At least, you think it's a toy. And the bulging pockets filled with the balloons she twists into animals for the children brave enough to come near. And the signs — she always carries a sign and you've at least seen one of those. Tall, thin, precisely printed letters, blue or black marker on white or yellow bristol board. Most of the letters are too small and too tight for anyone to read, but there are always a few words printed large enough that you can see them, even speeding past on Lakeshore Boulevard, thinking of getting home at the end of a long day.

The big letters always spell out a warning about the CN Tower that's both important and meaningless. *Don't go! Affront to Heaven!! Remember Wardenclyffe!* And she waves at you with a happy smile as you drive by.

That's right, now you remember her.

The day I took Billy to the CN Tower for the first and last time, her sign read, *Tesla's Truths Revealed!* Some of the tightly spaced letters on the tattered white cardboard looked like they spelled out equations but I didn't pay attention. Billy was crying. The clown had scared him when she had stepped in front of us on the outdoor walkway and I was annoyed. The last thing I wanted to do was send my five-year-old son back to his mother in Calgary with tales of a terrible summer visit.

The clown behaved as if Billy were laughing, though. She smiled at him with teeth the color of her waistcoat and reached into a pocket for a fistful of limp balloons that flopped in her hand like dead worms. "That's a good little fella," she said, then she stuck a balloon between her teeth, stretched it out and blew it up with one endless-seeming puff. I picked up Billy and he cradled against me.

Watching the giraffe take shape in the clown's quick hands, I didn't think that I was prolonging Billy's terror by keeping him close to the person who had frightened him. Instead, I was the one who was overwhelmed by remembering that once I had held my son with one hand and he had been shorter than my forearm, and that someday too soon he'd look down on me as I shrunk with age and I would never hold him again. I'm always amazed that something as full of life as a child can bring on such relentless thoughts of mortality. Opposites attract, I suppose, and some thoughts are magnetic in that way.

The clown handed Billy the giraffe — a sausage-like assemblage of long yellow balloons. He still had tears in his eyes but even at five he knew better than to turn down something for nothing and he took it, trying not to smile too soon after crying. He was growing up fast.

I decided not to escalate the situation. I gave Billy a comforting squeeze. "What do you say?" I prompted him.

"Don't go up there," the clown said. She still smiled but now she looked at me. "The little sprout knows."

One of my last rational thoughts of that day was that the clown was working for some other tourist attraction in the area. The miniature golf course, maybe. Or even the McDonald's across from the Tower's base. I was too polite to think she was crazy right from the start.

"Say, 'Thank you,' Billy," I prompted again, then started to move to the side to get around the clown and continue on our way.

But the clown bobbed in front of me and the monkey with the long arms around her shoulder seemed to struggle to keep its grip. "Twenty-seven lost souls dead in that abomination," the clown whispered. I could feel Billy tense in my arms, startled again.

"Once they started to pour that concrete they couldn't stop."

"Here we go, Billy," I said, and just started walking straight ahead, pushing past her.

But she followed, still talking, whispering, saying nonsense. I could hear her sign flip flop against her legs as she half ran to keep up with my long strides. "In they fell and the concrete swirled and the platform kept rising! That's how tall it is! Tesla knew! The top moves faster than the bottom! The Tower wants to twist but the cables keep it straight!" I started walking faster. "There's tension, you fool! The tip streaks through the Heaviside Layer and the eddies form!"

I ran up the steps leading to the glass-walled entrance walkway. I pushed against another woman heading in the same direction and saw from the corner of my eye that I had made her stumble. I had to slow, to turn and apologize.

"*The eddies!*" the clown shouted. "When the storm comes!" The woman who had stumbled saw the clown at the bottom of the steps and the wide-eyed look in Billy's eyes. "When the lightning *releases* the tension." I looked apologetic. The woman smiled at me—I still remember how unexpectedly warm and understanding that smile was — and she held open the heavy glass door so I could rush inside. "Twenty-seven lost souls dead and held captive and the storms it brings —"

The glass door swung shut behind me, cutting off the clown's ranting. The woman who had stumbled gave me a commiserating look, then hurried on. I glanced over my shoulder to see the clown shrug elaborately, then start to leave. The way the toy monkey's head bounced on her shoulder, it seemed to turn back to watch me. It looked sad, I thought. Then again, most tattered toy animals do. The lost love of a child and all that.

"Is she mad, Daddy?" Billy asked me. He still had a grip on his balloon giraffe.

"She's just having a bad day," I said.

"Like you and Mommy?"

"Yeah," I said as I carried him under the signs advertising all the tourist joys that lay ahead. Mommy and I had had our share of bad days. Which is why I was in Toronto and she was in Calgary and Billy was growing up like a ping-pong ball.

When we came to the stairway leading down to the Tower's main hall, I suddenly took the giraffe from Billy's hands. The clown had had those balloons in her mouth and I was thinking like my mother — who knew where the clown had been? "I'll buy you a proper giraffe when we go to the zoo," I told him. Billy didn't seem to mind and waved goodbye to the balloon animal as I stuffed it into a trash bin before getting on the escalator that took us down to the ticket counter.

As we waited in line, Billy standing on his own now, holding my hand, I saw from the signs behind the ticket counter that all the tourist attractions in the area were part of the same operation, so I realized that the clown couldn't have been working for anyone else in trying to dissuade me from going up the Tower. There was a young woman in some sort of a sci-fi jumpsuit standing by a futuristic elevator that took a separate line of ticket holders to a space travel attraction beneath the Tower. She looked bored, a student with an undemanding summer job. I asked her about the clown.

"You mean Eddie," she said. She didn't think that was the clown's real name. But since all the clown talked about was "the eddies," it seemed to fit.

"Why doesn't she like the CN Tower?" I asked. Billy was leaning away from me, swinging back and forth on my arm, secure in the knowledge that I would never let go of him.

"The story I heard was that her husband got killed when the Tower was being built."

I remembered what the clown had said. "Did he fall into the concrete?"

The student gave me an exaggerated frown that made me realize she thought I was a hundred years old. "Nobody fell into the concrete, sir. Everything she says is crazy."

The ticket line was slowly moving, taking me away from the student. I nodded good-bye and she shrugged, looked away, and I knew I had instantly passed from her mind. But she had been wrong about *everything* the clown said being crazy. Some of it, at least, made a kind of sense.

The comparative drawings of free-standing towers above the ticket counter stated that the CN Tower was 553 meters tall. That meant that as the world rotated, the top of the Tower travelled through a circle with a radius a few hundred meters larger than the circle the Tower's base moved through. Since both trips take twenty-four hours, more or less, and the Tower's top has to travel a greater distance in that time, then of course it moves at a faster speed. And in something as tall as the CN Tower, angled from the Earth's axis by reason of its northern location, the stress induced by the differing rates of rotational speed along its length *must* lead to Coriolis twisting — the same phenomenon that gives tornados their funnel shape and makes water spiral as it goes down a drain anywhere except at the equator. I asked at the ticket counter and a supervisor confirmed that steel cables do stretch up inside the Tower's three main supports precisely for the purpose of anchoring the structure against that twisting.

So the clown was right about the Tower being under constant tension. But what that had to do with Tesla, the weather, or twenty-seven imaginary people dead in the Tower's concrete, I hadn't the slightest idea. Probably neither did the clown.

After buying the tickets, I held Billy up so he could look out the elevator's glass walls for the fifty seconds it took to ascend to the Tower's first observation level. I was glad we had come early because there were storm clouds building over Lake Ontario and I guessed that within an hour they'd reach land and cut off the view. Billy pointed to the dark clouds obscuring the horizon and whispered, "Big sparks," as they flickered with lightning. Thunder and lightning had frightened him pretty badly before I finally had convinced him that lightning was only a big spark. When he had visited last Christmas, he had taken great delight in sliding his sock feet across the rug in my living room to give me a shock of static electricity. I knew he had taken my lesson to heart because he had invariably called the miniature sonic boom caused by the sparks' faster-than-sound travel, "Thunder." I'd jump, he'd giggle, and I'd wonder how I could ever bear to put him on a plane to go back to his mother.

The elevator operator—another bored student—told us to watch our step as we left the elevator. Billy squirmed in my arms and I let him slip down to the floor after the crowd of fellow passengers had dispersed around us. His little legs instantly took him toward the souvenir stand, but I intercepted him and deftly spun him around to the revolving doors that led to the outside observation deck.

The first thing I noticed when we stepped outside was that the storm was closer than I had thought. The wind made my light summer shirt flap at the sides and swept Billy's perfect fringe of blond bangs from his forehead. The second thing I noticed was that I was suddenly afraid of heights.

I had never been bothered by heights before. I spend most plane trips staring out the window. I had leaned out over the railing in this same observation deck before, perfectly aware that I could never dislodge the protective grilles that encased it even if I fell against them. But I had never been here before with a five-year-old. *My* five-year-old. And suddenly I felt my knees weaken as I saw his little form silhouetted against the backdrop of the city so many hundreds of meters below us.

Intellectually, I knew that the wind was not strong enough to blow Billy off his feet. Conclusively, I knew that Billy could never slip between the bars of the grilles that angled out over the city. But primally, I was flooded with the intense knowledge that my child was in danger and I grabbed at his shoulder so quickly and so tightly that Billy almost tripped.

He looked at me accusingly as I kept him close to me, against the inner wall of the deck. "It's too windy out here," I told him.

"I wanna look down," he said.

The muscles in my arms felt chilled. My legs felt numb. Once I had seen Billy start to run into the street after a ball and I had felt the same panic that was building in me now. "Inside," I said, and I scooped him up again, ignoring his renewed squirming.

I took him back to the revolving doors. Another tower employee stood outside them. She wore a dark blue nylon windbreaker over her white blouse. It flapped and fluttered more loudly than my shirt. She held a walkie-talkie and looked out at the storm rushing closer as her hair blew behind her in streamers.

"Getting pretty windy, eh?" I knew it was an inane statement as soon as I said it, but I was hoping she'd respond with something that would justify in some small way my unthinking need to get Billy inside.

"We're going to have to close this deck in a few minutes," she said. "But the upper deck is glassed-in."

"Higher?" Billy asked, eyes wide at the thought.

She smiled at Billy as she tried to push her hair down. "Another hundred and five meters."

"Wanna go, Daddy."

Great, I thought. The Metro Zoo was beginning to look especially attractive to me now. It was low and spread out. But as soon as we were indoors again, safe from the wind and the open deck, my growing unease left me as quickly as it had arrived. It was exposure to the outside that had disturbed me, I decided. Not height. Safe behind glass I was no longer fearful of some impossible accident befalling Billy.

"Wanna go *up*, Daddy." Billy tugged on my arm as if he were a little hunchback trying to ring a cathedral bell. The only reason I didn't hug him again is that he was too much fun to watch.

"Okay," I finally said. We stood in line for the elevator that ran up inside the Tower to the Space Deck. It was the last elevator ride we took that day.

On the way up, the phone on the elevator's control panel rang and the operator interrupted his monotone dissertation about the Space Deck — "the highest operational observation deck in the world" — to answer it. As he nodded at whatever he heard on the phone, I had to wonder how many *non*-operational observation decks there were in the world. I figured that who-ever wrote the lines for the Tower's employees was even more bored than the summer students were.

But as the operator hung up the phone, he didn't look bored anymore. It was a subtle change, but something he had been told had certainly sparked his interest in his job.

"The weather report calls for thunderstorms within the hour," the op-erator said as the elevator came to a stop. "So, we'll be closing the observa-tion decks in fifteen minutes." As if to punctuate the announcement, the elevator car shifted a few centimeters. The other people in the car laughed nervously. Billy held my hand more tightly.

"How much does the Tower sway?" someone asked.

The elevator doors opened. "At the Space Deck level, about one meter," the operator said. "Nothing to worry about."

The passengers began expanding out of the car. The area beyond was dark. There were metal staircases to climb to get to the glassed-in deck on the level above us. "What about lightning?" someone else asked.

"The Tower gets hit several times every time a storm moves over it," the operator said offhandedly. "But it's grounded so there's no danger to visitors and no interruption in the communications services the Tower pro-vides."

It was only after the elevator doors had closed behind us and Billy and I were on the stairs that I wondered why they bothered to close the decks if there was no danger. Closing the outdoor deck because of high winds made sense, but surely in a city the size of Toronto there would be enough people who'd enjoy the experience of riding out a thunderstorm in the middle of a thundercloud. Twenty years ago, I would have wanted to do it myself.

The only answer I could come up with was that, however small, there was *some* danger associated with being on the Tower during a lightning hit, which made me decide to walk Billy around the deck once, then immedi-ately get on the return elevator. Why wait the full fifteen minutes?

But then I saw the storm.

It was hypnotic. Even my hyperactive Billy stood still as he watched it. His hands were up by his face, resting on the railing along with his chin as we stared past the graceful arc of the Toronto Islands at the avalanche of storm clouds rushing at us, its darkness lit from within by the flickering glow of lightning crackling deep inside.

"It's a front," a voice said beside me.

I glanced to the side and saw the woman who I had made stumble as I had rushed away from the clown. She smiled at me, then pointed and traced the line of the storm clouds.

"See up above the cumulonimbus — the swirling of the altocumulus?"

I knew she was talking about the clouds, though I had long forgotten what their various names were. I guessed she meant the finely rippled streaks of white clouds that floated above the towering anvil-headed dark clouds that skimmed the surface of the lake. It was remarkable the amount of churning and twisting that could be seen in them, though they were still kilometres away. "You mean the white clouds above the dark clouds?" I said.

She nodded, not bothered by my ignorance. "The city's in a low-pressure area. That storm's a high-pressure area, and as it's rushing in at us, convection is sending mountains of air up into the higher atmosphere, causing those eddies you see in the, uh, white clouds."

I had been about to ask her if she were a weather reporter, if she were single, if she minded dating a divorced man with a five-year-old, and then she had said "eddies" and it had reminded me of the clown.

"That's what the clown was talking about," I said.

"The one you were trying to avoid down there?" she asked, still smiling.

"She said the Tower was" — I glanced down at Billy who remained oblivious to this conversation, transfixed by the storm — "dangerous when the eddies came. You think those are what she meant?" I nodded up at the white clouds.

"I doubt it," the woman said. "It's just wind and ice crystals." She held out her hand, offering to shake, and told me her name.

I shook her hand and told her mine. She smiled at Billy. "Is he your son?"

"For the summer and alternate holidays," I said. "The rest of the time he lives with his mother in Calgary." I watched her eyes carefully. The disclosure of my marital and child-rearing status didn't faze her. I had the sudden hope that my summer was about to become more interesting.

We talked a few more minutes—my plan for a quick departure from the deck was completely forgotten, and she carefully let me know of her own background: a high-school teacher from Toronto, also divorced, no children though she liked them, meeting her sister at the revolving restaurant on the main deck in an hour. "If it's still open," she added. "For some reason they don't like keeping the Tower open during a storm." She smiled again. I knew I could get to like that expression. "But I've always thought it would be fun to see a storm from the inside."

I agreed. Why not?

Then Billy brought us back to the present with a simple observation. "Look at the policemen, Daddy."

Policemen were not what I would expect to see on the Space Deck and I looked around in surprise. But except for a handful of other civilian visitors gawking at the storm, the deck was empty.

"Where do you see policemen, Billy?" I asked.

Billy pointed down. Straight down. "There," he said.

It took me a few seconds but I finally saw what he was pointing to. To the left of an old train roundhouse almost directly below us was a small, apparently derelict building in the middle of a grassy field. It had oddly rounded sides, seemed to stand on stilts, and looked like it was blocked off from view by high fences along the roads that bordered it so it could only be seen from the Tower. Old railway land, I knew. Worth a fortune if the economy ever improved. So it was probably some special type of old-fashioned railway building. And there *were* people by it. Little blue dots as small as the white dots practicing baseball beneath the slowly closing roof of the SkyDome.

"How do you know they're policemen?" I asked Billy.

"'Cause of their hats," he said matter-of-factly.

I stared down at the stream of people in blue who were leaving the derelict building. Running from it, actually, single file in almost a quicktime march. More like soldiers than police. "You can see their *hats*?"

The woman peered down beside me. Her shoulder brushed mine. "They have much sharper eyes at that age," she said.

Then we heard a garbled announcement on the public address system. "Attention, please. The Space Deck will be closing in five minutes. Please return to the elevator. Thank you."

The other visitors made sounds of disappointment, but the woman, as always, smiled again. I wondered what secret she possessed to look so eternally happy. "I think that means they'll be closing the restaurant, too," she told me.

"Is that good?" I asked.

She laughed. "You don't know my sister." Then she began to tell me of her sister's predilection for constantly complaining and I was laughing with her by the time we reached the top of one of the two staircases leading down to the elevator doors. There were about twenty people in front of us and we ended up halfway down the stairs. Except for a gray-haired couple behind us, we were the farthest back in line.

When the elevator doors opened again and the people on the stairs began to reflexively crush closer together in anticipation of crowding onboard, I heard the first thunder of the approaching storm. It was distant, but the acoustics of this central well within the Tower gave the long low sound an echo. The woman touched my arm. "Close your eyes," she said. I did, wondering what it would be like to kiss those smiling lips. "Can you feel that?"

It took a moment to realize what she meant, but then I did feel it. The Tower was swaying. I opened my eyes to find her looking directly at me. It was such a small moment, but we had shared it — the harbinger of many more shared moments to come, I hoped.

Then Billy tugged on my hand again. "C'mon, Daddy!" At the same time, the gray-haired man behind us cleared his throat. The stairs below us were clear and it appeared there was room for all in the elevator.

But the elevator was packed by the time we reached it. The operator stood on tiptoes and made a quick headcount. I was about to say that we could wait when another roll of thunder filled the well with deep echoes,

GARFIELD REEVES-STEVENS

accompanied by another sensation of swaying. The storm was coming even faster than I had guessed. I heard the gray-haired woman gasp behind me.

"Can you squeeze two more on?" the smiling woman asked the operator, then stepped to the side to usher the gray-haired couple forward.

The operator hesitated, but then must have seen what I saw—the gray-haired woman's face was ghost white and her hands dug into her gray-haired companion's arm like grasping claws. Neither of the two older people waited for the operator's invitation and simply burrowed into the already packed elevator.

"We'll wait for the next one," I told the operator, as if we had a choice.

He backed into the crammed elevator car and said, "Roundtrip takes two minutes." Then he stretched over the gray-haired woman's head for the control panel and the doors slid shut. The Tower swayed again and I heard a metallic thunk followed by a muffled chorus of discomfort from the descending elevator's passengers. Then there was silence and I was alone with my intriguing new friend. And Billy, of course.

The central stairwell felt twice as big without any other people in it. But in the silence I could hear the growing rush and whistle of the storm's wind. I checked on Billy to see how he was handling the situation. He looked bored. It was a good sign.

"This feels like an adventure," the woman said happily. "What do you think, Billy?"

Billy nodded dumbly at her.

"I think we should go sneak a peek at the storm," she said.

I glanced up the staircase. The open doorways leading to the Space Deck were darker now. The clouds must be even closer.

"You don't think it might be. . .?" I didn't want to use the "d" word again because this time I knew Billy was listening.

But the woman shook her head. "Just for a minute. And then we'll always be able to say we did it." She held out her hand. Billy beat me to it. We rushed up the stairs, our footfalls blending in with the rolling thunder and the rushing wind.

The view *was* spectacular. We could see a wall of rain sweeping across the stretch of water between the Islands and the shore. Lightning danced over the Island's trees and it took only a second's delay to hear the crack of each strike. Billy's eyes were wide with childlike awe. "Big sparks," he whispered.

The clouds billowed like the dust of an enormous explosion rushing to engulf us. I looked up past the overhang of the deck's low ceiling in time to see a final patch of distant blue sky, dusted with the swirling eddies of the delicate white clouds. Then the storm front was close enough that all I could see was a wall of black thundercloud bearing down on us. Breathtaking.

It was when a blazing ribbon of lightning flashed across the sky with an almost instantaneous crack of thunder and I felt Billy's hand squeeze mine that I realized we'd been standing on the deck for more than two minutes.

"Daddy. . .?" Billy said in a tiny voice.

I knew immediately what he wanted and I picked him up. For the briefest of instants, the woman had lost her smile and she nodded when I said, "We should go now."

We went to the doorway leading to the central well. It was pitch black. Not even a battery-powered emergency light lit the gloom. For a moment, I paused in the doorway waiting for a spill of light to burst from the elevator's opening doors. But the darkness remained impenetrable.

"Phone's ringing," Billy said.

I angled my head and concentrated to hear something other than the increasing howl of the wind and near-continuous echo of thunder.

"Something *is* ringing," the woman said. "It must be the phone by the elevator."

I kept what I wanted to say to myself. If even the emergency power was out, then how could the elevator work? We'd either have to ride out the storm huddling on the metal floor by the elevator, or walk down all—I cringed as I dredged up what the first operator had said on the glass-walled elevator—1360 stairs.

Then a pale yellow circle of light hit the stairs in front of me. The woman held a finger-sized flashlight from which her keys dangled. "We'd better let them know we're still up here," she said, then cautiously moved down the stairway, faintly illuminating each step before her. I held Billy tight to my chest, slid my free hand along the railing, and followed.

The weak light from the keychain picked out a phone handset on the wall beside the elevator. The shrill electronic chime of its ring was much louder now that we were closer. The woman lifted the handset and said "Hello" several times. In the dim light I could see her frown as she passed me the handset. The only thing I could hear was the sound of more wind howling, as if the other end of the line were a second abandoned handset dangling on the end of its cord, buffeted by the storm.

That was when Billy started to whimper. It wasn't that the woman and I were unthinking enough to say anything that might upset him, it was just that a five-year-old's sensitivity to the emotional state of those around him is even more finely developed than his eyesight. And I was worried.

I hugged Billy tightly with both arms and told him that everything was going to be all right.

"You don't suppose the operator came back, didn't see us, and thought we took the stairs, do you?" the woman asked.

"Thirteen hundred and sixty stairs?" I asked in reply.

"We're only fourteen floors above the main deck," she said. "That's not too unreasonable."

I didn't tell her that unreasonable had a different definition when you were carrying a frightened five-year-old.

"Maybe we should wait a bit longer," I said.

But the woman disagreed. "Feel the swaying?" she asked. I could. It was much stronger and more continuous than just a few minutes ago. And it certainly felt as if we were moving more than a meter in each direction. "They probably can't send the elevator through the shaft with that much movement."

"All the more reason to stay put," I said.

The woman stepped closer to me, as if she wanted to say something that Billy wouldn't be able to hear. "There's got to be some safety reason for why they close this deck during a storm," she said, and as if some stagehand had been waiting for a cue, the dark stairwell suddenly flashed with erratic, blinding-white flickers of light as a deafening metallic roar shook everything, including us.

Billy began to cry in earnest.

"I think I saw the entrance to the stairs over here," the woman said.

I followed the silhouette she made in the pale flashlight beam as she walked to the side. There was a door in an alcove with a large push handle and a prominent sign that identified it as an emergency exit only, with an alarm that would sound if it were opened.

More lightning flashed around us and the stairs and railings rattled violently as a whipcrack of thunder made Billy almost jump from my arms. He howled like the storm now, terrified. I told him it was only big sparks but he was beyond hearing anything I might say. I nodded at the woman. She pushed open the door. I braced Billy for the blare of the siren I expected to hear. But there was nothing.

The woman stood in the open doorway and moved her flashlight beam around. She picked out a metal landing directly ahead of her, from which red-painted metal stairs descended. A sign said the main observation deck was fourteen levels below us. Billy's wailing cries echoed more than the thunder in the smaller confines of the narrow stairwell. I thought I could carry him down fourteen floors without much trouble. I stepped onto the railing behind the woman just in time to see where her flashlight beam landed next.

On the bare concrete wall to the side was an emergency light fixture — two floodlight bulbs pointed in opposite directions, attached to a wall-mounted battery. Both bulbs were dark.

"Those things are supposed to be on continuous charge," the woman said. Then she moved her beam down to what was below the emergency light. It was a red-painted metal door, curved at the corners like the airlock in an old submarine. The sign on it said, AUTHORIZED PERSONNEL ONLY. But there was no warning of an alarm sounding if the door were opened. Instead it was locked with a metal latch bar and a large padlock so it couldn't be opened except by a key. I guessed the door led to a higher level of the Tower, probably for servicing the topmost antenna. Then the Tower swayed abruptly and the padlock shifted against the latch bar, rattling almost as if someone were pushing against the door from the other side.

Billy wailed, quaking against me. "We should hurry," I said. The woman nodded and I began to follow her down.

Every three landings brought us to a new number marker stencilled on the concrete wall. That was good because between the swaying, the thunder, and the rattle of the stairs as we descended, I doubted if I could have kept track of how many levels we had passed. It also gave me something to say to Billy. "Only ten more. . .only nine more. . ." By the time we had reached the halfway number seven, he had stopped his all-out crying. The swaying was lessening, too. Though the thunder was increasing.

Then, at level six, one peal of thunder was so loud I stopped moving down the stairs and tried to cover Billy's ears by jamming his head against my chest. The woman stopped in front of us and turned back to shine the rapidly fading flashlight in my face.

"That sounded like an explosion," she said. Her face was in darkness but I knew that she had finally lost her smile.

"Probably a direct hit of lightning," I said. "That's all. The kid on the elevator said the Tower gets hit a lot during storms."

The woman started to turn back. Billy was trembling against me, too frightened to cry now. Then a new sound echoed in the stairwell. Not an explosion of thunder this time, but a different noise—like the cracking of metal.

It was followed a moment later by a rhythmic clanging that slowly died. The first and only image that came to mind was of a padlock clattering down metal stairs after falling from a broken latch bar.

I saw the woman hesitate on the stairs, as if she were thinking the same thing I was about the red-painted airlock door eight levels above us. Then she began to hurry down the stairs again, flashlight beam bouncing crazily along the bare walls. My footsteps thundered right behind her, drowning out any other noise that might be coming from above us.

But at level four, even the mad crashing of our feet was not enough to mask the growing scream of the wind that chased us. Instinctively, as if drawing on reflexes buried deep in our memories, we stopped and grabbed the railing an instant before the wind hit us with a blast of cold and damp that had no place in summer.

Somehow, there was rain in that wind, too, and I felt it soak through my shirt, stealing the heat from me. The woman began to lead the way down again. If she said anything, I couldn't hear it. It was like running through a wind tunnel. All I was aware of was the storm.

On the second level, she slipped on the wet stairs. I saw the almost imperceptible flashlight beam swing to the side, then drop, leaving me only the briefest of instants to notice her silhouette angle to the side.

I stopped, daring to take one hand from Billy to push tendrils of rain-sopped hair from my eyes. I called her name, hearing my voice weakly echo over the constant shriek of the wind. I thought I heard her answer. I listened more carefully. And then I heard something more than the wind and the storm.

I heard footsteps. Distant, clanging on metal, coming from above.

I was beyond thought now. Whatever was happening, I only knew it wasn't *supposed* to happen. I peered into the darkness before me and saw only the padlock on the red metal door moving as if someone were pushing from the other side. I moved my foot slowly off the step I had stopped on, searching for the next. I felt a hand close over my ankle. I opened my mouth to scream.

But it was the woman, calling my name, slowly getting to her feet before me. Her hand travelled over my shaking arms, she leaned her head close to mine. I felt her cold wet hair slap against me in the swirling of the wind.

"Can you hear that?" she shouted into my ear. But I could barely hear her and I was in no mood to wait around trying to hear anything else.

"Run!" I shouted back.

So we did. And even without hearing them, I knew there footsteps above us, moving faster, coming closer, the whole way down.

I counted six landings and knew we must have arrived at the main deck because the floor was concrete now. I heard a metal clang at my side, felt my heart shudder, then saw the woman outlined in a doorway as lightning flickers played behind her. She waved at me and I rushed past her till I was once again on metal flooring surrounded by red-painted rails. This was where Billy and I had boarded the elevator for the Space Deck. The open doorway to the left opened into the main observation level. I could see light there, muted like twilight, broken by lightning flashes, but bright enough to see. I handed Billy to the woman and neither of them complained. I told them to run ahead, then I ripped the emergency exit sign from the door to the stairwell and jammed the edge of it between the bottom of the door and its threshold. I didn't know if it would do any good. I didn't really know why I had done it. But the woman had watched me and she didn't ask, so I knew that whatever half-formed images were going through my mind were also going through hers.

She handed Billy back to me and we ran away from the Space Deck elevator toward the main elevators so we could be rescued.

But there was no one there to rescue us. And there was no way to reach the main elevators.

The woman held onto the metal grilles that closed off the hallways leading to the main elevators and rattled them angrily. I was too tired to be mad. Instead I looked at the narrow openings in the walls and the tracks in ceiling and floor which anchored them. Their construction was the same as the metal grilles that lined the outside observation deck — tightly spaced metal bars that not even Billy could slip through.

"What are these doing here?" she asked, furious.

I guessed they were for crowd control — perhaps to keep restaurant patrons from leaving the area of the restaurant at night when the rest of the Tower was closed. But the woman shook her head. She looked so tired with her hair hanging in long, clumped strands. "The restaurant is two levels up," she said. "All they'd have to do is close off the central stairways."

Obviously, the security gates were here to keep *someone* from moving around the observation level when they weren't supposed to, but I didn't want to think who or why. All that mattered to me was somehow getting through them to the main elevators.

The woman looked at me. There wasn't fear in her eyes, which is all that *I* felt. Instead, there was sadness. A deep, inexpressible sadness.

"*Was* there someone else in the stairwell?" she asked.

I shook my head. How could there be? Then I felt the wind again.

We both snapped our heads in the direction of the Space Deck elevator, but nothing moved there. Even in the absence of emergency lighting, there was enough muted light from the storm outside to make that clear.

Billy shivered silently against me as the woman and I looked carefully around. Then she pointed to the source of the cold wind.

A revolving door leading to the outside observation deck was slowly moving, bringing cold air inside.

"We can go around," the woman said.

I stared at her, not wanting to understand.

"We can get to the other side of these gates by going around on the outdoor deck."

"What if the doors are locked on the other side?" It was the only reasonable question I could think to ask. Believe me, I had several more that were *un*reasonable.

She pointed again at the revolving door. "That one isn't."

I looked at the door. There was a walkie-talkie lying on the floor beside it. Whoever the last employees up here had been, they had left in a hurry.

A sudden flash of lightning blazed through the glass doors and windows looking onto the outdoor deck and the Tower shook with instant thunder. Billy whimpered.

Then we heard the bang of metal on metal. It came from the direction of the Space Deck elevator.

As if we were two minds in one body, the woman and I ran for the revolving door. There would be time to be rational about this later, I thought. It wasn't the first time I had been wrong that day.

With my first step onto the outdoor deck I knew what madness was. All around were seething, dark, and angry clouds. The howling wind drove rain into me with such ferocity I was afraid to open my mouth for fear of drowning. What air I breathed burned my nostrils with a sharp, electric scent. Thunder vibrated through my chest unceasingly. The deck splashed with thick sheets of water. The safety grilles shook and rattled as if outside some monstrous beast was eager to be released from its cage.

And I was afraid of heights again.

That last emotion was ridiculous, I knew. What heights? I couldn't see anything beyond the grilles except an endless dark fog. It was as if whatever made me fearful out there was not connected to altitude, but instead was something that could be felt only when I had stepped beyond the insulation of the glass windows and doors.

Glass *was* an insulator, I knew. I thought of tension. Of lightning being released. Of knowing my five-year-old son trembling in my arms was now surrounded by a metal cage in the midst of a lightning storm.

I couldn't breathe, I was so frightened. But the tiny form I carried gave me no choice.

I walked into the storm, eyes squinting, bent over, protecting my flesh and blood as I followed the woman around the curve of the deck, keeping one shoulder in constant contact with the concrete wall, not daring to look to the side or behind.

We passed a set of glass windows and doors, but they were on the same side of the inner security gates as we had been before. The woman waved me on. The wind became worse as we moved to the Tower's south side — the side that faced the lake and the storm's onslaught.

The rain was stinging. I looked down at Billy in my arms and his eyes were clenched shut. I felt tears come to my own eyes. How could I have done this to him? How could —

I bumped into the woman. She had stopped moving. I peered past her, into the driving rain, and saw why.

Ahead of us, a wide section of security grille had been hit by lightning and had collapsed inward in a jumble of twisted metal.

The woman said it was impossible for the grille to be hit — not with the grounding and lightning rods designed into the Tower. But I didn't listen. Ten feet beyond the impossible tangle was the revolving door that led inside to the main elevators, and the way to that door was impassable, except for a narrow strip of clear concrete at the lip of the deck, where there was no longer any security grille or rail between the Tower and an endless fall.

"Let's go back," the woman said. "We'll come at it from the other way."

I didn't have to say anything. I agreed by quickly turning and taking a step back the way we had come.

That was when the lightning hit the grille behind us. It was like being at ground zero.

When I opened my eyes again I realized I was sitting on the deck, slumped against the wall where I had been thrown by the explosive force of the strike. A jagged afterimage of a web of lightning was etched into my vision. For a moment I thought the wind had stopped blowing but then I realized that I couldn't hear anything, not even my own voice asking Billy if he were all right.

Billy just stared ahead, face slack, limp in my arms. He blinked when I desperately grabbed his tiny face and made him look at me, so the worst hadn't happened. But it was hard to imagine that there could be anything worse than what we were experiencing now.

Then the woman made me look at what the latest lightning hit had done. It *was* worse. The way behind us was now blocked by a second fallen tangle of security grilles. And this tangle had no clear path around it. Instead, part of the wreckage dangled over the lip of the deck like a wave about to crest and break.

The woman huddled against the wall and shook her head. She didn't want to go on. But all I could think of was another lightning hit on the grilles beside us, and what would happen when the electrified metal flew at us with the full might of the storm.

I steadied myself with one hand and slowly got to my feet. I pointed to the tangle of metal before us and the narrow path at its edge. It was our only hope. Billy's only hope.

I had tears in my eyes as I approached it.

Two meters.

That was all.

The path at the edge of the deck went only two meters, and then the rest of the deck was clear. I reached out and touched the part of the twisted grille closest to me. It was loose. I could make it shake though I couldn't hear it rattle. I tried to envision how I could cross those two meters while holding Billy, my feet treading on rainslicked concrete, combating the sudden shifts of the gusting wind, with only the loose grilles to hold onto.

I couldn't do it.

Then the woman knelt beside me. Somehow, with inner resources I can only guess at, she forced a shadow of her smile to her lips and held out her arms for Billy.

She would hold him, she was telling me, so I could go first. Then she would hold his arm and help him go halfway where I could reach him and pull him to safety.

If I don't slip, I thought. If Billy doesn't slip. If she doesn't slip. If lightning doesn't strike. There were too many ifs, but no more time.

I kissed Billy's head, relinquished him to the stranger with the magical smile, turned my back to the storm and the void, and with my heels only centimeters from the edge of the deck and three-hundred-and-forty-two meters of empty space, I began to push myself along the tangle of lightning-crumpled metal bars.

The silent wind was like a thousand grasping hands pulling me back. The grille I leaned against shifted and bounced as if it were about to cascade over the edge at any moment. The concrete was slippery. My drenched shirt caught on a jagged finger of metal. My hands were cramping with the cold. Each sliding step seemed to take hours. And then I fell — forward — and landed against the concrete of the unobstructed deck beyond.

I felt dizzy. The Tower wheeled around me, trying to throw me off. But I had made it. Now it was time to rescue my son.

First I ran to the revolving door to see if anyone had remained behind. The door was unlocked, slowly moving as the other had been. But the area by the main elevators was deserted. Lightning crashed somewhere above. I couldn't leave Billy on the deck. I ran back to the tangled grilles.

The woman knelt at the edge of the deck beyond the wreckage. One hand tightly grasped a thick bar of metal. The other held Billy's wrist.

I tried not to think about what we were about to do. I grabbed what I hoped was a secure shaft of metal on my end, then slid forward again, back to the void, and stretched out my hand.

The woman edged Billy forward, also keeping his back to the storm. But I could see in Billy that expression and posture I knew so well. He was exhausted. His knees were in danger of buckling any moment. I screamed at him to look at me, though I knew the thunder of the last strike had made him as deaf as I was. I leaned into the metal, feeling it shift beneath me, willing my arm and my hand to stretch to him.

The woman pushed him forward. Billy's eyes were squeezed shut. His mouth opened and closed in fearful gasps. Somehow I knew it was a blessing that he was so terrified he didn't know what he was doing, where he was. I heard his little voice in my mind. *Wanna go up, Daddy.*

No, I thought. Not now. I wouldn't let him slip away.

My trembling fingers hit his shoulder. I couldn't snag his shirt but the contact was enough to make him look up at me. He held out his hand to me. I could see him angrily, fearfully pull against the woman's grip, trying to get to me.

His foot slipped.

He started to flail his one free arm.

He hung over the void, his eyes burning into mine.

I screamed as I lunged at him. Whatever primal fury fueled this storm was nothing compared to what drove me forward to my son.

My hand reached his arm.

And when my fingers closed over his rain-chilled flesh no thunder or lightning could ever dislodge me. Ever.

I pulled him back.

He swung over empty space but I pulled him back. The ragged metal I leaned against ripped my shirt, tore my skin and shed my blood but I pulled my son back to me, to safety, and to life.

I held him as I held him when he was smaller than my forearm, fragile, tiny, but mine. Bound for a full life in which I will protect him from thunder and lightning and dark clouds and all that is bad.

But I had not done it alone. There was another life in my hands now. The woman who I had made stumble. The woman who had known about clouds. The woman who shared a moment with me and then risked her life to save my son.

I made Billy sit on the deck with his back against the wall, well away from any metal. I returned to the edge of the wreckage. The woman stood at her end, ready to follow the same narrow path to reach my hand.

She smiled at me.

Though her lips didn't move, I could hear her voice say that this was an adventure that we would tell our grandchildren. *Our* grandchildren. I could see the future I would share with this woman as I held out my hand to her and she took her first sliding step along the concrete.

That was when the eddies got her.

As soon as I saw them I knew that was what they were.

The instant the first gray hand closed on her shoulder.

The moment her eyes widened as she felt what had pursued us down the stairs grab her legs.

Pull her hair.

Rip her blouse.

Wrench her out into the storm where the others clambered over the undamaged grilles like spiders, tangled all together, as many descending the Tower from the outside as from the inside, hands reaching, pulling, grasping, *demanding*. . .

She held out both hands to me.

I could hear nothing but I could see my name form on her lips as she was passed from arm to arm, kicking, silently screaming, swung up from the deck, back to the others hooked onto the grilles, then tossed like something used and empty into the streaming clouds, to finally get her wish of experiencing a storm from the inside.

Then the eddies stared at me.

Every word the clown had said replayed in my mind.

They were human in form, though gaunt and gray. Men and women, different ages. I couldn't see all of them. I couldn't think to count them. But I knew there were twenty-seven of them, just as the clown had said. Lost souls. Trapped somewhere—in the Heaviside Layer, in Hell, in some electromagnetic limbo from which they could never escape except, perhaps, by changing the charges that held them. By releasing the tension.

Opposites attract, I thought, and most things are magnetic in that way, including the living and the dead.

The eddies began to move again, as if gravity had no dominion over them, hand over hand through the tangled grilles, across the intact grilles, coming closer relentlessly like the slow build of potential that will finally erupt in a bolt of lightning.

I felt the hair bristle on the back of my neck. My arms tingled as I saw the fabric of my shirt lift away from me. I saw their eyes, as mad and swirling and dark as the storm that had swallowed the woman.

I was frozen.

Trapped like iron filings in a magnetic field.

And the only release I would know was when the eddies reached me and took me and—

A tiny hand pulled on mine.

It was so unexpected that I turned my head from the eddies' eyes without knowing how impossible that action was.

Billy looked up at me. I couldn't hear him but I could understand the words his perfect lips formed.

"Wanna go home, Daddy."

It was all I needed.

I swept my son into my arms and ran for the revolving door.

I knew I mustn't look behind me and I didn't as I tore through the carpeted hallway toward the emergency exit by the main elevators. But as I opened that door I saw from the corner of my eye how the eddies massed against the glass walls and windows outside, arms sprawled as if an even greater force pushed them there against that insulating wall.

Then I saw one stumble out of the revolving door. The others, I knew, would follow. Whoever had added the inner security gates to the CN Tower's design had known, too.

There were no lights in the main stairwell, no way to know where I was or how much longer I must descend with Billy in my arms. And as I swung around the railings on each landing, lungs burning, legs on fire, I could feel the vibrations in the metal stairway. Other feet were running in that darkness.

Eventually, I came to understand that I would not win the race I ran. My arm would never lose its grip on Billy, but my legs were failing. If I stopped moving now, I knew, or even slowed, my legs would stop. But the eddies were powered by something other than flesh and blood and would never tire.

I gasped for breath. I begged Billy for forgiveness. Another ten steps, another five, and I would be finished. Everything would be finished.

Then I saw the first flicker of light below me.

I knew I wasn't anywhere near the bottom, but perhaps I was coming to a point where the emergency lights still worked.

My legs were useless stumps. I couldn't feel my feet. Whatever lights might be below me, they were too far to do any good.

Then the light flashed again and it was brighter, moving, coming closer. I screamed for help.

I collapsed to my knees on a landing, folding myself over my son. I felt the thrumming in the metal, the thunder of two sets of running feet, but which set was closer — ascending or descending — I couldn't tell.

I cradled my son. There was nothing left that I could do but love him.

Then a hand grabbed my head and pulled it up and I looked into a blinding flashlight. People were talking to me. I sensed others pushing past me, continuing up the stairs. I squinted. The man who held the flashlight carried in his other hand a long rod of glass wrapped with intricate coils of bare copper wire. And he wore a blue uniform, without markings of any kind. But I knew from his hat he was one of Billy's policemen, housed in the old-fashioned building hidden on old railway land.

I nodded at him as he asked me if I were all right. What he said next was a bit harder to read on his lips. "What did you see?" he asked.

I wasn't sure of much right then, but somehow I knew that if I told the truth, I'd be spending some time in that old-fashioned building myself, while someone convinced me otherwise.

"Nothing," I said. "The storm scared my son."

The man in blue with the glass rod told me to stay put. I laughed. I wasn't capable of doing anything else. Then he left me his flashlight and went up the stairs, following the others. The vibrations I felt in the metal after that made no sense.

I might have slept then, I'm still not sure. But eventually I became aware of the lack of vibrations in the stairs. My legs were sore but they worked again, and with Billy sleeping against my shoulder, I slowly walked the rest of the way down.

I came out in a concrete lobby with several doors leading to various parts of the Tower. A woman in blue directed me to a first-aid office. She carried a walkie-talkie and acted as if she had been expecting me.

Billy wasn't talking, which was good. I told the first-aid nurse about the lightning and nothing more. I could still hear the thunder reverberate in my ears — I feared I would be hearing it for a long time to come — but at least I was beginning to hear other sounds, too.

I ignored the nurse when she told me to go to another office for an interview after she had dressed the scrape across my ribs. I carried Billy along the same glass-walled walkway we had used to enter the Tower. The storm was almost over. The clouds were breaking up and there was a lot of blue sky showing through. Toronto weather is like that, I thought. Then I laughed again, much too loudly.

As I knew she would be, the clown was waiting for me when I reached the outdoor walkway, as if the insulating glass held some power over her as well. Her sign was unreadable now, completely smeared by the rain. But I didn't have to read it to know what it said.

"Storm came, didn't it?" she asked.

I nodded. Billy wriggled down from my arms but kept a tight hold on my hand.

The clown absently patted the head of her toy monkey and it seemed to shift so one ear would get the bulk of attention, as if it were itchy. "Twenty-eight lost souls dead in that abomination, aren't there?"

I nodded again. I knew they'd never find the woman's body, and they didn't.

The clown looked down at Billy. I was worried he'd be frightened again. But Billy let go of my hand and went to the clown and hugged her, grimy yellow waistcoat and all.

"That's a good little fella," the clown said. "*Now* the little sprout knows." I didn't try to pull Billy away from her. I guessed I knew where the clown had been after all.

A few months later I moved to Regina. It's 2000 kilometres from the CN Tower, 2700 kilometers from Wardenclyffe, Long Island where Nikola Tesla built a wooden tower that could create hundred-meter bolts of artificial lightning. For some reason, Tesla didn't want to send radio signals through the air. He wanted to send them through the ground and his tower was part of his plan to do just that. It was only fifty meters tall, but it looked a lot like the CN Tower. Maybe he knew something about what was waiting in the air, when conditions were exactly right. Maybe that's why people thought he was crazy.

I don't think he was crazy. That's why I'm living in a city so flat you can see a cab coming from the airport twenty minutes before it arrives, and when thunderstorms roll by, there's nothing around for hundreds of kilometers tall enough to reach up and streak through whatever's up there, trapped between heaven and earth, trying to find a way back.

Since I'm closer to Calgary, Billy can visit more often, too. He's still growing up too fast but I don't think he remembers much about our first and last visit to the CN Tower. About the only hint of what he went through is that he doesn't call lightning "big sparks" anymore, and from time to time he asks about the pretty woman with the nice smile, wondering if she's going to come back.

I'm sure she is. Whenever a summer storm blows off Lake Ontario and they close the CN Tower for no reason at all, I'm sure she comes back every time, along with all the others.

If you happen to be by the Tower on a day like that, ask the clown.

Ask the clown about the eddies.

Then do yourself a favor.

Go to the zoo.

Sometimes, in the Rain

by Charles Grant

Novelist, editor, and short story writer, Charles Grant is a towering presence in the field of dark fantasy. Three times winner of the World Fantasy Award and twice winner of the Nebula Award, he received the British Fantasy Society's Special Award for life achievement in 1987and in May of 2000 received the Lifetime Achievement Award from the Horror Writers Association.

As editor of the influential Shadows *series of anthologies, Grant championed the kind of literate fiction that came to be known as "quiet horror." This story, set in the peaceful surrounds of London, Ontario, is a fine example of the deceptively "quiet" story that sneaks up and grabs you when you least expect it. Following its initial publication in* Northern Frights 2 *it was reprinted in* The Year's Best Fantasy and Horror, *St. Martin's Press, 1995 (U.S.) and* Best New Horror, *Volume Six,* Raven, *1995 (U.K.).*

There was rain that day in London, in the last month of the year. A soft rain, not much to it, and most of the noise it made came from falling off the leaves, the eaves, from the tips of people's umbrellas and the brims of their hats as they hurried past the house and never saw me in the chair. I didn't mind. I wasn't after company. And I suppose, if they had looked, they wouldn't have seen me anyway. When it rains in December, you don't expect to see someone sitting on a porch.

So they passed me by and let me watch them until the soft rain became hard rain and the tires spit instead of hissed, and the leaves bowed instead of trembled, and the eaves filled with a harsh rushing sound that slammed against thin metal as the water sped down the spouts and gushed onto the grass at all the house's corners.

I shivered a little, pulled my overcoat closer to my throat, and kind of tucked my chin a little closer to my chest.

Though it wasn't really cold, the snow we've had gone and churned to mud, it wasn't exactly spring either, and the tips of my fingers tingled a little, and the lobes of my ears protested by slightly burning until I rubbed them and made them burn for a different reason. Then I huddled again, and watched the rain.

Sometimes, but only sometimes, you can see things out there.

When everything, and everyone, has been washed of color, when edges blur and perspective distorts and light catches a raindrop and makes it flare silver, you can see things.

I waited.

The footstep a few minutes later didn't startle me, nor did the creak of the railing when she sat on it, one foot firm on the floorboard, the other swinging ever so slightly in time to the breeze that had decided to sweep down the tarmac and drag the rain with it. I watched her without moving my head, didn't say anything, finally let my gaze drift back to the sidewalk, the street, the houses across the way that had no lights yet in any of the windows.

"If you catch pneumonia out here," she said at last, not looking at me, "I'm not going to be responsible."

I shrugged.

I didn't much care one way or the other about her feelings of responsibility.

"I mean it, Len. I'm tired of it. I've had enough."

The dangling foot kicked lightly at the rail spindles.

A man walked by, hunched over in a pea coat, baseball cap yanked down to his Clark Gable ears. He had an old pipe in his mouth, the kind whose stem curves down and away, and up again to the bowl. He stopped at the foot of the walk and squinted at the house.

"Oh, swell," she said. The foot stabbed now. "Just what I need."

I sniffed, loudly.

She wore a cardigan over what they used to call a spinster blouse, and she tucked her hands into its pockets, bulging them as she pushed her fists together for warmth. Her profile was half shadow, half rainlight, enough magic there to take away most of the wrinkles and most of the years. With her short hair and the fact that she'd been lean since the first day out of the womb, she could have been any age from thirty to sixty.

In half shadow.

In the rainlight.

It was the voice that gave her away; it had been used for too many years for too many things that seldom made her laugh.

The man with the pipe saw me, nodded a greeting, and trudged up the walk.

She rolled her eyes, stared at the roof to search for the strength to keep her from killing him before he reached the steps. Me, too, probably; me, too.

"Afternoon, Gracie," Youngman Stevens said politely. His right hand made a tipping-his-cap gesture which she acknowledged by nodding, just barely. He grinned. "Len, you trying to kill yourself or what?"

"I like the rain," I said flatly, still watching the street.

"Well," Gracie said, angry that I'd spoken to an old man like Youngman and not to my own sister. But she didn't move except to kick the spindles again.

The breeze finally reached me, fussed with my hair until I slapped at it to keep it down. Youngman grinned again; hell, he was always grinning. He grinned at the funerals of our enemies and our friends; he grinned when we took our table up at the Aberdeen; he grinned when his wife died in his arms three summers ago, down at the river, in Labatt Park.

He leaned against the post and pulled off his cap, slapped the rain off it, and jammed it on again. Then he took the pipe from his mouth and dropped it into his coat pocket. Shadow or no shadow, there was no mistaking his age—he wore it like a mask he intended to take off any day now, to reveal that, by damn, he was only seventeen. His cheeks used to be chipmunk puffed, his nose round instead of a bulb, his eyes deepset instead of sinking into his skull. He had a habit of pulling at the corner of his upper lip, as if he were pulling at the mustache he used to have. He pulled it now. It drove Gracie crazy.

"So listen," he said to me. "You thirsty or what?"

I almost laughed. "It's pouring, you old fart, or hadn't you noticed? How the hell can I be thirsty?"

Youngman stared at the rain from around the post. "You ain't drinking it, are you?"

I shook my head.

"So?" He lifted a hand. "You thirsty?"

Gracie stood, foot stamping hard, sounding loud in spite of the damp. "Why the hell don't you just leave him be?" She stomped to the door, yanked it open, and stood there. "You're going to kill him, and he's too stupid to know it."

The door slammed behind her.

Youngman and I exchanged looks.

The rain eased its roaring; it was back to soft again, back to quiet.

"Y'know," he said, staring at the door, "when we was married, me and that woman, she wasn't nearly this cranky. What the hell'd you do to her?"

"I lived," I answered simply.

He understood and looked away.

And I stood. Slowly. As if, after all these years, I still had to get used to just how tall I was. I had never stooped, and when the years came that suggested gravity take over and give me a rest, I refused the invitation. Some claim it makes me look younger, or that they can tell when I'm not doing so well because I look somehow shorter; and every time I go to the States, they always, dammit, ask if I ever played basketball.

I pushed my coat into place around various places on my body. My left leg was a little stiff, and I sure didn't feel like racing, but all in all, I felt pretty good. I leaned over and plucked my hat from the floor, smoothed the brim, and said, "If we hurry, we can stay just long enough that it'll be too late to come back for supper. Then we'll have to eat there."

He laughed. He and Gracie had been married for just about four years before she got fed up and left him and moved, of all places, out to Vancouver. Four years of Youngman doing most of the cooking; and when she returned to move in with me, if I didn't feel like cooking, we ate out. I never let her in the kitchen, and she didn't mind. There were lots of things she was stubborn about, my younger sister by a dozen years, but she knew she couldn't boil water without burning the bottom out of the pan. Never thought it necessary to learn the culinary arts, and so she hadn't, with a vengeance.

As he turned to lead us down the steps, I took his shoulder and held him. "What?" I asked.

He didn't look back.

"C'mon, what?"

He shook my hand off, lowered his head, and stepped into the rain.

I frowned, called something hasty over my shoulder in case Gracie was eavesdropping from the living room window, and hurried after him.

The rain was cold.

By nightfall, less than an hour or so away, it would freeze on the streets and pavement, and coat the dead grass white. Maybe snow by midnight, though it didn't feel like it yet; but it would make coming home a treacherous trip. I almost changed my mind. I knew what happened when folks like me fell. We look healthy, maybe; we look like we'll live forever. But bones bust too easily and healing isn't ever easy again, if we ever heal at all. The only thing that kept me moving was the thought of Gracie nagging at me to cook. Weather like this, she wouldn't go out on a bet. Then I'd have to listen to her all night.

By the time I caught up to him he was already on Dundas Street, heading west. A few cars on the road, the streetlamps already on, and the rain. Across the street a woman hurried up a walk with grocery bags hugged in her arms, a small dog racing up the steps ahead of her.

Youngman hesitated when he saw her.

Then I knew.

"Thought you saw her, right?" I said softly.

He didn't nod; it didn't matter.

We walked on.

Funny how it was, back when we thought we knew it all even when we suspected we didn't know a damn thing—funny, I guess, how this little old man was once a little young guy with not much going for him but good hands with wood, and how this woman came along to take Gracie's sting away. Funny how it happens, just when you think you've used it all up and there's nothing left but empty, and having drinks with your friends.

Funny.

A drop exploded on the back of my neck, like being stabbed with melting ice, and I shuddered, twisted my shoulders, and knew that when I got back, my sister would give me hell about not taking an umbrella.

"She was at the park," Youngman said as we reached a corner and habit forced us to check for traffic that was seldom there.

I made a sound, neither believing nor disbelieving.

"Not very clear," he went on, taking his time stepping up the next curb. His right hip was bad, but not as bad as his heart. Or mine. I don't know if she saw me.

"You go up to her?"

He looked at me, astonished. "You kidding? Scared the hell out of me, Len."

"You've seen her before."

"Scared the hell out me then, too."

We walked on.

Finally I couldn't stop the asking: "What do you think she wants?"

He didn't know, didn't have a clue, and we debated the possibilities over a couple of drinks, over supper, over a couple of drinks more; we talked about it to Maggie McClure—theoretically, of course and the Aberdeen's owner had no opinion one way or the other except that she was getting tired of hearing Youngman asking everybody in creation about seeing his wife, what the meaning was, or if he was really crazy.

"Christ, Youngman," she said, "don't you ever watch hockey or anything? Give it a rest, for God's sake. Ask me about the weather."

We didn't have to.

The rain did what it was supposed to for the rest of the night, and Youngman left before he was too drunk to walk. I sat alone for a while. I wasn't worried about ice or snow or finding my way back if I went over my limit. And I didn't laugh, as the others did, telling each other a new Youngman story.

Because sometimes, but only sometimes, you can see things in the rain.

I sat there and held the empty glass until Maggie suggested, very gently, it was time to go home.

I sat there, you know. I sat there out at that damn, goddamn hospital, and held Dad's swollen, darkening hand until the nurse told me twice visiting hours were over. But I couldn't let go. He was thin, he was pale, his lips moved and made no sound, his body shook once in a while, his eyelids bulged whenever he saw something in the dark where he lived. I sat there, thinking that I was damn near fifty, for God's sake, and it was right that Dad should be afraid and should need someone, even me, to hold his hand while he left. He wasn't going to last forever.

I had dozed.

I woke up.

Father didn't.

That was that.

"Len?"

I kind of snorted, shook my head, and grinned at Maggie. "Thinking," I said.

"About what? Winning a lottery?"

A shrug, a few bills on the table without counting, and I stepped outside, flipped up my collar, adjusted my hat, and started for home.

Cold; it was cold that night.

Raindrops caught the bare branches and froze into clear hanging flowers glittering in the streetlamp light; cars moved more slowly, a bus sounded huge and warm, and a pickup backfired softly in the distance; no people but me, and I wondered what the hell I thought I was doing when, instead of heading back to the house, I moved down the street, past the museums, the courthouse, and took the long sloping block down to the park.

The Thames is dark in winter daylight, rushing ebony at night, and the city above and behind, the houses across the way, didn't provide much light, only gave birth to shifting shadows. Especially under the trees that line the tarmac path following the river. I shivered a little and called myself too many kinds of fool to count, and decided, with a sigh that puffed a ghost in front of my face, that maybe it was time Youngman saw a doctor.

A moment later I thought maybe I should see one too.

Because she was there.

She wore a camel's hair coat, a small black hat on her auburn hair, and carried a white purse over one arm.

I would have known her anywhere: Edith Stevens, dead three years and looking no different than the last time I saw her when she was alive.

She was across the water, at the base of the concrete wall that kept the Thames from taking the homes above it. Barely seen in mist and shadow, but it was her, no question about it, and as my left hand reached out to grab the nearest bole to keep me standing, the rain came back and washed her away.

Just like that.

I stood there; I waited; I looked around slowly when someone touched my arm, and Gracie took my elbow, tugged a little, and led me away. She didn't say a word until we were nearly home, but I could feel it and it bothered me—my sister was afraid.

She asked me if I was drunk, and I told her I didn't think so, and told her what I'd seen. A little moan, a disgusted sigh, and we were finally inside, coat and hat hung in the closet, shoes off, socks off, me in my living room chair while she fussed in the kitchen.

Tea, a tray of cookies, napkins, sugar, and spoons.

She set them on a coffee table that separated our chairs, sat, and looked at me.

I smiled; I couldn't help it.

When we were young—or at least younger than we were—I was round and she was angles, but age had swapped our features. And for her age, though I'd never told her, she wasn't at all bad looking. It was the bile that made her ugly.

The front window was at my right shoulder, and as I sipped I looked out. Not much to see when the inside lights are on, only my reflection floating beneath black glass, and a faint cloud of white from the streetlamp down the block.

"What do you think she wants?" Gracie asked.

I couldn't believe it. No scolding, no sarcasm, no verbal whipping for the bad boy who walked around in the middle of a January night, courting pneumonia when he ought to damn well know better. It took me a while to find an answer.

"Gracie, I've had a few drinks, you know, and not a hell of a lot to eat. Edith is dead. She wasn't there, it was just the stories, you know how Youngman is."

She glanced out the window.

The rain had turned to sleet and was scraping at the pane.

For a minute there, I didn't think she was breathing.

"Gracie?"

Two breaths; two slow breaths.

"Do you know why I came back?"

I grinned. "Sure. To devil me into my grave."

Still looking out the window: "Because I thought you might need me. I don't know why. It wasn't much fun out there. You had Dad, and I had a couple of husbands after. . .him. But when they were all gone, I thought maybe you'd need me."

It wasn't in her face — that was as expressionless as one could get without wearing a mask; it was in the tone beneath the monotone, and I nearly choked.

I think she hated me.

She put her cup down, brushed some crumbs from her lap, and left the room. I didn't say anything because I couldn't think of anything to say. I suppose I could have protested that I did in fact need her, despite her carping and belligerence, if only because it was nice to have another person in the house to keep away the hours when the hours were all empty. She wouldn't have believed me, though.

I sat there for another hour, staring blindly out the window, and when I tried the tea again, it was cold enough to make me shudder. So I cleaned up, went to bed, and barely slept.

When I did, it was frightening.

Which not surprisingly left me cranky as hell the next morning, especially when I looked out and saw the goddamn rain.

Gracie and I fought over what to have for breakfast, what to wear to go to the market once the rain had let up enough to let us out of the house, what to watch on TV...name it, we snapped and bit and snarled about it. At one point, it got so ludicrous I started to laugh, and that only made it worse. By lunchtime, we couldn't stand to be in the same room together; by midafternoon, I had jammed myself into my chair with a book I didn't want to read and pointedly ignored her every time she stomped through; by dinner, I had had it. I grabbed my coat and hat from the hall closet, marched into the kitchen and said, "I'm going to the Aberdeen. There's frozen dinners in the freezer."

She was at the table, doing a crossword puzzle in the paper. She looked at me without raising her head. "We had an affair, you know."

I looked at the ceiling for deliverance. "What the hell are you talking about?"

"Youngman and I," she answered. And she smiled. "You never knew, did you."

"Oh sure," I said, buttoning my coat. "You flew in from Vancouver while I wasn't looking, hit the hay with him, flew back, and never said a word."

She shrugged. "A couple of times he flew out. A business trip, you know?" She touched the pencil point to her tongue, marked a square in the puzzle.

"Sure you did," I said, and walked out.

No; I slammed out.

The rain had eased, the cold had returned, and it took me forever to get to the pub because the sidewalk had turned to thin ice, the kind you can't really see until you're parked on your ass, wondering what the hell had happened. All the time, I fumed. I knew what she was trying to do—she wanted me and Youngman apart so she could have me to herself. It would, she'd be thinking, be fitting. I had had Dad; she would have me.

Jesus.

What I wanted then was a couple of stiff drinks, and Youngman's ear to bend until he slapped me a couple of times to bring me to my senses. But I had no sooner stepped inside, when Maggie grabbed my arm and turned me around.

"What?" I said, not believing I'd be thrown out before I'd even gotten in.

"That idiot," she said, nodding sharply toward the door. "He comes running in, says he's seen his damn wife again, shouts a hail and farewell and scares half my customers to death, and runs out again."

I tried to think, but Maggie wouldn't let me. She opened the door and gently nudged me to the sidewalk.

"Go get him, Len, before he kills himself, eh? He said he was going to Labatt."

I must have looked my age then, standing at the curb, the rain an evening mist. I was confused, I was unnerved, and I was more than a little frightened that Youngman would do something really stupid. And how was I supposed to stop him?

I hurried to the park as fast as my legs and the weather would let me, still half-burning over Gracie, and half-weeping over Stevens. I had seen it before, and kicked myself for not seeing it now—others my age, the age we all reach when we never think we will, finding not much left of the future and so go sneaking off to the past for something to hold on to when it was time for no future at all.

Like Dad had done with me.

Like Gracie wanted me to do with her.

I stumbled and grabbed a fencepost to keep from falling; I tripped over a curb and went down on one knee, crying out and not caring if anyone could hear; I hurried down the slope, under the overpass, and saw him on the wide grassy bank, not a foot from the water.

Rushing out of the night above, and into the night below.

No light on it at all.

"Hey!" I called weakly, out of breath, sagging against a tree, feeling the cold work up my arms. "Hey, you old fart, I need a drink, you coming?"

His cap was over his ears, his pipe in his left hand, his pea coat glittering as if it had been sewn with stars. He grinned at me, waved the pipe over his shoulder.

"Gotta go, Len," he said.

I shook my head. "Youngman, this is crazy. Please. Just get your sorry ass over here and we'll go have something to eat. Gracie's pissed at me, and I could use the company."

He laughed without a sound, and something dark moved behind him. "Sorry, Len."

"Stevens, dammit!"

A car slashed by, somewhere above us.

Youngman tucked his pipe into his pocket. "I finally figured it out," he said as the dark form met the light. "She's going to show me the way." A tilt of his head. "Gonna miss you, old friend."

I couldn't say it; I felt as if I were strangling.

Edith, camel hair coat and white purse, slipped her hand around his arm, and he pressed it lovingly to his side.

He grinned.

He waved quickly, and they turned their backs to me.

God, no, I thought; please, God, no.

Onto the river, then, and down; into the dark.

I stood there for a while, a couple of seconds, a couple of minutes, before I pushed myself away from the tree, too weary to be angry, too saddened to be scared.

I walked.

That's all; I just walked, and wondered about the funeral. No one would believe me, least of all Gracie, and I hoped that someone, and I knew it would be me, would arrange a memorial service for that stupid idiot in that stupid cap.

A siren exploded somewhere, not very far away, and for a moment my heart and lungs stopped because it sounded like Youngman.

And he was screaming.

I even looked back, mouth open, eyes wide, until I saw flashing lights streak around the corner at the top of the tarmac slope.

But the siren kept on screaming, and it sounded just like him, and I did my best to run, not getting very far because the heart, the lungs, and the legs just couldn't take it. I managed to get up to Dundas Street without stopping, managed to get three blocks more before I realized there were no sirens anymore, but the lights were still spinning, up there by the Aberdeen. I squinted, and counted two patrol cars parked nose-in at the curb, and an ambulance swept by me, making me jump away from the curb.

Maggie, I thought, finally shot a deadbeat customer.

I was wrong.

I went up there, and I was wrong.

When I hadn't come back, she had gone looking for me again. Maggie told me later she had been furious, nearly spitting, when I wasn't at my table. So mad she'd stepped off the curb without looking, and the truck hadn't stopped in time, braking and skidding on the rainmist ice-slick street.

I don't know if I actually passed out or just slid into a stupor, but the next thing I knew there was a funeral, there were people, there was Maggie McClure, there was silence. A day, a week, I don't know how long it was, but the rain stopped, and I spent most of my time packing her clothes to give to charity, or a church, I hadn't made up my mind.

That's when I found the letter—she and Youngman, years after their divorce, carrying on, practically coast to coast.

"Son of a bitch," I said in her empty bedroom. "Son of a bitch."

That, more than anything, made me remember the night they had died.

That, more than anything, made me remember the siren, made me wonder if that first wailing really had been Youngman screaming, because Edith knew.

I don't know.

But there's rain now, never snow, almost every day. It slips from the eaves and rushes along the gutters and no one ever looks while I sit on the porch and watch.

Funny how things are; I used to think it would be Dad who would come to show me the way when the way was open for me to take it.

Not now.

Sometimes, in the rain, I can see her across the street, standing beneath a pine tree, waiting for me to leave.

She isn't smiling, my Gracie.

She isn't smiling at all.

The Sloan Men

By David Nickle

Each volume in our series has featured work by David Nickle. "The Sloan Men," printed in NF2, was Dave's second foray into dark fantasy, following publication of his first such effort in volume one. The story was reprinted in Year's Best Fantasy and Horror, *St. Martin's Press, 1995 and was also adapted and filmed as an episode in the TV series* The Hunger. *In 1998 he and Edo van Belkom—another* Northern Frights *stalwart—were co-recipients of the Horror Writers Association's Bram Stoker Award, the world's top honor in the field of dark fantasy.*

M rs. Sloan had only three fingers on her left hand, but when she drummed them against the countertop, the tiny polished bones at the end of the fourth and fifth stumps clattered like fingernails. If Judith hadn't been looking, she wouldn't have noticed anything strange about Mrs. Sloan's hand.

"Tell me how you met Herman," said Mrs. Sloan. She turned away from Judith as she spoke, to look out the kitchen window where Herman and his father were getting into Mr. Sloan's black pickup truck. Seeing Herman and Mr. Sloan together was a welcome distraction for Judith. She was afraid Herman's stepmother would catch her staring at the hand. Judith didn't know how she would explain that with any grace: Things are off to a bad enough start as it is.

Outside, Herman wiped his sleeve across his pale, hairless scalp and, seeing Judith watching from the window, turned the gesture into an exaggerated wave. He grinned wetly through the late afternoon sun. Judith felt a little grin of her own growing and waved back, fingers waggling an infantile bye-bye. Hurry home, she mouthed through the glass. Herman stared back blandly, not understanding.

"Did you meet him at school?"

Judith flinched. The drumming had stopped, and when she looked, Mrs. Sloan was leaning against the counter with her mutilated hand hidden in the crook of crossed arms. Judith hadn't even seen the woman move.

"No," Judith finally answered. "Herman doesn't go to school. Neither do I."

Mrs. Sloan smiled ironically. She had obviously been a beautiful woman in her youth—in most ways she still was. Mrs. Sloan's hair was auburn and it played over her eyes mysteriously, like a movie star's. She had cheekbones that Judith's ex-boss Talia would have called sculpted, and the only signs of her age were the tiny crow's feet at her eyes and harsh little lines at the corners of her mouth.

"I didn't mean to imply anything," said Mrs. Sloan. "Sometimes he goes to school, sometimes museums, sometimes just shopping plazas. That's Herman."

Judith expected Mrs. Sloan's smile to turn into a laugh, underscoring the low mockery she had directed towards Herman since he and Judith had arrived that morning. But the woman kept quiet, and the smile dissolved over her straight white teeth. She regarded Judith thoughtfully.

"I'd thought it might be school because you don't seem that old," said Mrs. Sloan. "Of course I don't usually have an opportunity to meet Herman's lady friends, so I suppose I really can't say."

"I met Herman on a tour. I was on vacation in Portugal, I went there with a girl I used to work with, and when we were in Lisbon—"

"—Herman appeared on the same tour as you. Did your girlfriend join you on that outing, or were you alone?"

"Stacey got food poisoning." As I was about to say. "It was a rotten day, humid and muggy." Judith wanted to tell the story the way she'd told it to her own family and friends, countless times. It had its own rhythm; her fateful meeting with Herman Sloan in the roped-off scriptorium of the monastery outside Lisbon, dinner that night in a vast, empty restaurant deserted in the off-season. In the face of Mrs. Sloan, though, the rhythm of that telling was somehow lost. Judith told it as best she could.

"So we kept in touch," she finished lamely.

Mrs. Sloan nodded slowly and didn't say anything for a moment. Try as she might, Judith couldn't read the woman, and she had always prided herself on being able to see through most people at least half way. That she couldn't see into this person at all was particularly irksome, because of who she was—a potential in-law, for God's sake. Judith's mother had advised her, "Look at the parents if you want to see what kind of man the love of your life will be in thirty years. See if you can love them with all their faults, all their habits. Because that's how things'll be. . ."

Judith realized again that she wanted very much for things to be just fine with Herman thirty years down the line. But if this afternoon were any indication. . .

Herman had been uneasy about the two of them going to Fenlan to meet his parents at all. But, as Judith explained, it was a necessary step. She knew it, even if Herman didn't—as soon as they turned off the highway he shut his eyes and wouldn't open them until Judith pulled into the driveway.

Mr. Sloan met them and Herman seemed to relax then, opening his eyes and blinking in the sunlight. Judith relaxed too, seeing the two of them together. They were definitely father and son, sharing features and mannerisms like images in a mirror. Mr. Sloan took Judith up in a big, damp hug the moment she stepped out of the car. The gesture surprised her at first and she tried to pull away, but Mr. Sloan's unstoppable grin had finally put her at ease.

"You are very lovely," said Mrs. Sloan finally. "That's to be expected, though. Tell me what you do for a living. Are you still working now that you've met Herman?"

Judith wanted to snap something clever at the presumption, but she stopped herself. "I'm working. Not at the same job, but in another salon. I do people's hair, and I'm learning manicure."

Mrs. Sloan seemed surprised. "Really? I'm impressed."

Now Judith was sure Mrs. Sloan was making fun, and a sluice of anger passed too close to the surface. "I work hard," she said hotly. "It may not seem—"

Mrs. Sloan silenced her with shushing motions. "Don't take it the wrong way," she said. "It's only that when I met Herman's father, I think I stopped working the very next day."

"Those must have been different times."

"They weren't that different." Mrs. Sloan's smile was narrow and ugly. "Perhaps Herman's father just needed different things."

"Well, I'm still working."

"So you say." Mrs. Sloan got up from the kitchen stool. "Come to the living room, dear. I've something to show you."

The shift in tone was too sudden, and it took Judith a second to realize she'd even been bidden. Mrs. Sloan half-turned at the kitchen door, and beckoned with her five-fingered hand.

"Judith," she said, "you've come this far already. You might as well finish the journey."

The living room was distastefully bare. The walls needed paint and there was a large brown stain on the carpet that Mrs. Sloan hadn't even bothered to cover up. She sat down on the sofa and Judith joined her.

"I wanted you to see the family album. I think—" Mrs. Sloan reached under the coffee table and lifted out a heavy black-bound volume "—I don't know, but I hope. . .you'll find this interesting."

Mrs. Sloan's face lost some of its hardness as she spoke. She finished with a faltering smile.

"I'm sure I will," said Judith. This was a good development, more like what she had hoped the visit would become. Family albums and welcoming hugs and funny stories about what Herman was like when he was two. She snuggled back against the tattered cushions and looked down at the album. "This must go back generations."

Mrs. Sloan still hadn't opened it. "Not really," she said. "As far as I know, the Sloans never mastered photography on their own. All of the pictures in here are mine."

"May I. . .?" Judith put out her hands, and with a shrug Mrs. Sloan handed the album over.

"I should warn you—" began Mrs. Sloan.

Judith barely listened. She opened the album to the first page.

And shut it, almost as quickly. She felt her face flush, with shock and anger. She looked at Mrs. Sloan, expecting to see that cruel, nasty smile back again. But Mrs. Sloan wasn't smiling.

"I was about to say," said Mrs. Sloan, reaching over and taking the album back, "that I should warn you, this isn't an ordinary family album."

"I—" Judith couldn't form a sentence, she was so angry. No wonder Herman hadn't wanted her to meet his family.

"I took that photograph almost a year after I cut off my fingers," said Mrs. Sloan. "Photography became a small rebellion for me, not nearly so visible as the mutilation. Herman's father still doesn't know about it, even though I keep the book out here in full view. Sloan men don't open books much.

"But we do, don't we Judith?"

Mrs. Sloan opened the album again, and pointed at the polaroid on the first page. Judith wanted to look away, but found that she couldn't.

"Herman's father brought the three of them home early, before I'd woken up—I don't know where he found them. Maybe he just called, and they were the ones who answered."

"They" were three women. The oldest couldn't have been more than twenty-five. Mrs. Sloan had caught them naked and asleep, along with what looked like Herman's father. One woman had her head cradled near Mr. Sloan's groin; another was cuddled in the white folds of his armpit, her wet hair fanning like seaweed across his shoulder; the third lay curled in a foetal position off his wide flank. Something dark was smeared across her face.

"And no, they weren't prostitutes," said Mrs. Sloan. "I had occasion to talk to one of them on her way out; she was a newlywed, she and her husband had come up for a weekend at the family cottage. She was, she supposed, going back to him."

"That's sick," gasped Judith, and meant it. She truly felt ill. "Why would you take something like that?"

"Because," replied Mrs. Sloan, her voice growing sharp again, "I found that I could. Mr. Sloan was distracted, as you can see, and at that instant I found some of the will that he had kept from me since we met."

"Sick," Judith whispered. "Herman was right. We shouldn't have come."

When Mrs. Sloan closed the album this time, she put it back underneath the coffee table. She patted Judith's arm with her mutilated hand and smiled. "No, no, dear. I'm happy you're here—happier than you can know."

Judith wanted nothing more at that moment than to get up, grab her suitcase, throw it in the car and leave. But of course she couldn't. Herman wasn't back yet, and she couldn't think of leaving without him.

"If Herman's father was doing all these things, why didn't you just divorce him?"

"If that photograph offends you, why don't you just get up and leave, right now?"

"Herman—"

"Herman wouldn't like it," Mrs. Sloan finished for her. "That's it, isn't it?" Judith nodded. "He's got you too," continued Mrs. Sloan, "just like his father got me. But maybe it's not too late for you."

"I love Herman. He never did anything like. . .like that."

"Of course you love him. And I love Mr. Sloan—desperately, passionately, over all reason." The corner of Mrs. Sloan's mouth perked up in a small, bitter grin.

"Would you like to hear how we met?"

Judith wasn't sure she would, but she nodded anyway. "Sure."

"I was living in Toronto with a friend at the time, had been for several years. As I recall, she was more than a friend—we were lovers." Mrs. Sloan paused, obviously waiting for a reaction. Judith sat mute, her expression purposefully blank.

Mrs. Sloan went on: "In our circle of friends, such relationships were quite fragile. Usually they would last no longer than a few weeks. It was, so far as we knew anyway, a minor miracle that we'd managed to stay together for as long as we had." Mrs. Sloan gave a bitter laugh. "We were very proud."

DAVID NICKLE

"How did you meet Herman's father?"

"On a train," she said quickly. "A subway train. He didn't even speak to me. I just felt his touch. I began packing my things that night. I can't even remember what I told her. My friend."

"It can't have been like that."

Judith started to get up, but Mrs. Sloan grabbed her, two fingers and a thumb closing like a trap around her forearm. Judith fell back down on the sofa. "Let go!"

Mrs. Sloan held tight. With her other hand she took hold of Judith's face and pulled it around to face her.

"Don't argue with me," she hissed, her eyes desperately intent. "You're wasting time. They'll be back soon, and when they are, we won't be able to do anything.

"We'll be under their spell again!"

Something in her tone caught Judith, and instead of breaking away, of running to the car and waiting inside with the doors locked until Herman got back—instead of slapping Mrs. Sloan, as she was half-inclined to do— Judith sat still.

"Then tell me what you mean." she said, slowly and deliberately.

Mrs. Sloan let go, and Judith watched as the relief flooded across her features. "We'll have to open the album again," she said. "That's the only way I can tell it."

The pictures were placed in the order they'd been taken. The first few were close-ups of different parts of Mr. Sloan's anatomy, always taken while he slept. They could have been pictures of Herman, and Judith saw nothing strange about them until Mrs. Sloan began pointing out the discrepancies: "Those ridges around his nipples are made of something like fingernails," she said of one, and "the whole ear isn't any bigger than a nickel," she said, pointing to another grainy polaroid. "His teeth are barely nubs on his gums, and his navel. . .look, it's a slit. I measured it after I took this, and it was nearly eight inches long. Sometimes it grows longer, and I've seen it shrink to less than an inch on cold days."

"I'd never noticed before," murmured Judith, although as Mrs. Sloan pointed to more features she began to remember other things about Herman: the thick black hairs that only grew between his fingers, his black triangular toenails that never needed cutting. . .and where were his fingernails? Judith shivered with the realization.

Mrs. Sloan turned the page.

"Did you ever once stop to wonder what you saw in such a creature?" she asked Judith.

"Never," Judith replied, wonderingly.

"Look," said Mrs. Sloan, pointing at the next spread. "I took these pictures in June of 1982."

At first they looked like nature pictures, blue-tinged photographs of some of the land around the Sloans' house. But as Judith squinted she could make out a small figure wearing a heavy green overcoat. Its head was a little white pinprick in the middle of a farmer's field. "Mr. Sloan," she said, pointing.

Mrs. Sloan nodded. "He walks off in that direction every weekend. I followed him that day."

"Followed him where?"

"About a mile and a half to the north of here," said Mrs. Sloan, "there is an old farm property. The Sloans must own the land—that's the only explanation I can think of—although I've never been able to find the deed. Here—" she pointed at a photograph of an ancient set of fieldstone foundations, choked with weeds " —that's where he stopped."

The next photograph in the series showed a tiny black rectangle in the middle of the ruins. Looking more closely, Judith could tell that it was an opening into the dark of a root cellar. Mr. Sloan was bent over it, peering inside. Judith turned the page, but there were no photographs after that.

"When he went inside, I found I couldn't take any more pictures," said Mrs. Sloan. "I can't explain why, but I felt a compelling terror, unlike anything I've ever felt in Mr. Sloan's presence. I ran back to the house, all the way. It was as though I were being pushed."

That's weird. Judith was about to say it aloud, but stopped herself— in the face of Mrs. Sloan's photo album, everything was weird. To comment on the fact seemed redundant.

"I can't explain why I fled, but I have a theory." Mrs. Sloan set the volume aside and stood. She walked over to the window, spread the blinds an inch, and checked the driveway as she spoke. "Herman and his father aren't human. That much we can say for certain—they are monsters, deformed in ways that even radiation, even Thalidomide couldn't account for. They are physically repulsive; their intellects are no more developed than that of a child of four. They are weak and amoral."

Mrs. Sloan turned, leaning against the glass. "Yet here we are, you and I. Without objective evidence—" she gestured with her good hand towards the open photo album "—we can't even see them for what they are. If they were any nearer, or perhaps simply not distracted, we wouldn't even be able to have this conversation. Tonight, we'll go willingly to their beds." At that, Mrs. Sloan visibly shuddered. "If that's where they want us."

Judith felt the urge to go to the car again, and again she suppressed it. Mrs. Sloan held her gaze like a cobra.

"It all suggests a power. I think it suggests talismanic power." Here Mrs. Sloan paused, looking expectantly at Judith.

Judith wasn't sure what "talismanic" meant, but she thought she knew what Mrs. Sloan was driving at. "You think the source of their power is in that cellar?"

"Good." Mrs. Sloan nodded slowly. "Yes, Judith, that's what I think. I've tried over and over to get close to that place, but I've never been able to even step inside those foundations. It's a place of power, and it protects itself."

Judith looked down at the photographs. She felt cold in the pit of her stomach. "So you want me to go there with you, is that it?"

Mrs. Sloan took one last look out the window then came back and sat down. She smiled with an awkward warmth. "Only once since I came here have I felt as strong as I do today. That day, I chopped these off with the wood-axe—" she held up her three-fingered hand and waggled the stumps "—thinking that, seeing me mutilated, Herman's father would lose interest and let me go. I was stupid; it only made him angry, and I was. . .punished. But I didn't know then what I know today. And," she added after a brief pause, "today you are here."

The Sloan men had not said where they were going when they left in the pickup truck, so it was impossible to tell how much time the two women had. Mrs. Sloan found a flashlight, an axe and a shovel in the garage, and they set out immediately along a narrow path that snaked through the trees at the back of the yard. There were at least two hours of daylight left, and Judith was glad. She wouldn't want to be trekking back through these woods after dark.

In point of fact, she was barely sure she wanted to be in these woods in daylight. Mrs. Sloan moved through the underbrush like a crazy woman, not even bothering to move branches out of her way. But Judith was slower, perhaps more doubtful.

Why was she doing this? Because of some grainy photographs in a family album? Because of what might as well have been a ghost story, told by a woman who had by her own admission chopped off two of her own fingers? Truth be told, Judith couldn't be sure she was going anywhere but crazy following Mrs. Sloan through the wilderness.

Finally, it was the memories that kept her moving. As Judith walked, they manifested with all the vividness of new experience.

The scriptorium near Lisbon was deserted—the tour group had moved on, maybe up the big wooden staircase behind the podium, maybe down the black wrought-iron spiral staircase. Judith couldn't tell; the touch on the back of her neck seemed to be interfering. It penetrated, through skin and muscle and bone, to the juicy center of her spine. She turned around and the wet thing behind pulled her to the floor. She did not resist.

"Hurry up!" Mrs. Sloan was well ahead, near the top of a ridge of rock in the center of a large clearing. Blinking, Judith apologized and moved on.

Judith was fired from her job at Joseph's only a week after she returned from Portugal. It seemed she had been late every morning, and when she explained to her boss that she was in love, it only made things worse. Talia flew into a rage, and Judith was afraid that she would hit her. Herman waited outside in the mall.

Mrs. Sloan helped Judith clamber up the smooth rock face. When she got to the top, Mrs. Sloan took her in her arms. Only then did Judith realize how badly she was shaking.

"What is it?" Mrs. Sloan pulled back and studied Judith's face with real concern.

"I'm. . .remembering," said Judith.

"What do you remember?"

Judith felt ill again, and she almost didn't say.

"Judith!" Mrs. Sloan shook her. "This could be important!"

"All right!" Judith shook her off. She didn't want to be touched, not by anyone.

"The night before last, I brought Herman home to meet my parents. I thought it had gone well. . .until now."

"What do you remember?" Mrs. Sloan emphasized every syllable.

"My father wouldn't shake Herman's hand when he came in the door. My mother. . .she turned white as a ghost. She backed up into the kitchen, and I think she knocked over some pots or something, because I heard clanging. My father asked my mother if she was all right. All she said was no. Over and over again."

"What did your father do?"

"He excused himself, went to check on my mother. He left us alone in the vestibule, it must have been for less than a minute. And I. . ." Judith paused, then willed herself to finish. "I started. . .rubbing myself against Herman. All over. He didn't even make a move. But I couldn't stop myself. I don't even remember wanting to stop. My parents had to pull me away, both of them." Judith felt like crying.

"My father actually hit me. He said I made him sick. Then he called me. . .a little whore."

Mrs. Sloan made a sympathetic noise. "It's not far to the ruins," she said softly. "We'd better go, before they get back."

It felt like an hour had passed before they emerged from the forest and looked down on the ruins that Judith had seen in the Polaroids. In the setting sun, they seemed almost mythic—like Stonehenge, or the Aztec temples Judith had toured once on a trip to Cancun. The stones here had obviously once been the foundation of a farmhouse. Judith could make out the outline of what would have been a woodshed extending off the nearest side, and another tumble of stonework in the distance was surely the remains of a barn — but now they were something else entirely. Judith didn't want to go any closer. If she turned back now, she might make it home before dark.

"Do you feel it?" Mrs. Sloan gripped the axe-handle with white knuckles. Judith must have been holding the shovel almost as tightly. Although it was quite warm outside, her teeth began to chatter.

"If either of us had come alone, we wouldn't be able to stand it," said Mrs. Sloan, her voice trembling. "We'd better keep moving."

Judith followed Herman's stepmother down the rocky slope to the ruins. Her breaths grew shorter the closer they got. She used the shovel as a walking stick until they reached level ground, then held it up in both hands, like a weapon.

They stopped again at the edge of the foundation. The door to the root cellar lay maybe thirty feet beyond. It was made of sturdy, fresh-painted wood, in sharp contrast to the overgrown wreckage around it, and it was embedded in the ground at an angle. Tall, thick weeds sprouting galaxies of tiny white flowers grew in a dense cluster on top of the mound. They waved rhythmically back and forth, as though in a breeze.

But it was wrong, thought Judith. There was no breeze, the air was still. She looked back on their trail and confirmed it — the tree branches weren't even rustling.

"I know," said Mrs. Sloan, her voice flat. "I see it too. They're moving on their own."

Without another word, Mrs. Sloan stepped across the stone boundary. Judith followed, and together they approached the shifting mound.

As they drew closer, Judith half-expected the weeds to attack, to shoot forward and grapple their legs, or to lash across their eyes and throats with prickly venom.

In fact, the stalks didn't even register the two women's presence as they stepped up to the mound. Still, Judith held the shovel ready as Mrs. Sloan smashed the padlock on the root cellar door. She pried it away with a painful-sounding rending.

"Help me lift this," said Mrs. Sloan.

The door was heavy, and earth had clotted along its top, but with only a little difficulty they managed to heave it open. A thick, milky smell wafted up from the darkness.

Mrs. Sloan switched on the flashlight and aimed it down. Judith peered along its beam—it caught nothing but dust motes, and the uncertain-looking steps of a wooden ladder.

"Don't worry, Judith," breathed Mrs. Sloan, "I'll go first." Setting the flashlight on the ground for a moment, she turned around and set a foot on one of the upper rungs. She climbed down a few steps, then picked up the flashlight and gave Judith a little smile.

"You can pass down the axe and shovel when I get to the bottom," she said, and then her head was below the ground. Judith swallowed with a dry click and shut her eyes.

"All right," Mrs. Sloan finally called, her voice improbably small. "It's too far down here for you to pass the tools to me by hand. I'll stand back—drop them both through the hole then come down yourself."

Judith did as she was told. At the bottom of the darkness she could make out a flickering of light, just bright enough for her to see where the axe and shovel fell. They were very tiny at the bottom of the hole. Holding her breath, Judith mounted the top rung of the ladder and began her own descent.

Despite its depth, the root cellar was warm. And the smell was overpowering. Judith took only a moment to identify it. It was Herman's smell, but magnified a thousandfold—and exuding from the very walls of this place.

Mrs. Sloan had thoroughly explored the area at the base of the ladder by the time Judith reached her.

"The walls are earthen, shorn up with bare timber," she said, shining the light along the nearest wall to illustrate. "The ceiling here tapers up along the length of the ladder—I'd guess we're nearly forty feet underground."

Judith picked up the shovel, trying not to imagine the weight of the earth above them.

"There's another chamber, through that tunnel." Mrs. Sloan swung the flashlight beam down and to their right. The light extended into a dark hole in the wall, not more than five feet in diameter and rimmed with fieldstone. "That's where the smell is strongest."

Mrs. Sloan stooped and grabbed the axe in her good hand. Still bent over, she approached the hole and shone the light inside.

"The end's still farther than the flashlight beam will carry," she called over her shoulder. "I think that's where we'll have to go."

Judith noticed then that the tremor was gone from Mrs. Sloan's voice. Far from sounding frightened, Herman's mother actually seemed excited. It wasn't hard to see why — this day might finish with the spell broken, with their freedom assured. Why wouldn't she be excited?

But Judith couldn't shake her own sense of foreboding so easily. She wondered where Herman was now, what he would be thinking. And what was Judith thinking, on the verge of her freedom? Judith couldn't put it to words, but the thought twisted through her stomach and made her stop in the dark chamber behind Mrs. Sloan. A little whore, her father had called her. Then he'd hit her, hard enough to bring up a swelling. Right in front of Herman, like he wasn't even there! Judith clenched her jaw, around a rage that was maddeningly faceless.

"I'm not a whore," she whispered through her teeth.

Mrs. Sloan disappeared into the hole, and it was only when the chamber was dark that Judith followed.

The tunnel widened as they went, its walls changing from wood-shorn earth to fieldstone and finally to actual rock. Within sixty feet the tunnel ended, and Mrs. Sloan began to laugh. Judith felt ill — the smell was so strong she could barely breath. Even as she stepped into the second chamber of the root cellar, the last thing she wanted to do was laugh.

"Roots!" gasped Mrs. Sloan, her voice shrill and echoing in the dark. "Of course there would be —" she broke into another fit of giggles " — roots, here in the root cellar!" The light jagged across the cellar's surfaces as Mrs. Sloan slipped to the floor and fell into another fit of laughter.

Judith bent down and pried the flashlight from Mrs. Sloan's hand — she made a face as she brushed the scratchy tips of the two bare finger-bones. She swept the beam slowly across the ceiling.

It was a living thing. Pulsing intestinal ropes drooped from huge bulbs and broad orange phalluses clotted with earth and juices thick as semen. Between them, fingerlike tree roots bent and groped in knotted black lines. One actually penetrated a bulb, as though to feed on the sticky yellow water inside. Silvery droplets formed like beading mercury on the surface of an ample, purple sac directly above the chamber's centre.

Mrs. Sloan's laughter began to slow. "Oh my," she finally chuckled, sniffing loudly, "I don't know what came over me."

"This is the place." Judith had intended it as a question, but it came out as a statement of fact. This was the place. She could feel Herman, his father, God knew how many others like them—all of them here, an indisputable presence.

Mrs. Sloan stood, using the axe-handle as a support. "It is," she agreed. "We'd better get to work on it."

Mrs. Sloan hefted the axe in both hands and swung it around her shoulders. Judith stood back and watched as the blade bit into one of the drooping ropes, not quite severing it but sending a spray of green sap down on Mrs. Sloan's shoulders. She pulled the axe out and swung again. This time the tube broke. Its two ends twitched like live electrical wires; its sap spewed like bile. Droplets struck Judith, and where they touched skin they burned like vinegar.

"Doesn't it feel better?" shouted Mrs. Sloan, grinning fiercely at Judith through the wash of slime on her face. "Don't you feel free? Put down the flashlight, girl, pick up the shovel! There's work to be done!"

Judith set the flashlight down on its end, so that it illuminated the roots in a wide yellow circle. She hefted the shovel and, picking the nearest bulb, swung it up with all her strength. The yellow juices sprayed out in an umbrella over Judith, soaking her. She began to laugh.

It does feel better, she thought. A lot better. Judith swung the shovel up again and again. The blade cut through tubes, burst bulbs, lodged in the thick round carrot-roots deep enough so Judith could pry them apart with only a savage little twist of her shoulders. The mess of her destruction was everywhere. She could taste it every time she grinned.

After a time, she noticed that Mrs. Sloan had stopped and was leaning on the axe-handle, watching her. Judith yanked the shovel from a root.

Brown milk splattered across her back.

"What are you stopping for?" she asked. "There's still more to cut!"

Mrs. Sloan smiled in the dimming light—the flashlight, miraculously enough, was still working, but its light now had to fight its way through several layers of ooze.

"I was just watching you, dear," she said softly.

Judith turned her ankle impatiently. The chamber was suddenly very quiet. "Come on," said Judith. "We can't stop until we're finished."

"Of course." Mrs. Sloan stood straight and swung the axe up again. It crunched into a wooden root very near the ceiling, and Mrs. Sloan pried it loose. "I think that we're very nearly done, though. At least, that's the feeling I get."

Judith didn't smile—she suddenly felt very cold inside.

"No, we're not," she said in a low voice, "we're not done for a long time yet. Keep working."

Mrs. Sloan had been right, though. There were only a half-dozen intact roots on the cellar ceiling, and it took less than a minute for the two women to cut them down. When they stopped, the mess was up to their ankles and neither felt like laughing. Judith shivered, the juices at once burning and chilling against her skin.

"Let's get out of this place," said Mrs. Sloan. "There's dry clothes back at the house."

The flashlight died at the base of the ladder, its beam flickering out like a dampened candle flame. It didn't matter, though. The sky was a square of deepening purple above them, and while they might finish the walk back in the dark they came out of the root cellar in time to bask in at least a sliver of the remaining daylight. The weeds atop the mound were still as the first evening stars emerged and the line of orange to the west sucked itself back over the treetops.

Mrs. Sloan talked all the way back, her continual chatter almost but not quite drowning out Judith's recollections. She mostly talked about what she would do with her new freedom: first, she'd take the pickup and drive it back to the city where she would sell it. She would take the money, get a

DAVID NICKLE

place to live and start looking for a job. As they crested the ridge of bedrock, Mrs. Sloan asked Judith if there was much call for three-fingered manicurists in the finer Toronto salons, then laughed in such a girlish way that Judith wondered if she weren't walking with someone other than Mrs. Sloan.

"What are you going to do, now that you're free?" asked Mrs. Sloan.

"I don't know," Judith replied honestly.

The black pickup was parked near the end of the driveway. Its headlights were on, but when they checked, the cab was empty.

"They may be inside," she whispered. "You were right, Judith. We're not done yet."

Mrs. Sloan led Judith to the kitchen door around the side of the house. It wasn't locked, and together they stepped into the kitchen. The only light came from the half-open refrigerator door. Judith wrinkled her nose. A carton of milk lay on its side, and milk dripped from the countertop to a huge puddle on the floor. Cutlery was strewn everywhere.

Coming from somewhere in the house, Judith thought she recognized Herman's voice. It was soft, barely a whimper. It sounded as though it were coming from the living room.

Mrs. Sloan heard it too. She hefted the axe in her good hand and motioned to Judith to follow as she stepped silently around the spilled milk. She clutched the doorknob to the living room in a three-fingered grip, and stepped out of the kitchen.

Herman and his father were on the couch, and they were in bad shape. Both were bathed in a viscous sweat, and they had bloated so much that several of the buttons on Herman's shirt had popped and Mr. Sloan's eyes were swollen shut.

And where were their noses?

Judith shuddered. Their noses had apparently receded into their skulls. Halting breaths passed through chaffed-red slits with a wet buzzing sound.

Herman looked at Judith. She rested the shovel's blade against the carpet. His eyes were moist, as though he'd been crying.

"You bastard," whispered Mrs. Sloan. "You took away my life. Nobody can do that, but you did. You took away everything."

58

Mr. Sloan quivered, like gelatin dropped from a mold.

"You made me touch you. . .Mrs. Sloan stepped closer ". . . worship you. . .you made me lick up after you, swallow your filthy, inhuman taste. And you made me like it!"

She was shaking almost as much as Mr. Sloan, and her voice grew into a shrill, angry shout. Mr. Sloan's arms came up to his face, and a high, keening whistle rose up. Beside him, Herman sobbed. He did not stop looking at Judith.

Oh, Herman, Judith thought, her stomach turning. Herman was sick, sicker than Judith had imagined. Had he always been this bad? Judith couldn't believe that. Air whistled like a plea through Herman's reddened nostrils.

"Well, no more!" Mrs. Sloan raised the axe over her head so that it jangled against the lighting fixture in the ceiling. "No more!"

Judith lifted up the shovel then, and swung with all her strength. The flat of the blade smashed against the back of Mrs. Sloan's skull.

Herman's sobbing stretched into a wail, and Judith swung the shovel once more. Mrs. Sloan dropped the axe beside her and crumpled to the carpeted floor.

The telephone in Judith's parents' home rang three times before the answering machine Judith had bought them for Christmas switched on. Judith's mother began to speak, in a timed, halting monotone:

"Allan. . .and. . .I are. . .not. . ."

Judith smoothed her hair behind her ears, fingers tapping impatiently at her elbow until the message finished. She nearly hung up when the tone sounded, but she shut her eyes and forced herself to go through with it.

"Hi Mom, hi Dad." Her voice was small, and it trembled. "It's me. I know you're pretty mad at me, and I just wanted to call and say I was sorry. I know that what we did—what Herman and I did, mostly me—I know it was wrong. I know it was sick, okay? Dad, you were right about that. But I'm not going to do that stuff anymore. I've got control of my life, and. . .of my body. God, that sounds like some kind of feminist garbage, doesn't it? Control of my body. But it's true." With her foot, Judith swung the kitchen door shut. The gurgling from upstairs grew quieter.

"Oh, by the way, I'm up at Herman's parents' place now. It's about three hours north of you guys, outside a town called Fenlan. You should see it up here, it's beautiful. I'm going to stay here for awhile, but don't worry, Herman and I will have separate bedrooms." She smiled. "We're going to save ourselves."

Judith turned around so that the telephone cord wrapped her body, and she leaned against the stove.

"Mom," she continued, "do you remember what you told me about love? I do. You told me there were two stages. There was the in-love feeling, the one that you get when you meet a guy, he's really cute and everything, and you just don't want to be away from him. And then that goes away, and remember what you said? 'You'd better still love him after that,' you told me. 'Even though he's not so cute, even though maybe he's getting a little pot belly, even though he stops sending you flowers, you'd better still love him like there's no tomorrow.' Well Mom, guess what?"

The answering machine beeped again and the line disconnected.

"I do," finished Judith.

Farm Wife

by Nancy Kilpatrick

One of Canada's premier horror writers, Nancy Kilpatrick has appeared in each of our previous Northern Frights *anthologies. This short but highly effective story from our initial volume was prompted by some of Nancy's own non-urban experiences in her adopted country. "I came to Canada as a landed immigrant in 1970," she writes. "I've lived in different parts of the country, traveled to both coasts several times, and lived on a farm for a year. Noma in 'Farm Wife' is a composite of farm wives I've met: resourceful, practical, independent women who matter-of-factly take care of business. Noma, of course, takes it to the limit."*

Noma stationed herself at the back porch and propped the screen door open with her left foot. The sun hadn't set but one hour ago and already the Napanee sky was the color of ashes from the woodburner. Out past the pale tripod fencing and across the dying rye fields she saw Bert shuffling, Dog by his side. The sickness drained him. And left him hungry. Hungry all the time. Lord knows she fed that man a baker's dozen meals a day, but it was never enough. The more he ate, the thinner he got. Wasted. Just this morning she noticed he barely cast a shadow.

A mosquito trying to sneak into the house paused on her meaty upper arm. Yard was swarming with the last of 'em. She watched the bloodsucker poke its snout into a pore. "Want blood you'll get blood," she promised. Her skin began to itch bad but she made herself wait. Easy now. Ball the fist and knot the shoulder like her daddy had showed her. Noma's work-developed muscles tensed. She believed she could feel the strong blood forced up that chute.

The sucker went rigid.

Swelled to triple size.

Probably didn't even think about getting away.

She flicked the bloody corpse into the coming night and scratched her wound.

Noma shut the screen door but continued watching Bert make his way slowly toward the house. Sure is a stubborn man, she thought. Had been the forty-odd years she'd known him. Her daddy'd warned her, said it ran in Bert 's family, but she wouldn't listen. When Bert first come down with the sickness, she tried getting him over to the hospital. But he didn't trust city-trained doctors, didn't trust doctors at all, especially since his sister. Noma couldn't blame him, though. Seeing Ruby lying like milkweed fluff on those crisp sheets, color of white flour and brittle as dead leaves, eyes shot with blood and sunk back into her head, breath rank, gums shrunk up from the teeth like that... God, what a waste.

The doctors claimed it was some fancy kind of anemia. Gave her stuff but it didn't make the slightest bit of difference that Noma could see. Bert did the right thing in bringing her home. Ruby stayed upstairs in the room next to them, fading day by day, withering to less than nothing, just like Bert was now, until one morning when Noma took up eggs and bacon and found that Ruby had departed. "Best that way," Bert said. Noma had to agree.

And now it's him, she thought. As he reached the vegetable garden, even in the poor light she could see his bones pressuring the skin to set them free. His face wasn't more than a skull, with hardly any flesh for that pale hide to stretch across, and just a tuft of red on top. He lifted an arm and waved — she knew how hard that was for him.

As Bert reached the porch, Noma stepped out, ready to give him a hand up the steps, but he shrugged her off. You old curmudgeon, she thought. Even now, when he can use it most, he won't take no help. Well, that's just like a farmer, isn't it?

By the time she'd latched the screen door and closed and locked the inside one, he was at the refrigerator, dragging out the apple pie she'd baked this afternoon. He got a dessert plate from the cupboard and placed a hearty slice of pie on it. That slice went right back into the refrigerator. Out came the cheddar, and pure cream she'd whipped. He plunked himself down in front of the bulk of the pie, helped himself to a wedge of cheese the size of Idaho and scooped seven or eight kitchen spoons of milk fat onto the whole mess. She figured by eating so much, he fooled himself he wasn't sick.

"Cuppa coffee?" she asked.

He grunted and nodded but didn't pause.

Noma plugged in the kettle, but before the water got a chance to boil the pie tin was empty and he was back for that abandoned slice.

She measured freeze-dried coffee into two mugs — one twice the size of the other — and glanced out the window while she poured water over it. Gonna be cool tonight — October tended to be like that. Leaves on the willow been gone over a week; branches swayed in the breeze like a woman's hair. Might be a harvest moon come up, if the sky stayed clear. Low on the horizon. And full. She checked the calendar. Nope. Full moon tomorrow night. Be plenty to do come sunrise.

When Bert finished the pie be leaned his skinny self back in the chair and belched loud, then patted his stomach, or what used to be a stomach but had become so bloated he looked like he swallowed a whole watermelon. "Waste not want not," he said, and she agreed. She handed him his coffee and he took it to the living room. She heard the television; sounded like a sports show.

About eleven Noma put Dog out and they went upstairs. Bert tossed and turned, keeping her awake for a time, but she must have dozed off because she woke when she heard the stairs creak as he stumbled down. The refrigerator door opened and closed. Opened and closed again. Then the back door. She screen door slammed. She turned onto her side and pulled the feather pillow over her ear and went back to sleep.

Noma got up with the sun. Down in the kitchen she cleared the mess Bert had left. She opened the back door to let Dog in and fed him the scraps. The sky was packed with clouds the color of cow's brains, the air snappy. Farmer's Almanac promised frost tonight.

When breakfast was out of the way and she'd fed the chickens and pigs and milked the cows and turned them out to pasture, Noma harvested as much of the Swiss chard from the garden as she could — two and a half bushel baskets worth. She washed and blanched the iron-rich greens then stuffed them in airtight plastic bags that she sealed for the freezer. Bert hated chard, hated vegetables on principle, he said, but Noma couldn't get enough.

There was bed making, washing to do, some mending, lunch to get ready and eat, vacuuming, and a call to the feed store to see if that new corn and soya mix the pigs was in yet. It wasn't.

Around four Noma began supper. Hadn't seen Bert all day. Didn't expect to. Still, she cooked up a mess of chard, and a ton of beef stew, the way she'd made a big lunch and breakfast, just in case.

Around six the cows came back. She locked them up in the barn and on her way to the house looked across the rye. The fields had faded to the color of dry bone. No sign of Bert. Not surprising. Still.

Noma watched reruns of that show with the fat woman but it wasn't very funny this week. She crawled into bed early, not quite ten-thirty. She'd done all she could, all anybody could, but sleep wasn't about to help her out tonight.

The eaves creaked. The wind picked up and howled the way it can. The house her daddy left her was old but solid. Noma grew up here, married here, had her kids, buried her folks. Through every season, lean and plenty — she was used to the sounds.

But when Dog howled at the moon, well; Bert always looked after Dog. She went to the window at the back and was about to warn the mutt to settle himself or else but stopped. Dog wasn't making a peep now. He stood quivering, scruffy tail between his legs, ears back, about to bolt. And staring at Bert.

A cloud lifted from the bloated moon and Bert turned his face up. The sickness was all over him. Eyes flecked with red like the blood that spurts from a leghorn when you chop the head off. He'd turned into a skeleton and what flesh he had left the moon showed was a kind of whitewashed blue. "Noma," was all he said. He grinned at her and she saw his gums had receded; his teeth reminded her of the sharp teeth on the combine. But the worst of all was his shadow. It was gone.

"Ain't letting you in," she told him firmly.

His eyes got hard and fiery red like sumach fruit. He stepped up onto the porch, out of her sight. She heard him rattling the back door. "Noma," he called again, so pathetic it got to her.

Despite her better judgment, she went down to the kitchen and opened just the inside, keeping the screen door between them.

"Best you be off," she told him. He cocked his head to one side — that always softened her up. The yellow kitchen light gave him some color. "Noma," he whispered, like they were in bed together.

She shook her head but opened the screen door.

He was on her in a second, pitchfork teeth tearing into her throat. Noma'd always been a big strong woman, but he was stronger — she'd discovered that early in their marriage. This was more so. He stank like the compost heap and his skin rivalled the frosty air. It was plain enough, he was starving, she was supper.

He held her against the kitchen table. She felt the iron-blood being drawn from her like milk from a cow. Wasn't but one thing to be done, what her daddy had taught her.

Noma worked slow, tensing the muscles up from her legs, through her privates and stomach, her arms, chest and back. When that was done, she eased up a second. One final overall squeeze did tile trick.

Bert looked like he'd been slammed by a bale of hay. Blood gushed from his mouth, nose, and ears. His eyes popped wide. He swelled fast, the way the skin does when you're frying up chicken. A funny sound, kind of a cross between her name and a goose hissing, started to rise out of him but didn't get much of a chance.

Noma shook for a while but figured there wasn't much point to that. The clock over the stove read two-thirty. She glanced out the window. Frost had taken the Last of the chard. The waste of it troubled her.

The walls and ceiling were splattered, the floor slime. She cleaned up what she could of the gory mess, then opened the door. Dog bounded in, happy to gobble the scraps.

Noma dabbed alcohol on her neck and checked the clock again. Time to get herself to bed. Sunrise wasn't far off. Tomorrow there'd be plenty to do. Always is for a farm wife.

The Perseids

by Robert Charles Wilson

In his collection The Perseids and Other Stories *(Tor, 2000) author Wilson con-*
fided : "The story (and as a result virtually every story between these covers)
owes its genesis to Don Hutchison , editor of the long-running Canadian dark
fantasy anthology series Northern Frights. *I had not written a short story for*
many years when Don tapped me for a contribution to Northern Frights 3. *He*
allowed me the latitude to cross some genre borders (i.e. to mount a science
fiction engine in a horror-story chassis), and the result was this novelette, which
met with a surprisingly positive reaction."

"The Perseids" won the Aurora Award for Canadian short fiction in
1996 and was nominated for the Nebula Award and the World Fantasy Award
as well. It formed the title story of Bob's first collection, which included "The
Inner Inner City" (Northern Frights 4) *and "Plato's Mirror"* (Northern Frights
5). The collection itself was honored as a New York Times *"Notable Book of the*
Year".

T he divorce was finalized in the spring; I was alone that summer.

I took an apartment over a roti shop on Bathurst Street in Toronto.
My landlords were a pair of ebullient Jamaican immigrants, husband and
wife, who charged a reasonable rent and periodically offered to sell me grams
of resinous, potent *ganja*. The shop closed at nine, but most summer nights
the couple joined friends on a patio off the alley behind the store, and the
sound of music and patois, cadences smooth as river pebbles, would drift
up through my kitchen window. The apartment was a living room facing
the street, a bedroom and kitchen at the rear; wooden floors and plaster
ceilings with rusting metal caps where the gas fixtures had been removed.
There was not much natural light, and the smell of goat curry from the kitchen
downstairs was sometimes overwhelming. But taken all in all, it suited my
means and needs.

I worked days at a second-hand book shop, sorting and shelving stock, operating the antiquated cash register, and brewing cups of yerba mate for the owner, a myopic aesthete of some sixty years who subsisted on whatever dribble of profit he squeezed from the business. I was his only employee. It was not the work I had ever imagined myself doing, but such is the fortune of a blithe thirty-something who stumbles into the recession with a B.A. and negligible computer skills. I had inherited a little money from my parents, dead five years ago in a collision with a lumber truck on Vancouver Island; I hoarded the principal and supplemented my income with the interest.

I was alone and nearly friendless and my free time seemed to stretch to the horizon, as daunting and inviting as a desert highway. One day in the bookshop I opened a copy of *Confessions of an English Opium-Eater* to the passage where de Quincey talks about his isolation from his fellow students at Manchester Grammar School: "for, whilst liking the society of some amongst them, I also had a deadly liking (perhaps a morbid liking) for solitude." Me, too, Thomas, I thought. Is it that the Devil finds work for idle hands, or that idle hands seek out the Devil's work? But I don't think the Devil had anything to do with it. (Other invisible entities, perhaps.) Alone, de Quincy discovered opium. I discovered Robin Slattery, and the stars.

We met prosaically enough: she sold me a telescope.

Amateur astronomy had been my teenage passion. When I lived with my parents on their country property north of Port Moody I had fallen in love with the night sky. City people don't understand. The city sky is as gray and blank as slate, faintly luminous, like a smouldering trash fire. The few celestial bodies that glisten through the pollution are about as inspiring as beached fish. But travel far enough from the city and you can still see the sky the way our ancestors saw it, as a chasm beyond the end of the world in which the stars move as implacably and unapproachably as the souls of the ancient dead.

I found Robin working the show floor at a retail shop called *Scopes & Lenses* in the suburban flatlands north of the city. If you're like me you often have a powerful reaction to people even before you speak to them: like or dislike, trust or fear. Robin was in the *like* column as soon as she spotted me and smiled. Her smile seemed genuine, though there was no earthly reason it should be: we were strangers, after all; I was a customer; we had these roles to play. She wore her hair short. Long, retro paisley skirt and two earrings in each ear. Sort of an art-school look. Her face was narrow, elfin, Mediterranean-dark. I guessed she was about twenty-five.

Of course the only thing to talk about was telescopes. I wanted to buy one, a good one, something substantial, not a toy. I lived frugally, but every couple of years I would squeeze a little money out of my investments and buy myself an expensive present. Last year, my van. This year, I had decided, a telescope. (The divorce had been expensive but that was a necessity, not a luxury.)

There was plenty to talk about. 'Scopes had changed since I was teenager. Bewilderingly. It was all Dobsonians, CCD imagers, object-acquisition software.... I took a handful of literature and told her I'd think about it. She smiled and said, "But you're serious, right? I mean, some people come in and look around and then do mail order from the States...." And then laughed at her own presumption, as if it were a joke, between us.

I said, "You'll get your commission. Promise."

"Oh, God, I wasn't *angling*...but here's my card...I'm in the store most afternoons."

That was how I learned her name.

Next week I put a 10-inch Meade Starfinder on my Visa card. I was back two days later for accessory eyepieces and a camera adapter. That was when I asked her out for coffee.

She didn't even blink. "Store closes in ten minutes," she said, "but I have to do some paperwork and make a deposit. I could meet you in an hour or so."

"Fine. I'll buy dinner."

"No, let me buy. You already paid for it. The commission — remember?"

She was like that.

Sometime during our dinner conversation she told me she had never looked through a telescope.

"You have to be kidding."

"Really!"

"But you know more about these things than I do, and I've looked through a lot of lenses."

She poked her fork at a plate of goat cheese torta as if wondering how much to say. "Well, I know telescopes. I don't know much astronomy. See, my father was into *telescopes*. He took photographs, 35mm long exposures, deep-sky stuff. I looked at the pictures; the pictures were great. But never, you know, through the eyepiece."

"Why not?" I imagined a jealous parent guarding his investment from curious fingers.

But Robin frowned as if I had asked a difficult question. "It's hard to explain. I just didn't want to. Refused to, really. Mmm...have you ever been alone somewhere on a windy night, maybe a dark night in winter? And you kind of get spooked? And you want to look out a window and see how bad the snow is but you get this idea in your head that if you open the curtain something truly horrible is going to be out there staring right back at you? And you know it's childish, but you still don't open the curtain. Just can't bring yourself to do it. You know that feeling?"

I said I'd had similar experiences.

"I think it's a primate thing," Robin meditated. "Stay close to the fire or the leopard'll get you. Anyway, that's the way I feel about telescopes. Irrational, I know. But there it is. Here we are on this cozy planet, and out there are all kinds of things—vast, blazing suns and frigid planets and the dust of dead stars and whole galaxies dying. I always had this feeling that if you looked too close something might look back. Like, don't open the curtain. Don't look through the 'scope. Because something might look back."

Almost certainly someone or something was looking back. The arithmetic is plain: a hundred billion stars in the galaxy alone, many times that number of planets, and even if life is uncommon and intelligence an evolutionary trick shot, odds are that when you gaze at the stars, somewhere in that horizonless infinity another eye is turned back at you.

But that wasn't what Robin meant.

I knew what she meant. Set against the scale of even a single galaxy, a human life is brief and human beings less than microscopic. Small things survive because, taken singly, they're inconsequential. They escape notice. The ant is invisible in the shadow of a spruce bud or a clover leaf. Insects survive because, by and large, we only kill what we can see. The insect prayer: *Don't see me!*

Now consider those wide roads between the stars, where the only wind is a few dry grains of hydrogen and the dust of exploded suns. What if something walked there? Something unseen, invisible, immaterial — vaster than planets?

I think that's what Robin felt: her own frailty against the abysses of distance and time. *Don't look. Don't see me. Don't look.*

It was a friend of Robin's, a man who had been her lover, who first explained to me the concept of "domains."

By mid-September Robin and I were a couple. It was a relationship we walked into blindly, hypnotized by the sheer unlikeliness of it. I was ten years older, divorced, drifting like a swamped canoe toward the rapids of mid-life; she was a tattooed Gen-Xer (the Worm Oroborous circling her left ankle in blue repose) for whom the death of Kurt Cobain had been a meaningful event. I think we aroused each other's exogamous instincts. We liked to marvel at the chasm between us, that deep and defining gulf: Wynona Ryder vs. Humbert Humbert.

She threw a party to introduce me to her friends. The prospect was daunting but I knew this was one of those hurdles every relationship has to jump or kick the traces. So I came early and helped her clean and cook. Her apartment was the top of a subdivided house in Parkdale off Queen Street. Not the fashionable end of Queen Street; the hooker and junkie turf east of Roncesvalles Avenue. Rent was cheap. She had decorated the rambling attic space with religious bric-a-brac from Goodwill thrift shops and the East Indian dollar store around the corner: ankhs, crosses, bleeding hearts, gaudy Hindu iconography. "Cultural stew," she said. "Artifacts from the new domain. You can ask Roger about that."

I thought: Roger?

Her friends arrived by ones and twos. Lots of students, a few musicians, the creatively unemployed. Many of them thought black was a party colour. I wondered when the tonsure and the goatee had come back into style. Felt set apart in jeans and sweatshirt, the wardrobe-for-all-occasions of another generation. But the people (beneath these appurtenances: people) were mostly friendly. Robin put on a CD of bhangra music and brought out a tall blue plastic water pipe, which circulated with that conspiratorial grace the cannabis culture inherits from its ancestors in Kennedy-era pre-history. This, at least, I recognized. Like Kennedy (they say), unlike Bill Clinton, I inhaled. But only a little. I wanted a clear head to get through the evening.

Robin covered a trestle table with bowls of kasha, rice cooked in miso (her own invention), a curry of beef, curry of eggplant, curry of chicken; chutneys from Kensington Market, loaves of sourdough and French bread and chapatis. Cheap red wine. There was a collective murmur of appreciation and Robin gave me more credit than I deserved — all I had done was stir the pots.

For an hour after dinner I was cornered by a U. of T. poli-sci student from Ethiopia who wanted me to understand how Mao had been betrayed by the revisionists who inherited his empire. He was, of course, the son of a well-to-do bureaucrat, and brutally earnest. I played vague until he gave up on me. Then, cut loose, I trawled through the room picking up fragments of conversation, names dropped: Alice in Chains, Kate Moss, Michaelangelo Signorile. Robin took me by the elbow. "I'm making tea. Talk to Roger!"

Roger was tall and pale, with a shock of bleached hair threatening to obscure the vision in his right eye. He had the emaciated frame of a heroin addict, but it was willful, an aesthetic statement, and he dressed expensively.

Roger. "Domains." Fortunately I didn't have to ask; he was already explaining it to a pair of globe-eyed identical twins.

"It's McCluhanesque," one twin said; the other: "No, *ecological*...."

Roger smiled, a little condescendingly, I thought, but I was already wondering what he meant to Robin, or Robin to him. He put out his hand: "You must be Michael. Robin told me about you."

But not me about Roger. At least not much. I said, "She mentioned something about 'domains' — "

"Well, Robin just likes to hear me bullshit."

"No!" (The twins.) "Roger is *original*."

71

It didn't take much coaxing. I can't reproduce his voice—cool fluid, slightly nasal—but what he said, basically, was this:

Life, the biological phenomenon, colonizes domains and turns them into ecologies. In the domain of the ocean, the first ecologies evolved. The dry surface of the continents was a dead domain until the first plants (lichens or molds, I suppose) took root. The air was an empty domain until the evolution of the wing.

But domain theory, Roger said, wasn't just a matter of biology versus geology. A living system could *itself* become a domain. In fact, once the geological domains were fully colonized, living systems became the last terrestrial domain and a kind of intensive recomplication followed: treetops, colonizing the air, were colonized in turn by insects, by birds; animal life by bacteria, viruses, parasites, each new array creating its own new domain, and so *ad infinitum*.

What made Roger's notion original was that he believed human beings had—for the first time in millenia—begun to colonize a wholly new domain, which he called the gnososphere: the domain of culture, art, religion, language. Because we were the first aboard, the gnososphere felt more like geology than ecology: a body of artifacts, lifeless as a brick. But that appearance was already beginning to change. We had seen in the last decade the first glimmerings of competition, specifically from the kind of computer program called "artificial life," entities that live—and evolve—entirely in the logarithms of computers, the high alps of the gnososphere. Not competing for *our* ground, obviously, but that time might come (consider computer "viruses"), and—who knows?—the gnososphere might eventually evolve its own independent entities. Maybe already had. When the gnososphere was "made of" campfire stories and cave paintings it was clearly not complex enough to support life. But the gnososphere at the end of the twentieth century had grown vast and intricate, a landscape both cerebral and electronic, born at the juncture of technology and human population, in which crude self-replicating structures (Nazism, say; Communism) had already proven their ability to grow, feed, reproduce and die. Ideologies were like primitive DNA floating in a nutrient soup of radio waves, television images, words. Who could say what a more highly evolved creature—with protein coat, nucleus, mitochondria; with eyes and genitals—might be like?

We might not be able to experience it at all, since no single human being could be its host; it would live through our collectivity, as immense as it was unknowable.

"Amazing," the twins said, when Roger finished. "*Awesome.*"

And suddenly Robin was beside me, handing out tea, taking my arm in a proprietary gesture meant, I hoped, for Roger, who smiled tolerantly. "He is amazing, isn't he? Or else completely insane."

"Not for me to say," Roger obliged. (The twins laughed.)

"Roger used to be a Fine Arts T.A. at the University," Robin said, "until he dropped out. Now he builds things."

"Sculpture?" I asked.

"*Things.* Maybe he'll show you sometime."

Roger nodded, but I doubted he'd extend the invitation. We were circling each other like wary animals. I read him as bright, smug, and subtly hostile. He obviously felt a powerful need to impress an audience. Probably he had once impressed Robin—she confirmed this later—and I imagined him abandoning her because, as audience, she had grown a little cynical. The twins (young, female) clearly delighted him. Just as clearly, I didn't.

But we were polite. We talked a little more. He knew the book store where I worked. "Been there often," he said. And it was easy to imagine him posed against the philosophy shelves, long fingers opening Kierkegaard, the critical frown fixed in place. After a while I left him to the twins, who waved me goodbye: "Nice meeting you!" "*Really!*"

When I was younger I read a lot of science fiction. Through my interest in astronomy I came to sf, and through both I happened across an astronomer's puzzle, a cosmological version of Pascal's Wager. It goes like this: If life can spread through the galaxy, then, logically, it already has. Our neighbours should be here. Should have been here for millennia. Where are they?

I discussed it, while the party ran down, with the only guest older than I was, a greying science-fiction writer who had been hitting the pipe with a certain bleak determination. "The Oort cloud," he declared, "*that's* where they are. I mean, why bother with planets? For dedicated space technologies—and I assume they would send machines, not something as

short-lived and finicky as a biological organism—a planet's not a really attractive place. Planets are heavy, corrosive, too hot for superconductors.
Interesting places, maybe, because planets are where cultures grow, and
why slog across all those light years unless you're looking for something as
complex and unpredictable as a sentient culture? But you don't, for God's
sake, fill up their sky with spaceships. You stick around the Oort cloud,
where it's nice and cold and there are cometary bodies to draw resources
from. You hang out, you listen. If you want to talk, you pick your own
time."

The Oort cloud is that nebulous ring around the solar system, well
beyond the orbit of Pluto, composed of small bodies of dust and water ice.
Gravitational perturbation periodically knocks a few of these bodies into
elliptical orbits; traversing the inner solar system, they become comets. Our
annual meteor showers—the Perseids, the Geminids, the Quadrantids—are
the remnants of ancient, fractured comets. Oort cloud visitors, old beyond
memory.

But in light of Roger's thesis I wondered if the question was too nar-
rowly posed, the science fiction writer's answer too pat. Maybe our neighbors
had already arrived, not in silver ships but in metaphysics, informing the
very construction and representation of our lives. The cave paintings at
Lascaux, Chartres Cathedral, the Fox Broadcasting System: not their
physicality (and they become less physical as our technology advances) but
their intangible *grammar*—maybe this is the evidence they left us, a ruined
archeology of cognition, invisible because pervasive, inescapable: they are
both here, in other words, and not here; they are us and not-us.

When the last guest was gone, the last dish stacked, Robin pulled off her
shirt and walked through the apartment, coolly unselfconscious, turning
off lights.

The heat of the party lingered. She opened the bedroom window to
let in a breeze from the lakeshore. It was past two in the morning and the
city was relatively quiet. I paid attention to the sounds she made, the rustle
as she stepped out of her skirt, the easing of springs in the thrift-shop bed.
She wore a ring through each nipple, delicate turquoise rings that gave back
glimmers of ambient light. I remembered how unfamiliar her piercings had

seemed the first time I encountered them with my tongue, the polished circles, their chilly, perfect geometry set against the warmer and more complex terrain of breast and aureole.

We made love in that distracted after-a-party way, while the room was still alive with the musk of the crowd, feeling like exhibitionists (I think she felt that way too) even though we were alone.

It was afterward, in a round of sleepy pillow talk, that she told me Roger had been her lover. I put a finger gently through one of her rings and she said Roger had piercings, too: one nipple and under the scrotum, penetrating the area between the testicles and the anus. Some men had the head of the penis pierced (a "Prince Albert") but Roger hadn't gone for that.

I was jealous. Jealous, I suppose, of this extra dimension of intimacy from which I was excluded. I had no wounds to show her.

She said, "You never talk about your divorce."

"It's not much fun to talk about."

"You left Carolyn, or she left you?"

"It's not that simple. But, ultimately, I guess she left me."

"Lots of fighting?"

"No fighting."

"What, then?"

I thought about it. "Continental drift."

"What was her problem?"

"I'm not so sure it *was* her problem."

"She must have had a reason, though—or thought she did."

"She said I was never there." Robin waited patiently. I went on, "Even when I was with her, I was never *there*—or so she claimed. I'm not sure I know what she meant. I suppose, that I wasn't completely engaged. That I was apart. Held back. With her, with her friends, with her family—with anybody."

"Do you think that's true?"

It was a question I'd asked myself too often.

Sure, in a sense it *was* true. I'm one of those people who are often called loners. Crowds don't have much allure for me. I don't confide easily and I don't have many friends.

That much I would admit to. The idea (which had come to obsess

Carolyn during our divorce) that I was congenitally, hopelessly *set apart*, a kind of pariah dog, incapable of real intimacy...that was a whole 'nother thing.

We talked it around. Robin was solemn in the dark, propped on one elbow. Through the window, past the halo of her hair, I could see the setting moon. Far away down the dark street someone laughed.

Robin, who had studied a little anthropology, liked to see things in evolutionary terms. "You have a night watch personality," she decided, closing her eyes.

"Night watch?"

"Mm-hm. Primates...you know...proto-hominids...it's where all our personality styles come from. We're social animals, basically, but the group is more versatile if you have maybe a couple of hyperthymic types for cheer-leaders, some dysthymics to sit home and mumble, and the one guy — you — who edges away from the crowd, who sits up when everybody else is asleep, who basically keeps the watches of the night. The one who sees the lions coming. Good night vision and lousy social skills. Every tribe should have one."

"Is that what I am?"

"It's reassuring, actually." She patted my ass and said, "Keep watch for me, okay?"

I kept the watch a few minutes more.

In the morning, on the way to lunch, we visited one of those East Indian/West Indian shops, the kind with the impossibly gaudy portraits of Shiva and Ganesh in chrome-flash plastic frames, a cooler full of ginger beer and coconut pop, shelves of sandalwood incense and patchouli oil and bottles of magic potions (Robin pointed them out): St. John Conqueror Root, Ghost Away, Luck Finder, with labels claiming the contents were an Excellent Floor Polish, which I suppose made them legal to sell. Robin was delighted: "Flotsam from the gnososphere," she laughed, and it was easy to imagine one of Roger's gnostic creatures made manifest in this shop — for that matter, in this city, this English-speaking, Cantonese-speaking, Urdu-speaking, Farsi-speaking city — a slouching, ethereal beast of which one cell might be Ganesh the Elephant-Headed Boy and another Madonna, the Cone-Breasted Woman.

A city, for obvious reasons, is a lousy place to do astronomy. I worked the 'scope from the back deck of my apartment, shielded from streetlights, and Robin gave me a selection of broadband lens filters to cut the urban scatter. But I was interested in deep-sky observing and I knew I wasn't getting everything I'd paid for.

In October I arranged to truck the 'scope up north for a weekend. I rented a van and Robin reserved us a cabin at a private campground near Algonquin Park. It was way past tourist season, but Robin knew the woman who owned the property; we would have the place virtually to ourselves and we could cancel, no problem, if the weather didn't look right.

But the weather cooperated. It was the end of the month — coincidentally, the weekend of the Orionid meteor shower — and we were in the middle of a clean high-pressure cell that stretched from Alberta to Labrador. The air was brisk but cloudless, transparent as creek water. We arrived at the camp site Friday afternoon and I spent a couple of hours setting up the scope, calibrating it, and running an extension cord out to the automatic guider. I attached a 35mm SLR camera loaded with hypersensitized Tech Pan film, and I did all this despite the accompaniment of the owner's five barking Yorkshire Terrier pups. The ground under my feet was glacier-scarred Laurentian Shield rock; the meadow I set up in was broad and flat; highway lights were pale and distant. Perfect. By the time I finished setting up it was dusk. Robin had started a fire in the pit outside our cabin and was roasting chicken and bell peppers. The cabin overlooked a marshy lake thick with duckweed; the air was cool and moist and I fretted about ground mist.

But the night was clear. After dinner Robin smoked marijuana in a tiny carved soapstone pipe (I didn't) and then we went out to the meadow, bundled in winter jackets.

I worked the scope. Robin wouldn't look through the eyepiece — her old phobia — but took a great, grinning pleasure in the Orionids, exclaiming at each brief etching of the cave-dark, star-scattered sky. Her laughter was almost giddy.

After a time, though, she complained of the cold, and I sent her back to the cabin (we had borrowed a space heater from the owner) and told her to get some sleep. I was cold, too, but intoxicated by the sky. It was my first attempt at deep-sky photography and surprisingly successful: when the photos were developed later that week I had a clean, hard shot of M100 in Coma Berenices, a spiral galaxy in full disk, arms sweeping toward the bright center; a city of stars beyond counting, alive, perhaps, with civilizations, so impossibly distant that the photons hoarded by the lens of the telescope were already millions of years old.

When I finally came to bed Robin was asleep under two quilted blankets. She stirred at my pressure on the mattress and turned to me, opened her eyes briefly, then folded her cinnamon-scented warmth against my chest, and I lay awake smelling the hot coils of the space heater and the faint pungency of the marijuana she had smoked and the pine-resinous air that had swept in behind me, these night odors mysteriously familiar, intimate as memory.

We made love in the morning, lazy and a little tired, and I thought there was something new in the way she looked at me, a certain calculating distance, but I wasn't sure; it might just be the slant of light through the dusty window. In the afternoon we hiked out to a wild blueberry patch she knew about, but the season was over; frost had shrivelled the last of the berries. (The Yorkshire Terriers were at our heels, there and back.)

That night was much the same as the first except that Robin decided to stay back at the cabin reading an Anne Rice novel. I remembered that her father was an amateur astronomer and wondered if the parallel wasn't a little unsettling for her: there are limits to the pleasures of symbolic incest. I photographed M33 in Triangulum, another elliptical galaxy, its arms luminous with stars, and in the morning we packed up the telescope and began the long drive south.

She was moodier than usual. In the cabin of the van, huddled by the passenger door with her knees against her chest, she said, "We never talk about relationship things."

"Relationship things?"

"For instance, monogamy."

That hung in the air for a while.

Then she said, "Do you believe in it?"

I said it didn't really matter whether I "believed in" it; it just seemed to be something I did. I had never been unfaithful to Carolyn, unless you counted Robin; I had never been unfaithful to Robin.

But she was twenty-five years old and hadn't taken the measure of these things. "I think it's a sexual preference," she said. "Some people are, some people aren't."

I said — carefully neutral — "Where do you stand?"

"I don't know." She gazed out the window at October farms, brown fields, wind-canted barns. "I haven't decided."

We left it at that.

She threw a Halloween party, costumes optional — I wore street clothes, but most of her crowd welcomed the opportunity to dress up. Strange hair and body paint, mainly. Roger (I had learned his last name: Roger Russo) showed up wearing a feathered headdress, green dye, kohl circles around his eyes. He said he was Sacha Runa, the jungle spirit of the Peruvian *ayahuasqueros*. Robin said he had been investigating the idea of shamanic spirit creatures as the first entities cohabiting the gnososphere: she thought the costume was perfect for him. She hugged him carefully, pecked his green-dyed cheek, merely friendly, but he glanced reflexively at me and quickly away, as if to confirm that I had seen her touch him.

I had one of my photographs, the galaxy M33, enlarged and framed; I gave it to Robin as a gift.

She hung it in her bedroom. I remember — it might have been November, maybe as late as the Leonids, mid-month — a night when she stared at it while we made love: she on her knees on the bed, head upturned, raw-cut hair darkly stubbled on her scalp, and me behind her, gripping her thin, almost fragile hips, knowing she was looking at the stars.

Three optical illusions:

1) Retinal floaters. Those delicate, crystalline motes, like rainbow-hued diatoms, that swim through the field of vision.

Some nights, when I've been too long at the 'scope, I see them drifting up from the horizon, a terrestrial commerce with the sky.

2) In 1877, Giovanni Schiaparelli mapped what he believed were the canals of Mars. Mars has no canals; it is an airless desert. But for decades the educated world believed in a decadent Martian civilization, doomed to extinction when its water evaporated to the frigid poles.

It was Schiaparelli who first suggested that meteor showers represent the remains of ancient, shattered comets.

3) Computer-generated three-dimensional pictures — they were everywhere that summer, a fad. You know the kind? The picture looks like so much visual hash, until you focus your eyes well beyond it; then the image lofts out, a hidden *bas-relief*: ether sculpture.

Robin believed TV worked the same way. "If you turn to a blank channel," she told me (December: first snow outside the window), "you can see pictures in the static. Three-dee. And they move."

What kind of pictures?

"Strange." She was clearly uncomfortable talking about it. "Kind of like animals. Or bugs. Lots of arms. The eyes are very...strange." She gave me a shy look. "Am I crazy?"

"No." Everyone has a soft spot or two. "You look at these pictures often?"

"Hardly ever. Frankly, it's kind of scary. But it's also...."

"What?"

"*Tempting.*"

I don't own a television set. One summer Carolyn and I had taken a trip to Mexico and we had seen the famous murals at Teotihuacan. Disembodied eyes everywhere: plants with eyes for flowers, flowers exuding eyes, eyes floating through the convolute images like lost balloons. Whenever people talk about television, I'm reminded of Teotihuacan.

Like Robin, I was afraid to look through certain lenses for fear of what might be looking back.

That winter, I learned more about Roger Russo.

He was wealthy. At least, his family was wealthy. The family owned Russo Precision Parts, an electronics distributor with a near-monopoly of the Canadian manufacturing market. Roger's older brother was the corporate heir-designate; Roger himself, I gather, was considered "creative" (i.e, unemployable) and allowed a generous annual remittance to do with as he pleased.

Early in January (the Quadrantids, but they were disappointing that year) Robin took me to Roger's place. He lived in a house off Queen West — leased it from a cousin — a three-story brick Edwardian bastion in a Chinese neighborhood where the houses on each side had been painted cherry red. We trekked from the streetcar through fresh, ankle-high snow; the snow was still falling, cold and granular. Robin had made the date: we were supposed to have lunch, the three of us. I think she liked bringing Roger and me together, liked those faint proprietary sparks that passed between us; I think it flattered her. Myself, I didn't enjoy it. I doubted Roger took much pleasure in it, either.

He answered the door wearing nothing but jogging pants. His solitary silver nipple ring dangled on his hairless chest; it reminded me — sorry — of a pull-tab on a soft drink can. He shooed us in and latched the door. Inside, the air was warm and moist.

The house was a shrine to his eccentricity: books everywhere, not only shelved but stacked in corners, an assortment too random to categorize, but I spotted early editions of William James (*Psychology*, the complete work) and Karl Jung; a ponderous hardcover *Phenomenology of the Mind*, Heidegger's *Being and Time*. We adjourned to a big wood-and-tile kitchen and made conversation while Roger chopped kohlrabi at a butcher-block counter. He had seen *Natural Born Killers* at a review theatre and was impressed by it: "It's completely post-post — a deconstruction of *itself*—very image-intensive and, you know, florid, like early church iconography...."

The talk went on like this. High-toned media gossip, basically. After lunch, I excused myself and hunted down the bathroom.

On the way back I paused at the kitchen door when I heard Roger mention my name.

"Michael's not much of a watcher, is he?"

Robin: "Well, he is, actually — a certain kind of watcher."

"Oh — the astronomy...."

"Yes."

"That photograph you showed me."

"Yes, right."

That photograph, I thought. The one on her bedroom wall.

Later, in the winter-afternoon lull that softens outdoor sounds and amplifies the rumble of the furnace, Robin asked Roger to show me around the house. "The upstairs," she said, and to me: "It's so weird!"

"Thanks," Roger said.

"You know what I mean! Don't pretend to be insulted. Weird is your middle name."

I followed Roger's pale back up the narrow stairway, creaking risers lined with faded red carpet. Then, suddenly, we were in another world: a cavernous space — walls must have been knocked out — crowded with electronic kibble. Video screens, raw circuit boards, ribbon wire snaking through the clutter like eels through a gloomy reef. He threw a wall switch, and it all came to life.

"A dozen cathode ray tubes," Roger said, "mostly yard-sale and electronic-jobber trash." Some were black and white, some crenellated with noise bars. "Each one cycles through every channel you can get from cable. I wired in my own decoder for the scrambled channels. The cycles are staggered, so mostly you get chaos, but every so often they fall into sync and for a split second the same image is all around you. I meant to install a satellite dish, feed in another hundred channels, but the mixer would have been...complex. Anyway, I lost interest."

"Not to sound like a Philistine," I said, "but what is it — a work of art?"

Roger smiled loftily. "In a way. Actually, it was meant to be a ghost trap."

"Ghost trap?"

"In the Hegelian sense. The *weltgeist*."

"Summoned from the gnososphere," Robin added.

I asked about the music. The music had commenced when he threw the switch: a strange nasal melody, sometimes hummed, sometimes chanted.

It filled the air like incense. The words, when I could make them out, were foreign and punctuated with thick glottal stops. There were insect sounds in the background; I supposed it was a field recording, the kind of anthropological oddity a company called Nonesuch used to release on vinyl, years ago.

"It's called an *icaro*," Roger said. "A supernatural melody. Certain Peruvian Indians drink *ayahuasca* and produce these songs. *Icaros*. They learn them from the spirit world."

Ayahuasca is a hallucinogenic potion made from a mixture of *Banisteriopsis caapi* vines and the leaves of *Psychotria viridis*, both rainforest plants. (I spent a day at the Robarts looking it up.) Apparently it can be made from a variety of more common plant sources, and *ayahuasca* churches like the *Uniao do Vegetal* have popularised its use in the urban centres of Brazil.

"And the third floor," Robin said, waving at the stairs dimly visible across the room, "that's amazing, too. Roger built an addition over what used to be the roof of the building. There's a greenhouse, an actual greenhouse! You can't see it from the street because the facade hides it, but it's huge. And there's a big open-air deck. Show him, Roger."

Roger shook his head: "I don't think it's necessary."

We were about to leave the room when three of the video screens suddenly radiated the same image: waterfall and ferns in soft focus, and a pale woman in a white skirt standing beside a Datsun that matched her blue-green eyes. It snagged Roger's attention. He stopped in his tracks.

"*Rainha da Floresta*," he murmured, looking from Robin to me and back again, his face obscure in the flickering light. "The lunar aspect."

The winter sky performed its long procession. One clear night in February, hungry for starlight, I zipped myself into my parka and drove a little distance west of the city—not with the telescope but with a pair of 10X50 Zeiss binoculars. Hardly Mount Palomar, but not far removed from the simple optics Galileo ground for himself some few centuries ago.

I parked off an access road along the ridge-top of Rattlesnake Point, with a clear view to the frozen rim of Lake Ontario. Sirius hung above the dark water, a little obscured by rising mist. Capella was high overhead, and to the west I was able to distinguish the faint oval of the Andromeda galaxy, two-million-odd light years away. East, the sky was vague with city glare and etched by the running lights of airliners orbiting Pearson International.

Alone in the van, breathing steam and balancing the binoculars on the rim of a half-open window, I found myself thinking about the E.T. paradox. They ought to be here...where are they?

The science fiction writer at Robin's party had said they wouldn't come in person. Organic life is too brief and too fragile for the eons-long journeys between stars. They would send machines. Maybe self-replicating machines. Maybe sentient machines.

But, I thought, why machines at all? If the thing that travels most efficiently between stars is light (and all its avatars: X-rays, radio waves), then why not send *light itself*? Light *modulated*, of course; light alive with information. Light as medium. Sentient light.

Light as domain, perhaps put in place by organic civilizations, but inherited by — something else.

And if human beings are truly latecomers to the galaxy, then the network must already be ancient, a web of modulated signals stitching together the stars. A domain in which things — entities — creatures perhaps as diffuse and large as the galaxy itself, creatures made solely of information — live and compete and maybe even hunt.

An ecology of starlight, or better: a *jungle* of starlight.

The next day I called up Robin's sf-writer friend and tried out the idea on him. He said, "Well, it's interesting...."

"But is it possible?"

"Sure it's possible. Anything's possible. Possible is my line of work. But you have to keep in mind the difference between a possibility and a likelihood." He hesitated. "Are you thinking of becoming a writer, or just a career paranoid?"

I laughed. "Neither one." Though the laughter was a little forced.

"Well, then, since we're only playing, here's another notion for you. Living things — species capable of evolving — don't just live. They eat." (Hunt, I thought.) "They die. And most important of all: they reproduce."

You've probably heard of the hunting wasp. The hunting wasp paralyses insects (the tarantula is a popular choice) and uses the still-living bodies to incubate and feed its young.

It's everybody's favorite Hymenoptera horror story. You can't help imagining how the tarantula must feel, immobilized but for its frantic heartbeat, the wasp larvae beginning to stir inside it...stir, and feed.

But maybe the tarantula isn't only paralysed. Maybe it's entranced. Maybe wasp venom is a kind of insect ambrosia — *soma, amrta, kykeon*. Maybe the tarantula sees God, feels God turning in hungry spirals deep inside it.

I think that would be worse — don't you?

Was I in love with Robin Slattery? I think this narrative doesn't make that absolutely clear — too many second thoughts since — but yes, I was in love with Robin. In love with the way she looked at me (that mix of deference and pity), the way she moved, her strange blend of erudition and ignorance (the only Shakespeare she had read was *The Tempest*, but she had read it five times and attended a performance at Stratford), her skinny legs, her pyrotechnic fashion sense (one day black Goth, next day tartan miniskirt and knee socks).

I paid her the close attention of a lover, and because I did I knew by spring (the Eta Aquarids...early May) that things had changed.

She spent a night at my place, something she had been doing less often lately. We went into the bedroom with the sound of *soca* tapes pulsing like a heartbeat from the shop downstairs. I had covered one wall with astronomical photographs, stuck to the plaster with push pins. She looked at the wall and said, "This is why men shouldn't be allowed to live alone — they do things like this."

"Is that a proposition?" I was feeling, I guess, reckless.

"No," she said, looking worried, "I only meant...."

"I know."

"I mean, it's not exactly *Good Housekeeping*."

"Right."

We went to bed troubled. We made love, but tentatively, and later, when she had turned on her side and her breathing was night-quiet, I left the bed and walked naked to the kitchen.

I didn't need to turn on lights. The moon cast a gray radiance through the rippled glass of the kitchen window. I only wanted to sit a while in the cool of an empty room.

But I guess Robin hadn't been sleeping after all, because she came to the kitchen wrapped in my bath robe, standing in the silver light like a quizzical, barefoot monk.

"Keeping the night watch," I said.

She leaned against a wall. "It's lonely, isn't it?"

I just looked at her. Wished I could see her eyes.

"Lonely," she said, "out here on the African plains."

I wondered if her intuition was right, if there was a gene, a defective sequence of DNA, that marked me and set me apart from everyone else. The image of the watchman-hominid was a powerful one. I pictured that theoretical ancestor of mine. Our hominid ancestors were small, vulnerable, as much animal as human. The tribe sleeps. The watchman doesn't. I imagine him awake in the long exile of the night, rump against a rock in a sea of wild grasses, shivering when the wind blows, watching the horizon for danger. The horizon and the sky.

What does he see?

The stars in their silent migrations. The annual meteor showers. A comet, perhaps, falling sunward from the far reefs of the solar system.

What does he feel?

Yes: lonely.

And often afraid.

In the morning, Robin said, "As a relationship, I don't think we're working. There's this *distance*...I mean, it's lonely for me, too...."

But she didn't really want to talk about it and I didn't really want to press her. The dynamic was clear enough.

She was kinder than Carolyn had been, and for that I was grateful.

I won't chronicle the history of our break-up. You know how this goes. Phone calls less often, fewer visits; then times when the messages I left on her machine went unreturned, and a penultimate moment of drawing-room comedy when Roger picked up her phone and kindly summoned her from the shower for me. (I pictured her in a towel, hair dripping while she made her vague apologies—and Roger watching.)

No hostility, just drift; and finally silence.

Another spring, another summer—the Eta Aquarids, the Delta Aquarids, at last the Perseids in the sweltering heat of a humid, cicada-buzzing August, two and half months since the last time we talked.

I was on the back deck of my apartment when the phone rang. It was still too hot to sleep, but *mirabile dictu*, the air was clear, and I kept the night watch in a lawn chair with my binoculars beside me. I heard the ring but ignored it—most of my phone calls lately had been sales pitches or marketing surveys, and the sky, even in the city (if you knew how to look), was alive with meteors, the best display in years. I thought about rock fragments old as the solar system, incinerated in the high atmosphere. The ash, I supposed, must eventually sift down through the air; we must breathe it, in some part; molecules of ancient carbon lodging in the soft tissue of the lung.

Two hours after midnight I went inside, brushed my teeth, thought about bed—then played the message on my answering machine.

It was from Robin.

"Mike? Are you there? If you can hear me, pick up...come on, *pick up!* [Pause.] Well, okay. I guess it's not really important. Shit. It's only that...there's something I'm not sure about. I just wanted to talk about it with someone. With you. [Pause.] You were always so *solid*. It thought it would be good to hear your voice again. Not tonight, huh? I guess not. Hey, don't worry about me. I'll be okay. But if you—"

The machine cut her off.

I tried calling back, but nobody answered the phone.

I knew her well enough to hear the anxiety in her voice. And she wouldn't have called me unless she was in some kind of trouble.

Robin, I thought, what lens did you look through? And what looked back?

I drove through the empty city to Parkdale, where there was no traffic but cabs and a few bad-tempered hookers; parked and pounded on Robin's door until her downstairs neighbors complained. She wasn't home, she'd gone out earlier, and I should fuck off and die.

I drove to Roger's.

The tall brick house was full of light.

When I knocked, the twins answered. They had shaved their heads since the last time I saw them. The effect was to make them even less distinguishable. Both were naked, their skin glistening with a light sheen of sweat and something else: spatters of green paint. Drops of it hung in their wiry, short pubic hair.

They blinked at me a moment before recognition set in. I couldn't recall their names (I thought of them as Alpha and Beta) — but they remembered mine.

"Michael!"

"Robin's friend!"

"What are *you* doing here?"

I told them I wanted to talk to Robin.

"She's real busy right now — "

"I'd like to come in."

They looked at each other as if in mute consultation. Then (one a fraction of a second after the other) they smiled and nodded.

Every downstairs light had been turned on, but the rooms I could see from the foyer were empty. One of Roger's *icaros* was playing somewhere; the chanting coiled through the air like the winding of a spring. I heard other voices, faintly, elsewhere in the house — upstairs.

Alpha and Beta looked alarmed when I headed for the stairs. "Maybe you shouldn't go up there, Michael."

"You weren't *invited*."

I ignored them and took the steps two at a time. The twins hurried up behind me.

Roger's gnostic ghost trap was switched on, its video screens flashing faster than the last time I had seen it. No image lingered long enough to resolve, but the flickering light was more than random; I felt presences in it, the kind of motion that alerts the peripheral vision. The icaro was louder and more insinuating in this warehouse-like space, a sound that invaded the body through the pores.

But the room was empty.

The twins regarded me, smiling blandly, pupils big as half-dollars. "Of course, all this isn't *necessary*—"

"You don't have to *summon* something that's already *inside you*—"

"But it's *out there*, too—"

"In the images—"

"In the *gnososphere...*"

"Everywhere...."

The third floor: more stairs at the opposite end of the room. I moved that way with the maddening sensation that time itself had slowed, that I was embedded in some invisible, congealed substance that made every footstep a labor. The twins were right behind me, still performing their mad Baedeker.

"The greenhouse!" (Alpha.)

"Yes, you should see it." (Beta.)

The stairs led to a door; the door opened into a jungle humidity lit by ranks of fluorescent bars. Plants were everywhere; I had to blink before I could make sense of it.

"*Psychotria viridis,*" Alpha said.

"And other plants—"

"Common grasses—"

"*Desmanthus illinoensis*—"

"*Phalaris arundinacea*—"

It was as Robin had described it, a greenhouse built over an expansion of the house, concealed from the street by an attic riser. The ceiling and the far walls were of glass, dripping with moisture. The air was thick and hard to breathe.

"Plants that contain DMT." (The twins, still babbling.)

"It's a drug—"

"And a *neurotransmitter.*"

"N,N-dimethyltryptamine...."

"It's what dreams are made of, Michael."

"Dreams and imagination."

"Culture."

"Religion!"

"It's the *opening*—"

I said, "Is she drugged? For Christ's sake, where is she?"

But the twins didn't answer.

I saw motion through the glass. The deck extended beyond the greenhouse, but there was no obvious door. I stumbled down a corridor of slim-leaved potted plants and put my hands against the dripping glass.

People out there.

"She's the *Rainha da Floresta*—"

"And Roger is *Santo Daime*!"

"All the archetypes, really...."

"Male and female, sun and moon...."

I swiped away the condensation with my sleeve. A group of maybe a dozen people had gathered on the wooden decking outside, night wind tugging at their hair. I recognized faces from Robin's parties, dimly illuminated by the emerald glow of the greenhouse. They formed a semi-circle with Robin at the centre of it—Robin and Roger.

She wore a white t-shirt but was naked below the waist. Roger was entirely naked and covered with glistening green dye. They held each other at arm's length, as if performing some elaborate dance, but they were motionless, eyes fixed on one another.

Sometime earlier the embrace must have been more intimate; his paint was smeared on Robin's shirt and thighs. She was thinner than I remembered, almost anorexic.

Alpha said, "It's sort of a wedding—"

"An *alchemical* wedding."

"And sort of a birth."

There had to be a door. I kicked over a brick and board platform, spilling plants and potting soil as I followed the wall. The door, when I found it, was glass in a metal frame, and there was a padlock across the clasp.

I rattled it, banged my palm against it. Where my hand had been I could see through the smear of humidity. A few heads turned at the noise—including, I recognized, the science fiction writer I had talked to long ago. But there was no curiosity in his gaze, only a desultory puzzlement. Roger and Robin remained locked in their peculiar trance, touching but apart, as if making room between them for...what?

No, something *had* changed: now their eyes were closed. Robin was breathing in short, stertorous gasps that made me think of a woman in labor. (A *birth*, the twins had said.)

I looked for something to break the glass—a brick, a pot.

Alpha stepped forward, shaking her head. "Too late for that, Michael."

And I knew—with a flood of grief that seemed to well up from some neglected, swollen wound—that she was right.

I turned back. To watch.

Past understanding, there is only observation. All I know is what I saw. What I saw, with the glass between myself and Robin. With my cheek against the dripping glass.

Something came out of her.

Something came out of her.

Something came out of her and Roger, like ectoplasm; but especially from their eyes, flowing like hot blue smoke.

I thought their heads were on fire.

Then the smoke condensed between them, took on a solid form, suspended weightless in the space between their tensed bodies.

The shape it took was complex, barbed, hard-edged, luminous, with the infolded symmetries of a star coral and the thousand facets of a geode. Suddenly translucent, it seemed made of frozen light. Strange as it was, it looked almost obscenely organic. I thought of a seed, an *achene*, the dense nucleus of something potentially enormous: a foetal god.

I don't know how long it hovered between their two tensed bodies. I was distantly aware of my own breathing. Of the hot moisture of my skin against the greenhouse glass. The *icaro* had stopped. I thought the world itself had fallen silent.

Then the thing that had appeared between them, the bright impossibility they had given birth to, began to rise, at first almost imperceptibly, then accelerating until it was suddenly gone, transiting the sky at, I guessed, the speed of light.

Commerce with the stars.

Then Robin collapsed.

I kicked at the door until, finally, the clasp gave way; then there were hands on me, restraining me, and I closed my eyes and let them carry me away.

She was alive.

I had seen her led down the stairs, groggy and emaciated but moving under her own volition. She needed sleep, the twins said. That was all.

They brought me to a room and left me alone with my friend the science fiction writer.

He poured a drink.

"Do you know," he asked, "can you even begin to grasp what you saw here tonight?"

I shook my head.

"But you've thought about it," he said. "We talked. You've drawn some conclusions. And, as a matter of fact, in this territory, we're all ignorant. In the gnososphere, Michael, intuition counts for more than knowledge. My intuition is that what you've seen here won't be at all uncommon in the next few years. It may become a daily event—a part, maybe even the central part, of the human experience."

I stared at him.

He said, "Your best move, Michael, and I mean this quite sincerely, would be to just get over it and get on with your life."

"Or else?"

"No 'or else.' No threats. It doesn't matter what you do. One human being...we amount to nothing, you know. Maybe we dive into the future, like Roger, or we hang back, dig in our heels, but it doesn't matter. It really doesn't. In the end you'll do what you want."

"I want to leave."

"Then leave. I don't have an explanation to offer. Only a few ideas of my own, if you care to hear them."

I stayed a while longer.

The Orionids, the Leonids: the stars go on falling with their serene implacability, but I confess, it's hard to look at them now. Bitter and hard.

Consider, he said, living things as large as the galaxy itself. Consider their slow ecology, their evolution across spans of time in which history counts for much less than a heartbeat.

Consider spores that lie dormant, perhaps for millennia, in the planetary clouds of newborn stars. Spores carried by cometary impact into the fresh biosphere (the *domain*) of a life-bearing world.

Consider our own evolution, human evolution, as one stage in a reproductive process in which *human culture itself* is the flower: literally, a flower, gaudy and fertile, from which fresh seed is generated and broadcast.

"Robin is a flower," he said, "but there's nothing special about that. Roger hastened the process with his drugs and paraphernalia and symbolic magic. So he could be among the first. The *avante-garde*. But the time is coming for all of us, Michael, and soon we won't need props. The thing that's haunted us as a species, the thing we painted on our cave walls and carved into our pillars and cornices and worshipped on our bloody altars and movie screens, it's almost here. We'll all be flowers, I think, before long."

Unless the flower is sterile — set apart, functionally alone, a genetic fluke.

But in another sense the flower is our culture itself, and I can't help wondering what happens to that flower after it broadcasts its seed. Maybe it wilts. Maybe it dies.

Maybe that's already happening. Have you looked at a newspaper lately?

Or maybe, like every other process in the slow ecology of the stars, it'll take a few centuries more.

I cashed in my investments and bought a house in rural British Columbia. Fled the city for reasons I preferred not to consider.

The night sky is dark here, the stars as close as the rooftop and the tall pines—but I seldom look at the sky.

When I do, I focus my telescope on the moon. It seems to me that sparks of light are gathering and moving in the Reiner Gamma area of Oceanus Procellarum. Faintly, almost furtively. Look for yourself. But there's been nothing in the journals about it. So it might be an optical illusion. Or my imagination.

The imagination is also a place where things live.

I'm alone.

It gets cold here in winter.

Robin called once. She said she'd tracked down my new number, that she wanted to talk. She had broken up with Roger. Whatever had happened that night in the city, she said, it was finished now. Life goes on.

Life goes on.

She said she got lonely these days and maybe she understood how it was for me, out there looking at the sky while everyone else sleeps.

(And maybe the watchman sees something coming, Robin, something large and terrible and indistinct in the darkness, but he knows he can't stop it and he can't wake anyone up....)

She said we weren't finished. She said she wanted to see me. She had a little money, she said, and she wanted to fly out. Please, she said. Please, Michael. Please.

God help me, I hung up the phone.

Fourth Person Singular

by Dale L. Sproule

Dale Sproule's "Fourth Person Singular" appeared in Northern Frights 2. *Not surprisingly, it was one of the stories from that volume chosen by the late, great author/editor Karl Edward Wagner to appear in his* Year's Best Horror *series from DAW Books. Following Wagner's tragic, untimely death the DAW series was terminated and none of our stories were thus honored. Those of us who knew Karl well knew what great taste he had in literature, so it is a pleasure to be able to reprint one of the stories he so admired.*

E very night since I was seven years old he's swooped down at me out of the darkness of sleep: a pale, skeletal boy with thin arms thrust out like wings, eyes like white domes in black craters, mouth open as he screams acceleration.

His name is Wren.

And he is the mad eye of the fourth person singular
   of which nobody speaks
   and he is the voice of the fourth person singular
   in which nobody speaks
   and which yet exists
   with a long head and a foolscap face

and the long mad hair of death
of which nobody speaks
And he speaks of himself and he speaks of the dead. . .
-    Lawrence Ferlinghetti, "HF"

It's been over thirty years and the images haven't even begun to fade. Maybe writing it down will help exorcise my ghosts.

In 1961, when I was six and my brother, Wren, was nine, we would huddle together on his bed pulling his thick blue bedspread over our heads on those nights when the screams came from the basement. Several times each year, tortured voices wavered up the heat ducts, sometimes sounding like men, sometimes women. Sometimes they would wail for hours although one night, a single excruciating plea of "stop!" was followed by silence. Wren and I put our ears to the metal vent in the hardwood floor, listening for more, but instead heard the door downstairs slamming and Dad stomping up the stairs. I barely had time to scramble back to my room and pull up my covers before my door swung open and Dad came in and kissed me goodnight.

He smelled like the stuff they use to clean hospitals, the scent of pine heightened until it makes your nose smart and your eyes water.

Smashing, cursing sounds told me he was going into Wren's room. Dad hardly ever came upstairs, so he didn't remember Wren's forty or fifty model airplanes hanging on fishing line from the bedroom ceiling; a network of filaments like a massive spiderweb.

The next morning at breakfast, Dad spoke. "Renfield," he said, being the only person who ever used my brother's full name, "I want you to take down those airplanes."

"You broke four of them," Wren replied sullenly.

A spoonful of cornflakes stopped en route to my lips as I watched Wren mirror Dad's stare, a shrunken reflection of our father's stubbornness and passionate intensity.

"Move them or suffer more losses than you already have. Understand?"

"Yes, sir," he muttered, playing it safe for once. My relief slipped out in a sigh. Then, with no more trepidation than saying "pass the milk", Wren asked, "What is that screaming we always hear coming from the basement?" I wanted to grab my brother by the shoulders and shake him and shout "Shuttup you idiot! This man made Mom disappear. He'll make you disappear too and then I'll be alone with him. Don't leave me alone with him!" But I didn't move, didn't breathe.

Looking up from his magazine, Dad sounded genuinely puzzled. "Screaming?" He turned to me. "Have you heard screaming, Barrymore?"

Avoiding Wren's glare, I said, "No, Dad."

"He hears it just like me. Tell him, Bear."

I couldn't.

An interminable silence later, Dad suggested, "I have a proposition for you, Renfield. Come into the basement with me when I get home from work tonight and I will show you everything there is to see."

I hoped Wren would somehow read the silent plea in my eyes, but without according me even a scornful glance, he flipped his long black hair out of his eyes and said, "Naw. Guess I don't want to know all that badly."

"We will see." Dad nodded, then looked at us one by one. "Neither of you have mentioned this imaginary screaming to anyone outside of this house, have you?"

"No," I answered, hoping Wren would chime in and we would speak in a single voice like we once did.

Instead, my brother wondered aloud, "How could we tell anybody, if you won't let us out of the house, Dad?"

"You sneak out sometimes while I am at work during the day. I found that yellow plastic bowl you left beside the garage the other day."

We had used the bowl to feed our neighbour's Irish setter. Their house was around the bend in the road and we never wandered that far, so we'd never been close enough to overhear the dog's name. Going over to inquire might start them asking why we weren't in school. So I blessed the dog with a second name; Robin, like in that song Mom used to sing.

"When the red, red robin comes bob, bob, bobbing along..."

The lecture droned on, "...going out any more. I have to trust you to be good boys," Dad gave Wren a fatherly smile and tousled his hair. "If you told anyone about this screaming, they would quite likely send you to a psychiatrist. Do you know what the psychiatrist would do? Perform a lobotomy operation. Just like they did to my father. They drilled a hole in his forehead, inserted a knife, and sliced off the front of his brain. We don't want anyone doing that to you, now do we? I want my family safe and sound. Keeping your mouth and eyes and ears shut is the best way to stay safe and sound, Renfield."

"I thought keeping the door shut was the best way."

"Are you being smart?"

"No sir. You told us. . ."

"Do not ever get smart with me."

"Yes, s. . ."

"Mouth SHUT, correct?"

Wren nodded.

Dad got up and walked straight out the kitchen door. My brother and I listened to the rattling of locks and latches, the departing footsteps, the uneven rumble of the Rambler's engine and the crunching of gravel as Dad backed out the driveway. Then Wren said, "I'm going down to the base-ment. You wanna come?"

I shook my head and pouted. "You'll scream," I warned.

"Huh?"

"Going down there will make you scream like all the others."

"Dad goes down there," said Wren. "He doesn't scream."

I trailed my brother upstairs, unable to muster a better argument than his. We struggled to lift the window in his bedroom.

"Get something to prop it open!"

I brought the wastebasket from the bathroom and watched as he climbed onto the porch roof. His legs, his head, and finally his hands seemed to sink into the greenery as he climbed down the trellis.

After a few scary minutes by myself, I decided to follow, but on my way out, I hit the wastebasket with my shoulder and the window came shud-dering down at me. Certain I was about to be decapitated, I threw myself back into the room, escaping with no worse injury than bruised elbows and a sore bum.

I'd seen the wastebasket bounce off the gutter into the yard, where Dad was sure to find it. My struggles to open the window couldn't budge it.

Had I locked my brother out forever? I had no idea what to do next. Break the window? I scanned the room for a tool, in case it came to that. On the floor were clothes and empty boxes from his model planes, but no balls, bats or other outside toys. Being too young to assemble the many models Dad had given me as gifts, I'd passed mine along to Wren who had thrown out the cars and boats, but added the airplanes to his collection.

I looked up. Even if I could reach them, Wren would kill me for throwing one of his planes through the window. I'd once broken a wing on a model he was working on. He didn't talk to me for a week.

I looked down. I was standing on the furnace grate. Kneeling beside it, I tried unsuccessfully to pry it out of the floor. Then, lying flat on my stomach, I put my lips to the open vent. "Wren? Are you down there?" I shouted timidly. Receiving no answer, I yelled again and again. When I stopped, I could hear my own small, hollow voice still echoing through the ductwork.

The door behind me opened and I whirled, surprised that Wren had found another way in. But it wasn't Wren.

Dad stared down at me, his face blank and grey as usual. He was still in his blue suit as if going off to work but he obviously hadn't gone.

"We were. . .uhhm. . .playing hide 'n' seek," I stammered, unable to lie quickly or convincingly enough. "I'm IT. Wren is hiding."

Wordlessly, Dad turned and headed back down the stairs.

How had I failed to hear him return? Dad must have read our minds again. He must have parked the Rambler on the road and snuck into the house on tiptoes.

I lay there on the cold floor until Dad called me for supper hours later. Wren wasn't there. Hopefully, he'd seen Dad coming and run away. I never asked, never spoke at all, never even looked up from the canned spaghetti cooling and congealing on my plate. Dad sent me to my room.

I curled on my bed, clutching my knees to my chest as I listened for my brother's screams. There were screams; although not those of a child. A man's voice gibbered and wept for a long time before his screaming started.

It was loud at first, his voice gradually weakening, becoming hoarse and merging with the rustling of leaves in the nearby trees, the rushing of water in the creek, the pumping of my own heart.

Wren was in bed when I peeked in on him next morning.

Needing to know if he was alive, I slipped through the doorway, crept up beside the bed, reached out and tentatively touched him on the shoulder. He didn't move. I shook harder, then tried to roll him onto his back, but he resisted.

"Go away," he said in a voice I barely recognized.

"Are you hurt?" I whispered.

"He made me watch."

"But he didn't hurt you?" I asked.

"He made me watch." Wren said again. "Now go away."

"What did you see?"

"The screams. I saw the screams."

"Who was screaming?" I asked.

He didn't answer so I grabbed his shoulder again, shook harder, asked more loudly, "Who was it? Why were they screaming?"

"Breakfast," said a man's voice from behind me. Dad had stuck his head in. I turned and saw him smiling warmly. As suddenly as he'd appeared, he went away and I heard a number of distinct thumps as he descended the stairs two at a time.

Dad must have heard me asking Wren about the screams, which, even from the sanctuary of my bedroom, sounded full of pain and fear. I didn't really want to know what the screams looked like. I didn't want to talk to Wren anymore. I didn't want to go downstairs for breakfast. I didn't know what to do.

Wren got up and I followed him down to the breakfast table. My brother stared vacantly at me as we sat down, although I'm sure he didn't see me. Dad whistled and made "a hearty breakfast" of bacon and eggs. I concluded he hadn't heard me asking about the screams. Dad chattered throughout the meal about nothing in particular.

The next few weeks were lonely. The only time I saw Wren was at supper. After we ate, Dad would present him with a new model plane.

Wren added it to the stack against the wall at the bottom of the stairs before retreating to his privacy. After a while, my brother began to act like himself again. The tower of boxes shrank, then disappeared.

I went to his room, but Wren was so caught up in the process of building his new models that he hardly talked to me. So I stopped visiting. The next day the banging and hammering sounds began. Wanting him to know how hurt and offended I was, I refused to give into my curiosity. He didn't seem to notice. One afternoon as I was just about to give in and visit him, Wren appeared at my door.

"Come see my invention."

I did.

His model airplanes had been taken down and were heaped in and around his closet. A single plane hung from the knob at the bottom of the light fixture in the centre of the ceiling. Leading from there into the corner where Wren stood on top of his bed, was what looked like a railway track which Wren had constructed out of coathangers. At the end of the track, hung another plane. Wren reached up and grasped it firmly.

"Watch this," he said, hurling the projectile as hard as he could. I could actually hear it whistle through the air as it flew across the room and collided with the stationary plane. Bits of plastic sliced through the air in every direction and I turned away, covering my eyes.

"What'dya think?" he asked.

"Uhmm, neat, I guess."

"It's the neatest thing ever," he corrected. "I'll show you again."

I watched Wren untwist the lines, dropping the wreckages carelessly to the floor, before replacing them with new airplanes.

"You know what this is called?" he asked just as he was about to throw the second plane.

I shook my head.

"A dogfight." Smash.

"What is?" I puzzled, as Wren replaced the casualties with new sacrifices.

"Airplane battles. No kidding. I dunno why. A birdfight would make more sense. Or flying tiger fight. But it's called a dogfight. Wanna try?"

I could barely touch the fuselage with my fingertips let alone grab hold of the plane.

"Can you make the string longer?"

Wren shook his head. "Took forever to get everything just right. Don't wanna start over."

I couldn't throw very hard. On my first attempt the plane ended up flying in circles around the target after missing completely. Wren let me try again. I managed to break one strut off the propellor on the target plane. Wren laughed. I stomped out, leaving my brother to the bewildering and solitary pleasure of destroying the only thing he'd ever cared about.

A month later, Dad took him downstairs for a second time.

The screams went on for longer than usual that night and I imagined I heard more than one voice wailing. I didn't recognize either of them though.

Wren was withdrawn the next day, but not at all as bad as he'd been that first time. He even came to breakfast. Dad had made pancakes.

"What do you want for your birthday on Sunday, Barry?"

"It's my birthday?"

"Seven years old. Both my boys are growing up."

I didn't respond.

"If you don't ask for something I can hardly get it for you, can I? What would you like?"

"A puppy?"

"You know we don't have pets in this house. Don't be so stupid. Now what would you really like?"

I shrugged.

"Would you like to come to the basement and see what daddy does downstairs?"

"A colouring book."

"We could have a party down there. All three of us."

"He says he wants a coloring book instead, Dad," Wren cut in, the boldest I'd seen him since his first trip to the basement. "I don't think Barry's old enough. He wouldn't understand."

Dad pushed his plate of uneaten pancakes into the center of the table and wiped his lips with a napkin. Then he stood, not moving from his place at the table, and stared at me.

I'm sure Dad saw that I was crying, no matter how hard I tried to hide it.

With a nod, he grunted, "Perhaps," then strode to the door and out.

"Why can't I have a puppy?" I sobbed once he was gone.

"He'd kill it. He killed Robin, you know?"

I didn't know. I hadn't been outside in weeks.

"He keeps the body in the basement," Wren continued.

"Maybe it was another dog that looked like Robin."

"I'm sorry, Barry," Wren said, coming around the table to give me a hug. "I'd get you a puppy if I could."

Wren's hammering resumed late the next morning, but he wouldn't let me see what he was up to. "Secret," he explained.

That Saturday, Dad brought home a yellow cake with red writing on white icing. It spent the night in the fridge.

Sunday at noon, Dad brought out the cake, singing "Happy Birthday" as he carried it to the table. He watched for my reaction and I pretended that it was a big surprise. He smiled and kissed the top of my head.

"I guess I should get some candles to put on there," Dad said.

"Aren't you supposed to light the candles before you sing?" asked Wren.

"I think there's some in the hutch. Be right back," Dad continued, as if my brother hadn't said a word. He went into the dining room to look for them.

Wren saw me staring at the top of the cake and said, "What are you looking at?"

"The words."

"What for? He'll never let us learn to read."

Wren had been to grade one but I'd never gone to school. Dad said that insolence and apathy were all we would learn in school. Teachers know nothing about respect, he would say. How to give it or how to earn it. I'd like to teach the teachers, he would say. And he would laugh.

When Dad returned with the candles, he also brought my presents; a stack of coloring books and what seemed like a hundred packages of crayons. I picked one of the coloring books off the pile and studied the cover wondering if I could learn to read by studying those letters. If I looked at them long enough, would it suddenly come to me and start making sense? I looked at the second coloring book down. It was blue with a cartoon dog on the cover.

"You like Huckleberry Hound, Barry? Did I pick you some good ones?"

"What's Hucklederry Hound?"

Dad put his hands on his knees and bent down to look me in the face. He smiled broadly. "Like on TV?"

"Barry's never seen TV, Dad."

"Yes, I have," I protested.

"Well, you can't remember it, can you, twerp?"

I had no answer to that one.

Dad just kept smiling. "Maybe that's what I should buy for Christmas. A television set, a family present."

Wren and I nodded eager assent.

"Now let's get back to that party," Dad grinned as he held a little box of candles beside his ear and shook it.

After I blew them out, Dad asked, "What'd you wish for?"

"That Mom would come back."

"Oh." Dad's smile disappeared. He busied himself cutting big pieces of cake, then said, "I have to go to work."

"It's Sunday," I protested as he was leaving, but Wren held a finger to his lips.

"Shhh. Let's just eat."

Wren gave me the biggest piece and I crammed a big forkful into my mouth. After a minute I looked up at Wren, who simply sat with his empty hands face down on the table on each side of his plate. He stared at the cake without eating any. After a few more bites my appetite disappeared.

"What's the matter?"

"I got you a present," Wren said.

"Why didn't you bring it to the party?"

"Party? This isn't a real. . .aw, hell Barry. Dad wouldn't have liked it, that's all. I got you something he wouldn't have liked, so you have to keep it a secret. Okay?"

"What is it?"

"Guess."

"I dunno. What color is it?"

"Mostly black. But his tail and one foot are white."

Was Wren talking about some sort of stuffed toy? Where would he have found such a thing?

"C'mon. I'll show you."

I followed my brother to his bedroom which looked empty except for the pile of plastic which had once been model airplanes. The carpet was squishy underfoot.

Wren saw me looking down and said, "He messed the floor."

"Who did?" I said, starting to get genuinely excited. Had Wren some- how smuggled in a real puppy? He started hauling something out of the closet. A box? A cage? No. . .a big piece of plywood; with a puppy nailed to the wood by its paws.

"His eye is gunky," Wren was explaining. "I thought you could fix it with that big green marble you were showing me the other day."

Not wanting to believe what I saw, I asked, "Is it dead?"

Wren was offended. "He WAS dead. Now he's your puppy."

I covered my mouth with my hand, not knowing what to do.

Wren kept talking, earnestly, desperately, "It feels a bit funny when you scratch him behind the ears. And he has these little white bugs crawl- ing around in his fur."

My brother was making a sincere effort to give me what I wanted. I knew that. I could see love and concern in his eyes, hear it in his voice. Wren cared about me. But then, so did Dad.

". . .maybe we should give him a bath."

"Did you kill it?"

"What?"

"The puppy. Did you kill it?"

"I FOUND him. Beside the road. Alone. He needs someone to love him. Somebody like you."

I wanted to thank him, but I felt like throwing up.

"I thought we could name him Razzmatazz. Why don't you. . ."

I turned and ran to my room, slamming the door behind me. I leaned against the door and burst into tears.

Wren pounded and pushed on the door. "Barry? Are you okay? What's the matter, Bear? Don't you like him? What's wrong?"

Realizing that Wren genuinely didn't know what was wrong, I braced my feet against the side of my dresser. My socks left red footprints on white paint. I remembered how I felt when Wren said, "He messed the floor." Now I knew what he meant. "Go away!" I screamed.

But he didn't go away. Nor did he try to break in. He kept knocking and asking what was the matter until I stood up and yelled. "Because the stupid puppy is dead and that's the dumbest present anybody ever got and you're the dumbest brother anybody ever had! Now leave me alone!"

Without another word, Wren went away.

I couldn't sleep. Sometime in the middle of the night, I snuck into his room to apologize.

"Wren?" I whispered, stepping into absolute darkness.

I stood there and listened for the sounds of his breathing. Nothing. I brought my hands up defensively with each cautious step, half expecting to run into something in the middle of the room.

As I approached the bed, feeble moonlight sliding through the crack at the edge of the curtain allowed me to see that the bedspread was still pulled all the way up, neat as could be. I backed up to the door and flicked on the light. The room was empty.

I walked through the rest of the house in darkness, everywhere except the basement. Then I went back upstairs.

Maybe Wren had run away. Maybe I had driven him away.

Wren wasn't just my brother, he was my protector, the only thing between me and Dad. Between me and the basement.

He didn't show up for breakfast.

"Where's Renfield?" asked Dad.

I shrugged.

That day, the pounding and hammering started again. This time it reverberated through the whole house. I couldn't tell where it was coming from and I was afraid to call out for Wren, in case it was actually Dad again.

When Wren didn't show up at dinner, Dad asked me, "Where's your brother?"

"Said he wasn't hungry."

"Is he sick?" Dad pushed his chair back and walked to the stairs.

"Said he was tired. He's sleeping."

"You're sure he's not sick?"

I nodded. Dad came back to the table.

"You bring him up some dinner later."

I nodded again and ate the rest of my meal in silence.

Dad wouldn't accept the same explanation a second time. I had to decide what to do.

As far as I knew, Wren had only one exit; the window in his room. He'd been outside to get me the puppy so it followed that he must have managed to pry the window back open.

After Dad went out that night, I got up and went to Wren's room. I entered in darkness, in case Dad was lying in wait again. Ready to catch us again.

There was a gust of cold air. The window was open. A new airplane was hanging from the light fixture. The wind slammed the door behind me as I walked to the centre of the room.

"Wren?" I yelled, turning circles as I stumbled back toward the light switch. Flick. A second plane slid along the track. Crash. But no one was there to throw it. The room was empty, except for me. Except for me and the airplanes, now swaying silently on their strings; two wreckages dangling from their strings.

"Wren!" I screamed, lurching from the room.

I searched the whole house calling his name; checking every door and window; looking in closets and cupboards, behind curtains, even in places I knew were too small for him to fit.

I flopped face down on the sofa and was still sleeping there when Dad found me, hours later, and carried me up to bed.

At breakfast the next morning, Dad put my bowl of cereal down in front of me. "Where's Renfield, son?"

My throat tightened up like it was stuck with airplane model glue.

Able to neither swallow nor talk, I shook my head.

"We're a tight-knit family. You two are always together. Your brother wouldn't have left without telling you where he was going. Where was he going, Barrymore?"

"I. . .don't. . ." my words seeped out.

"What are you afraid of, son? Do you think he's gone to the police? Is that it? Are you afraid they'll send him to a psychiatrist and slice up his brain?"

It hadn't occurred to me. Suddenly I was truly afraid for my brother.

Dad's moist brown eyes oozed fatherly love as he reached out, cupping my whole jaw in his big hand. "I can't protect him if I don't know where he is. You tell me, so I can bring him home safely."

The air felt so warm and thick I could hardly breathe. "I don't know," I said. "I've been looking for him."

"You don't know?" Dad asked. "If you don't know, who does, Barrymore?"

"I don't. . ."

"Tell me where he is, son."

"I don't. . ."

"Tell me!"

As I shook my head, tears ran down my cheek into his cupped hand. He let me go. Then he got up and stared out the window, into the morning sunshine. "What are we going to do? We can't call the police."

Recalling his story of where the police would send him, I nodded.

"But if the police find him and Renfield mentions that he has a brother, they might come looking for you I'm. . .I'm going to have to hide you. I'll put you in the basement. Won't let them look in the basement. This wrecks my plans. I was going to have guests tonight. Damn that boy."

Dad's stare made me feel transparent, like he could see the fear gushing around inside me. "Let's go. Before the police get here."

I bolted from my chair, planning to lock myself in the bathroom, but Dad caught me before I reached the stairs. "What the hell is the matter with you? I'm doing this for your own protection. To keep you safe and sound."

I squinted in the bright sunshine as he carried me out to the porch, then down the steps to the basement door. He inserted a key in the lock and the door swung open, letting some darkness out. But somehow no light came back in when we entered.

Dad didn't even turn on the light when he pushed the door shut behind us. The air was cold. My legs swung with the rhythm of his stride as I pried at the hairy arm clamped around my chest and listened to my father's footfalls clop across bare concrete.

Abruptly, he stopped and reached up. As a light directly above us blazed on, I struggled to get free.

"Am I going to have to strap you down like I did to Renfield? Like I did to your mother?" Peering through the incandescence of my fear, I saw a table; a giant version of the puppy board, its wood was riddled with nail holes and covered with dark splotches.

Dad spun me around to face a wooden wall. No, it was an upright board; like the table, except with belts instead of nails to hold someone by their arms and legs.

The board wasn't propped up from behind, it was nailed to a beam above us. As I stared up at the ceiling, I could make out something else; some sort of metal track, like the one in Wren's room. My gaze slid along it into an impenetrable darkness. This had to be where Wren got the idea to build his track. I wondered what sorts of things my father sent rumbling toward whomever was strapped to the board. Things that made people scream.

My gaze searched the perimeter of our pool of light. I saw shapes along the wall. Just jars and bottles, I finally realized; milk bottles, pop bottles. Maybe there were horrible things in them. I couldn't tell.

On the other end of the table was a workbench. It was painted green, just like the one at our old house. All of Dad's tools were hung up neatly along the wall above it; I'd never seen pliers and drills before, so I didn't know what they were. But I had seen knives, and there were lots of knives; some funny ones with big square blades and some hook shaped ones and some really skinny ones along with all the regular knives. There were a few empty spaces at the bottom. I wondered if Dad had brought some down for me.

Dad put his arm around my shoulders and walked me up to the edge of the table. I backed away, but he held onto my upper arms and turned to face me. Crouching down, he looked me in the eyes and smiled. He shook me very gently for emphasis as he spoke. "It's a father's responsibility to protect his family. I'll teach you how to make people respect you, Barrymore. Because people who respect you will never hurt you. There's only one person you should fear. You know who that is?"

Wide eyed, I answered, "You, sir?"

He laughed and kissed me. "No, Barrymore. It's you. That's right. People hurt themselves sometimes, son. Even kill themselves. Like your mother. She could have lived as long as she wanted. But she knew I couldn't let her go to the police. So, you see? For all intents and purposes, her own hand held the knife that slit her throat. She killed herself. I guess she didn't have enough respect for herself. I loved her, just like I love you and Renfield. I would never hurt either of my boys. But I have to teach you not to hurt yourselves."

As he stood up again, I heard a whistling sound like the ones during the dogfights in my brother's bedroom. Dad noticed the sound at the same time I did, only he had to turn around in order to see what I saw; Wren soaring toward us, his arms straight out to the sides like wings. In one hand, he held a fireplace poker and in the other, a knife. My father and I stood transfixed.

Any sound the metal shaft of the poker might have made as it plunged into Dad's throat was drowned out by a terrible thump and clatter of the ropes breaking free of their guides. My brother flew overhead, his body slamming into the plywood board. The knife clattered at my feet.

I bent down and tried to turn Wren onto his back. His head lolled loosely, just as the dead puppy's head had done two nights earlier. But how could Wren be dead? He wasn't bleeding or anything.

Dad was bleeding. He was lying on his side and I could see the tip of the poker coming out the back of his neck.

"Wren?" I said, but he didn't answer.

I remembered somebody saying that when a person is dead, they stop breathing. And I couldn't see Wren's chest going up and down like it usually did when he pretended to be dead. I put my ear to his mouth and listened as hard as I could. His lips were cold. I could hear a breathing sound, I was sure of it! As it got louder I realized that the sound wasn't coming from Wren.

I looked at my father, half expecting him to pull the implement from his neck and stand up, but he didn't move.

The sound was coming from deep in the gloom of the basement. A voice? I sat up, holding my own breath as I peered into the darkness.

It was a voice of a sort; the growl of a dog floated toward me, turning into a whimper.

"Robin?" I said. And the big red dog stuck his head around the edge of the board and sniffed at Wren's hair. It licked my dead brother's face. Then it staggered toward Dad and started lapping blood off the floor.

"Robin! Don't!"

Wren had told me Robin was dead. He'd seen the body. But Wren was wrong.

The dog's tail pounded against the wooden table leg as I stood up. He began walking slowly towards me. I reached out to push him away. His fur felt stiff, the same way the puppy had felt a day or two earlier.

Backing away from the dog, I looked at the bodies of my father and brother. "How long will *you* stay dead?" I whispered. Then I turned and scrambled toward the line of sunlight streaming in through the door which was standing slightly ajar.

Sensing Robin close behind me, I looked back. In the light, he looked worse than he had when I'd first seen him — horribly skinny and his fur was all matted and crusty.

Robin followed me when I ran. His limp prevented him from catching up, but he was still there every time I glanced back. The dog on my heels kept me running. I don't remember stopping. I don't think I ever stopped.

Although my brother has been dead a long, long time now, he comes back night after night; as cold and familiar as the moon.

Slow Cold Chick

by Nalo Hopkinson

"Slow Cold Chick" is perhaps the only Northern Frights story to have had both an airwave and a print debut, having been commissioned by and performed on CBC Radio (The Canadian Broadcasting Corporation) prior to book publication. Like her award-winning first novel, Brown Girl in the Ring, *Nalo Hopkinson's story employs Afro-Caribbean culture, language, and sensibilities within the northern setting of her adopted home of Toronto. It is soon to be reprinted in her first short story collection,* Skin Folk, *Warner Aspect Books, 2001.*

They'd cut off the phone. Blaise slammed the receiver back into its cradle. "Oonuh couldn't wait just a little more?" she asked resentfully of the silent phone. "I get paid Friday, you know." Now she couldn't ask her mother if to put milk or water in the cornbread. Chuh. Blaise flounced into the kitchen and scowled at the mixing bowl on the counter.

Mummy used milk, she was almost sure of it. Blaise poured milk and oil, remembering her mother's home-made cornbread, yellow-warm smelling, hot from the oven, with butter melting more yellow into it. Yes, Mummy used milk.

And eggs. And Blaise didn't have any. "Damn." It was almost a week until pay day. She made a sucking sound of irritation. Frustration burned deep in her chest.

A movement through her kitchen window caught her eye. From her main floor apartment, Blaise could easily see the Venus-built lady in the next door garden. The Venus-built lady's cottage always gave the appearance of having just popped into existence, unexpected and anachronistic as Doctor Who's call box.

Chocolate-dark limbs peeking out of her plush white dressing gown, the Venus-built lady waded indolently through rioting ivy, swollen red roses, nasturtiums that pursed into succulent lips. Blaise had often thought to ask the beautiful woman what her name was. But to meet the eyes of someone so self-possessed, much less speak to her...

Branches laden, an otaheite tree bobbed tumescent maroon fruit, so low that the lady could have plucked them with her mouth. Blaise's mother sometimes sent her otaheite apples from Jamaica, but how did the tropical tree flourish in this northern climate?

As ever, the Venus-built lady's gingered brown hair flung itself in crinkled dreadknots down her back, tangled as lovers' fingers. Blaise had chemically straightened all the kinks out of her own hair.

The Venus-built lady was laying a circle of conch shells around a bed of bleeding hearts. She reached out to caress the plants' pink flowers. At her touch, they shivered delicately. Blaise looked down at her own dull brown hands. The Venus-built lady's skin had the glow of full-fat chocolate.

The woman bent and straightened, bent and straightened, leaving a pouting conch shell behind her each time, until pink echoed pink in a circle around the bleeding hearts. Blaise thought of the shells singing as the wind blew past their lips.

The lady turned away from the flower bed and swayed amply up her garden path. As her foot touched the first step of the cottage, a fat, velvet-petalled rose leaned beseechingly towards her. She tugged the rose from its stem and *ate* it. Then she opened her gingerbread door and sashayed inside.

Weird. Blaise imagined a spineless green grub squirming voluptuously in the heart of the overblown rose. And an avid mouth descending towards it. She shuddered. *I don't want to eat the worm.*

It had gotten hot in the apartment. The fridge burped. Distractedly, Blaise opened it.

There was an egg huddling in one of the little cups inside the fridge door. Where had that come from? Exactly what she needed. She was reaching eagerly for it when a stench from deep inside the fridge slid into her nostrils; a poisonous, vinegary tang. The scotch bonnet pepper sauce she'd made, last year sometime? was rotting in its glass jar. The pepper crusting the jar's lid had begun to corrode the metal. A vile greenness bloomed on the surface of the red liquid. Blaise kissed her teeth in disgust and dumped the mouldering sauce into the sink.

Cornbread now.

The egg was a little too big for its cradle, a little rounder than eggs usually were. Blaise picked it up. Its cold, mercurial weight shifted in her palm, sucking warmth from her hand. She cracked it into the bowl. With a hollow *clomp!* a mass disappeared below the surface of the liquid.

A sulphur-rot stench filled the kitchen. "Backside!" Blaise swallowed a wave of anger. A bubble of foetid air popped from the depths of the bowl. Blaise grimaced and began to pour the swampy goop down the drain. The tainted milk and oil mingled with the pepper sauce.

Something rubbery thumped into the mouth of the drain and lay there. It was small and grey and jointed. A naked, fully formed chicken foetus. Blaise's gorge rose. When the thing moved, wallowing in the pepper sauce remaining in the sink, she nearly spewed the coffee she'd drunk that morning.

"Urrrr..." rattled the cold-grown chick. Slowly, slowly, it extended a peeled head on a wobbly neck. Its tiny beak was thin as nail parings. Its eyes creaked open, stretching a red film of pepper sauce from lid to lid. It shrieked tinnily as the pepper made contact with its eyes. Frantically it shook its head. Its pimply grey body contorted in agony. It shrieked again. Fighting revulsion, Blaise grabbed a cooking spoon and scooped it up.

"Shh, shh." She wadded a tea towel in her free hand and deposited the bird into it. It wailed and stropped its own head against the tea towel. Its cartilaginous body writhed against her palm. Her skin crawled.

"Arr..." the chick complained. Blaise filled the cooking spoon with water and trickled it over the grey, bald head. The bird fought and spluttered. Reddened eyes glared accusingly at Blaise.

"Make up your mind," she flared. "You want fire in your eyes, or cool water?" The chick tried to peck. Blaise hissed angrily, "Well here, then, take that!"

She scooped some drops of pepper sauce from the sink with her fingers and flicked it at the bird's head. It yowped in indignation. Then, worm-blind, a tiny grey tongue snaked out of its mouth and licked some of the pepper sauce off its beak. "Urrrr...." This time it didn't seem to mind the taste of the pepper. It licked it off, then blinked its burned eyes clear.

Its body a blur, it shook the water off. It sat up straight in her palm, staring alertly at her. It seemed a little bigger. It did have a few feathers after all, Blaise must have just not noticed them before.

Her anger cooled. She'd let loose the heat of her temper on such a little thing.

The chick opened its mouth wide; Blaise nearly dropped it in alarm. Its hungry red maw looked bigger than its head.

Well, it had seemed to like the pepper, after all. Blaise scraped stringy threads of it out of the sink and dangled them in front of the cold chick's beak. It gaped even wider, begging to be fed. She let slimy tendrils fall. Red threads wriggled down the bird's throat. Ugh.

The chick swallowed, withdrew its pinny head into its ugly neck, and closed its eyes.

"That do you for now?" Blaise asked it.

The chick purred, a low, rattling sound. It radiated heat into her hand. It wasn't so ugly, really. She tucked its warmth close to her breast.

Someone knocked at the door. Blaise gasped, jolted out of her peaceful moment. She dumped the chick into a soup bowl. It squawked and toppled, legs kicking at the air. "Stay there," she hissed, and went to answer the knock.

It was the guy next door, lanky and pimply in a frowsty leather jacket. "Hi there, Blaise," he leered. "Whatcha up to?"

The red tongues of his construction boots hung loose and floppy. He was gnawing on the gooey tag end of a cheap chocolate bar, curled wrapper ends wilting from his fist.

"Nothing much," Blaise replied.

Tethered by a leash through its studded leather collar, the guy's ferret humped around and around in sad circles at his feet. Something about its furtive slinkiness brought to mind a furry penis with teeth.

The guy took a hopeful step closer. "Want some company?"

Not this again. "Um, maybe another time." She remained blocking the doorway, hoping he'd get the point. The ferret sneezed and rubbed fretfully at its snout. Oh, goody: the guy next door's ferret had a head cold. Gooseflesh rose on Blaise's arms.

"What, like this evening, maybe?" asked the guy. His eyes roamed eagerly over her face and body. The familiar steam of stifled anger bubbled through Blaise. Why couldn't he ever take a hint? She wished he'd just dry up and fly away.

There was a thump from the kitchen. The ferret arched sinuously up onto its hind legs, its fur bristling. Blaise turned; her blood froze cold. A creature something between a chicken and an eagle was stalking menacingly out of her kitchen. It was the cold chick, grown to the size of a spaniel. Its down-feathered neck wove its raptor's head in a serpentine dance. Its feet had become cruel, ringed claws. It stared at her with a fierce intelligence.

The guy goggled. "What the...?"

At the sound, the chick's fiery-red comb went erect. Nictitating membranes slid clear of its eyes, which glowed red. Blaise felt a peppery warmth flood her body briefly. Frightened, she stepped aside. The chick turned its gaze full on the guy. It hissed, a sound like steam escaping. The guy next door looked down at it, and seemed immediately held by its stare. He whimpered softly. Heat danced between the chick and the guy next door, then he just, well, *vaporized*. In a second, all that was left of him was a grey smear of ash on the hallway carpet, and a faint whiff of cheap chocolate.

"Oh, my God," Blaise said, feeling frantically for the open doorway.

The ferret growled. The chick pounced. Blaise leapt out of the way. Jesus, now they were between her and the way out.

The ferret wound itself around the creature. The chick's beak slashed. The ferret yipped, sneezed. Drops of ferret blood and mucus flew. The cold chick flexed a meaty thigh to slice a talon through the ferret's middle. The ferret arched and writhed in extremis. Knots of bloody intestine trailed from its belly. The cold chick twisted its head between the cruel tines of its beak. Blaise heard the ferret's neck snap. Holding it down with its claws, the cold chick began to devour the ferret with a wet crunching sound. Blaise could hear her own panicked sobbing.

The chick sucked up looped coils of gut with little chirps of pleasure. Then it *blurred*. When Blaise could see it clearly again, it was the size of a rotweiler. Its feathers had sprouted into rich burgundy and green plumes. It snapped up the rest of the ferret, then crouched in the doorway. It looked at her, and Blaise knew it would burn her to death. A keening sound came from her mouth. Heat washed over her, but then the membranes slid down over the chick's open eyes. Blaise could still see its piercing stare, slightly opaqued.

"Mmrraow?" it enquired fondly. It had a satisfied look on its beaky face.

It wasn't going to eat her. It had done this to please her, and now the guy next door was really dried up and gone. "That isn't what I meant," Blaise wailed. The chick cocked its head adoringly at the sound of her voice.

Blaise sat down heavily in her tattered armchair, trying to figure out what to do next. The chick groomed, rattling its beak through its jewel-coloured feathers. Its meal was still altering its body. It blurred again, it morphed. Four clawed, furred front legs sprouted to replace its chicken feet. The chick cockatrice looked down at its own body, stomped around experimentally on its new limbs. It made a chuckling noise. Would it have stayed a slow, cold chick if it hadn't eaten the ferret? Or the burning pepper sauce?

It belched, spat up a slimy black thread; the ferret's leash. It pounced on the leash and started worrying at it. Sunlight danced motes of colour through its plumage. It was very beautiful. And it would probably need to feed again soon.

I not going to be second course, Blaise thought. She moved to the door. Happily torturing the leash, the cockatrice ignored her. She grabbed her jacket from its peg and locked her door behind her. She left the apartment.

The clean fall air cleared her mind a little. The animal shelter, yeah, they'd come and take the beast away.

She had to pass the Venus-built lady's garden on the way. There was a man in the yard with his back to her: a slim, bald man with a wiry strength to his build. Shirtless, he was digging beside the otaheite tree. His tanned shoulders made a "v" with the narrowness of his waist. With each thrust of the shovel, corded muscles flexed like cables in his arms and back. Blaise slowed to admire him. He pumped the shovel smoothly into the earth with one bare, sturdy foot, but something stopped it from sinking any further. He went down on one knee and began tenderly pulling up clods of dirt, crumbling them between his fingers. Blaise crept closer to the gate and craned her neck to see better. The man sniffed at the dark soil in his hands and poured a handful of it down his throat. His adam's apple jumped when he swallowed.

Was everybody eating something strange today? All Blaise had wanted was cornbread.

The man looked round, saw her, and grinned. It was a friendly expression; there were well-worn smile lines pared into his cheeks. She grinned back. His lean face had the rough texture of chipped rock. Not handsome, but striking.

He reached into the womb of soil again and tugged out the rock that had stopped his shovel. His fingers flexed. He crushed the rock between them like a sugar cube and reverently licked up the powdery bits.

The cottage door opened, letting the Venus-built lady out. She had changed into a sweater and close-fitting jeans that made her hips heart-shaped. She had a basket slung over one shoulder. A smile broke onto the man's face the way the stone had cracked between his fingers. He offered a stone-powdered palm. "It's sweet," he said in a voice like gravel being ground underfoot. "The fruit will be sweet too."

The Venus-built lady smiled back. Then she looked at Blaise. "So come and help us then, nuh?" she asked in a warm alto that sang of the tropics, "instead of standing there staring?"

Blaise felt heat warming her face.

But what about the cockatrice?

The problem was too big for her to deal with for the moment. With an "Um, okay," she chose denial. She let herself into the garden, trying shyly to avoid eye contact with either of them. "What you doing?"

"Getting the otaheite tree ready for winter," the man replied. "It won't last out in the open like this."

"I bury it in the soil every winter," the Venus-built lady told her. "Then I dig it up in summer, and it blooms for me by the fall."

"And that works?"

"It works, yes," the Venus-built lady replied. "It bears, and it feeds my soul. Is a flavour of home. You going to help me pick, or you want to help Johnny dig?"

Standing this close to her neighbour, Blaise could taste the warm rose spice of her breath. Even her skin had the scent of the roses she ate. Blaise looked at Johnny. He was resting comfortably on the shovel, watching both of them. He grinned, jade eyes bright.

Who to help? Who to work close beside? "I will help you pick for now," she told the Venus-built lady. "But when Johnny get tired, I could help him dig."

Johnny nodded. "The more, the merrier." He returned to his task.

The otaheite apples seemed to leap joyfully from their stems into the Venus-built lady's hands. She and Blaise picked all the fruit, ate their fill of maroon-skinned sweetness and melting white flesh, fed some to sweaty Johnny as he dug. The woman owned a flower shop over in Cabbagetown. "Is called Rose of Sharon," she laughed. "Sharon is my name." Blaise inhaled her flower-breathed words.

Johnny was a metalworker. He pointed proudly at Sharon's wrought iron railings. "Made those."

His ruddiness came from facing down fire every day. Blaise imagined him shirtless at the forge, forming the molten iron into beautiful shapes.

"I need help at the shop," Sharon told her. "You don't like the job you have now, and you have a gentle hand with that fruit you picking. You want to come by Monday and talk to me about it?"

Blaise thought she might like to work amongst flowers, coaxing blooms to fullness. "Okay. Monday evening," she replied.

She and Johnny dug out most of the soil from around the tree's roots while Sharon steadied its trunk. Then all three of them laid the tree in its winter bed, clipped its branches and covered it with soil.

"Goodnight, my darling," whispered Sharon. "See you soon." The bleeding hearts quivered daintily. The roses dipped their weighty heads.

The sun was lowering by the time they were done. The shelter would be closed, but probably the cockatrice was asleep by now. Blaise stood with Sharon and Johnny beside the giant's grave that held the otaheite tree. She ached from all the picking and digging; a good hurt. Johnny put a hand lightly on her shoulder. She felt the heat of it through the fabric. He smelt of sweat and fire and earth. On Johnny's other side, Sharon took his free hand. She and Johnny kissed, slowly. They looked into each other's eyes and smiled. Sharon slid an arm around Blaise's waist. Blaise relaxed into the touch, then caught herself. Ears burning, she eased away, stood apart from the warmth of the two.

"I should go now," she said.

Sharon replied, "Johnny likes to take earth into himself. Soil and rock and iron."

"What?"

"It's what I crave," Johnny told her helpfully. "And plants nourish Sharon. What do you eat?"

"How you mean? I don't understand."

Sharon said, "You must know the things that nourish you. Sometimes you have to reach out for them."

No, that couldn't be right. The bird birthed of the heat of Blaise's anger had eaten as it pleased, and it had turned into a monster.

"Um, I really have to go now. Things to take care of."

"Something we can do?" Johnny asked. Both his face and Sharon's held concern.

Blaise looked at this man who ingested the ore he forged, and the woman to whom flowers gave themselves to be supped. She took a deep breath and told them the story of the cockatrice.

Blaise's hallway still had the oily smell of cheap chocolate, burnt. She stepped guiltily around the ash smear on the carpet. "This is my place."

"Careful as you go in," Sharon warned.

The apartment was close and hot. It reeked of sulphur. Blaise flicked on the light.

The tv had been gutted. It lay crumpled on its side, a stove-in, smoking box.

"Holy," Johnny growled. The couch was in shreds, the plants steamed and wilting. The casing of the telephone was melted, adding its own acrid smell to the reek.

Blaise could feel the tears filling her eyes. Sharon put an arm around her shoulders. Blaise leaned into the comfort of Sharon's petal-soft body and sobbed, a part of her still aware of Sharon's rosiness and duskiness.

A bereft screech; a flurry of feathers and fur and heat; a stinking hiss of pepper and rotten eggs. The cockatrice rammed full weight into Blaise and Sharon, bearing them to the floor. Sharon rolled out, but the cockatrice sat on Blaise's chest. Its wordless howl carried all the anguish of *Mummy gone and leave me,* and the rage of *Oh, so she come back now? Well, I going show her.*

Blaise cringed. The cockatrice spat a thick red gobbet at her face. It burned her cheek. The drool smelled like rotting pepper sauce. Blaise went cold with horror.

Suddenly the creature's weight was lifted off her. Johnny was holding the cockatrice aloft by its thick, writhing neck. Blaise scrabbled along the floor, putting Johnny between herself and the monster. Johnny's biceps bulged; the rock-crushing fingers flexed; the cockatrice's furred hindquarters kicked and clawed. It spat. Johnny didn't budge. Fire had met stone.

"Kill it for me, Johnny, do." Blaise shoved herself to her feet.

"Oh God, Johnny; you all right?" Sharon asked.

"Yes," he muttered, all his concentration on the struggle. But his voice rang flat, a hammer on flawed steel.

The cockatrice thrashed. Blaise's belly squirmed in response. The animal made a choking sound. It was dying. Blaise felt warmth begin to drain from her body. Her heat, her fire was dying.

"You have to go," Blaise whispered at it. "You can't do as you want, lash out at anything you don't like."

Sharon gripped Blaise's shoulder. Where was the softness? Sharon's hand was knotted and tough as ironwood. "You want to kill your every desire dead?" she asked.

The cockatrice sobbed. It turned a hooded look of sorrow and rage on

Blaise. Then it glowered at Johnny. Blaise saw the membranes slide back from its eyes. She lunged at it.

Too late. The heat of its glare was full on. The air sizzled, and Johnny was caught. Sharon screamed. Johnny *glowed*, red as the iron in his forge fires.

But he didn't melt or burn. Yet. Blaise could see him straining to break the pull of the cockatrice's glare, see him weakening. Her beast would kill this man.

"Bloodfire!" Furious, she charged the cockatrice, dragged it out of Johnny's grasp. She heard Johnny crash to the floor.

The cockatrice glared at her. Hot, hot. She was burning up with heat, with the bellyfires of anger, of wanting, of hunger.

"Talk to it," Sharon told her. "Tell it what you want."

Blaise took a step towards the cockatrice. Bird-like, it cocked its head. It mewed a question.

"I *want*, " she said, her voice quaking out the unfamiliar word, "to be able to talk what I feel." God, fever-hot. "I want to be able to say, *you hurt me.*" The cockatrice hissed. "*Or I'm not interested.* " The cockatrice chortled wickedly. "Or," Blaise hesitated, took in a burning breath, "*I like you.* "

The cockatrice sighed. It leapt into her arms, its dog-heavy weight nearly buckling her knees. Its claws scratched her and its breath was rank, but somehow she held it, feeling its strength flex against her. She held the heat of its needing body tight.

Suddenly, it shoved its beak between her lips. Blaise choked, tried to drop the beast, but its flexed claws held her tightly. Impossibly, it crammed its whole head into her mouth. Blaise gagged. She could feel its beak sliding down her throat. It would sear her, like a hot poker. She fought, looking imploringly at Sharon and Johnny, but they just sat on the floor, watching.

Blaise tried to vomit the beast out, but it kept pushing more of itself inside her. How, how? It was unbelievable. Her mouth was stretched open so wide, she thought it would tear. Heat filled her, her ribs would crack apart. The beast's head and neck snaked down towards her belly. Its wings beat against her teeth, her tongue. Her throat, it was in her throat, stopping her air! Terrified, she pulled at the cockatrice's legs. It clawed her hands away. With a great heave, its whole bulk slid into her stomach. She could feel its muscly writhing, its fire that now came from her core. She could breathe, and she was angry enough to spit fire.

"What oonuh were thinking!" she raged at them. "Why you didn't help me!"

Johnny only said, "I bet you feel good now."

Oh. She did. Strong, sure of herself. Oh.

Sharon leaned over Johnny and blew cool, aloe-scented breath on his blisters. Blaise admired the way that the position emphasized the fullness of her body. Johnny's burns healed as Blaise watched. "I enjoyed your company this afternoon," she said to them both. Simple, risky words to say with this new- found warmth in her voice.

Sharon smiled. "You must come and visit again soon, then."

Blaise giggled. She reached a hand to either of them, feeling the blood heat of her palms flexing against theirs.

Horror Story
by Robert Boyczuk

We like to think that one possible reason for the success of the Northern Frights *series is our genuine appreciation for all brands of genre fiction. We have featured stories that could, and sometimes did, appear in science fiction magazines and other stories that could, and sometimes did, appear in mystery magazines provided they had a dark and/or fantastic element. Robert Boyczuk's suspenseful "Horror Story" is one heck of a hard-boiled police procedural yarn, but one with a decided difference. Bob's original title was "The Killer in the Filing Cabinet." We thought that made it seem too much like a straight whodunnit, so we re-titled it "Horror Story," for reasons that the reader will find apparent.*

The third murder happened at a dumpy motel on Lakeshore Boulevard, just off the Gardiner Expressway. The Lakeview Inn. A real hole, peeling paint and pigeon shit everywhere. Meyers sat hunched in his car, parked behind two cruisers, staring at the scene through the curve of his windshield. The motel was a way station for the down and out, for transients, junkies, prostitutes and their johns — rooms to let by the week, day or hour. Meyers was familiar with its water-stained walls, its florid, torn curtains, its grey, sway-backed mattresses. When he'd worked vice, he'd been here on at least half a dozen calls. Bright yellow tape, snapping in late autumn gusts, closed the entrance way. The uniforms had sealed off the parking lot even though it was empty. Leaves scudded across the cracked asphalt. Through the big plate-glass window of the office he could see the sad-eyed, East Indian woman who worked the front desk. She was flanked by a couple of detectives, pads open, scribbling impassively as she talked.

Christ, how could this be happening?

I knew, Meyers wanted to tell them. *I knew the call was coming.* But what could he have said? That this morning, while scrambling eggs for Sarah, he'd seen the killer outside his kitchen window? No, not seen. Not clearly, anyway. More a silhouette flitting between houses, an indistinct, half-formed image, flat mask for a face with only the eyes clear, two tiny pinpricks of ruby light, blazing points that pulsed with the rhythm of his own heartbeat.

Twice before he'd seen the shadow, each time just before the call had come. This morning had been the third.

There was no fucking way he could tell them. *A shadow?* they'd ask in disbelief, then laugh. *You saw a shadow?* And the Staff Inspector would call it stress, and replace him with someone who could no more help the case than Meyers could help seeing his shadow. Perhaps if had explained earlier, in the beginning....

Shit, no. Even then they'd have figured he was nuts. He couldn't have told them about the dark figure that stalked the edges of his world, that lurked just outside the periphery of his vision. Nor about the file folder he carried with him all the time now, that sat on the passenger seat of his car. A folder he'd pulled from the dust-grimed filing cabinet in his basement when he'd first understood the pattern. Christ almighty! He stared at the folder. It had been an exercise. Just a fucking exercise!

Meyers' hands trembled; a trickle of perspiration ran down his temple, clung to the edge of his jaw.

Even the Scotch didn't seem to be helping. He had dawdled, let the others leave the Operations Room before him, telling them he had to make a quick call, that he'd meet them at the Lakeview; and when they'd all gone, he pulled the mickey from his desk drawer, taken a stiff pull on it, then slipped it into his pocket. Now the smokey bottle weighed heavily in his hand again, its stubby, black cap atop the folder on the passenger seat. Ducking so the cops in the office couldn't see him, he took another slug, screwed the cap back on, then tossed it into the glove compartment, snapping the door shut with his elbow. He wiped the sleeve of his overcoat across his mouth and climbed from the car.

Halfway along the boxy, white-washed block of rooms, a door stood open; figures swam through the murkiness inside, a uniform standing watch outside. Meyers ducked under the police tape, walked unsteadily across the lot. He nodded brusquely at the officer, sucked in a big breath and plunged inside the room.

Luckas' bulky form loomed up, blocked the view. He held a half-eaten cinnamon roll in his left hand; a coffee steamed in his right. "About time you got here."

At first Meyers couldn't see anything. Then, as his eyes adjusted to the dim light, he saw either end of the bed, Luckas' girth still blocking its middle. A pair of arms and legs was all he could see, the body spreadeagled by black straps wound around wrists and ankles, the straps secured to the four thick wooden feet of the bed. A leather jacket, jeans, and a pair of ragged underwear had been neatly laid out on a chair near the head of the bed. Leather biker boots sat on the floor at the foot of the bed. On the far wall, the words, *Once upon a time* had been painted in blood. Meyers throat tightened.

"Thought we'd have to send someone out to look for you," Luckas smirked.

Meyers brushed past him.

Like the others, this victim had been splayed like a pinned insect. Two lines had been neatly incised at the top of his chest, and wadded, blood-soaked kleenex had been stuffed inside to distend the skin below the incisions into the shape of small breasts. He had been emasculated, his penis and scrotum cut away, a crude vagina formed and the flaps of skin held in place by several large safety pins. The sheets beneath him were black with dried blood. His thin, parted lips had been slathered with bright red lipstick, and, beneath his open eyes, exaggerated dark circles had been painted in mascara that gave him a plaintive, questioning look, sad and bewildered, as if he couldn't quite believe what he'd become. His eyes seemed to stare at Meyers, asking him, *Why? Why did you do this to me?*

Christ. The bitch had done it again. Something inside Meyers crumpled like a tissue crisped by a flame. He felt the blood drain from his face.

"No signs of struggle," Luckas said. He took a big bite out of his roll, a thick line of cream bleeding onto his chin. He nodded towards the wall.

No shit, Meyers thought. No fucking shit. Stun guns don't leave marks. But he couldn't tell them about the 40,000 volt gun; not yet. They'd think it was too fucking weird that he knew. They'd just have to figure it out themselves. Forensics would pick it up eventually. Wouldn't they?

"Put on your gloves. You've been elected to baggie detail," Luckas said, grinning. He put his coffee down on an end table, pulled an extra-large, zip-lock baggie from the pocket of his rumpled jacket and shoved it at Meyers. "You can begin with the garbage pail in the washroom. That's where his balls are. Oh, and look before you pour yourself a drink," Luckas said stuffing the bag in Meyers' hand. "His dick is in a dixie cup by the sink."

But then, Meyers already knew that, didn't he? That was the way he'd written it.

Alone. Everyone else had gone home long ago.

The lights of the Operations Room at Metro Headquarters burnt brightly, painfully. Meyers turned on every one of them when he'd felt the darkness pressing against the window panes like a slavering beast. Against the utter black, the unnatural brilliance dazzled him, made his head spin. Meyers snatched his glass from the desk, Scotch slopping over the side and watering his hand. It was his fourth—no fifth. He took a big swig, let the warmth of the liquid wash down his gullet, quell his jangling nerves, blunt the glare of the lights. Then his hand fell, the thick bottom of the glass clacking loudly against desktop, making him jump. He released the glass, watched it wobble for a second, then settle.

Two folders lay on his desk.

One was old, shedding fibres along its edges, its cover stained, dog-eared. The other folder was new, unmarked, drawn from the supply cabinet that afternoon.

Meyers opened the fresh one. He stared at the white sheets, filled with crisp, orderly lines of black type. The crime scene report he'd written earlier today. Clean, neat, methodical. The murder reduced to simple, comprehensible facts:

Arriving at the scene at 10:45 a.m., I found the victim, subsequently identified as Ronald Kurt Aikmen, in room 12 at the Lakeview Inn. The subject sustained numerous sharp force injuries, including massive incisions in his pelvis and chest. Coagulated and dried blood stained the bed and surrounding carpet, principally near the pelvis of the victim. Cordura straps had been looped around the wrists and ankles of the decedent and secured to the feet of the bed. The victim was naked with the exception of a leather vest. Lividity was fixed and rigor mortis was fully established. To the right of the bed, a flannel shirt, leather jacket, and jeans had been neatly arranged on a chair...

He poured himself another shot, a smaller one; he threw it back. The tremor in his hand seemed to diminish infinitesimally. Goddamn if he couldn't have used this earlier, when he'd had to bag that guy's nuts.

Meyers slapped the folder closed. The bottle clicked against his glass as he poured himself a double this time. A moment later the burning liquid curled into his throat. Yeah. That seemed to do the trick.

He fingered the other folder; its cover was filled with scribbles, names and phone numbers, cryptic notes made to himself that no longer made sense, and the name of a recommended restaurant to which he'd never had the chance to go. It was an exercise he'd done at the seminar in Pennsylvania, nearly seven years ago. Something he'd almost forgotten, stuck in a filing cabinet in his basement, along with miscellany of his life: tax returns, receipts, warranties and bills, birth and marriage certificates, the deed to his house, a yellowing envelope containing his only citation in an otherwise undistinguished career at Metro.

He flicked the folder open.

Inside were several sheets with his cramped handwriting, all in pencil. On its index tab he'd written the name *VICKI* in large, dramatic letters, then underlined the name twice. It had been his project, an exercise in creating a psychological profile for a serial killer. While the other cops at the workshop had struggled to imagine a killer, his had flowed easily, naturally. But then, he'd always liked that sort of thing, making stuff up. Like the stories he'd woven for Sarah soon after they started dating. At first he'd thought it was kind of weird, the way she'd insisted, late at night when they were settled into the pocket of warmth beneath the quilt, that he tell her a story. But, much to his surprise, he found he had a talent for storytelling. For imagining things he'd never seen.

Vicki is a white female, in her early to mid-thirties; she keeps herself in good shape. Personal appearance is very important to her. Parts of her residence, however, are disordered. She has split into half a dozen distinct personalities, all with different and sometimes conflicting needs (though bits of each leak through into the other's life). Two personalities dominate, one meticulous and organized, who keeps an immaculate home, a woman who has no close friends but many acquaintances, and seems to be searching for stability – and is possibly even married; the other a careless, often slovenly, thrill seeker, insensible to threat and oblivious to danger, though acutely aware of her other half's attitudes towards her – and often resentful of them. When living this second aspect of her personality, she frequents local bars, strikes up conversations with complete strangers, takes them to their homes or hotel rooms.

Vicki is the only daughter in a family of men. From an early age she was raped repeatedly by her father and brothers, suffering severe beatings in the process. What Vicki remembers of the women in her family is unflattering: she sees her mother as an ineffectual, withdrawn woman who suffered similar abuse at the hands of the male members of the family, and slipped into alcoholic or drug induced stupors to numb her pain. Most importantly, perhaps, Vicki came to see her mother as a passive, non-threatening, creature. From this stems her desire to remake the people in her world into equally non-threatening entities...

Meyers' teacher at the FBI's road school had dismissed these preliminary notes as contradictory, an unlikely blend of psychological traits. Too clever, he had called Meyers' work, designed only to fool his fellow students, and of little use in real life. There was simply not enough information available on women serial killers to justify his portrait.

Vicki. Meyers could see her clearly in his mind's eye, just as he had all those years ago. Short cropped blonde hair. A severe, narrow face. Grey, washed out eyes, flat and lifeless, shoulders stooped and withdrawn, begging to be ignored, left alone. Except... except when she hunted; then her eyes shone, glittered like chips of ice, cold and dark and predatory. As they did now in his imagination. She smiled at him, a sly mocking thing that made him shudder.

No! He slammed a fist down on the desk. You're not real! I made you up!

He shook his head, trying to dislodge the picture of her, but only succeeded in making the room spin.

Christ, he thought, panicky, staring at the sheet. Christ almighty! Sweat rolled down his temple, collected in the small of his back. He pulled his hand from atop the page, leaving a dark palm print in its centre. An absurd notion occurred to him: he wondered if perhaps no serial killer, not a single one, had ever existed except in their files, that it was the fact of the files that had given them shape and meaning and life.

Swallowing, he turned the pages, lifting the pieces of paper like he'd have lifted the sheet from a corpse in the morgue, until he came to the descriptions. His mock crime scene reports. The third one began,

The victim, an unidentified white male, approximate age 30, was discovered in room 3A of the Sandylot Hotel by the chambermaid. The decedent was naked with the exception of a leather vest. Cordura straps had been used to bind the subject to the bed. Minor bruising was observed on the victim's upper right shoulder and two large sharp force injuries were evident on the victim's upper chest and lower pelvis. A leather jacket, jeans and boots had been arranged neatly on a chair to the right of the bed...

There were still three more reports left in the folder. They were only supposed to write two reports, but Meyers had enjoyed the assignment so much he'd written six. *Six.* Meyers' stomach felt like a knot being pulled tight. He grabbed the mickey, turned it upside down over his glass, and was rewarded with only a thin trickle, two, maybe three, drops. Empty. Goddamn empty.

The bottle banged into Meyers' wastepaper basket, spun the pail until it fell to its side flinging its contents onto the floor, spilling rubbish everywhere.

In his head, Meyers heard the echo of Vicki's mocking laughter.

Sarah was in bed when Meyers got home.

Swaying only slightly, he tiptoed into the room. Close now, he could see she breathed deeply, regularly. Her clothes were scattered about the room, and, weaving between bed and dresser, he picked them up, one by one, a silk blouse and a linen skirt in a pile near the closet, a serge jacket thrown carelessly across the foot of the bed, one arm brushing the floor. Her clothes were expensive, impeccable, beautiful. Like she was. In her late thirties, and she could still turn heads. Meyers placed each item carefully on a hanger and smoothed it, his fingers thick and coarse against the fine material.

"David?" Her voice weighted by sleep. She stirred, propped herself up on an elbow, blonde hair spilling over her shoulders and across her small, perfect breasts. In the cross-thatched shadows of their room her face was hidden, her expression veiled, unknowable. Meyers stepped over to the bed and gently brushed back her hair until he could see the pale oval of her face. But in the dark it wasn't the face he remembered, its lines and edges were different, deeper, hardened. The face of a stranger. How long since he had last looked at it closely?

"You've been drinking." She pushed his hands away, like she was disgusted. "Dammit, David," she said, her voice tired, resigned. "You're going to kill yourself."

"Just a quick one. After work."

She drew her lips into a tight line; her eyes narrowed. She looks pissed, more pissed than usual. "I waited an hour." Her voice was cool, not angry, more detached than anything, as if her words belonged to a different scene, a different couple. "Where were you?" she asked, staring at the sheets, the wall, the open closet, anything but him.

Then it hit him. *La Piazza.* Her favourite restaurant on Bloor. Christ, how could he have forgotten? He was supposed to have met her there for lunch. Then drive her to the garage where they were going to pick up her old Tercel. He'd forgotten all about it when the call on the latest victim had come in that morning.

"Sorry." He dropped numbly onto the edge of the bed, moving his hand towards her again, but she continued to recede. "Work, you know —"

"Shit, David! I had to take a cab to the garage, and I didn't have enough money with me to pay for the work. They had to replace the whole bumper. They almost wouldn't let me have the car." She pulled herself into a sitting position, away from him, crossing arms over her breasts. "I had to promise them you'd come by tomorrow with the rest of it."

"Don't worry. I'll take care of it. Tomorrow."

She frowned, but said nothing.

"We had another one today."

She stiffened, and her voice sounded strained, not frightened exactly, but tense, breathless, as if she was struggling to control it. "You know I don't like hearing about these things."

She thought his work gruesome. At home, she skipped past the stories of murder and mayhem in the papers, flicked the remote whenever they came on the news. But the Scotch had loosened his tongue.

"Just south of here. Along the Lakeshore."

Pulling up her legs, she wrapped her arms around her shins, flattening her breasts. "David, please—"

"The Lakeview Motel. You must know it." Meyers stared at the curve of her muscled calf. "You jog past it all the time."

Her eyes darkened. "Jesus. What did you have to tell me that for? You know I hate hearing about these things!" She shuddered.

"No reason to worry. You're safe." Reaching up, he placed his hands on her arms. Cool. Her skin was cool, like that of a fresh corpse. He began rubbing her arms, trying to put some warmth back in them, but she shrugged free of his grip, edged backwards. He let his hands drop to the bed. "She's only interested in men."

"She?"

Meyers panicked; he pushed off of the bed, staggered over to the dresser, clutched it for support. Christ. What the fuck was he thinking? He hadn't told anyone yet. They were only beginning to suspect. But no one had seriously suggested the killer was a woman yet. "He? She?" He tried to shrug nonchalantly. "Whoever."

"You said *she*. A woman."

"I did?" Meyers lowered his head, swallowed. He decide to bite the bullet. "Yeah. I think so, anyway." He shrugged. "It would answer a lot of questions."

Sarah nodded gravely in the dark; she seemed infinitely distant. A mystery deeper than any of the ones he confronted every day. If only he could apply the same methods to his own life...

Christ, yes! Why hadn't he thought of it before? He was an investigator, a problem solver, a simple fact that had somehow eluded him before. It was only a matter of finding the proper clues to untangle Sarah's motivation, to understand what needed to be done to keep them from drifting even further apart, to repair the damage time and indifference had done. A strange optimism flushed him, a crazy hope. "Listen," Meyers said in a sudden rush, stumbling back towards the bed. "Let's go away, huh?" His words were quick, excited, his hands extended. "When all of this is over. I'll take some time. We'll go away somewhere nice. What do you think?" Meyers meant it, really meant it this time, though he was not sure how to say it convincingly, how to make the words sound real instead of like the drivel that came out of the telvision. Jesus, he hadn't told her a story in years. Even though he knew she loved them. When had that all stopped? Why had it stopped? He couldn't remember. It had just faded, disappeared without a trace. But he'd make up for it. Had to make up for it.

He reached out, thinking he might tell her about the folder he'd pulled from the filing cabinet in the basement, about the shadows. About his monster. But she jerked back reflexively, eyes wide, surprising him. Could she smell his fear, sense in her own groping way the weight of his responsibility, the guilt leaking out from around his edges. "Sarah?"

She blinked, pulled the sheets up around her, then looked away. "You know I hate to hear about this stuff."

His heart, thumping expectantly an instant ago, withered. He let his hands fall to his sides. It was too late for stories. It was too for anything. How could he have believed that he might unburden himself to her? Silence had grown too strong a habit between them, become too much part of their lives. He was alone in this. Turning, he walked to the door, paused, hand on the jamb. "I've got some reports to go over."

She nodded distantly, but he could see she wasn't really listening, hadn't really listened to him in years. Some actions had no motivation that could be understood; like random, pointless, murders, some feelings couldn't be solved.

Three days later the shadows gathered again.

ROBERT BOYCZUK

Meyers stared out the fourth floor hallway window by the vending machines, the coins in his hand forgotten, his attention focussed on the small square opposite the station. Not a square, really, more an interruption in the face of abutted office towers, an indentation in which a few low-slung concrete benches had been scattered around two large, ugly concrete planters. The space was empty, the awnings of an adjacent bar trembling in the breeze, the day bright and relentless, casting sharp dark lines that sliced the world into strange, distended planes. Beneath the arching branches of a denuded oak, in its shadows, blackness in the form of a human shape uncoiled, twisting and turning like a grub in black earth.

Meyers stomach flip-flopped; his coins clattered to the floor.

The shadow solidified like an egg hardening in a frying pan; colours sprang up along the thing's edges, ran along it like spikes of flame. Clamping his jaw shut and fighting a rising panic, Meyers willed it to still, to cease its restless stirring. The tendons in his neck tightened with his concentration.

His efforts were having an effect. The shadow's growth slowed, became sluggish, then stopped. He felt the tug of it against his will, fighting to take on shape. Vicki's shape. But, if the thing didn't grow, neither did it shrink. A standoff. Sweat collected on his brow, ran down along his temples; he trembled. If only he could hang on, he might yet drive it back into the recesses from which it sprang.

"DTs got you?"

The words jolted Meyers. A hand clasped his shoulder, making him jerk like he'd been shocked. He blinked rapidly, his eyes suddenly watering as if they stung. His attention wavered then dissolved, his eyes cutting to Luckas who had spoken, then back to the tree. But in the moment of his lapse, the shadow had completed its metamorphosis. A woman stood there, wrapped in a long coat blacker than the deepest shadows. Her face was shaded by the broad brim of a hat, but her head was angled towards him. Two crimson points for eyes, watching him. She waved. The bitch waved!

Meyers' shoved past Luckas, ran towards the stairwell.

"Asshole." Luckas' word pursued Meyers as he took the steps two at a time. He broke out into the bitter fall light of the day and loped heedlessly across the street, ignoring the squeal of tires and the angry honks.

Gone. She'd fled. The square was deserted.

Meyers looked up and down the canyon of office towers. Nothing. Not a Goddamned thing. A few pedestrians strolling in the distance, carrying shopping bags, office workers in suits but no overcoats hustling from heated building to heated building, an older man walking a terrier. And doors. Dozen of doors, any one of which she could have slipped through.

"Fuck!" The shout burst from him; several people glanced over, then looked away quickly, hurrying past, and Meyers was suddenly aware he was standing there in the square, jacketless, his shoulder harness visible for all to see.

She was gone. And there was nothing he could do but return to the Operations Room and wait for the next call. This time it would be a security guard, a deserted office building, and common hardware-store string in large, crude stitches in place of safety pins.

The call came early the next morning.

"Rise and shine, asshole," Luckas said when Meyers picked the phone up, the big man taking obvious delight in waking Meyers. But Meyers was up, had been up most of the night, sitting at the dining room table with his file spread out before him. In a way it was preferable to contemplating the insuperable barrier of Sarah's back. "We got another one. The night watchman in the Hunter-Thompson Building. Fifth floor washroom. Jesus, doesn't this guy ever sleep?"

Half listening to Luckas, Meyers lifted a sheet of paper. *The fourth victim, the security guard at Dominion Securities,* began the report, *was found the day after the previous murder.*

He crumpled the page in his fist, let it fall to the floor. The phone was back in its cradle, but Meyers couldn't remember hanging it up. The Hunter-Thompson Building. He'd been in the building a few times, the last time maybe two years ago. To pick up Sarah who'd been working as a copy editor for a trade publication, something to do with concrete. Had she worked on the fifth floor? He couldn't remember. Christ, he'd even used the washroom there, once.

Half an hour later, Meyers' heart was hammering, his pulse pounding in his neck, as he walked through the glassed-in lobby of the building. But even when he stepped off the elevator on the fifth floor, he couldn't be sure if this was where Sarah had worked; if it was, the partitions had been changed, the furniture moved. He followed a trail of police tape to the washroom.

"You look like shit," Luckas said. He half-leaned, half-sat against a long vanity with four sinks, flipping idly through a pad filled with scribbles. "The photographer's not here yet."

Meyers ignored him; instead his eyes flicked over the scene, the smashed mirrors, the smears of blood over the tiled floor, the guard's feet sticking out from the last stall, the metal trash can with the mess spilling out of its flap. A fucking mess. He took another step into the room and glass ground loudly under the soles of his shoes.

"Lucked out this time," Luckas said, grinning.

"What?" Meyers blinked stupidly. He'd been trying to remember if the mirror had been on this side of the washroom he'd used. Christ, all these places looked the same.

"We maybe got a witness," Luckas said tapping his pad with a thick forefinger. "A cleaning lady. She said she saw someone leaving just as she was coming in for her shift. A *woman*."

Meyers heart froze; he stared at Luckas, every atom in his body seemed to quiver, every sense intensified, painfully aware of the buzz of the fluorescent lights, of the intermittent drip from the closest tap.

"Can you fuckin' believe it? A broad's been doing this." Luckas shook his head ruefully. "The cleaning lady didn't get a good look at her face. Short, pale, thin. Orange, spiky hair. Carrying a black case. Leather dress and jacket, she said."

Christ Jesus. It wasn't Vicki. Not the Vicki he'd described, anyway. He'd never imagined her with the hair or the leather skirt and jacket.

"Oh, and she said some weird shit about her eyes, like they glowed or something." Luckas snorted.

Meyers' stomach fluttered, like he'd hit a dip on a rollercoaster.

Luckas flipped his pad closed. With his free hand he pulled something from his pocket, flicked his wrist. The thing shot across the washroom, struck Meyers squarely in the chest and dropped to the floor between his feet. A pair of latex gloves in a plastic package. "Come on," Luckas said cheerfully. "Let's get to work."

Eleven p.m. and Sarah wasn't home.

Meyers sat in the wingback chair by the door, a small bottle of Scotch balanced on its arm, rolling his glass with the tips of his fingers, back and forth, watching the amber liquid pitch first one way then the other.

His tongue tingled from too many drinks.

Something was buzzing inside Meyers' head. He tried to rub it away by pressing the glass of Scotch against it, but the glass felt hot, scalding hot against his temple, and he dropped it, liquor and ice splashing the papers scattered at his feet and going all over the rug. He knew he should clean it up, Sarah would go nuts, her favorite rug. He slid down out of the chair and gingerly touched the glass. Cool, now. He needed a rag, but was too drunk to want to get up again; he shrugged out of his shirt, began blotting up the liquor, bunching ice cubes in the folds. The thing in his head was still angry at him, like a wasp on a hot summer's day bumping into the windowpane. How could he fucking work with this shit going on? He pressed the damp of his shirt to his forehead, felt the chill go deep, breathed fumes of Scotch. There, that was all right, that was the ticket. He glanced up, hearing a click from somewhere in the house, some mechanism, the furnace, the water heater, switching on. Shadows everywhere, closing in on the lamplit oval where he was sitting; but when they felt the pressure of his stare, they oozed back several inches, like frightened oil.

The report. He had to see his report again. Dropping his shirt, he moved the strewn pages around, sheet sliding on sheet, mixing them even more. Then he spotted it, the one he wanted, a brown streak on its upper right corner, smudges of chocolate from a candy bar he'd been eating when he first wrote it years ago. He snatched it up, stuck it in front of his face. It was hard to read, his tiny crabbed handwriting swimming like an army of spiders across the sheet.

The fifth victim is a salesman on his bi-annual trip to Toronto. His body was discovered in the bathtub of his room in the Sutton Place Hotel...

He thought about Sarah alone in the house all day, his filing cabinet collecting dust in the basement. Bored, she might have noticed it one day, pulled open the drawer searching for something, anything....

Jesus, what was he thinking?

Sarah was nothing like Vicki. Was she? He'd met her parents several times, and they were both normal, stable people, not like the parents of the killer in his profile.

Unless....

A vague memory drifted through his mind like the snatches of a half-remembered song. A late night shortly after he'd met Sarah, before she'd given up drinking, two or three bottles of wine into the evening and a slurred recollection about her childhood, about her...step-parents? Had she called them that? Or was he imagining it, constructing and reconstructing the memory as he had the killer in his file, as they did now in the Operations Room, piecing the portrait together bit by bit until it matched his own?

No! Not Sarah! Christ, he was a cop. He'd been trained to identify the signs, would have recognized such darkness long ago, seen it for what it was. And have helped her. He was always willing to help, wasn't he? He shook his head to clear away the creeping fog.

But what that left him with was, a ghost, a phantom. A paper killer.

Where are you, Sarah? he wondered.

On hands and knees, his glass cradled in one fist, he crawled back to the chair and the bottle of Scotch miraculously still balanced on its arm.

"David?"

Meyers opened his eyes, and the light made his head throb; his mouth was dry, filled with the gummy residue of Scotch. He sat in the wingback chair, something hard pressed between the arm of the chair and his thigh. A glass. His empty glass.

"David, I'm leaving."

He lifted his head, and a spike of pain shot through his neck, blazed in his skull. Colors danced madly before him; the radio blared loudly in the background. Who had left it on? "What?" he croaked; everything was too dazzling, too loud, a hash, and he couldn't make it settle into any kind of sense.

"I didn't want to sneak off. I wanted you to know."

His eyes snapped into focus. Sarah stood by the open door, a look of disgust on her face. Her gaze wandered over the scattered sheets, the stained carpet, the wadded mass of his shirt. "I'll pick up the rest of my things later," she said. Bending, she lifted her suitcase. Then, she was gone, vanished, like she'd never been there in the first place. He hadn't seen her turn, walk out the door, but she wasn't there.

Meyers heaved himself to his feet, staggered forward, crashing into the doorframe, his head spinning, the muscles in his legs rubbery and unwilling. His vision blurred, then cleared, in time to see Sarah climb into her Toyota. The new front bumper glinted blackly against the fading red paint of the car's exterior. Meyers blinked, looked through the windshield. Behind Sarah, in the back seat, a shadow rose, like someone sitting up, but it was a silhouette, an emptiness darker than tar, its only clear feature two pupilless, glowing ovals in the centre of her face, eyes that expressionless red colour you'd sometimes get in pictures taken with a flash. Eyes staring blankly at Meyers. Asking...asking for what? Christ, he thought, trembling uncontrollably. Christ almighty.

The engine started, and the headlights flared in the night, blinding him, making him raise his arm across his eyes.

"Sarah! No! Stop!"

Her car backed out, its lights raking the front of the house as it swung into the road.

Meyers stumbled back into the house, crashed through the bedroom, the hallway closet, the kitchen, until he found his jacket on the back of a chair. He rifled the pockets, looking for his keys. Not there. He began his frantic search again, tearing through the house, his head throbbing, his heart hammering, his stomach heaving. But the keys weren't anywhere.

By the time he found them dangling from the ignition of his car, it was too late, she'd been gone nearly five minutes and there was no hope of catching her.

The phone in the Operations Room trilled, and Meyers jumped a little, just as he had every time it rang that morning.

He felt like shit. His head throbbed unmercifully; he shivered, sweat peppering his forehead, running freely beneath his arms. It rang again, and Meyers shuddered. Standing in front of the corkboard, he pretended to study the sheets of paper tacked to the board, the psychological profile of the killer. Behind him, he heard a sigh, the creak of leather shoes, the click of the receiver being lifted.

"Yeah?" Luckas' rough voice, sounding bored. "Yeah, okay. I got it. We'll be right there." The sound of the receiver being dropped back into its cradle.

"Number five," Luckas announced to the room.

Meyers turned with the others, watched Luckas shake his head; he looked pissed, like this time he'd been insulted personally. "The Erskine Hotel," he said gruffly. "Jesus, can you believe the balls?"

The Erskine Hotel. A block away. Only a block.

Meyers knew the place, because once he'd spent a weekend there with Sarah. Just for the hell of it. *Let's be good to ourselves*, she'd said, giggling. She'd always been that way, impulsive where Meyers was methodical. It was one of the things he had loved about her. Her impetuousness. He'd capitulated, gave in to her whim. They'd taken the Oriental Suite, complete with Japanese teak furniture, hinged, painted screens, a hot tub with woven mats next to it, and a king-size water bed with an ornate headboard. They'd ordered champagne. Sitting across from him in the tub, he'd thought it would be fun to watch the soft-core porno movies on the tv, but she'd shaken her head, then said, "Tell me a story."

And in the midst of swirling jets of heated water, with the inspiration of the implausible setting and the wine coursing through his veins, Meyers had told her stories, one after another, as if they would never end...

The body had been carved up in the same way as the others. But this time it had been dumped in the hot tub, an empty champagne bottle and two shattered glasses beneath it. Around the tub the killer had arranged two black lacquered screens, their panels filled with the pink cherry blossom trees, long-necked cranes, and incomprehensible Japanese ideographs.

What was happening?

Meyers barely managed to stagger through the day. Three times he'd slipped away to call everyone he could think of: Sarah's parents, her few friends, the fitness club to which she belonged, even the people at the store where she'd worked last year during the Christmas holidays. But no one had heard from her. Or if they had, they weren't telling him. When he spoke to her mother, he tried to sound calm, as if this was nothing more than a small spat. But when she began to flip out, Meyers told her that he was sure Sarah was all right. Knew that she was fine. For an instant he thought about telling her. But Christ, what could he say, that he was worried her daughter had been kidnapped by a shadow? He made reassuring noises, promised to call her her the moment he heard anything, made her promise the same thing. And in all this he lost his nerve to ask her about Sarah's past, to confirm or refute his hazy, alcohol-laden recollection of what she'd said about her adoption.

At six p.m. they finished with the scene, and Meyers stepped from the hotel into an overcast day, dark, snarled clouds blotting out the lowering sun.

Jesus, he was tired. He hadn't slept well in days, not at all in the last twenty-six hours. He felt giddy, light-headed. People hurried past, clutching their coats tightly around them, holding their hats firmly on their heads against an bitter, blustering wind. Meyers moved forward, travelling on a wave of numbing energy, an enervated momentum that pushed at his back like a large, insistent hand, driving him ahead, across the street to Headquarters and the underground parking lot. He found himself in his car, his hands clutched tightly on the wheel to keep them from shaking.

Where now?

Home. He'd go home.

But without Sarah, the word *home*, the whole concept, seemed empty, pointless. Repellant. His stomach churned apprehensively. Bad idea. Maybe he'd just drive around for a while, to get his bearings. To calm down. Stop somewhere for a quick one. A drop to help him think things through. His mouth watered. Yeah, that was what he needed. Sarah would understand, wouldn't she? How could she fault him for doing what he had to? He imagined the sting of Scotch sliding down his throat, its perfume seeping into his brain, blunting the edges of his jagged world. He fumbled for the keys he'd dropped on the passenger's seat, stuck them in the ignition, pulled the car out of the lot.

He drove through two intersections; at the third, the light went yellow. He pulled up to the crosswalk just as the first drops of rain pattered onto his windshield. Then it began pissing down, sluicing off his windshield in tiny streams that blurred the outside world. Meyers stared out, unseeing, into the wash of colours. A patch of red across the street snagged his attention.

Red like Sarah's car.

He flicked on his wipers, forced his eyes to focus.

On the opposite side of the intersection, idling at the stoplights, was a Tercel, its front bumper too new for the rest of the car, its driver an outline.

The shadow.

Christ Jesus! Meyers' heart stuttered, stalled.

It was her. Alone in Sarah's car.

The figure was sitting upright, clearly visible, dead black where there should have been some detail, some hint of colour, of flesh, but there was only absolute, undifferentiated black. And two tiny red glimmers for eyes.

As the light went green and the Tercel pulled away, Meyers spun his steering wheel around—then stomped on his brakes to keep from tee-ing into a beige Bonneville that trundled into the intersection behind the Toyota, drifting past like it was moving in slow motion. By the time he managed to pull a u-turn, the Tercel was two blocks ahead. Meyers hit the gas, swung around the Bonneville, just making the next light, and closed on the Tercel, his breath coming hard, but beginning to get a grip, to think coherently, to feel a strong, gleeful confidence. No way she was going to lose him now. He'd cuff her, beat her, blow holes in her if he had to, whatever it took to make her return Sarah. Panic tightened his chest when he realized he left his gun behind. No, no, wait. The glove compartment. He'd stuck it there that morning. He punched open the compartment, keeping an eye on the Tercel, and groped inside it, felt weighted leather, the familiar grip. Fucking A! He was down with it this time.

A block ahead, the Tercel sped up and turned right. Maybe she'd spotted him. Shit! Meyers swung after her, cutting across the apron of a gas station with a big painted sign out front proclaiming NO AIR, some guy in a greasy coverall cursing at him, and sped along a residential street, houses here and there among the clusters of low-rise apartments, and every fifty feet or so a diseased-looking sapling planted on the narrow median. The Tercel was still a block ahead, and before Meyers could cut much of the distance, it turned again. By the time he rounded the corner, it had pulled ahead nearly two blocks, separated from him by three cars. He slammed his hand against the steering wheel in frustration, so hard pain spiked his wrist, and he leadfooted the gas, blowing through a stop sign.

They were in some kind of industrial park.

Ahead, the Tercel's right taillight flashed once, then it disappeared, unhurriedly, around the corner. Meyers honked, roared past a white sedan, his wheels squealing as he took the corner and —

— tromped on his brakes.

A dead end.

A short street lined with squat, red-brick buildings, concrete stairs leading up to metal doors, narrow margins on which cars had been parked haphazardly under NO PARKING signs, crammed in between dented, green dumpsters. And at the very end, facing him, a bar, a glaring neon sign low along its front, parts burnt out, others flickering and buzzing angrily, red in a border of white: *Vicki's Place*. The Tercel was parked under the sign, jammed between two other cars, the door on its driver's side open. Meyers thought about the last crime scene report he'd written for his project, about the final victim, a bartender.

His stomach went cold. Lifting his foot off the brake, he let his car roll forward, fat drops of rain thumping on the roof and splattering on his windshield. He angled in behind the Toyota, blocking it.

Meyers switched off the engine, climbed out of his car into the downpour. Shoulders hunched against the rain, he sidled up to the bar's entrance, a blistered wooden door, and listened. Nothing but the staccato pattering of rain. Cautiously, he pushed the door open. It swung inward easily.

Just inside was a small foyer with flimsy, plywood walls. He stepped in, paused, hand on the inner door. He sniffed the air, a whiff of something underneath the smell of stale beer and urine, something trickling past him that, at first, he couldn't quite place, a familiar smell. Sarah's perfume. Christ Jesus, Sarah's perfume! Pushing open the door, he stumbled into the gloom of the bar.

The room was long and narrow, the wall on the left covered in a burgundy wallpaper that had faded to the colour of dried blood, beneath which were scattered half a dozen small round tables and plastic chairs with splayed legs. On the other side was a long mahogany bar, the only clear illumination in the entire room coming from its far end, a small table lamp, its porcelain base cracked and its shade askew, sitting on the polished surface of the bar where it curved back towards the wall. The place was deserted, except — except for the far corner, where a lone woman sat at a small table, legs crossed, a cigarette dangling from her fingers, its smoke curling away into the hovering shadows.

She lifted her hand, took a drag. The tip of the cigarette glowed bright red and her eyes blazed too, burning intensely for an instant, then diminishing with the cigarette's retreating glow as she lowered her hand. "I've been waiting for you, David," she said, smiling, smoke sliding listlessly from between her lips. Her face was pale, bloodless, her teeth small and sharp and perfect.

Christ Almighty, it was her. Vicki. But not as he'd imagined her, as he'd written her. She'd changed. Remade herself. Cropped and colored her mousy hair into a spiky orange tangle; exaggerated her soft, unassuming features with dramatic, uneven slashes of ruddy blush, green eye shadow and black lip gloss; replaced her baggy, shapeless clothes with a skin-tight leather skirt and zippered vinyl vest, a leather biker's jacket hanging from the back of her chair. And she held herself with none of the uncertainty and fear he'd imagined for her, but with the sort of corrupt assurance Meyers had seen in the countless punks he'd busted. She beckoned to an empty chair next to her.

Meyers' head spun. This couldn't be real, couldn't be happening. He closed his eyes and opened them. But the bitch was still there, still smiling. Christ, what was he doing here? Sarah. He was here for Sarah. But his legs trembled, failed him, as if they'd developed a life of their own, as if the only way they would work was if he turned and let them carry him out of this fucking bar as far and as fast they could.

"Sarah sends her regards."

Rage suffused Meyers; he staggered forward, came to a swaying halt in front of the table, his fists bunched. Behind the woman, the shadows seemed to stir themselves in response, thickened like a congealing gravy, closing in. He ignored them.

"Sarah," Meyers sputtered, his voice rough, almost unintelligible; his face burnt like it had been splashed with acid. Here, near the table, an overpowering smell curled into his nostrils, sweet and sickly and nauseating all at once, made his throat constrict and his gorge rise. The coppery smell of blood.

"Ah, that got your attention." She laughed lightly, carelessly, like a child.

Back by the wall Meyers caught sight of a body on the floor, arms and legs splayed. The blood in his own body stilled, froze in his veins. He stared, but shadows clung to it like a thousand dark spider webs, cocooning it, making it impossible to see with any clarity.

"Don't worry," Vicki said cheerfully, nodding at the figure. "The bartender. Looks like it's self-serve for the next little while." She laughed again.

"Answer my question!"

"Sarah's safe." Leaning forward, she stubbed out her cigarette in a chipped ashtray and Meyers caught the rising scent of Sarah's perfume. "Or is for now. As long as you treat me right."

The anger drained from Meyers; despair filled the space it had vacated. How did you fight a shadow, a phantom? He felt helpless before her, as helpless as he had in his disintegrating marriage. He went limp, collapsing into the empty chair, cupping his head in his hands. "What... what do you want from me?" His words were choked.

A glass scraped across the table. He looked up. Two fingers of Scotch in a dirty tumbler in front of him. He hadn't noticed it before. He stared at her. And suddenly noticed something he hadn't seen before. She looked like Sarah. Christ, he'd never realized, even when he'd pictured her years ago. But Sarah was there, in the shape of her mouth, the lift of cheekbones. And he was too, Vicki's eyes identical to those that stared back at Meyers from the mirror every morning. It was like he was looking at their child.

"I need a small favor, David. It's nothing really. Something you've done before...."

Something he'd done before? Meyers gaped at her, at the cold, dead flesh cloaking the monster. His monster.

Uncrossing her legs, she reached into the pocket of her jacket, the leather of her skirt creaking as she shifted. "Here."

She dropped a pencil in front of him, smoothed out a folded piece of paper next to it. It was blank. She stood and her heels ticked across the linoleum, stopped behind him. He felt her lean over his shoulder, could hear her breathing, only it wasn't the breath of a slight woman, but ragged and huge, in and out, in and out, like an enormous, shuddering bellows; moist air licked the side of his face in warm, nauseating waves. In it he could smell the beast, her distinctive reek, the stink of the putrid organs she had carved like trophies from corpses—and the dust from his file, laced with the stench of his own fear and uncertainty, of long sleepless nights, of unhappiness, anger and failure. The room heaved beneath him, began a long, slow, lazy spin.

Reaching past him, she dragged the glass of Scotch closer, until the odor of the alcohol rose into his nostrils, merging with the stench, became so twisted, one in the other, that it was impossible to separate the two smells. She worked the pencil into the cold claw his fingers had become. In a voice that could have been Sarah's, she whispered, "Tell me a story."

Via Influenza

by David Annandale

Playwright and short story writer David Annandale was born in Winnipeg in 1967 and, with the exception of a few years in Paris, has lived there most of his life. He completed his PhD on horror fiction and film at the University of Alberta, and currently teaches film and literature at the University of Manitoba. David reports that he got the idea for "Via Influenza" from asking himself many of the same questions his protagonist does, wondering about the stories behind disused roads and forgotten buildings.

The meaning of roads is fragile.

Derek had become aware of this some time ago. Initially, he thought it was an urban phenomenon, but that was only because it was in the city that he had first noticed it. He'd been driving through a part of Winnipeg he didn't see often, just northwest of the city centre, when grey brick and concrete had suddenly made him pull over. He got out of the car and began snapping pictures. Of the factory: nameless, windows grimed with years, and had they ever been clean? and was there such a thing as a new factory? Of the shops across the street: named but faded under grey, pawn shop and parts shop and café, indistinguishable, Pepsi signs hung when they still used molasses, and were the shops ever open? And did anyone actually come here? That was the question that took over. Surely not, the answer seemed to be. There was no one around. The factory was silent. The shops were shut in the middle of a weekday afternoon. The only cars Derek could see were in transit. The road could only be for taking people *through* here, not *to* here. But then why come here at all? What did the road mean in this context? What did it mean at all?

He wanted his pictures to ask these questions. He doubted anyone could answer them, nor did he want that. The questions were the important thing. They forced a new look, a new perspective on the viewer. That was no bad thing.

If it worked, that is. But Val said it did. The critics said so too. So he'd continued his study, finding more and more city streets that were irrelevant to the districts they went through.

A week ago, he discovered that rural roads could be just as meaningless, just as easily. It struck him while he and Val were driving back from her sister's farm. The roads gridded off to the horizon, a thin layer, gossamer fragile, overlaying the prairie's implacable monotony. He realized how easy it would be to get lost. Here the roads lost meaning completely. They weren't just rushing past pointless locations on the way to somewhere else. They were going nowhere. Derek made another study.

It was Val who suggested the next step.

"Why not combine the two?" she asked.

"What do you mean?" Derek sipped his sherry. It was Friday. It was spring. They were home from work, and the weekend beckoned.

"You've done the urban series and the rural series. Now do one of both."

"Um, and how precisely—"

"Ghost towns."

Derek sat and blinked at his wife for a few moments. She smiled at him. She twiddled one of her paintbrushes around her fingers, her expression loving, yes, but smug? Oh, that too.

"Ghost towns," Derek repeated. Of course. The perfect combo. The lost web of prairie road plus the city, shut down and back turned for good and all. "Can you give me a single valid reason why I didn't think of that?" he asked.

"Certainly. You're just not as quick as I am, that's all." Her smile became a grin.

He mirrored her. "Is that right?"

"Yes it is."

"So suppose you tell me where I'm going to find just the right town. I would imagine that most former town sites are fields now. Wouldn't look like much."

Her grin turned into something that might have been a leer if it hadn't been both too elegant and too evil. Derek's fingers twitched for a camera. That look, backdropped by a late May's evening window, deserved better preservation than his memory could offer.

"Suppose I do." Val reached behind her easel and produced a folder. She sauntered over to where Derek sat on the couch and tossed the folder into his lap. She sat down next to him as he opened it.

Inside he found a sheaf of photocopies. He picked up the first. It was a newspaper article from 1918. "Influenza Epidemic in Pierton," he read. He glanced at Val. "Never heard of the place."

She sighed. "Of course not. Keep reading."

He turned to the next piece. "Pierton Quarantined." Then the next: "Pierton Decimated." Then there was a map, locating Pierton in Snow Valley, not far from Roseisle. "What happened?" he asked Val.

"What do you think?"

He stared. "They died?"

She nodded.

"*All* of them?"

"So I gather. Any survivors must have moved away."

"A whole town." Derek shook his head. "Doesn't seem possible."

"There was an influenza pandemic at the time, Derek. It killed more people than World War I."

"The flu?"

"The flu."

He whistled. "Glad we licked that charmer. My God, this sounds so *medieval*." He frowned. "You've done a lot of digging. You've *got* to have an ulterior motive."

She rubbed up against him, purring. "Your artistic well-being isn't reason enough?"

"Hardly."

She ran a finger down his cheek. "I'm so transparent."

"I'm so smart."

She chuckled and reached over to turn over the map. There was one more clipping underneath. It was from the July 23, 1968 edition of the *Winnipeg Tribune*. "Artists to Set Up Colony in Ghost Town."

"Ah," Derek smiled. "Now I understand. And did they?"

"If they did, they didn't stick it out for very long. But this is what makes me think the town's worth checking out, if a project like that was doable as recently as '68. Look," she pointed to the third paragraph. "Says here a lot of the buildings were stone."

"Highly unusual."

"Yes it is. But lucky for us, eh? There should be more than just a field."

Derek took her hand and caressed it. "Tell me. Just how much self-interest is behind your sudden inspiration for *my* next career move?"

She leaned in and nibbled his earlobe. "Call it a happy confluence of interests."

"Is that right?"

"That's right."

"Like this one?"

"Like this one."

They headed out to Pierton late Saturday morning. It was sunny when they left, but the horizon was frowning before they'd been on the road for an hour.

The irony of the trip appealed to Derek. They were travelling purposefully, giving a road meaning, in order to find that meaning's loss.

He folded the map. "Know the way?" he asked Val.

"For now." She overtook a dawdling Geo. "I'll probably need you to navigate once we get near Roseisle."

Derek nodded. "Incidentally, why are you so interested in the colony?"

"Well, you know how you've been working on the absence of meaning?"

"Yes."

"I'm playing with the reverse. I want to work with sites with a history. Art history is even better. And if most of the evidence is gone, and I have to bring the history back, then better still."

"I'll bet it's times like this you wish we lived in Europe."

"More history, you mean."

"Of the kind you want."

Val shrugged. "There's probably more around than we might think. It just fades away more easily here."

The clouds were waiting for them when they reached Snow Valley. The shift from prairie was a surprise, but just subtle enough not to be an ambush. Grasslands took over from cultivated fields. Clumps of trees camouflaged some of the early ground rolls. Then the road dipped, quite suddenly, and there were lots of trees, and they were into the valley. There were hills, virtually invisible from outside. Once you were here, though, they made their presence known and final. Rounded and hunched with age, they remembered Pangaea. They crowded around the car and drew the clouds down. The light changed from white to grey, then darker. Derek looked at the hills. He could almost hear them whisper: *History? Oh, we can tell you a thing or two about history. Just wait. Just you wait.* The hiss, he knew, was just the wind. He knew.

"Looks like rain," Val commented. She sounded like she sensed a need for intervention by the mundane, and so had supplied it herself.

"Um," said Derek. He wasn't sure he wanted to break the atmosphere, to interrupt the hills' concentration.

They came to a crossroads. Val stopped the car. "Could you check the map?" she asked.

Derek unfolded it. Lines ran over the land, doubtful as a palimpsest. "Left," he said, and Val turned onto gravel so old and disused it had mostly sunk back into the mud. Derek made a note to take a shot of the road, meaning fading to trace.

The road turned into a clump of trees, then dipped again, and levelled off in a shallow bowl. In it was the corpse of Pierton.

Val slowed the car down to a crawl.

A number of buildings were still standing, or at least were distinct ruins. Most of the roofs had caved in, and some walls had collapsed into cascades of stone. Derek saw a barn, one of the few wood structures still around, leaning at a forty-five degree angle. The scatter of the buildings implied a past presence of other roads, but there was only this one now. It went through the middle of Pierton, but then, coming out the other side, it stopped. Over. Gone beneath the grass.

Val stopped the car. She gestured at the field before them. "End of the road," she said.

Derek was already fumbling for the right lens, thinking Oh perfect, perfect. Perfect. "I have to tell you, honey," he said. "When you pick them, you don't kid around."

"No point in half measures."

"True enough." He got out of the car and stretched. He checked the clouds. They were a very dark grey now, with black in some formations. Definite low-light conditions.

"How long do you think we have?" Val asked.

"Before the rain? I don't know. Could start any moment, I'd say. Do you know what you want to see?"

"I want to look inside some of the buildings."

"Okay," said Derek. "Well I want to get some exterior shots while I still can. I'll come find you or meet you back here if it starts to bucket. Deal?"

"Deal." She picked up her sketching pad and headed off towards the nearest intact house.

Okay, Derek thought, what first? He looked around. The hills were still keeping close track of him. He decided to start with them. These wouldn't be road shots, but they could establish context. He began with focusing on the top of the hills, where the clouds were so low they were a lid over the valley. As he clicked the shutter, the wind came up, as if the hills resented his returning of the gaze. The breath was chill and sharp, a scalpel through his sweater.

He worked the view down, over the trees on the slopes, some leafed, some budding, some still the palsied claws of winter. Down, over the grass, already green, shaded richer yet by the darkly filtered light. And then the road, fading with a whisper into its grave.

When he turned around to take his first shot of Pierton itself, something flickered in the corner of his left eye. He had a sliver impression of a fragment of grey gauze, barely darker than the surrounding air, candleflame dancing. It was gone when he moved his head.

He shrugged, raised his camera— And there it was again: visible through the viewfinder, but not when he looked directly at the corner where it moved. Fatigue, he thought. Has to be. He couldn't feel the lower eyelid twitch he would have expected. But fatigue it must be, and he pushed the shutter release for proof.

He tried to ignore the grey as he blanketed the town with shots. But it was always there, flutter flutter, film ribbon. It didn't stay put either. It skittered to different sections of the frame, and of his vision. Up left, down right, skating the periphery, sometimes flicking in from the edges, but never upfront, never face to face.

Keep 'em guessing.

Concentrate, Derek told himself. It would be a crime to waste such a perfect location with half-assed shooting. He made his thoughts focus beyond the viewfinder, past the flicker, to the town. He wanted to imagine the life that had been here, so he could better photograph its loss.

He walked slowly up the road, clicking, clicking, stealing souls. And so here: a rounded pile of stone going drowning in the grass, going down for the third time. And here: a store? Yes, could be. A store, bigger than the houses, roofless walls, windows the idiot glare of empty space. And here: the church, spire gone except for a broken molar base, and behind it—

—the cemetery. Derek was almost able to forget the flicker. There were only a couple of graves still visible, and Derek wondered who it had been who had warranted stone markers. The two graves were close enough together that he could keep them both in frame if he wanted to, but far enough apart that the distance, the absences, the loss, could not be missed. This, this was the centre to which his pictures had been moving. Here were the milestones for the end of all roads. Here even the ending was fading. Barely more than trace already, it disappeared from the land as it vanished from memory. In less than a century, there would be nothing left at all. Not even the presence of loss, the signs of death. Just the green, silent and smug in its reclamation.

So what, Derek wondered, was he doing with his photographs? Hardly a resurrection. Preservation? Perhaps. But he liked to think it was a bit more than that. He wasn't exactly keeping memories alive. He hadn't lived here. He didn't know what would be authentic to remember. But he was creating new memories. People could see his pictures. They could think about Pierton and its deaths, and maybe imagine the helplessness as disease spread its wings over your home, slamming down the little piece of history you were trying to make, putting an end to all future stories and erasing the old. But here was Derek, hero of the lens, freezing the closing images of final extinction, keeping at least the end alive a bit longer.

Wasn't that a form of life? If not a resurrection, at least a haunting? He liked to think so.

He raised the camera. One last exterior shot. Then he'd have covered the whole town. He centred on emptiness, but kept one stone at bottom left, isolated and cold under a grim sky, and click — and the flicker vanished and behind him, a fluttering rattle like the wings of a huge moth.

His shoulders spasmed, tension a steel trap. The wind blew colder, the hand of a glacier slowly wrapping its fingers around him, closing into a fist. His chest locked, refusing him breath.

"Derek?"

The moth sound stopped. Derek whirled with a shocked grunt. But it was only Val, who didn't ask him what the hell his problem was, only Val, who was looking pale and rattled and no better off than he was.

"Val?" he asked back, all mixed up with concern for her and relief that he wasn't alone anymore.

She inhaled, deep and shuddering. "Derek, there's something I need you to see." She took his hand with one just as cold. In a numb clasp, she pulled him out of the graveyard.

She led him around the church, across the road, and toward one of the three houses that still stood firm and whole. The roof sagged slightly, but wasn't going anywhere. There was glass over the dark windows, eyes that were not glazed and blank but secretive, brooding. The clouds leaned in closer, putting pressure on the hills. Old gods jostled for a better look.

Derek saw the house come for him, expand and open its mouth wide. Swallow. They were inside. The wind, whining shrill, dug at the windows' weak spots.

"It's downstairs," said Val.

Derek squeezed her hand, giving and seeking reassurance. They moved to the cellar steps, and breath held, went down.

Light oozed in, limp and grey, through narrow rectangles. It was just enough to reveal the secrets. Skeletons spread out over the floor. Derek counted six. Two were laid out neatly, side by side, in one corner. Three others sprawled and jumbled as if tossed. One of them appeared to have fallen down the stairs. The sixth was huddled against the far wall.

"My God," Derek whispered. This wasn't just a reminder of meaning's end. It was the end itself, laid bare and grinning.

"It must be the artists," said Val. She too spoke quietly. You never knew.

Derek nodded. "Must be," he agreed. Decades old as it clearly was, this death had to be more recent than the town's. "But I don't understand. Why wasn't there a follow-up article? Why were they left like this? Didn't anybody know?"

"Maybe not. They might not have been local. Perhaps no one knew to miss them here."

"Maybe," Derek conceded. Val had to be right. One way or another, Pierton had kept this to itself.

Val picked her way over the bones to the crouching skeleton. She knelt beside it. "Come here," she said.

Derek braced himself, stepped off the cellar steps and weaved through death. "What is it?" he asked when he reached Val.

"Look." She pointed.

The skeleton's hands clutched a large stone. Ceramic shards littered the floor. On the wall were the remains of a tile mosaic. Whatever the picture had been, it had been smashed into jigsaw mystery. Some of the pieces showed a faint blue in the gloom. Others were grey, but whether from art or grime, Derek couldn't tell.

"I don't think this was originally part of the house," said Val.

"Meaning?"

"Meaning I think it was made and smashed by the same people. These people."

Derek looked around. Skulls stared back, the darkness of their sockets as deep and full of despair as a final sigh. He decided that it was time to go. His nerves and imagination were taut over barbed wire, and if he heard any strange noises now, he would lose it. Simple as that. He didn't care about the town's mysteries anymore. He didn't care about its construction, or its honored graves, or its life, or its demise. It didn't matter. There were meanings here, dead but lingering, and they could hurt him if he saw them. He didn't want to learn. "What I think we should do," he said, not even trying to keep his voice steady, "is leave. I take some pictures of the scene, and we go to the police and tell them about this, and we show them the pictures. But we leave. Now."

Val stood up, hugging herself against cold breaths. The wind crept downstairs to see them. "Yes," she agreed.

They went back to the stairs. Val waited near the top while Derek mounted the flash and began to record the cellar's memory. Four shots, he thought. Four shots and I'll have it, everything that counts in this place on film. Four shots and we're gone. And so from left to right, panorama, don't worry about the aesthetics, just get it and flash, flash, flash, flash—

Something outside started to bang. It was the sound of solid metal against hollow. Metronomic, twice a second, bang bang bang bang bang. Derek and Val looked at each other, eyes linking their fear directly, and then they scrambled up the steps and out of the house.

Run for that car.

The banging was sourceless. It rode the wind, beating from whatever direction it chose, sometimes from all. It would come closer, but never close enough to show its hand. It called on the clouds. With a rear and a roar, they opened up. Blackness poured down, torrential and drowning. Derek staggered as the rain smashed onto him. It drove the gravel deeper into its grave. The road turned to mud. And bang bang bang bang, all the way to the car, as Val fumbled with the keys, as Derek, rainblind, fell into the passenger seat, as the wheels spun, flinging gumbo. Bang bang bang, as the tires gripped, as Val turned the car around, as she accelerated through the white sheets of water. Bang bang bang—

It stopped the instant Pierton disappeared from view.

Back in Winnipeg. Back in their apartment. Back in dry clothes. Warm. Cozy. Safe. So they talked about it. A little.

"Do you think we were hallucinating?" Derek asked. They had both heard the banging.

"Seems a little unlikely, doesn't it?" Val seemed sorry to have an objection, no matter how reasonable. "I mean, that we would both spontaneously imagine the same thing?"

Derek grimaced. She was right, of course. But that was no comfort. "Then what...?" he asked, not quite in despair, not quite in fear, but helpless just the same.

"I don't know," Val sighed.

They sat and stared at each other for a few minutes, each waiting for the other to solve the dream and wake them up.

"Okay," said Derek, trying for a collaboration. "Well something had to cause it—"

"—it did come right before the storm—"

"—so the weather—"

"—the wind—"

"—caught a door or something on a loose hinge—"

"—and banged it back and forth," Val finished, smiling.

Derek smiled back. There. They had done it. Here was the explanation. It made perfect sense. They were back in the logical again.

Back in the rational.

Warm. Cozy. Safe.

Derek didn't sleep a wink that night.

And on Sunday, Derek went into the darkroom for the reckoning. He was nervous about developing the films, for reasons that he knew were stupid, since it had all been explained. Didn't matter. He was still nervous, and if he was going to be silly about the pictures, he didn't want Val to see.

Anyway, he suspected that she was wrestling with the same jitters. She had moved her easel and paint out of the living room and into the spare bedroom she used as a studio, and closed the door. Derek had felt a nibble of unease when he'd seen a tube of blue paint in her hand.

He got to work. He concentrated on the pure mechanics of developing. He refused to look at negatives or anything else until all the prints were complete. He didn't need to fuel his imagination with small or still-forming images, thanks all the same. He kept his eyes moving, letting them rest on a developing photograph only long enough to make sure he wasn't making any stupid mistakes. He didn't break for lunch. Nerves fought with appetite, and won.

Val's door was still shut when he finally emerged from the darkroom, prints in hand. It was early evening, but the overcast sky made it later. Derek glanced out the living room window and had to shake himself. For a moment he'd thought the clouds were the ones from Pierton. Watch it, he warned himself.

He sat down on the sofa. Took a breath. Ready? he wondered. Not really, he answered. Too bad. Here we go. He looked at the first picture.

The grey was there. Flicker immobilized, it was a faint gauzy wash, smirking in a corner. He'd been braced for it, or so he thought. But the chill still stabbed down to the marrow.

He looked at the next picture. The grey was there too. Different location, different shape, different texture, but there. And on the next one. And the next. And the next. All the way through, up until the last exterior shot, when he had finished covering the town and had heard the rattle of wings. By contrast, the shots of the skeletons were reassuringly normal.

He went through the pictures again, looking for the magic clue that would make everything mundane again. He didn't find it. Instead, he froze, fingers poised, breath arrested. He was looking at the first shot he took, before the grey, of the hills and the sky. The clouds looked out of the picture, straight at him, and even without faces, they were smiling significantly. Derek bit his lip. He turned his head, slowly, slowly, plenty of time for a prayer, and looked out the window.

The clouds were the same. He hadn't imagined it. Every shape, every frown, exactly the same as in the picture. Reality was suddenly a road whose meaning was evaporating, and Derek couldn't get off. He looked away from the window and shoved the prints, snakes, off his lap. They fell, shushing, to the floor.

He got up. He took a step back. He wanted to move around the couch, away from the pictures, away from the window and the sky. He wanted to go to Val. But the pictures weren't quite done yet. He noticed how two of the prints had fallen, how the two fragments of grey connected. He sighed, fatalistic. He should have seen it coming. He went to the kitchen, got some scissors, came back to the living room, and got to work.

It was easier than he thought. Some of the pictures, the ones where the grey was close to a corner, didn't need cutting. The puzzle fit itself together under his hands. He didn't know what to expect, or what to hope for, or even whether he should hope at all. But there was no point in fighting this, he thought. If nothing else, some kind of meaning might emerge to counter the entropy he was feeling.

He slotted the last piece into place and leaned back. He started to shiver. The grey formed a face. It was sheer, contorted, and screaming. Head back, mouth open to tear tendons. Inside the mouth, details collided into a shape he couldn't understand. The town orbited in angled fragments, debris in a tornado. The sense of movement was unmistakable, a vortex, a spiralling in to that shape inside the scream.

What was he looking at? With its agony and its transparencies of flesh, it was what he imagined the picture of a ghost would look like. Ghost town, he thought. Ghost of the town? No, not right. The shape in the mouth, now vaguely familiar, said no. Not of the town. Then what? The town's death?

He started. Where were these thoughts coming from? The grade of this road he was on was getting steeper, aiming for vertical, down into the dark, and the meanings he was hitting were not his, and they were corroding the ones he did own. He needed to get away before free fall. He shuffled back on his knees.

Too late. Wind hit the window, and he knew where he had seen that shape before. In pictures, of course. Grey ones. Ones taken using an electron microscope. It was a virus.

Influenza. The town's killer. His shivers almost prevented him from standing up. Influenza, the defanged plague. Could a pandemic have a ghost?

Then: as he stumbled back, body trying to find an expression for his fear, the picture began to flake. The grey face lifted off the prints like ash in a breeze, twirling, little dust devil, then slinging itself up, over his shoulder, and behind.

Then: the sound came back, the rattle of the moth, the clacking of wings, the wracking of phlegm, choking the throat, drowning the lungs.

Derek tried to scream, but his voice, deep in the tunnel, falling and lost, only whispered "Val."

The last of the face flaked away, and this time he spun with it, watched the cinders, followed their road as they drifted right through his wife's closed door.

Denial was too big, a block of concrete expanding in his chest. It burst through when he heard the crash. It came out as "*Val!*", loud this time, a shredding cry that still, still, could barely compete with the rattle.

Derek threw open the door. The face was waiting for him, staring back in blue and grey from Val's easel. The same face, striated by the reimaged mosaic. Here it rose as a pain cloud from the roofs of the culled town. And as he ran to her, Derek saw. He saw. He saw what had claimed meaning for its own to kill as it saw fit. Not peripheral vision this time, but dead centre, in your face and here I am: a grey figure, no longer flickering fragments, but doubly recreated. Brought back, its death a liberation, its very movement a smile, it danced out the closed window and into the welcoming storm. It spread racketing wings to fly down the new roads opened to it.

"Val," Derek moaned. Third time, last time. He crouched beside her. His shivering was of a different order now, the product of something much more fatal than fear. And Val turned to look at him, her eyes all wrong and shining.

Her skin was already reddening with the first fever flush of the end.

Ice Bridge

by Edo van Belkom

Prolific writer and editor Edo van Belkom is a familiar name to Northern Frights *readers. When our fourth volume received a complimentary review in* The Magazine of Fantasy and Science Fiction, *author/reviewer Elizabeth Hand singled out this story to comment that it read like something "worthy of the young Stephen King." Interestingly, Edo's submission is neither a supernatural tale or even a traditional horror story. It is, however, a bonafide Northern Fright.*

The continuous diesel-driven thrum of the loader was only occasionally drowned out by the crash of logs being dumped into place. The loud noise was followed by the faint groan of metal and the slight rumbling of frozen earth as the truck dutifully bowed to accept its load.

Rick Hartwick mixed his coffee with a plastic stir-stick and walked casually toward the far end of the office trailer. At the window, he blew across the top of his steaming cup and watched his breath freeze against the pane. Then he took a sip, wiped away the patch of ice that had formed on the glass, and watched his truck being loaded one last time. As always, the loader, a Quebecois named Pierre Langlois, was making sure Rick's rig was piled heavy with spruce and pine logs, some of them more than three feet in diameter. Langlois liked Rick, and with good reason. Every other week throughout the season, Rick had provided Langlois with a bottle of Canadian Club. He'd been doing it for years now, ever since he'd called a loader an asshole during a card game and wound up driving trucks loaded with soft wood and air the rest of the winter.

He'd been lucky to hang on to his rig.

The next winter he began greasing Langlois' gears with the best eighty proof he could find and since then he'd never had a load under thirty tonnes and only a handful under thirty-five.

He owned his rig now, as well a house in Prince George.

As he continued to watch the loading operation, Jerry Chetwynd, the oldtimer who manned the trailer for the company came up behind Rick and looked out the window. "That's a good load you got going there."

"Not bad," said Rick, taking a sip.

"Are you gonna take it over the road, or take a chance on the bridge?"

Rick took another sip, then turned to look at the old man. They said Chetwynd had been a logger in the B.C. interior when they'd still used ripsaws and axes to clear the land. Rick believed it, although you wouldn't know it to look at him now, all thin and bony, and hunched over like he was still carrying post wood on his back. "Is the ice bridge open?"

Chetwynd smiled, showing Rick all four of the teeth he'd been able to keep from rotting out. "They cleared the road to MacKenzie last night and this morning," he said. "But the company decided to keep the bridge open one more day seeing as how cold it was overnight."

Rick nodded. Although the winter season usually ended the last two weeks of March, a cold snap late in the month had lingered long enough for them to keep the bridge operating a whole week into April. And while they'd been opening and closing the ice bridge across Williston Lake like a saloon door the past couple days, the few extra trips he'd been able to make had made a big difference to Rick's finances — the kind of difference that translated into a two-week stay at an all-inclusive singles resort on Maui.

"Anyone use the bridge today?"

Chetwynd scratched the side of his head with two gnarled fingers. "Not that I know of. Maybe an empty coming back from the mill. Harry Heskith left here about an hour ago... But he said he wasn't going to risk the ice. Said the road would get him there just the same..."

"Yeah, eventually," Rick muttered under his breath.

The ice bridge across Williston Lake was three kilometres long and took about four minutes to cross. If you took the road around the lake you added an extra fifty kilometres and about an hour's drive to the trip. That might have been all right for Harry Heskith, with a wife, mortgage, two-point-three kids, and a dog, but Rick had a plane to catch.

Maui was waiting.

"Up to you," Chetwynd said, shrugging his shoulders as he handed Rick the yellow shipping form.

The loader's throaty roar suddenly died down and the inside of the trailer became very quiet.

Uncomfortably so.

Rick crushed his coffee cup in his hand and tossed it into the garbage. "See you 'round," he said, zipping up his parka and stepping outside.

"If you're smart you will," said Chetwynd to an empty trailer. "Smart or lucky."

The air outside was cold, but nothing like the -35 Celsius they got through January and February. Between -15 and -35 was best for winter logging — anything colder and the machinery froze up, anything warmer and the ground started getting soft. The weather report had said -15 today, but with the sun out and shining down on the back of his coat, it felt a lot warmer than that.

Rick slipped on his gloves and headed for his rig, the morning's light dusting of snow crunching noisily underfoot.

"You got her loaded pretty tight," he called out to Langlois, who had climbed up onto the trailer to secure the load.

"Filled the hempty spaces wit kindling," Langlois said with obvious pride in his voice.

"Gee, I don't know," chided Rick. "I still see some daylight in there."

"All dat fits in dare, my friend, is match sticks hand toot picks," Langlois' said, his French-Canadian accent still lingering after a dozen years in the B.C. interior.

Rick laughed.

"You know, I uh, I 'aven't seen you in a while and I been getting a little tirsty... You know what I mean?"

Rick nodded. Of course he knew what Langlois meant. He was trying to scam him for an extra bottle before he went on holidays, even though he'd given the man a bottle less than a week ago.

"I'll take care of you when I get back next week," Rick said, knowing full well he wouldn't be back for another two.

Langlois smiled. "Going somewhere?"

"Maui, man," said Rick, giving Langlois the Hawaiian 'hang loose' sign with the thumb and little finger of his right hand.

"Lucky man... Make sure you get a lei when you land dare."

"When I land," Rick smiled. "And all week long."

The two men laughed heartily as they began walking around the truck doing a circle check on the rig and making sure the chains holding the logs in place were tight and secure.

"You load Heskith this morning?" Rick asked when they were almost done.

"Yeah."

"What do you figure you gave him?"

"Plenty of air," Langlois smiled. He had struggled to pronounce the word *air* so it didn't sound too much like *hair*.

"How much?"

"Twenty tonnes. Maybe twenty-two."

"He complain about it?"

"Not a word. In fact, he ask me to load him light. Said he was taking the road into MacKenzie."

Rick shook his head. "Dumb sonuvabitch is going to be driving a logging truck into his sixties with loads like that."

"Well, he's been doing it twenty years already."

"Yeah, and maybe he's just managed to pay off his truck by now, huh?"

"He seem to do okay," Langlois shrugged. "But it's none of my business anyway, eh?"

"Right," said Rick, shaking his head. The way he saw it, truck logging was a young man's game. Get in, make as much as you can carrying as much as you can, and get out. So he pushed it to the limit every once in a while. So what? If he worked it right he could retire early or finish out his years driving part-time, picking and choosing his loads on a sort of busman's holiday.

They finished checking the rig.

Everything was secure. "How much you figure I got there?" asked Rick, knowing Langlois could usually estimate a load to within a tonne.

"Tirty-six. Tirty-seven."

"You're beautiful, man."

Langlois nodded. "Just get it to the mill."

"Have I failed you yet?"

"No, but dare will always be a first time."

"Funny. Very funny."

There was a moment of silence between them. Finally Langlois said, "So, you taking it over the ice?"

"The bridge is open isn't it."

"Yeah, it's *open*."

Rick looked at him. Something about the way he'd said the word *open* didn't sit right with him. It sounded too much like *hope* for his liking. "Did Heskith say why he wasn't taking the bridge?"

"Uh-huh," Langlois nodded. "He said he had no intention of floating his logs to the mill."

Rick laughed at that. "And I got no intention of missing my flight."

Langlois nodded. "Aloha."

For a moment, Rick didn't understand, then he smiled and said, "Oh, yeah right. Aloha."

The interior of the Peterbilt had been warmed by the sunlight beaming through the windshield. As Rick settled in he took off his hat and gloves and undid his coat, then he shifted it into neutral and started up the truck. The big engine rattled, the truck shivered, and a belch of black smoke escaped the rig's twin chrome pipes. And then the cab was filled with the strong and steady metallic rumble of 525 diesel-powered horses.

He let the engine warm-up, making himself more comfortable for the long drive to the mill. He slipped in a Charlie Major tape, and waited for the opening chords of "For the Money" to begin playing. When the song started blaring, he shifted it into gear and slowly released the clutch.

His first thought was how long it took the rig to get moving, as the cab rocked and the engine roared against dead weight of the heavy load. It usually didn't take so long to get underway, Rick thought. Must be a bit heavier than Langlois had figured.

Inch by inch, the truck rolled forward. At last he was out of first and into second, gaining small amounts of momentum and speed as he worked his way up through the gears.

A light amount of snow had begun to fall, but it wasn't enough to worry about, certainly nothing that would slow him down.

The logging road into MacKenzie was wide and flat, following the southern bank of the Nation River for more than a hundred kilometres before coming upon the southern tip of Williston Lake. There the road split in two, one fork continuing east over the ice bridge to MacKenzie, the other turning south and rounding the southern finger of Williston Lake before turning back north toward the mills.

Rick drove along the logging road at about sixty kilometres an hour, slowing only once when he came upon an empty rig headed in the opposite direction. Out of courtesy, he gave the driver a pull on the gas horn and a friendly wave, then it was back to the unbroken white strip of road cut neatly through the trees.

The snow continued to fall.

When he turned over the Major tape for the second time he knew he was nearing the bridge. He hated to admit it, but a slight tingle coursed through his body at the thought of taking his load over the ice.

When Rick first began driving logging trucks the idea of driving across lakes didn't sit all that well with him. To him, it was sort of like skydivers jumping out of perfectly good airplanes — it just wasn't right. Six-axle semi-trailers loaded with thirty-five tonnes of logs weren't meant to be driven over water — frozen or otherwise.

It was unnatural...

Dangerous.

But after his first few rides over the ice, he realized that it was the only way to go. Sure, sometimes you heard a crack or pop under your wheels, but that just made it all the more exciting. The only real danger about driving over the ice was losing your way. Once your were off the bridge there were no guarantees that the ice beneath your rig would be thick enough to support you. And if you did fall through, or simply got stuck, there was a good chance you'd freeze to death while searching for help.

Even so, those instances were rare, and as far as Rick knew, no one had ever fallen through the ice while driving over an open bridge.

And he sure as hell didn't intend to be the first.

Up ahead the roadway opened up slightly as the snow-trimmed trees parted to reveal the lake and the ice bridge across it. In the distance, he could see the smoke rising up from the stacks of the three saw mills and two pulp mills of MacKenzie, a town of about 5,000 hardy souls.

He turned down the music, then shut it off completely as he slowed his rig to a stop at the fork in the road.

He took a deep breath and considered his options one last time.

Across the lake at less than three kilometres away, MacKenzie seemed close enough to touch. But between here and there, there was nothing more than frozen water to hold up over thirty-five tonnes of wood and steel.

He turned to look down the road as it curved to the south and pictured Harry Heskith's rig turning that way about an hour before, his tracks now obscured by the continuing snowfall.

The road.

It was Heskith's route all right...

The long way.

The safe way.

But even if Rick decided to go that route, there were no guarantees that the drive would be easy. First of all he was really too heavy to chance it. With its sharp inclines and steep downgrades there was a real risk of sliding off the snow-covered road while rounding a curve. Also, although it hadn't happened to him yet, he'd heard of truckers coming across tourists out for Sunday drives, rubbernecking along their merry way at ten or fifteen kilometres an hour. When that happened, you had the choice of driving over top of them, or slamming on the brakes. And on these logging roads, hard braking usually meant ending up on your side or in the ditch, or both. And that might mean a month's worth of profits just to get back on the road.

But even if he *wanted* to take the road, it would mean spending another hour behind the wheel and that would make him late for his flight out of Prince George. Then he'd miss his connecting flight out of Vancouver which meant...

No Maui.

And he wasn't about to let that happen, especially when he'd been told that the resort he'd be staying at discreetly stocked rooms with complimentary condoms.

Man, he couldn't wait to get there.

He looked out across the lake again. The snow was still falling, but a light crosswind was keeping it from building up on the ice. He could still clearly see the thick black lines painted onto the ice surface on either side of the bridge. With those lines so visible, there was really no way he could lose his way.

He took one last look down the road, thought of Heskith heading down that way an hour ago and wondered if he'd catch up with good ole Harry on the other side.

If he did, maybe he could race him into Mackenzie.

The thought put a dark and devilish grin on Rick's face.

He slid the Charlie Major tape back into the deck, turned up the volume and shifted the truck into gear.

"Here goes nothing," he said.

The rig inched forward.

It took him a while to get up to speed, but by the time he got onto the bridge he was doing fifty, more than enough to see him safely to the other side.

The trick to driving over the ice was to keep moving. There was incredible amounts of pressure under the wheels of the rig, but as long as you kept moving, that pressure was constantly being relieved. If you slowed, or heaven forbid, stalled out on the ice, then you were really shit-out-of-luck.

He shifted into sixth gear, missed the shift and had to try again. Finally, he got it into gear, but in the meantime he had slowed considerably and the engine had to struggle to recover the lost speed.

Slowly the speedometer's red needle clawed its way back up to sixty, sixty-one, sixty-two...

And then he heard something over the music.

It was a loud sound, like the splintering of wood or the cracking of bone. He immediately turned down the music and listened.

All he could hear was the steady thrum of his diesel engine.

For a moment he breathed easier.

But then he heard it again.

The unmistakable sound of cracking ice.

It was a difficult sound to describe. Some said it was like snow crunching underfoot, while others compared it to fresh celery stalks being snapped in two. Rick, however, had always described it as sounding like an ice cube dropped into a warm glass of Coke—only a hundred times louder.

He looked down at the ice on the bridge in front of him, realized he was straddling one of the black lines painted on the ice and gently eased the wheel to the left, bringing him back squarely between the lines.

That done, he breathed a sigh of relief, and felt the sweat begin to cool on his face and down his back.

"Eyes on the road," he said aloud. "You big dummy—"

Crack!

This one was louder than the others, so loud he could feel the shock waves in his chest.

Again he looked out in front of his truck and for the first time saw the pressure cracks shooting out in front of him, matching the progress of his truck metre for metre.

Finally Rick admitted what he'd known all along.

He was way too heavy.

And the ice was far too thin.

But 20/20 hindsight was useless to him now. All he could do was keep moving, keep relieving the pressure under his wheels and hope that both he and the pressure crack reached the other side.

He stepped hard on the gas pedal and the engine responded with a louder, throatier growl. He considered shifting gears again but decided it might be better not to risk it.

He firmed up his foot on the gas pedal and stood on it with all his weight.

The engine began to strain as the speedometer inched past seventy... He remained on the pedal, knowing he'd be across in less than a minute.

The sound grew louder, changing from a crunching, cracking sound to something resembling a gunshot.

He looked down.

The crack in front of the truck had grown bigger, firing out in front of him in all directions like the scraggly branches of a December birch.

"C'mon, c'mon," he said pressing his foot harder on the gas even though it was a wasted effort. The pedal was already down as far as it would go.

Then suddenly the cracking sound grew faint, as if it had been dampened by a splash of water.

A moment later, crunching again.

Cracking.

He looked up. The shoreline was a few hundred metres away. In a few seconds there would be solid ice under his wheels and then nothing but wonderful, glorious, hard-packed frozen ground.

But then the trailer suddenly lurched to the right, pulling the left-front corner of the tractor into the air.

"C'mon, c'mon," Rick screamed, jerking back and forth in his seat in a vain attempt to add some forward momentum to the rig.

Then the front end of the Peterbilt dipped as if it had come across a huge rent in the ice.

"Oh, shit!"

The tractor bounced over the rent, then the trailer followed, each axle dipping down, seemingly hesitant about coming back up the other side, and then reluctantly doing so.

And then, as if by some miracle...

He was through it.

Rolling smoothly over the ice.

Solid ice.

And the only sound he could hear was the throaty roar of his Peterbilt as he kept his foot hard on the gas.

He raced up the incline toward the road without slowing.

When he reached the road, he got off the gas, but still had plenty of momentum, not to mention weight, behind him.

Too much of both, it seemed.

He pulled gently on the rear brake lever, but found that his tires had little grip on the snow-covered road. His rear wheels locked up and began sliding out from behind.

He turned the wheel, but it was no use.

He closed his eyes and braced himself for the rig to topple onto its side.

He waited and waited for the crash...

But it never came.

Suddenly all was quiet except for the calming rattle of the Peterbilt's diesel engine at idle.

Rick opened his eyes.

He breathed hard as he looked around to get his bearings.

He was horizontal across the highway, pointed in the direction he'd come.

He looked north out the passenger side window and saw the puffing smokestacks of MacKenzie, and smiled.

He'd made it.

Made it across the bridge.

The moment of celebration was sweet, but short-lived...

Cut off by the loud cry of a gas horn, splitting the air like a scream.

He turned to look south down the highway.

Harry Heskith's rig had just crested the hill and was heading straight for him.

Rick threw the Peterbilt into gear, stomped on the gas and popped the clutch.

The rig lurched forward, but he was too slow and too late.

All of Heskith's rear wheels were locked and sliding over the snow like skis. Heskith was turning his front wheels frantically left and right even though it was doing nothing to change the direction he was headed.

And then as he got closer, Rick could clearly see Heskith's face. What surprised Rick most was the realization that the old man was shaking his fist at him.

Shaking his fist, as if to say he was a crazy fool for taking the bridge.

But as the two trucks came together, all Rick could think of was how *he'd* been right all along.

The dangers of the ice bridge had all been a cakewalk compared to —

A Voice in the Wild

by Hugh B. Cave

This year we had the fun and privilege of helping celebrate Hugh Barnett Cave's 91st birthday. This extraordinary man, active as ever and still at the peak of his form, has been a professional author for over seven decades. Last year alone saw publication of four Cave short story collections and one new novel, The Dawning, Leisure Books, 2000. *Forthcoming novels include* The Evil Returns: Mindstealer Leisure Books, 2001 *and* The Caverns of Time Leisure Books, 2002. *In addition, short stories by Hugh, both new and reprint, appear at the rate of ten or so a year in various anthologies. The following tale was written at our request, its Ontario wilderness background based on fishing expeditions Hugh used to take with his friend,* Black Mask *pulp editor Ken White. The background is real, the characters (we hope) are fictional.*

A fter the fourth bank robbery, in which they shot and killed a guard, the two of them drove north to Sudbury, then west on 17 along the north coast of Lake Huron. Their destination was a small town named Bridge from which Luke, before turning to a life of crime, had once embarked on a canoe trip into the wilderness with some adventurous pals.

Luke knew an outfitter in Bridge from whom they could rent wilderness gear and a canoe. Their car, which had not been used in the holdups and would not betray them, they could safely leave in his care. What they would do was hide out in the wilderness for a while, living off the land. Then when sufficient time had passed for the hue and cry to die down, they could return to civilization with money enough for a life of leisure.

All this had been planned out in detail a month or so before the robberies. What they had not planned on was getting drunk near Webbwood and raping a young woman when they found her and her boyfriend in a broken-down pickup truck beside the road at night. Emile had shot the boyfriend, then both of them had raped the girl. And then, of course, it had been necessary to kill her too, or she would have described them when questioned.

The outfitter said, "There's a feller here name of Charley you could use as a guide, if you like. He has a camp way back in there and is travelin' alone. You want to talk to him?"

"Why not?" Luke said, he and Emile agreeing it might be a good idea to have someone along who knew the lakes and portages, and could do the cooking. But Charley turned out to be a Cree Indian probably as old as the two of them put together, and they declined his services.

"Well," old Charley said with a shrug, "if you run into any trouble in there, I'll be pretty close behind you, I expect. Good luck, anyway."

They talked about that and other things their first night in the wilderness, with two lakes and two portages behind them. The outfitter had provided them with a lightweight tent, backpacks full of staples, fishing gear, and, of course, the canoe. Finding the canoe awkward at first, they had been forced to spell each other frequently over the portages. But each had quickly learned how to flip the craft upside down, lower it onto his shoulders, and stride along with it. Now with the tent up on the shore of the third lake and a cozy fire glowing in front of it, they finished their first wilderness meal of fresh-caught trout.

Trolling for fish while paddling, they had caught more than enough trout to know that with a whole string of such lakes in the wilderness ahead, they need not fear going hungry. While sharing the first of several bottles of whiskey they had brought along, they felt safe enough to reminisce.

"That girl," Luke said. "She was a bit of all right, eh? Told me her name was Michelle." Luke was twenty-seven and well over six feet, with dark hair that he had let grow long so that it framed his face. Not a bad-looking face unless you were turned off by thin lips, a sharp nose, and rather piercing dark eyes. "Michelle," he repeated, nodding. "Bit of an all-right name too, eh? Too bad their truck didn't break down closer to Bridge, or we might have figured out a way to bring her along for company."

Lifting his long-fingered hands to the back of his neck, Luke fumbled with the clasp of a gold necklace he had taken from the girl's dead body. After a moment of struggle he managed to get the clasp open and hold the prize out in front of him. Then, peering more closely at the heart-shaped golden locket dangling from it, he said with a frown, "Hey! You suppose this could be one of those with—"

Clutching the locket, he brought it closer to his dark eyes. And seeing for the first time that it was hinged, he employed a thumbnail to snap it open.

Inside was a tiny photograph of the girl and her boyfriend.

Luke turned it so his companion could see it. "Looka this, will you," he said with a grin. "We got somethin' to remember her by!"

Emile leaned forward to peer at the photo. A year younger than Luke, he was several inches shorter but larger around the middle, with close-cropped yellow hair and pale blue eyes. "Both of 'em, hey? Did she tell you what his name was?"

"Jeffrey. She said his name was Jeffrey and they were gonna be married in the fall."

"Michelle and Jeffrey, huh? And you're wearin' 'em 'round your neck. You think you oughta be doin' that, Luke?"

"Why not?" Luke shrugged. "You got his belt on."

Emile looked down at the leather band around his pudgy middle. True, he had taken it from Jeffrey's dead body after Luke shot the fellow. But it was the best brown belt he had ever seen, made of real leather but soft, with a handsome design carved or pressed into it. Why not, for God's sake? Jeffrey wouldn't be needing it any more.

Funny, he thought. Luke had shot the boyfriend and was wearing the girl's necklace. He, Emile, had shot the girl and was wearing the boyfriend's belt. Should be the other way round, huh?

A rustling sound behind him near the water's edge caught his attention and he jerked his head around. The sound came closer, as though someone or something were crawling through a clump of grass there. Frowning, he reached for the Beretta Model 70 that was never more than inches from his gun-hand. Each man carried one.

Taking aim, Emile squeezed the trigger.

The sound of the shot shattered the stillness and sent echoes bouncing over the lake. The brush stopped moving. Emile got to his feet and with the eight-shot automatic still clutched in his hand, went striding toward the water's edge. The light from the fire showed him what he had killed. With a whoop of triumph he snatched up and waved a small porcupine.

Striding back to the fire, he dropped his prize at Luke's feet. The bullet had all but taken its head off. "Some shot, hey?" he gloated.

"A real good one," Luke conceded.

"Even that old Cree Indian couldn't do better, I bet," said Emile, and kicked the dead porcupine aside before sitting down again.

Next day Emile and Luke used their auto pistols four more times as they crossed the third lake and walked their rented canoe and gear over the third portage to lake number four. There was no reason not to, they told each other. They had plenty of ammunition and were entitled to at least a little pleasure here in the wilderness.

From the canoe Emile shot a small otter that surfaced within range, hitting it squarely between the eyes. On the portage, while his companion trudged behind him with the canoe, he spotted a Canada owl on a dead branch overhanging the trail and sharpened his shooting skills on that. Then when Emile took over the canoe, Luke whooped with delight on knocking a hawk out of its nest—it fell behind them on the trail—and later in killing a skunk that waddled unsuspecting from the brush ahead of him.

Again that night they sat at a fire in front of their tent and talked about their careers. About the banks they had robbed, the guard they had killed, the girl named Michelle and her boyfriend, Jeffrey.

Again Luke removed the heart-shaped locket from his neck so they could look at the photo in it.

Again they bemoaned the fact—aloud—that they had not been able to bring Michelle into the wilderness with them.

"Geez," Luke said, pushing grimy fingers through his long dark hair while shaking his head. "With her along I wouldn't mind bein' stuck in here awhile."

"Me neither," agreed his pudgy companion. "But at least we didn't bring that old Indian along. Can you imagine havin' him in our hair every minute?"

They lived on the fish they caught, plus bannock, some packaged soups, powdered eggs and other basics with which the outfitter in Bridge had stuffed their backpacks. One day Luke managed to kill a small deer with his hand-gun, and they ate that for several meals. Another time Emile shot a duck and they ate that.

Other creatures they shot for amusement while telling each other it made sense to hone their skills whenever an opportunity presented itself.

Each new day brought such opportunities. An oversized turtle plodded into their camp one evening. A gray bit of fluff called a Canada jay betrayed its nesting site one afternoon by voicing its loud "Ka-whee!"

Luke shot the turtle and laughed when it flipped over on its back and struggled for two full minutes to right itself before dying.

Emile shot the jay and threw up his hands in self approval as it dropped onto the trail amid a flutter of soft gray feathers.

Then on the fifth day they came to a lake that pleased them, and after paddling across it and finding a likely campsite, decided to go no farther.

"To hell with more walkin'," Luke said. "This here's as good as we'll find, and far enough in for us to be safe. I say we set up a camp here, make real beds with pine boughs and stuff, and use some of these boulders for a decent fireplace. We already know the lake's full of fish."

The lake was indeed alive with fish. Caught by trolling as they had pad-dled across it, eleven large trout lay in the bottom of the canoe at that mo-ment. To celebrate their decision Emile raised his Beretta, took aim at a large green frog that watched them from a nearby lily-pad, and squeezed the trig-ger. The frog burst into fragments.

By nightfall they had settled in and were seated around a fire with an-other bottle of the whiskey they had brought along. And when drunk enough they talked again of their accomplishments.

Of the banks they had robbed.

Of the guard they had killed.

Of the young woman, Michelle, and her fiancé, Jeffrey.

"Let's see that locket again," Emile said, putting a hand out. "Lookin' at her in the photo ain't as good as havin' her here, o' course, but it's better'n nothin'."

Luke took off the necklace and opened the locket, helping himself to a long look at the photo before handing it over. "What the hell," he said then. "Let's have a look at what you got from those two. I never did really look at it."

Emile unbuckled the belt and passed it over. "I ain't swappin'," he warned. "It may be a bit snug on me, but that's the best belt I ever owned."

After a while they ran out of memories and, being too drunk to talk any more, turned in.

Most of the following day they spent sleeping off hangovers, though late in the afternoon they devoted an hour or so to fishing. As the day waned, Luke carried a collapsible canvas bucket down to the shore for some water and, while scooping it full, saw a canoe on the lake. Wide-eyed with astonishment, he straightened up and watched it glide toward him for a moment, then shouted for Emile, who came running.

The man so skillfully wielding the paddle was the Cree they had been introduced to by the outfitter in Bridge. As he stepped ashore and drew his craft up on the sand, he frowned at them. He was no threat to their safety, of course. Even without the weapons they carried, they could have handled with ease anyone that old.

"You been followin' us?" Standing tall, with arms folded across his big chest, Luke made the question a challenge.

"Following you?" The old fellow seemed puzzled. "There is only one way through these lakes, friend. All of us must use the same portages." He peered past them at the camp they had set up. "But you are planning to remain here awhile, no?"

"That's right," said Emile, adding pointedly, "and we got here first, mister."

"Charley. My name is Charley, and I will not trouble you." The Cree lifted his aged shoulders in a shrug. "For tonight only will I be stopping here, then with break of day I will be on my way again. He turned as though to look across the lake at the way he had come. "I knew you were ahead of me, of course. You left your mark on every portage. Dead things, everywhere." Bending over his canoe to lift out a lightweight one-man tent, he muttered something else that sounded to Luke like "God's creatures."

"What?" Luke snarled. "What's that you said?"

The Cree glanced up over a shoulder. "I said good night," he replied with a shrug. Then after turning his canoe over on the sand, so in the event of rain it would not collect water, he swung the tent onto one shoulder, picked up a backpack, and walked away, evidently in search of a suitable place to spend the night.

Luke and Emile returned to their campfire and prepared an evening meal of trout. When finished, they carried their soiled tin plates and cooking utensils down to the lake to clean them. Dusk had descended. As they squatted side by side at the water's edge, scrubbing the gear with sand, they heard a sound that caused them to stop work and look to their left along the shore.

Their unwelcome guest, Charley Cree, was singing. Or was it chanting? He was doing something with his vocal chords, at any rate. With night coming down, the sound knifed eerily through the stillness.

It was still doing that when they finished their cleaning up and returned to their fire. As their talked turned again to the deeds they were so proud of, the chanting became an intrusion that could not be tolerated.

"Come on," Luke said angrily. "We gotta shut him up!"

Together the tall dark man and the short blond one descended to the lake again and made their way along the shore toward the glow of Charley Cree's fire. Reaching it, they found him seated cross-legged on a dark blanket beside it, his arms folded on his chest, his upper body swaying back and forth as the chant poured from his aged lips.

"You!" Luke snarled. "What are you doin', for God's sake? Tryin' to wake up the whole of creation?"

The chanting ceased, and the Cree looked up at them in silence.

"How the hell you expect anyone to sleep around here with all that racket goin' on?" Emile demanded. "What's it for, anyways?"

In a voice not nearly as loud, the Indian replied with a shrug, "I talk with the spirits."

"What spirits?" Luke asked in anger.

"Those of my people. We—my people—always talk with them when we have problems."

"Well, not tonight you don't," Luke snarled. "Not with us needin' our sleep. You keep it up and you'll get an answer from this, see? And nobody way the hell back in here will ever know what happened to you." Reaching into his pocket, he produced the Beretta automatic with which he had killed the bank guard and Jeffrey. "You got that, old man? You hearin' me good?"

Charley Cree gazed at the weapon in silence for a few seconds, then moved his grizzled head slowly up and down. "I am finished, anyway," he said.

"All right," Luke said. And to Emile, "Come on, let's get out of here. This guy gives me the creeps."

There was no more chanting. The only intrusive sound after that was made by Luke himself when, seeing what he thought was an eagle above the treetops, he lay flat on his back by their fire, took careful aim with his Beretta, and tried to shoot it down. He either hit it or badly startled it, for while it did not plummet to earth as he hoped, it did stagger in flight and drop a few feet before recovering and soaring away.

"Shit," Luke said. "I'm losin' my touch."

"Can't win 'em all," said his companion. "Come on now. We oughta hit the hay if we're gonna try for some fish in the mornin'."

Charley Cree appeared to be gone when they went down to the lake in the morning. At least, his canoe was gone from where he had left it. They could not see his campsite from that stretch of shore to know whether the tent, too, had disappeared.

"We trollin', or should we cut some poles?" Emile asked. The outfitter in Bridge, probably guessing they were not sportsmen, had not provided them with fly-rods, only with lines and hooks, plus a few lures in case they were unable to find bait at times.

"Trollin's easier," said Luke. "But wait'll we're out a ways."

With the short one in the bow and the tall one in the stern, they paddled out onto the lake. The sun was just coming up. On the opposite shore, tall evergreens stood black as etchings against a crimson sky. When he felt the water was deep enough, Luke tied one end of his line to a thwart, fastened a lure to the other end, and dropped the lure into the water. Emile did the same. In a moment both lines were taut as the canoe continued more slowly on course with only a gentle gurgling sound to disturb the morning stillness.

Nothing happened.

Bored, Luke began a conversation. The usual conversation. About the accomplishments they were so proud of. About the bank robberies, and their encounter with the young couple in the disabled pickup truck. About what a shame it was that they had been forced to kill the young woman rather than bring her here into the wilderness with them. "Damn it, we should've brought her," Luke said. "It would've been worth the risk."

Suddenly the line he had fastened to his thwart tightened with a jerk and began vibrating like a plucked guitar string. Then Emile's, in the bow, did the same. The talk ceased, and each man eagerly became an angler.

But as they reached for their lines to haul in what was causing the twitching, their outstretched arms abruptly froze.

"What the—" The fishing forgotten, Luke began clawing with both hands at his neck, where the necklace he had taken from the dead girl had suddenly come alive.

"Hey!" shouted Emile, dropping his line to claw with both his hands at the belt he had taken from the girl's dead boyfriend.

It, too, had suddenly begun to tighten.

Luke let out a yell, too, and then had no breath left for yelling as the necklace tightened like a hangman's noose about his throat. It shouldn't have been strong enough to do that, he told himself as panic gripped him. It was only a thin band of gold and should be a cinch to break. But he couldn't break it. The band was already so tight around his neck, there was no way he could even get his clawing fingers behind it. Every second it became tighter.

Now it was like a ring of steel, seemingly determined to cut his head off. Struggling with it in vain, his arms, hands and head going through a pantomime of contortions, he was so short of breath he could not even cry out.

In the bow of the canoe, the performance was being duplicated, except that Emile struggled with the band about his middle. The belt. The handsome, soft-leather belt he had taken from the body of the dead girl's dead fiancé. It had been a bit constrictive about his pudgy waist from the start, with no flap to spare, no extra holes. Now it was becoming tighter every second.

"My God, Luke, what's happenin'?" he screamed at his companion.

Luke had no breath with which to respond. Luke was no longer even struggling. His mouth was open as though gasping in vain for air. The necklace was so deeply buried in his throat, it was all but invisible. Even the locket containing the two miniature photographs seemed about to disappear into an ever deepening fissure of flesh.

Meanwhile the lines continued to jerk, though perhaps, like the necklace, they too should have broken under such stress, and now there was a kind of rhythm or synchronization in the way they were jerking. As though the two fish on the ends of them were working as a team to turn the canoe over.

Neither Luke nor Emile noticed. In the stern, Luke's face was turning purple as the golden noose about his throat became ever more tight. In the bow, a flap of leather with four empty holes in it now dangled from the belt tightening about Emile's tortured middle. Both men struggled feebly in silence, having no breath left with which to cry out.

Suddenly the two lines quivered in a climactic tug, and the canoe turned over with a convulsive gurgle.

The craft was still upside down and obviously empty moments later when a second canoe, with Charley Cree paddling, appeared around a wooded bend of shore and came gliding out into a blaze of golden sunlight. It continued to jerk and twitch, however, as the hooked trout that had overturned it struggled to free themselves.

Coming alongside the overturned craft, the Cree leaned sideways to put a hand on it, then lifted his grizzled head and gazed up at the sky. "Thank you," he murmured. "Thank you for answering this humble one's prayer."

He felt the jerking then. Guessing what was causing it, he investigated, and after a moment of maneuvering located the twitching lines. Very gently he drew the two hooked fish to the surface.

"As for you," he said as he released them, "you did well, though I think those two were disposed of anyway and drowning them was probably not necessary. Go now, and be content."

Hello, Jane, Good-Bye

by Sally McBride

Toronto writer/editor Sally McBride's short fiction has appeared in Asimov's SF, The Magazine of Fantasy and Science Fiction, Tesseracts, Realms of Fantasy *and numerous other sf and fantasy publications. Sally won the Aurora Award in 1995 for her novelette "The Fragrance of Orchids"* (Asimov's May 1994). *That story received Hugo and Nebula award nominations and received an honorable mention in 13th annual edition of* The Year's Best Science Fiction. *The following story was submitted to us following a challenge to Sally that we considered her too nice a person to be able to write a truly tough, truly nasty piece of fiction. As the reader will discover, she's one lady who knows how to meet a challenge.*

"Count backwards from fifteen, please, Angie."

Angie's brain doesn't just lie placidly in its bone cup, it moves and breathes. Not a lot, just enough so I know it's paying attention.

"Fifteen, fourteen, thirteen, twww..w...wwelve, eleven...ten—"

"Okay Angie, that's fine. Super."

Yes, her brain is paying attention, but it can be fooled.

Angie is a chubby sixteen-year-old with smooth pale skin and small, bright blue eyes, and a nervous mother in the visitors' lounge. Her father is most likely at work; not the type to take time off for something like this.

Angie's straight sandy hair will grow back after we pop the cut-out doorway back onto the top of her head and sew her scalp back up. She'll look like a skinhead for a while, but maybe her boyfriend will like that, maybe the other kids will think she's cool.

Better than epilepsy, isn't it, honey?

"Suction. Thanks, Kim."

I've got a good team. They're quiet, brisk, efficient. Quick on the uptake. At first a couple of them didn't like working for a female doctor, but they came around. I'm good. And my nurses are the best, they're on my side; we've done quite a bit of this sort of thing together.

I love it. God, I love it.

"Angie, can you tell me what you're thinking right now?" I can see her face in the mirror, and she can see mine. The edge of the green plastic dam separates her pasty little face from what's going on in her open skull. She can't move her head at all, but her eyes slide around, looking at me and away, flicking around as much of the operating theatre as is in her view, then back, shyly, to me. She licks her lips. She's scared, but she's doing fine.

"What'm I thinking...?"

Her face goes a little softer. Her eyes look at something, a little memory that's popped to the surface.

Her snub nose crinkles a bit. "I smell french fries," she says. "And vinegar... no, now it's gone."

The rounded tip of the electrode wand moves fractionally, gently padding along the skin of her brain like a tiny finger checking for blemishes, as if it were Angie delicately confronting a nascent pimple, getting ready to deal with it.

Leave it or squeeze it out?

I prefer to think of it as the paw of a cat, padding silently in search of mice in the mind's hidden crevices. The device is the perfect extension of my hand, my eye, my desire. I have tamed electricity to my personal will.

A smile creeps over her face. "It's Trish!" She's giggling."Oh, God, I can't talk about this... It's just like I'm *there*, wow... Trish, she can't handle booze, right? It's a party for Bruce ...she falls in Bruce's lap, right? Like, she's had too many —" And now her voice changes. She isn't just telling the story, she's living it. "Bruce, take it *easy*! Trish, come on. Let's go to the bathroom. Bruce, you asshole, help her up." Angie is still giggling. I wonder how many beers she's had? It's a fun memory, harmless, though her parents wouldn't like it.

Leave it there. Leave it and go on.

"Suction here, Kim. Time?"

"Nine nineteen, Barb."

We're all on first-name basis here, none of this Doctor Bell shit. My people respect me, I respect them; simple.

Angie's face blanks out for a moment. Her lips slacken. The electrode moves. I do love this, I do love it all so. . .

What we're doing here on this Tuesday morning in Operating Room 6 of Jubilee Hospital is eliminating epilepsy from this girl's life. No more seizures, no more medication. A normal, healthy life for an average young woman, a middle-class white girl with a so-so future, but shouldn't she have a life without disease?

Outside is a cold morning, snow in flurries whipped hard by the Manitoba wind. Inside is a haven of light and warmth and gleaming sterility. My world.

I know where it is, the little bit of brain tissue that must be destroyed. And I'll get to it, I'll get to it and have time for coffee before doing my rounds. But not just yet.

Move the electrode. Move it again, a millimetre at a time would be too much, too gross; I'll not wantonly rampage across Angie's life. But I know I'll find that little something tucked away, something she doesn't realize is still there. Most people have something they don't want to remember.

Angie, in the mirror, suddenly looks alert. Her heart rate leaps, her respiration stops, held in, then off she goes. Yes.

Yes, this is it. This is what I want.

"Hold her down, ladies. Let's find out what's happening."

Kim and Mattie lean into it. Angie's fighting hard; but for the head clamps she'd be off the table and out the door, wires trailing.

"No!" she screams, her voice high and childish. She's trying to pull her knees together, trying to twist her body away from the hands holding her down. "I'll tell Mommy! I'll — ah!" Another scream, cut off. Amazingly, a red patch flares on her cheek as if a phantom hand has slapped her. Then she goes silent, panting, her heart rate sky-high, her lips clamped shut as if a big heavy hand is over them.

I want very much to shut my eyes and take it all now. But the electrode must not move away from this sweet spot, this precious little node locked in Angie's cerebrum. If I'm going to get it I have to concentrate, trust that Mattie and Kim will do their part and trust me in turn. I'll enjoy it later, at home. Angie won't miss it; no, not at all.

She didn't even know it was there.

The buried traumas are the best. When they've been encysted deep and long, aging like brandy in a barrel, they taste the sweetest.

Angie is reliving the rape as we watch. It enters my brain as it exits hers, and I can even catch a little echo of what her father is feeling as he ravages his child. It's a very good session, very exciting. Who would have thought that ordinary little Angie Pitney would contain such delicious buried treasure?

"Well," I say as Angie lapses into unconsciousness and her heart rate levels out, "let's not let that come back. What do you say, ladies? Shall I excise this little bit of nastiness?"

Mattie and Kim, releasing their grip on Angie, nod as one. They see it my way, as always. Mattie must have some idea of what I do, but she doesn't care. She trusts me. Mattie can be elbow-deep in any sort of physical horror, but mental anguish knocks her sideways. To her, I'm purging these children of pain, cleaning them and making them well. How I do it is not her business. She keeps the others in line.

"Sue?"

Sue is my sterile nurse, new to this, and at first she won't look up from her tray of instruments.

"Sue? Are we in agreement?"

She nods then, gulping, and looks up at me. She's crying, her eyes spilling over as she gives me the kind of look I imagine a shepherd would give a burning bush.

"All right then. Probe, please."

The area will be heat-coagulated by the application of a controlled radio frequency current. It will never pop up out of Angie's psyche again. It won't need to: it's safe with me now.

When I was a girl, I'd get impressions from people: vague, shadowy pictures and emotions. They wouldn't stay, they vanished like fish in a lake. It didn't seem like anything special to me, and I never told anyone about it.

I knew I was destined to be a doctor when I grew up, I never wanted to be a nurse like the other little girls. I knew even then that I had to be the one in control, the one with her hands on the very essence of life.

As I learned more and took up neurosurgery, the belief that I was doing much more than empathizing with my patients sank in. I was *living* their memories. The electrical currents generated in connection with my work boosted the signal, as it were; I could capture what I wanted and keep it.

At first it frightened me, just as it does Sue to see me at work; then I learned to love it. I think there may be something wrong with me, something deep inside my own skull's cellar, but I'm functional, aren't I? Successful, in fact—even happy. I know what I'm doing. And what is wrong with that?

I'm the stereotypical image of the lady doctor, driven and loveless, burying herself in her career. Sex is a mundane, tedious exercise. I don't like to be touched. Driving is better, and I love to escape to midnight highways and see how fast my Mercedes will really go. Fast is good. Music is wonderful; the right aria, the right voice.

Drugs are good, and I've developed a fondness for certain uppers I can get in my professional capacity. I like to feel my brain race and burn and send off sparks like a screaming engine, knowing all along that it's different from anyone else's brain—it can do things that defy reason.

But *this* is the best. This quiet, sterile plundering of another's mind. The savoring of sweetness and pain that comes later. It's a pleasure that is all mine.

At home, I strip off my thin leather driving gloves and throw them on the credenza. It's dark out, the early frigid dusk of the north, and the drive was boring and stressful, past interminable petty accidents. Benita has laid a fire as she always does in the winter, after her cleaning and polishing duties. I never see her, she does her work and goes home.

Bending, I touch a match to the paper and watch the flames rise, feel the heat flare. The tension in my thighs as I crouch before the fire triggers something, and the next thing I know I'm on my back on the carpet, groaning as the stolen memory pounds its way into me, just as little Angie's father pounded his way into her. Past the defences, past the helpless, yielding flesh, right to the heart of *self*. For it's happening to me, *I'm* doing it, *I'm* feeling it from both sides, and it's strong, so strong...And it is mine, mine to enjoy as often as I want. How I would love the chance to get *his* brain under my hands, cracked open like an egg. What if I could get my own?

Afterwards, there's the glow of brandy, and as I watch the golden swirling liquid I think of what I do. What it means. If I were to announce this odd phenomenon, try to study it clinically and publish papers, then it wouldn't be mine any more. I'd be the one helpless under the electrodes, and I wouldn't like that, would I? So it's a moot question really. I have no intention of studying it.

I watch the news, then go to bed and enjoy Angie one more time.

"Jane Doe" lies under the sheet on the operating table, her head braced and shaved. She's seven, as near as can be determined. Records of her birth have yet to be found, and she's never been to school. Malnourished, thin, yet wiry as if her muscles have been tempered somehow, in some crucible of pain.

When she was brought in a ripple of shock went through the hospital like a physical thing, a wave of pity and horror. How could anyone treat a child so? How could the poor thing possibly have survived? There was hushed talk in the cafeteria and lots of speculation over the internal e-mail as people compared news broadcasts they'd seen, vied with one another to provide sordid morsels of information.

It got to the point where my initial reaction of pity was swamped under by the gossip. She's just another case, a brain-damaged child exhibiting symptoms that make my attentions necessary. Her cult-member parents, sub-human dregs at best, are beyond reparations now; the adults having taken the coward's way out: suicide.

Sue is readying the drill, Mattie and Kim bustle around. This time all we're going to do is drill some burr-holes in likely spots and pop the electrodes in for preliminary testing.

Jane Doe's charts tell me that she is unable to speak, though not for any organic reason. It has been determined that the epileptic seizures she experiences are probably the result of an infant brain inflammation, probably brought about by abuse, subsequent infection and lack of care. Her body has been brought to the edge of destruction by the tortures she has suffered, but fortunately it has not been permanently disabled. Her mind, though....

Ah, her mind.

"All right, ladies, time to get to work."

Jane Doe has been prepped and sedated already, and since she's to be awake during the procedure there is no need of an attending anesthetist. The brain itself has no pain receptors, so a local to the scalp is all that's needed. Sue can do that. Jane seems relaxed. Her respiration is slow and even, her eyes open and staring dreamily at the ceiling. Over the past few days in the hospital, many of her injuries have started to heal, and the swelling around her eyes and jaw has gone down. She might even be pretty some day.

Silence reigns as we work, except for monosyllabic orders and observations. We're like a planetary system, myself the sun, my ladies the planets securely in my orbit, little Jane the rogue comet to be studied as she flashes through our space.

The pattern of burr-holes might look random to the uninitiated observer, but it isn't. I'll be dropping my lures into several areas today, the way an Inuit hunter might fish from many holes in the Arctic ice, in hopes of catching a succulent seal. What is swimming under Jane's battered skull?

"Sue," I ask, "when was Jane's last seizure?"

"Oh two fifty-five," she responds. "Just over six hours ago."

"Duration?"

"Twelve minutes, thirty-three seconds."

"Okay. I'm going to insert the electrodes now, but we'll wait till they're all in place before running any current. Mattie, you're all set up? I want copies of the data sent to my office as well."

"No problem, Barb."

The hair-thin wires go in with no resistance. Jane stares at the ceiling, completely unresponsive, seeing who knows what. Telemetry aids the slight adjustments for exact positioning, in the amygdala, the cerebrum, the locus ceruleus and more. I'm casting my net wide.

I'm thankful that no electrocardiogram is monitoring my heartbeat right now. I know that if I spoke, my voice would betray my excitement, my impatience.

But when the current is initiated, there is almost no response at all.

It doesn't make sense. The electrodes are well within the centres of memory and emotion, as well as conscious thought; there must be something. Have her experiences left no impression at all? Is she so far gone that her mind is scrambled?

Now I wish I had gone ahead and opened her skull. I'd have more latitude to hunt with an electrode wand in my hand. For a moment there's a hot, clear image in my mind of my hands thrusting deep into the grey jelly, digging through Jane's brain up to my wrists, but it's nothing new. I always want to do that.

Perhaps, because the child is mute, she can't tell me her memories as they are drawn up, perhaps for that reason they can't come to me. But that doesn't seem likely; I've had other patients whose speech centres have been affected and it's made no difference. In fact, the impressions are invariably more sensual, more detailed in the areas of touch and smell.

Mattie, Kim and Sue exchange looks. I can sense their doubt, just as they can sense my anger and frustration. Sometimes I grow impatient with my role as goddess, and wish my ladies would vanish and leave me alone with my prey.

"Sue, I want sequential pulses. Start with the amygdala and move out."

That got something. "A little more power, if you please."

More, but nothing definite. There was a feeling like the sigh of wind through a high tree, thousands upon thousands of fluttering leaves making a rushing whisper in my head.

I also notice a flutter within Jane's amygdala, as I anticipated; a precursor to an epileptic seizure. "Did we get that? We'll have Jane back in here in a week or so, when she's strong enough, and take care of that."

A general lessening of the tension passes among my nurses. They like to be reminded of why we're here.

"Give me one more, Sue. Up it to point 3."

I see the motion of Sue's hand on the regulator out of the corner of my eye, and almost before it has a chance to register I find myself flat on my back on the white tiled floor.

My ears are ringing and my vision has narrowed to a black point. Mattie's voice wavers in and out as she sits me up and leans me precariously against the gurney leg. I feel her soft strong arm supporting me.

"Barb! Barb, what happened? It's okay, Sue's closing her up, don't worry, just take it easy — "

The blackness expands, sparkling at the edges. My lips are numb, and I feel intensely shaken and dizzy. Mattie has pulled my mask down, I can feel cold air on my face. I feel as though I have been flooded with something, like a rush of black water, or a howl of icy wind. Nothing like this has ever happened before.

In a few minutes I'm able to stand and leave the operating room. Little Jane lies on the table, her eyes turned toward me. She's awake and aware, and she's watching me with interest. Her eyes are bright in their bruised pits. Her lips are moving silently as if she's singing to herself, or repeating a word over and over, opening and closing.

"You want me to call Dr. Thom to look you over?"

I shake my head. It hurts. "No, Mattie, thanks. I'll be all right. I skipped breakfast this morning. I guess I've just been overdoing things." I give her a rueful smile which she seems to take as assurance that I really am all right. "I'm going to head home, though, okay?"

"Yes indeed. Put yourself to bed. Doctor's orders." I can feel her eyes on me as I head for the scrub room to doff my gown and gloves.

Just before I pass out the door, I hear a breathy little whisper from Jane. "Good-bye, good-bye..." She flashes me a tiny smile. It's eerie. It makes her seem *less* pathetic, not more, for some reason I can't fathom.

All the way home I keep well within the speed limit. My head feels as if it is going to explode. What have I got in there? What came over from Jane Doe to me?

I'm reluctant to light the fire that Benita has laid. Not afraid, I don't allow myself to be afraid. I can handle whatever it is; it's just more of the same after all, and like a connoisseur of wines I know how to take a sip and spit the rest out.

First I fix myself a sandwich—I really did skip breakfast—and then I take off all my clothes and lie on my bed. I keep it warm in my bedroom, so I don't need blankets. I don't like the feel of blankets touching me. As my breathing slows I start to feel the familiar tingle between my legs, the yearning that grows until it cannot be denied.

I know I'm in for a fast ride today, a bumpy ride. Maybe a crash. I can feel my lips pull back into a smile as I close my eyes. The possibility of a crash is like adrenalin to me, like the best upper in the world.

"All right. Come and get me."

It's like turning on a radio that is tuned between stations. Static fills my ears, hissing and throbbing as if powered by some vast generator pouring current into my head. There's nothing I can do to stop it now. I'm not afraid. I'm not afraid.

Then it's as if a weight has dropped onto me from a great height. A big heavy *thing*, not a body but a force. I'm quite familiar with the weight of men, the heavy bodies of rapists and pederasts crushing the breath out of their victims—out of me—and this isn't it.

It's grinding down on my chest and abdomen, leaving my legs and arms free. I can barely breathe. My arms fly back over my head, crashing into the headboard before halting locked behind me, as if caught in a very strong hand. My legs spread wide, drawn apart by that same rough force, my feet bent down into a ballerina's *pointe* and secured.

The static increases until I can barely think, but I'm past thinking now. I feel a point of heat come down and singe my breasts, licking along in a pattern, a pentagram sprawling sloppily across my belly. Looking down I can see round red welts on my skin, springing up as I watch. The heat and the pain spiral and stink, burning, and then are overcome by a crooning voice.

I feel my body rock and swing as if someone is dancing me around. The crooning turns into a song, a broken lullaby mumbled by a madwoman.

I swing, and then the arms let go and I'm falling free.

And then they all come in. All the Janes.

She's spent years creating the personalities that inhabit me now. Seventeen of them, and they take their turns with me over the next hours, each one different from the last, each one no preparation for the next. Jane — the core of the Jane personality — has been forced to become very inventive. I stop enjoying it after number five.

My own body is in league with the things inside me, and I'm tearing myself apart. I can feel the muscles rip, the flesh sizzle, the bruises flare and seep under my skin.

"My name is Gregor." He's a forty-something male built like a wrestler. Gregor is who Jane turns into when she's alone with the younger ones. He snaps my knuckles with gleeful force.

"I'm Susie," lisps a shy voice. "Will you play with me?" Susie is an artist who paints things in blood, her own blood. Layer upon layer of Susie's art covers the walls of Jane's room.

There's the screamer, the one who has no name, because all she does is scream. It drowns out everything else for a while. She's pushed aside by Auntie Crissy, who is able to do very nice things indeed with some of the toys in the room.

More follow; none of them listen to me. They are mine now, mine to keep in my head, but they won't listen. They won't stop. They won't let me go.

At last, at the very centre, is Jane. The real Jane who has no name and no identity, only the fearsome intelligence that has built this army of selves around it.

I see her at the end as my eyes give out, just as she was on the operating table, holes drilled in her skull. Wires trailing like reins, like veins, into my hands, my head, my soul.

Her lips are moving, she's saying good-bye, good-bye, good-bye. Thank you, doctor. Very softly, and with a smile on her swollen lips. Good-bye and good riddance.

Imposter

by Peter Sellers

Peter Sellers founded and edited Canada's critically-acclaimed Cold Blood *anthology series. His stories have appeared in every major mystery magazine and numerous crime and dark fantasy anthologies. He's smart enough to know that crime doesn't pay–at least not enough–so he's a freelance advertising writer by day and a crime writer by night. Perhaps it's late night inspiration that produces work like "Imposter" (originally titled "The Vampires Next Door") concerning the apartment dweller whose new neighbors turn out to be more experienced blood-suckers than his landlord. It's a very funny story but, just when you think that's all it is, it takes an abrupt turn into serious nightmare territory. (Did we forget to tell you that Peter writes ad copy for a local funeral home?)*

T he vampires next door were having a party. It didn't happen often. Generally they were pretty quiet neighbours. Nathan hardly knew they were there half the time. But once every two or three months they'd have friends in and things would get a little livelier.

From the beginning, Nathan wondered what the parties were like. Did vampires dance? If so, what kind of music did they play? Were the conversations intricate and philosophical discussions or shallow and transitory chit chat? Were charades popular? Nathan even tried to envision what they served as canapés. He already knew how the bar was stocked.

The morning after the second of the vampires' parties, Nathan found an empty plasma bag lying in the hall between the vampires' front door and the incinerator room. It was then around ten in the morning and the empty bag must have been lying there since before dawn, making Nathan wonder how many people had seen it on their way to the elevators and the office but had simply pretended it wasn't there.

Nathan went back into his apartment, put on the rubber gloves he used for washing dishes, and picked up the empty bag. He took it into the incinerator room and dropped it and the gloves down the chute. Then he washed his hands for a long time under very hot water.

The night of the vampires' first party, Nathan had been very nervous. He knew the fear was irrational. After all, the vampires had told him all the things he needed to do in order to stay safe. Still, there he was, living next door to a couple of undead things that survived by drinking human blood. And they were having company. He was terrified.

He tried telling himself it was no different than living next to a couple with any other dietary quirk. Vegetarians perhaps, or Catholics who ignored Vatican II and still ate fish on Friday. Or people who always ate the middle of the Oreo first, or who ate the red Smarties last. He tried thinking that way, but it didn't really help.

The vampires had been very good about preparing Nathan for their first party. Three days before, they came to Nathan's apartment for a visit. They brought a bottle of Bordeaux dated 1837 and they sat on the sofa holding hands. Every once in a while one or the other would laugh at something that was said and their fangs would peek briefly from behind their burgundy lips causing Nathan to suppress a shudder.

"We're going to have a party," Bianca told him.

Nathan's jaw dropped. "A party? Like an open house? For the neighbors?" He couldn't help wondering if anyone else in the building knew.

"No, silly," Bianca said. Laughter. Fangs. "For our old friends."

"Friends?"

"Yes," Mikhail told him. "Some friends from uptown. Some friends from other parts of the country. And some friends who just flew in from overseas."

Nathan smiled weakly. "And boy are their arms ever tired," he said.

Mikhail looked confused. "Yes," he said in his rumbling tones, "the strain it puts on the muscles here..." He started to indicate areas of the upper arm and shoulder when Bianca laid her hand on Mikhail's wrist and stopped him.

"It's an old joke," she said.

"Oh," Mikhail said, looking embarrassed. Nathan figured he came as close to blushing as a vampire ever could.

"The party will be Friday night," Bianca said.

The thirteenth, Nathan thought. Figures.

"We're expecting a large number of guests. We'll try and be as quiet as possible, the parties seldom become rowdy unless an infiltrator is found. Then things can get out of hand. If you're planning to be home that night, we advise you to take several precautions." Then she described in detail how Nathan could use crosses and garlands of fresh garlic to keep any overly enthusiastic partygoers at bay.

"But I don't take these precautions with you."

"That's because of our arrangement. Unfortunately, our friends aren't all as," she paused, hunting for the right word, "*avant garde* as we are. If you're careful, the worst that should happen will be the odd annoying phone call. You'd perhaps be best not to answer the phone at all that night."

The next day, Nathan bought several crosses in a variety of sizes from a Christian supply store he found in the Yellow Pages. Then he went to his local grocer and bought all the garlic buds they had. The grocer looked at him oddly as Nathan piled up the fragrant vegetables on the counter.

"I'm making soup," Nathan said.

The grocer nodded. "Thought maybe you were worried about vampires or something," he said. "Course, you make a soup with this much garlic, you'll keep more'n them suckers away." He laughed, showing wide, uneven teeth.

Nathan smiled back unhappily and walked home with his packages.

As it turned out, the party was one of the most subdued Nathan had ever lived beside. There were some peculiar noises, what he thought was the flapping of leathery wings outside his window, and what sounded like a large dog sniffing loudly at the base of his front door, but for the most part he was not bothered.

At two in the morning his phone did ring, as Bianca had told him it might, and a cold, hypnotic voice said, "Come next door and be the life of the party." But the call was abruptly cut off and Nathan unplugged the phone and sat up on the sofa for the rest of the night.

Nathan hadn't realized at first that his new neighbors were vampires, although it was unusual to have people moving in after midnight. He'd heard them thumping and banging in the halls and he recognized the universal cries of the do-it-yourself mover. "A little to the left." "Hangonhangonhangonhangon!" "Just let me get a better grip."

He went out into the hall to have a look and that's when he got his first glimpse of Bianca.

Her back was to him, clad entirely in black, with lustrous hair, the blackest Nathan had ever seen, falling almost to her slender waist. She wore snug black designer jeans, Nathan spent a long time trying to read the label, and black leather boots reached up almost to her knee. She was moving backwards toward the open door of the apartment next to Nathan's, and she was struggling with an awkward-looking box. As she moved she was giving directions to two men who followed her carrying a large dark wooden chest, like a long low sideboard, with ornate brass handles.

They were big, fierce looking men and Nathan hoped they hadn't noticed him looking so longingly at the woman's behind. He stepped forward. "Let me help," he said, grabbing the other end of the awkward box in the woman's arms.

She shot him a look of consternation. Sensing that perhaps she was new to the big city and uneasy about strange men offering assistance in the middle of the night, Nathan said, "I live next door". He pointed to his apartment and smiled at her with such bland innocence that she let him take some of the weight of the box. Nathan's knees buckled and the smile left his face. He'd expected linens or something, but it felt like there was an anvil in there. He struggled forward, expecting any second to feel something in his stomach tear apart.

They brought the box into the living room and set it down, Nathan dropping his end with a grunt and a crash the neighbors below must have loved. The woman set her end down as gently as a mother laying a newborn's head on a pillow. Nathan wondered how many hours she'd spent on a Nautilus machine to be able to do that.

The two men followed them into the apartment and set the sideboard against the dining room wall. "That's it," the woman said. "That's everything." She turned her gaze to Nathan and his heart swelled. He'd never seen eyes so black and he instantly fell in love. "Thank you, Mr..."

Nathan held out a hand. "Nathan," he said. "Since we're going to be neighbors, just call me Nathan."

"My name is Bianca." She took Nathan's hand. The night outside was edging down toward freezing, and she'd been working without gloves so her hands were cold. Releasing Nathan's grip, she indicated the two men with her.

"This," she said, pointing to a tall man with heavy shoulders, a handsome face deeply lined by the elements and eyes nearly as dark as her own, "is my husband Mikhail." Mikhail looked at Nathan with penetrating intensity and bowed slightly and briskly. "And this is our friend, Raoul." She drew the second syllable out so that the name sounded like an abbreviated howl. Raoul was, Nathan thought, the hairiest man he'd ever seen, his eyes sandwiched between a thick beard and heavy overhanging eyebrows.

Raoul immediately turned to Mikhail and grunted something, and then stalked out of the apartment.

"You must excuse Raoul," Bianca said. "He's a little lacking in the social graces. He's something of a lone wolf."

Nathan nodded. "Well," he said, "I better be going too. If there's anything else you need, I'm right next door."

"Must you go?" Bianca edged closer to him, her tongue moistening her upper lip.

"Won't you stay for a little nightcap?" Mikhail's voice was rich and textured, like a Slavic Richard Burton. "After all we're your new neighbors and you can give us a little taste of life in the building." There was something about the way Mikhail said it, and the way Bianca was rubbing her cold hands over Nathan's chest, that made him nervous.

"That's awfully nice of you," Nathan said, "but I have to work tomorrow, and it's so late..." He began backing toward the door.

"Oh? And what work do you do?" Bianca asked, although it sounded to Nathan like a polite cocktail party question.

"This makes a lot of people uncomfortable, but I work at a blood bank," Nathan said. "Testing blood."

Bianca pulled back from Nathan as if she'd been stung. He'd had that reaction before from women who thought his job was disgusting. He couldn't understand it, really. What he was doing was very important. What with all the horrible bacteria swimming around in the world's blood streams he, and those like him, were all that stood between national health and pandemia. So he wasn't surprised when Bianca drew away. He *was* surprised when he looked at her face, and then at Mikhail's, and saw a level of interest he'd never witnessed before.

"What exactly do you do," Bianca purred, "with the blood?"

"Well," Nathan confessed, "I don't actually do the testing. But they look for HIV, Tay-Sachs, sickle cell, syphilis, you name it, before they store it or ship it out for operations, transfusions, whatever. Naturally, they don't want to keep the bad stuff. That's my job. I'm in charge of disposal. There's a joke around the lab, there's always bad blood between me and everyone else."

Bianca laughed and Mikhail smiled ever so slightly. Then Bianca placed a hand on Nathan's elbow and steered him to the door with a strength that made him increase his estimate of how much time she'd spent in the gym. "But we must let you get some sleep. You have important work. And Mikhail and I have much to discuss about arrangements here in our new home."

The arrangements were made plain to Nathan two days later. Mikhail and Bianca invited him over for a drink and, they said, a chance to get better acquainted. Nathan wasn't entirely comfortable after their peculiar behaviour of the other night, but he found himself curiously unable to refuse.

Nathan sat in a very comfortable arm chair and looked at Mikhail and Bianca on the sofa. "So," he said with a smile, "now it's my turn." He took a sip of the wine they offered him. It had turned, but he tried not to show it. After all, unless the label was a gag, the bottle was over 150 years old. "What do you guys do for a living?"

Mikhail and Bianca looked at one another for quite some time. It was obvious to Nathan that they were trying to figure out how to answer, or even if they should. Maybe I shouldn't have asked, he thought. Maybe they do something really weird or gross. Maybe they're worm pickers and that's why you never see them during the day. Maybe they run a phone sex business. He mentally kicked himself. But just as he was about to try and steer the conversation in a new direction, Bianca turned her eyes from Mikhail to him.

"We're vampires," she said simply. Just like that. Flat out and straight faced. Like she was telling the guy at the deli how much smoked meat she wanted.

Nathan stared at her. "Pardon me?"

"We're vampires."

"You know, the undead," Mikhail added, by way of helpful explanation.

Nathan started to laugh. "You guys," he said, slapping his knee with a loud flat sound. "The clothes, the crazy hours. Look, if you don't want to tell me what you do, I understand. Everybody has secrets. It's okay with me."

Bianca shook her head. "We're not kidding, Nathan. We're really vampires."

There was something in her tone that made Nathan stop laughing. He'd heard of people who called themselves vampires. Little groups of fringe dwellers, the kind of wingnuts you found clinging like barnacles to the underside of any big city. People who drank the blood of animals or licked it from small wounds opened in one another's chests and fingertips, late at night, in the glow of dripping candles, often for sexual reasons.

Nathan looked at the thick crimson richness of the wine in his glass and felt queasy. Maybe they were being serious. Maybe they did consider themselves vampires. Maybe they were the kind of lunatics he'd really rather not have living next door, the kind he certainly didn't want to spend the evening with in idle chatter while they sized up which of his veins to open first. He started calculating how far it was to the front door.

Mikhail leaned forward suddenly. "We'll prove it to you," he said brightly.

"That's okay!" Nathan threw up his hands and shrank back. "If you say you're vampires, hey, who am I to argue?" He looked at his watch. "Whoa, where does the time go? I really...I gotta...I..."

Mikhail waved off his objections. "No, no," he said. "We must prove it to you. We sense, very strongly, that you are not sure in here." He touched the middle of his chest. "We will not rest easily if we feel there is any doubt."

Nathan was frantic. "I don't doubt! I don't doubt! Please don't feel you have anything to prove on my account."

"But we will," Mikhail barked. "Look!" Then he and Bianca pulled their lips back in exaggerated wedding photo grimaces and their fangs gleamed.

Nathan stared at the teeth. He had expected something more dramatic. He didn't say anything for the longest time, and Mikhail and Bianca's eyes darted uncertainly back and forth. As the silence lengthened, their upper lips began to tremble from the strain and a tear squeezed out of the corner of one of Mikhail's eyes.

"So what?" Nathan asked finally. "Those teeth you can probably pick up for ten bucks at a costume shop. I've got a pair at home that look every bit as good as that." It was true. Nathan's teeth had been provided by the cousin of a friend of his brother, who worked in the movie make-up and special effects business. Nathan had worn them to a Hallowe'en party and knew they looked every bit as real, if not more so, than what he was looking at now.

Bianca and Mikhail lowered their lips back over their fangs and Mikhail rubbed his jaw. "You want more proof?" Bianca couldn't entirely hide her displeasure at Nathan's disbelief. It showed in her eyes, but not in her voice. "Very well. Then we need you to do one small thing for us. With your hands."

Involuntarily, Nathan's fingers curled up as he imagined her sucking beads of crimson from their trembling tips. He started to shake, but neither Mikhail nor Bianca moved towards him. Instead she kept talking in her soft, hypnotic way. "Just take your hands," she said, "and place the index finger of one hand over the index finger of the other, at right angles, to make the shape of the...you know...the..." She waved a hand in the air to fill in the word.

"Shape of the cross, you mean," Nathan said. He had never in his life hit a woman, unless you counted Melissa Levinson when he was seven, but simply saying that word made him understand the feeling. Bianca's head snapped back and she grunted as if he had driven a vicious blow to her abdomen.

"Ahh!" Nathan cried. He felt like a heel. "I'm so sorry. I didn't think..."

"It's alright," Bianca said weakly. "Please, when I say ready, make the sign."

She reached over and took Mikhail's hand. They looked at one another again, this time with more sadness than Nathan thought he had ever seen, and then Bianca turned to him and nodded. "Ready." Nathan lifted his hands, index fingers extended, and he made the sign of the cross in the air in front of him.

It was as if a bolt of lightning had blasted from his fingers and hammered the two vampires back into the sofa cushions. They arched their backs and howled, trying desperately to avert eyes that were held riveted to Nathan's fingers. Their faces flushed red and the veins in their necks stood out, pulsing as if they would burst. Nathan stared in awe at the two writhing, groaning wild eyed figures who squirmed and convulsed before him. He was so mesmerized by what was happening that he forgot for a moment that he was causing it. Then his gaze fell for an instant to his hands and with a cry he yanked his fingers apart as if they were burned. Mikhail and Bianca slumped onto the sofa, leaning panting against one another, tears rolling down their faces as the brilliant red faded gradually returning them to their usual pallor.

"Wow," Nathan said. "That was something." The question remained, what? It was an impressive display, true. But it could have been acting. It could have been autosuggestion. If these people believed so deeply that they were vampires, they could have this kind of reaction automatically. He figured they probably had the idea so firmly fixed in their minds that if they went outside during the daytime, they'd break out in hives in about five seconds. But there was no way they'd crumble to dust.

As if he read Nathan's thoughts, Mikhail rose and walked toward him. Normally, Mikhail stood very tall and erect. But now he stooped and lumbered forward unsteadily and when he held out his hand it shook as if he were a thousand years old. "I sense you still don't believe. Take my hand."

Nathan reached out unsurely and took hold. If Mikhail was acting, he was awfully good. His grip was still strong and he half pulled Nathan to his feet, then he put his hand around Nathan's shoulder and walked him to a large cloth covered object hanging on the wall. Nathan had figured it was a painting they wanted protected from the sunlight, but Mikhail pulled a cord at the side and the cloth fell away, revealing a large gilt framed mirror.

Nathan stared into it. He felt Mikhail's hand clamped on his shoulder. He felt Mikhail's cool and trembling body next to his own. He heard Mikhail's rasping breath at his ear. But when he looked in the mirror he was quite alone.

Nathan glanced sideways. Mikhail. He looked in the mirror. No Mikhail. He shut his eyes and opened them again. Still no Mikhail in the mirror. "Oh my God," he said. And that's when he broke for the door.

Somehow, Mikhail got there first and Nathan hit him on the dead run. It was like running into a moose. Nathan wound up sitting on the floor, shaking his head in an effort to clear it, and looking up at the imposing vampire who reached a hand down to him. "We will not hurt you," Mikhail said. And he bent down and jerked Nathan to his feet. "We have a deal for you. A proposition."

"What kind of proposition?"

"We want you to supply us with blood," Bianca said in a voice that made Nathan's testicles contract.

Involuntarily, Nathan's hand flew to his neck. Bianca and Mikhail both laughed. "Not from your body, you foolish man," she said. "From where you work. Instead of throwing all that rejected blood away, bring some of it home to us."

"What?" Nathan asked in disgust. "You can't drink that blood."

"Whyever not?" Bianca asked, looking at him in puzzlement.

"Because it's bad. Diseased. It'll make you sick. It'll kill you."

Bianca laughed. "But, Nathan, we're already dead. More or less. What would hurt you can sustain us."

Nathan shook his head. "I don't like it."

"You'll get used to the idea."

"Well," he sighed, "I used to deliver pizzas. I guess it's not really that much different. But why are you doing this?"

"The old way is no good anymore," Bianca said with a wistful smile. "It lacks dignity. And besides, nowadays people aren't as superstitious as they were in the old days. And they all know what they're doing. With the books, and the movies, and on television even, everyone knows about vampires. Do you think if people started showing up with holes in their necks and bloodless veins they wouldn't come after us right away? We'd die horrible, helpless deaths."

"Writhing around with big sticks through our chests," Mikhail added, leaning forward in his seat and jabbing his finger at Nathan's chest for emphasis. "Pinned like butterflies to a cork board. Spewing blood, our eyes bursting." He sat back again, content to let Nathan dwell on the images.

"And don't believe what they say about vampires, either. We don't hate our half-lives, really. We don't have to worry about getting older, about sagging or wrinkles. I haven't colored my hair in over 260 years. And we never have to use aerobics or stair climbers to stay trim. True, we don't tan, but that's no longer good for you anyway. And the diet really isn't bad."

"Oh," Mikhail said, "the diet is wonderful. The variables of blood varietal, vintage and geographic region make for an astounding array of taste sensations. And every so often you hit upon a truly rare specimen and it's an experience any gourmet would sell his soul to sample."

Nathan struggled to control his nausea, the bile pressing frantically against the back of his clenched teeth.

"We just believe in changing with the times," Mikhail said.

"Even vampires have to evolve," added Bianca. "Will you help us?" She looked longingly at him. "If not..." She reached out and ran a cold, soft hand along the side of his neck.

Nathan started supplying blood to the vampires next door the following Monday. Smuggling the tainted samples out was easier than he expected, although with his liquid cargo hidden under his trench coat he felt like it was Prohibition and he was on his way home from the speakeasy.

And, as Bianca had predicted, he did get used to it. That was, in part, because he realized he had no choice. If he didn't supply them with blood, they'd take it. From him. Also, they were being very civilized about the whole thing. Preferring a life of middle class domesticity to one of terrorizing the city and condemning others to their fate.

For well over a year, everything went without a hitch. Nathan delivered every day. The vampires even created a card system. They'd leave one under his door every night, shortly before dawn. It would indicate the order for the day and Nathan would fill it as best he could, noting which particular requests he'd been unable to meet and making it up the following day. He wondered what Mr. O'Sullivan, the milkman he remembered from his youth, clanking from house to house in his white trousers and black bow tie, would think of Nathan and the hideous red pop he delivered now. Lord, how times have changed, Nathan thought to himself as he passed another day's supply into Mikhail and Bianca's eager hands.

Delivering blood got to be as routine as shaving or having lunch. And, after the first half dozen, the parties got to be that way too. But as Nathan's fear diminished, his curiosity increased. And so it was that when the vampires next door announced their latest gathering, Nathan decided he simply had to go, invitation or not.

He knew it would work. For over a year he'd studied two vampires up close. He knew how they talked and acted. He had teeth every bit as good looking as theirs. He knew Mikhail and Bianca would not be happy to see him, but he also knew they wouldn't expose him as an imposter to their friends and risk losing their safe source of supply. He knew the power he had in his fingers, how that simple sign of the cross could immobilize any vampire long enough to let him get away should things go wrong. And he also knew he wouldn't stay long in any event. Pop in, check it out, then head home. A daring commando strike on the vampire bash.

He prepared his apartment as usual with crosses and garlic, for protection when he returned home. He left the door unlocked for quick entry. Then he got himself ready. He wore black Levi's and black western boots, and a grey T-shirt beneath a dusty rose sport shirt. Then, of course, the teeth. He combed his hair and checked the fangs in the mirror, gave himself the thumbs up, and went out into the hallway.

He was about to knock on the vampires' door when a sudden thought occurred to him. Suppose no one arrived this way. Suppose they just materialized from under the door in a puff of smoke, or fluttered through the bedroom window on leathery bat wings. Oh well, he reasoned, those options weren't open to him. So he raised his hand and knocked, hoping no one inside would notice that he hadn't buzzed up from the lobby.

The door opened almost immediately by a young woman with short orange hair and large gold earrings. "Hi," she said, her kewpie doll eyes studying him and her lips forming a tentative smile. "I only just got here," she said. "It looks like quite a party. I've never been to one of these before."

"Neither have I. Can I come in?"

"Oh, sorry." She stepped back and Nathan entered, jumping in his skin at the sound of the door closing behind him.

"My name's Lucy." Nathan turned to se the orange-haired girl holding out a hand to him. He didn't want to touch her, knowing his hands would be too warm, but he wasn't sure how to avoid it without being rude. Finally he reached out quickly and gave her hand a light swift shake. Her hand felt clammy but she didn't react to the warmth he had feared would give him away.

"Do you know Bianca and Mikhail well?"

Nathan almost blurted out that he'd supplied the blood for the party, but caught himself in time. "Not really. But I better find them and say hello. Excuse me."

He made his way into the apartment. It was full of vampires. For an instant, Nathan had a dread thought that they would know automatically that he was not one of them. In the way he'd heard that gays could tell about each other. But there were only the usual casual glances one partygoer gives to another, unfamiliar face. There were vampires on the sofa, leaning against the walls, sitting on the seats and arms of the chairs. It seemed like any normal, casual gathering although everyone was drinking something that looked vaguely like cranberry cocktail and there were no chips and dip in sight.

Nathan headed for the kitchen. As with most of the parties he'd ever been to that was the liveliest room. It was solid vampires, many of them making their way to the two Coleman coolers filled with plasma bags, others pushing their way back through the crowd, drinks held aloft, calling, "Excuse me. Pardon me, please." That was where Nathan abruptly came face to face with Bianca.

At first it was as if she didn't know who he was. He was undoubtedly the last person she ever anticipated seeing at her party so placing him took a while. Then her face drained a shade paler. "What are you doing here?" she hissed.

Nathan smiled, proudly displaying his fangs. "Just checking it out. It's actually pretty dull, just a bunch of half-dead people sitting around talking."

"Many of them haven't seen each other in a hundred years and more. They're catching up. But if you don't leave this might get more exciting than you'd like."

"I'll be fine," he said, smiling and holding up his two index fingers like six guns.

Bianca shook her head and said simply, "I can't protect you here. No one can. Please, leave now. Before it's too late."

Nathan felt a hand on the small of his back and the chill of it shot through his shirts. "Oooh," a voice murmured, "who's this Bianca? He's dishy."

Nathan looked around and saw a vampire of about his own age, plunging neckline, short skirt, and dangerously sharp heels. "I'm Ruby," she said. "What's your name?"

"Nathan," he said, reflexively smiling wide enough to show her his fangs.

"You're new," she said.

He nodded. "This is my first party."

"No. New to this, uh, life," she said. "I can always tell."

Suddenly Nathan was overcome by panic. What had he hoped to accomplish? How close was he to being caught? Did Ruby know? Even Bianca couldn't protect him. He turned to her, trying to sound calm. "It was a lovely party. Thanks, but I have to go." Bianca looked at him very sadly. "Excuse me."

His impulse was to just shove his way through the crowd, bulldoze to the door. But he knew he'd never make it. He swallowed hard and eased past the revelers as inconspicuously as possible. God, if only he could turn himself into a wisp of smoke and vanish that way. He felt beads of sweat stand out on his forehead and he realized it had never occurred to him before, do vampires sweat? Thinking about it made it worse.

Somehow, Nathan managed to stay calm as he inched forward. The door, though, seemed to have been moved much further away than it was when he came in. It got closer and closer with agonizing slowness as Nathan waded through the blood-drinking throng. He was almost there when he suddenly felt a hand clutch his arm and someone whisper in his ear, with a feral excitement that chilled him, "We've got an imposter."

Nathan froze. If he hadn't been so frightened he would have screamed. He felt tears beginning to build behind his eyes and felt the hand on his arm begin to turn him back until he faced into the apartment. "Come on, Nathan," Ruby said. "Come back. We've got ourselves an imposter."

It took a few seconds for the meaning of the words to sink in. They had an imposter and it wasn't him. There was another one at the party. Nathan almost wept now, but with relief. Unthinkingly, he let Ruby propel him towards the kitchen and it was only after a few steps that he began to wonder who the other imposter was.

Then, outside the kitchen door, at the centre of a seething knot of vampires, was the orange-haired girl who'd opened the door for him. She was held fast, arms and legs, by at least half a dozen different eager guests, where their fingers pressed her flesh it showed true vampire white. But her eyes were wide with panic, her mouth open and a terrified keening was all that came out. It made Nathan's knees go weak.

Nathan looked at Ruby whose eyes glittered. "How do you know she's an imposter?" he asked in a whisper.

Ruby didn't take her eyes off the struggling girl. "Someone spilled a glass of blood on her and she used the name of the deity."

It took Nathan some time before he understood this further, and he only just stopped himself from repeating the error by muttering aloud, "Oh, she said Jesus Christ." Lucy managed to turn her head in his direction and their eyes met. He tried to give her a look of sympathy but her keening rose in intensity and Nathan understood right away. She recognized him as like her. Perhaps she thought he could help her. Perhaps she thought she could expose him in return for her freedom. He had no idea which.

"How did she get in here?" he asked.

"Doesn't matter. But she's here. And she's ours now. It's always so much better when this happens. And I think she likes you." Then Ruby was moving forward, dragging Nathan with her. "Look out," she said. "Let me through." She drew Nathan up to within three feet of the captive. He could smell the fear of her.

Then Ruby was talking again, this time to the hungering crowd. "This is Nathan. It's his first party. And he's new. He gets the first bite."

This sent Lucy into a new frenzy of anguished struggle. More hands reached in to hold her fast, two of them gripping her head and wrenching it to the side exposing the vein on her neck. Her face was flushed red with her terror and her struggling.

Nathan was frozen. Oh God, why didn't he stay home? He extended the index fingers of his hands and looked down at them but knew they were as useless as a water pistol against the horde. They'd simply bring him down from the rear. The door was unreachable, the crowd pressed in around him and from somewhere a chant went up that built and built as Lucy struggled in vain. "Bite! Bite! Bite! Bite!"

Ruby leaned forward and whispered in Nathan's ear. "Go ahead, Nathan. Bite."

Nathan took one last look around for an avenue of escape but there was none. Then he looked into Lucy's stricken eyes, tried to tell her with his gaze how sorry he was. He stared at the fat vein bulging in the side of her neck. He listened to the ravenous chanting. Bite! Bite! Bite! He said a short and silent prayer. Then Nathan shut his eyes and opened his mouth very wide.

Wild Things Live There

by Michael Rowe

In his introduction to this book Michael Rowe explained the genesis of his story "Wild Things Live There," the title of which we have appropriated as an intriguing alternative to the accurate but predictable Best of Northern Frights. *One of the many things we liked about this story was that it was set in a real Ontario town, that of Milton–a town in which the author once lived. With only a little encouragement from us, Michael wrote a second Milton terror tale, "Red Mischief," which appeared in* Northern Frights 4, *and began a series of Milton horror stories, transforming his old home base into the most fiend-haunted, werewolf-ridden, vampire-infested real estate outside of Jules de Grandin's Harrisonville, New Jersey and Charles Grant's Oxrun Station. What sets Michael's series apart is that Milton is not a fictional location. You can actually go there–if you dare.*

L ast night, I woke to the sound of fingernails scratching on the glass of my bedroom window eight floors above the ground, and for a moment I was eleven years old and back in Milton, and Mrs. Winfield had found me like she said she would.

Just before I opened my eyes, I heard a low, muddy chuckle, but the sound tattered away into the darkness. The room was silent, except for the pounding of my own heart and my wife's soft breathing. I reached across the bed and felt for her. The sheets were drenched in sweat, and Claudia had moved as far to the other side of the bed as she could. I saw the soft skin of her shoulder and her long blonde hair, both touched by moonlight. Claudia knows about my nightmares. She tried to wake me once during one of them, before we were married. When she laid her cool fingers on my chest, my dream shifted and I felt claws moving like a murderous caress towards my throat. I saw yellow eyes before I woke, and smelled sulphur. When she touched me, I began to scream. I think Claudia was as frightened as I was. When she had calmed me, Claudia gave me some Xanax from her private pharmacy of pills, and I fell into a sleep so deep that I woke the next afternoon feeling like there were ice picks methodically tearing my brain apart, strip by strip.

"How's your head?" she asked me sympathetically when I came into the living room. Through the haze of my pain, I caught a glimpse of myself in the bathroom mirror. "Do you want a Tylenol, Randy?"

"What are you, Claudia?" I said irritably. "My pusher? Drugs to make me sleep, drugs to keep me awake. Drugs for headaches..."

"I wish I had something to alter your mood," she said crisply. I must have winced, because her eyes darkened with concern. "Poor baby." She reached over and brushed my hair out of my eyes. "Do you want to talk about your dream?"

"I can't remember it," I lied, and I dropped the memory of my nightmare into the dark green waters of my subconscious. Years later, Claudia told me that she decided then and there to marry me, if only to protect from the monsters that visited me in the hours before dawn.

I pushed back the damp sheets and walked naked to the window of the bedroom. The bloated October moon hung low and orange over English Bay, and the West End was bathed in amber light. From our eighth floor apartment on Pendrell Street, I saw the Sylvia Hotel to the left, and the dark mass of Bowen Island and the mountains in the distance. We were one block from Stanley Park, but the park, with it's caves and ravines, disturbed me. It reminded me of the escarpment behind Auburn. Claudia was born in West Vancouver, and everything about the city was a joy to her. We skied at Whistler, and we took her father's boat out on weekends. But I never came to love Stanley Park. Wild things lived there: raccoons, foxes, and lately, worse. Stanley Park has become a dangerous place to walk after dark, when creatures crueller and more hostile than animals stalked and waited with lethal patience behind trees and boulders. I've always associated muggings and murders with the East, with Toronto. But nothing is immune, not even a paradise like Vancouver.

I peered out the window and looked down the wall of our building. There was nothing to see except the worn brick. The glass of the bedroom window was grimy at its base. There were vertical smudges near the latch.

They could have been caused by anything at all, I told myself. Shivering, I reached for my robe on the chair by the bed. I would call the management of our building in the morning. Christ knows, we pay enough for clean glass. I didn't like the smudges. In the moonlight, they look too much like fingerprints.

Although I traded the muted brick-reds and greys of southern Ontario for the vivid blues and greens of Vancouver nearly fifteen years ago, I was born in Milton, and I will always carry the flinty soil of southern Ontario within me, however long I live in British Columbia. I grew up in a small town called Auburn, nestled between Milton and Campbellville, at the foot of the Halton Hills, near the forests and gorges of the Niagara escarpment. My father died when I was five, and I was raised by my mother and my Aunt Etna. Both Mum and Aunt Etna were from Milton, but my grandfather gave my mother a farmhouse in Auburn when my father died, and I grew up there surrounded by women. There wasn't much to Auburn except a general store and a United Church, so I attended the J.M. Denies School on Thomas Street in Milton. After school, I would bike down Main Street to Tremaine Road, then west down the number 5 Sideroad towards home.

Every town has at least one house that children don't want to pass in the dark, especially on nights when the moon is out and riding. In Milton, it was Mrs. Winfield's house on Martin Street. Everyone in town knew that it was bad news. Nobody said "haunted," because they knew that Mrs. Winfield lived there, and a house couldn't be haunted by something living, could it? Mrs. Winfield had been a widow since God wore short pants. In a small Ontario town, removed by many miles from a major city, the fabric of life is shot through with legend. In a town like Milton, where gossip was mother's milk, the legend of Mrs. Winfield was nearly an epic.

Rumor had it that one night, back in the 1920's, she'd killed Mr. Winfield with an axe. Just cut him up into small pieces and stored him, cured and salted, in her icebox. Rumor further had it that she'd fed off him for months, one chunk at a time, and that she'd made mincemeat tarts and headcheese with what was left. But this was just ugly gossip, as my mother pointed out. The town constable called on Mrs. Winfield, and she was as nice and sweet as she could be. My mother and Aunt Etna told me that she'd wrung her hands and sobbed that he'd never been a reliable man, always away on business, and that one day he left and told her he wasn't coming home.

A local Catholic priest, formerly of Holy Rosary Church and dead these many years, claimed that he'd had tea at her home in an attempt to convince her to attend church now that she was alone. She'd invited him into her parlor, given him tea and tarts, after which he was violently ill. He refused to speak about Mrs. Winfield until the day he died.

But Mrs. Winfield wasn't from Milton. She was an outsider who'd moved there with her husband in 1914. When Mr. Winfield vanished she kept to herself, which was almost impossible to do in a small town. But she paid her taxes and hired a man to keep the outside of her house looking nice. Her shutters were always closed, and she never came to the door for her milk or her newspaper. What could the town do? No one ever saw Mrs. Winfield in church, and that bothered the town worthies, but there was no law against being godless.

One afternoon in early September, the second day of school, I was sitting at the kitchen table with my best friend, Patrick Cross. We were eating warm ginger cookies, and we each had a glass of milk. We heard Aunt Etna's old brown Buick on the gravel outside.

"It's your aunt," said Patrick.

"Duh," I answered him. "Of *course* it's my aunt, Einstein." Patrick was my best friend, but he was a little slow sometimes. We heard Aunt Etna open the door, and moments later she walked into the kitchen and put two bags of groceries on the counter.

"Hi, Aunt Etna!" I called out.

Usually she ruffled my hair and gave me a wet kiss, but this time she just looked at me and said, "Randy, don't you have homework?"

I looked up at Aunt Etna, and saw that her face was pale. Her hair seemed damp around the edges, and she looked sick.

"It's only four o'clock Aunt Etna. Patrick and I are going outside to play."

"Don't you sass me, boy!" Aunt Etna snapped. "You just go upstairs and do your homework right away!" I almost fell out of my chair. I'd never heard Aunt Etna raise her voice to me in my life. She must have noticed, because her voice softened a little. "Patrick can go up with you if he wants, and stay for dinner if he'd like."

"Thank you ma'am. I would," said Patrick winsomely. Everybody's parents loved Patrick.

"Randy, where's your mother?" Aunt Etna asked me. She sat down heavily in her chair beside the stove.

"She's in the garden," I replied. "Aunt Etna, what's wrong?"

"Nothing, dear," she said. "You two run upstairs now and let me talk to your mother."

In my room, I said told Patrick to keep it down.

"Ssshhh!" I whispered.

"Why?" Patrick asked. I crossed my room on tiptoes, Patrick following, also on tiptoes, and I opened the latch to my bedroom window. My mother's flower garden was directly beneath the window, and I leaned out to hear what Aunt Etna was saying.

"...right outside of Ledwith's," Aunt Etna gasped. "I was just standing there with the groceries, and she walks right toward me!"

"Etna!" Mother said in a shocked voice.

"As God is my witness," said Aunt Etna, crossing her heart. "What could I do? I said hello! I *had* to. It was the only polite thing to do."

"What happened then?"

"She looks right at me," Aunt Etna went on.

"Mrs. *Winfield?*" My mother sounded like she didn't believe Aunt Etna.

"As surely as I see you standing there."

"Jesus Christ," said my mother, who never took the Saviour's name in her life.

"And for a minute there, everything got a little dark." Aunt Etna shivered, though the September light was still warm. "Her eyes," Aunt Etna marvelled. "She had the strangest eyes. For a minute there, I could have sworn they were yellow, then they were just green. But...different."

"What do you mean different?"

"Nothing a body could put a finger on," Aunt Etna said nervously, "but different. About as human as an animal's eyes."

They were silent for a moment, then I heard my mother's voice again.

"You tell Randy about this?" my mother said.

"No," Aunt Etna replied. "I sent him upstairs with Patrick."

"Don't say a word about this to him, Etna, I swear. I don't want him going near that old woman, and you know how he gets with his questions."

"I won't," Aunt Etna said. She and my mother embraced, and held each other for a long time.   When they drew apart, I heard my mother say, "God, I wish Phil were still alive." She rarely spoke of my father, and something in her voice made me feel as though I were intruding on some grief that I wasn't a part of. I drew away from the window.

"That was *so* weird," Patrick said.

"It sure was," I agreed. I went over and turned my record player on. I put a Rolling Stones 45 on the turntable and cranked the volume until my mother called up and told me to *turn that gosh darned racket down, Randy!* and we went down to dinner, pausing to wash our hands in the upstairs bathroom because we knew she'd ask, and my mother always seemed to know when we hadn't.

As I drifted off to sleep that night, I heard my mother and Aunt Etna sitting in front of the fireplace, talking in hushed whispers about what Aunt Etna had seen outside of Ledwith's grocery store that afternoon.

The following Friday, quite by accident, I met Mrs. Winfield myself. I passed her on my bicycle as she shuffled down Martin Street, moving in that sludgy way that old people have, as though they had forgotten how to move. A twig caught in my spoke, and I nearly lost control of my bike. When I brought it to a wobbling halt, I almost fell on the sidewalk in front of her. She was looking down, so I didn't see her face.

"Good afternoon ma'am," I said, doing a fair imitation of Patrick's brilliant politeness. I still couldn't see her face, and I was curious too. I wanted to see if what Aunt Etna had said about her eyes was true or not.

She stopped then, and slowly raised her head to look at me. Her eyes were milky green, caught in a web of wrinkles around heavily hooded lids. She looked about a hundred years old. Her eyes widened slightly, and for a moment I thought I felt the air about me chill. Mrs. Winfield smiled, but somehow it wasn't the happy, senile smile of an old woman. Her teeth were yellow and twisted, and they seemed sharp, crueller somehow than the teeth of an old woman ought to be.

"Hello, Randy Murphy," she said, her voice like dry sand at noon. "You certainly are growing up to be a big boy." She said it in the same way that she might discuss a cut of lamb at a butcher's shop, and I again felt the cold and darkness that Aunt Etna had mentioned that night in the garden.

"How do you know my name?" I whispered. "I've never met you before."

"I know all the children's names," Mrs. Winfield said. "I've watched you all grow up, you know. I take an interest."

She smiled again, as though we both knew that there was a double meaning behind the perfectly innocuous old-lady words she'd selected. I mumbled something about having to get home for dinner, and took off on my bike as though wolves were snapping at my pedals. I rode away in the opposite direction from Auburn, because I remember thinking that she might follow me, I didn't want her to know where I lived.

That night, I dreamed I was walking through Mrs. Winfield's yard, with the full moon floating above me like the angry yellow eye of God. I dreamed that it was following me as I moved. I dreamed that I looked up at one of the windows and saw things slithering in the shadows behind filthy glass. I heard sighs and soft giggling, but it didn't sound happy or good in the dream, just cruel and unspeakably malevolent. When I tried to move away from the glass, I couldn't. You know how dreams are.

Then I saw Mrs. Winfield's face at the window. She glared at me with her red eyes and her mouth full of ripping teeth, her face covered with bristling brown hair, and she said, "Welcome, Randy Murphy. You're a *big* boy now, aren't you? Come inside."

When she reached up with her yellow-clawed hand and scratched on the glass, I woke up screaming. Yes—Christ, peal after peal until my mother came running in and grabbed me. She shook me and shouted at me to wake up. *Etna, he's hysterical!* she shouted at my aunt, not because she was angry but because I was screaming to wake the dead.

I slept in my mother's bed that night, but I stayed awake for hours afterwards, watching the door. I knew, deep inside, that the thing in the window of Mrs. Winfield's house on Martin Street wouldn't be bothered by my mother one bit.

That fall, we had a scare in Auburn. A little red-haired girl named Audrey Greystone was found about three miles out of town. She'd been murdered and...played with.

Aunt Etna said it was a pervert, probably from Toronto. A week later, they caught some tramp in Warner's field whacking off in broad daylight, and you can bet your ass they slapped that one in handcuffs and hauled him off for safe-keeping. We had our transients in Auburn and Milton, and our town drunks, but this one was a stranger and the only thing worse than a stranger in a small town is an old stranger amusing himself in public a week after a child-murder. There was no comfort for the Greystone family, but the town wanted to believe that the monster from the world outside Milton who had invaded their lives was locked up and awaiting justice. There was talk of lynching, talk of cutting off the old party's hands, and his thing, too. So the town constable did right by taking him away. But mostly, there was relief that the killer had been caught, and the kids could have a safe Halloween after all.

Patrick and I were a little old for Halloween, but it was my favorite time of year, Patrick's too. I loved the spicy air, the smell of leaves dying, apples and woodsmoke. In those days, you were still allowed to burn your leaves, and that smell was my favorite of all. I loved the way pumpkins looked in the windows, winking fire through their slashed eyes.

I was a pirate, and Patrick was a white rabbit. My mother made my costume out of a pair of old red bloomers and an old dinner jacket of my Dad's. She had to convince me that it was O.K. to wear her earrings. I'd seen pictures of pirates with earrings, but it still felt weird.

After we'd done our trick-or-treating, we hiked across the fields that separated Auburn and Milton. We'd taken in quite a haul, and we couldn't resist dipping into our stash on the way home, even though Mum would've taken a strip off us if she'd known we were eating our stuff before she checked it. She always worried about razor blades in apples.

There were scrubs of trees here and there at the foot of the escarpment, and small hills and caves. We called them Indian caves. Patrick and I had built tree forts there every summer since we'd been old enough to lift a hammer. The moon was brilliant that night, like a fire in the sky. The stars sparkled like diamonds against black velvet. It wasn't as if we couldn't see, because we saw *everything*.

We ran across the fields, laughing and talking about nothing at all, the way best friends do. Patrick jumped up and down like a rabbit, which made his white satin ears flop, and we both laughed harder.

People asked me afterwards why I didn't hear the man behind us, but I don't think he wanted us to hear him. And I think he knew how to keep that from happening. I remember I was looking over Patrick's shoulder when I saw something like a hulking black shadow separate itself from the copse of trees behind us. It grabbed Patrick and pulled him backwards into the trees. I might have run at this point, but when I heard Patrick screaming, all I could think about was how everyone picked on him at school for being slow. For some crazy reason I had this idea that it was Billy Macadoo or Dave Carruthers waiting for the perfect chance to beat holy hell out of Patrick. I was a big kid at eleven, and I always stuck up for him.

So I charged into the trees, fists swinging, ready to settle this bullying shit for all time. Patrick was struggling and screaming. By the time it registered that whatever had Patrick was taller than either Butch or Billy, I was deep into the darkness of the trees. I caught a powerful whiff of sweat and stale body waste. Something reached out a hand and smashed me hard across the head. I saw a shower of stars explode in front of my eyes, and I was falling, falling, with no ground beneath my feet.

I woke in pain. I could barely open my eyes, but I realized that I was naked, and my wrists and ankles were tied. The ropes cut into my flesh. Patrick was lying a few feet away, also naked and tied. He was unconscious.

"This is where I come to play," said a harsh voice to my left. I tried to turn, but the blinding pain in my head which surged forward with the effort made the bile rise in my throat. The man came around and stood in front of me. He was compact and well-muscled, and covered with tattoos. His hair was close-cropped, like they do it in a prison or an asylum. He was rubbing the front of his trousers.

I looked up at his face. He had cold little eyes and dark eyebrows. He grinned at me, and a long stream of drool hung from his bottom lip like a silver web. I felt my bowels empty themselves under me, and the stink of it drifted up to me. I gagged. I think that's when my last shred of hope that this was a dream disappeared. He reached down and flicked my nipple with his fingernail.

"*Bad* boy!" he hissed. "*Baaaad* boy made a mess!" He grinned even wider as he said it, showing a mouthful of decayed teeth, and I knew I was going to die.

"Please don't hurt me," I whispered. Patrick wasn't moving.

"I'm going to play with you, not hurt you," he giggled. "I like you very, very much!" He squealed with laughter.

As the pain in my head subsided to a rhythmic throbbing, I became aware of the subterranean coldness of the room. I saw that the light came from torches on the wall, and that the ceilings were oddly high, and vaulted. I saw a stone staircase winding upwards and disappearing into the gloom. I had seen cellars before, but never one like this.

"Is this a church?" I whispered, as much to myself as to the madman looming in front of me. "Where are we?"

"I come here," he sing-songed. "Through the hole in the hill nobody ever sees. Through the tunnel I found in the caves. Sometimes I bring friends to play with." He giggled again, and covered his mouth with his filthy fingers, like a sour child eager to tattle. "Friends like the little girl with the pretty carrot hair. Friends like you."

He fumbled in the dirty grey canvas rucksack at his feet. I hear the sound of metal scraping on stone. He turned slowly, and I saw that he held a carving knife. The blade was clotted with gore, and what looked like matted red hair.

"I like to cut," he whispered. "I cut, and cut, and cut. But first I like to play and have fun. Watch."

He stuck out his tongue, and ran the blade across it's tip. Blood spurted from the wound, and he rolled his eyes in ecstasy. He was smiling. I screamed, then, pain be damned. I shrieked and shrieked, and he shrieked right along with me, except his shrieks were interrupted by wild fits of giggling. He did a little dance, slapping his knees.

Then suddenly, he stopped. He cocked his head to the side, towards the stairs.

"Shut up," he whispered fiercely, but I was long past being able to shut up. He turned towards me and swung his fist in my face. "Shut the fuck *up!*"

The shock of the blow made me stop screaming, and I tasted copper in my mouth. He dropped the knife beside me and scuttled off towards the stairway. "Who's there?" he screamed. "Who's that?"

And then I heard it too. Slow, measured footsteps coming down the staircase towards us. The click of shoes on worn stone.

The man backed up with a look of stupid surprise on his coarse features. He fumbled for the knife on the floor beside me. He found it, and grasped it's handle, holding it out in front of him as though it were a sword. He was blocking my view of the staircase, but I heard the footsteps stop. The torches flared.

I heard the man babble something, but I couldn't make it out. Then he began to levitate. That's what I saw. His feet just left the floor, and he drifted up towards the vaulted ceiling. I heard him squeal again, and this time he sounded terrified. I blinked, and I knew that I was seeing something that couldn't be happening. People didn't float in the air, even mad giants with knives, who held the power of life and death over small children.

I heard another voice then, old and dry, and cold as ice. *Corrupt* is a word I'd use today, but at eleven I just remember thinking that I'd rather take my chances with the man hanging suspended in front of me. At least he was human. Whatever owned that voice was not.

"Callers," chortled the voice appreciatively. "Surprise visitors. How very nice."

The heels of the man's boots still obscured most of my vision, but I could see the hem of a black skirt, and black stockinged legs in black shoes walking towards me. I heard that slow, measured click, and saw sparks fly where the heels of the shoes struck the stone floor.

"Somebody found my trap door," scolded the ancient voice. "Nobody's ever found that trap door. Not for, oh, hundreds and hundreds of years." And then, a ghastly underground laugh that made me think of creatures squatting by open graves, devouring corpses. The man above me began to spin lazily in circles, and his knife arm hung limply at his side. He began to scream.

"I like to cut sometimes too," said the voice, addressing the whirling madman in the air above me. "Show me how *you* do it."

And then I saw the man's knife hand jerk upwards, as though it were attached to a string. He plunged the knife into his belly. The shrieks that came from him as the knife reared and plunged into him, and cut upwards, will be with me to my dying day.

The thing screamed with laughter, rocking back and forth. The man spun madly in the air and his blood sprayed across the walls like a geyser. Then, suddenly, the spinning stopped and the man crumpled to the floor. The knife clattered against the flagstones. What was left of him lay on the ground, quivered once, then stopped.

I looked up then, and what I saw was a hundred million times worse than anything I'd seen.

"Hello, little Randy Murphy," said Mrs. Winfield. Her face was streaked with the dead man's blood. As I watched, she licked some of it off her lips. She brought her face close to mine, and I smelled sulphur on her breath. Her eyes weren't milky green anymore. They were incandescent yellow. Her glance flickered across Patrick, unconscious beside me. She licked her lips again, smearing the blood.

"Rude to invite yourselves," she scolded. "Rude to come to an old lady's house at night and scare her half to death."

And then she began to change.

She...shrivelled. That's the only way I can describe it. I saw a snake shed its skin once by rubbing against a rock. Mrs. Winfield's skin just...fell off. Her face turned brown, and the wrinkles deepened until they looked like craters in her face. She opened her mouth, and as I watched, her teeth grew long and sharp. She licked them with a tongue that was now easily a foot long, and purple. She shrugged out of her black dress, and stepped out of her shoes.

She stared at me with her blazing yellow eyes. Her hideous breasts sagged to her belly, and her misshapen arms, roped with sinew, ended in long-fingered claws. Her mouth stretched into a nightmare rictus, and I realized she was smiling.

"I usually have to go out to eat," she said. She shambled over to Patrick, and traced a razor-sharp nail down his naked back. At that moment, I prayed to God that Patrick was dead, and wouldn't wake up to see this nightmare thing standing over him. Blood spurted from the cut on his back. The creature smiled. And to my horror, I saw Patrick stir, and heard him moan.

"I like the animals better alive," it croaked. And then it began to eat.

Patrick's screams of pain and terror blended into one scarlet blood-drenched sheet of sound. That's what I hear in my nightmares. Patrick screaming, and the awful wet ripping sounds of that...thing...killing him, bite by bite.

I think I was screaming then, too, but I don't think I was terrified anymore. I don't think I felt anything except the pressure of my sanity straining to break. The world turned red, then black. Then I felt nothing, saw nothing.

I woke up in Milton District Hospital, a white world inhabited by angels dressed in white robes, holding silver instruments and whispering sweet words to me about shock, and trauma, and sleep. My mother was there, and Aunt Etna, and I knew that Mrs. Winfield had killed and eaten me, and that I was in heaven.

I felt a cold sting in my upper arm, then I slept again, deeply and without any dreams.

I was in the hospital for six weeks. I missed a lot of school, and a psychiatrist from Hamilton worked with me every day so that I could understand what had happened.

The town constable explained to me that Mrs. Winfield had called him in hysterics. Apparently, she had gone downstairs to her basement to look for her kitty-cat, and discovered three bodies. She was quite upset. No one expects to make a discovery like that on Halloween night after coming home from a walk.

The constable explained to me that Mrs. Winfield's storm-cellar door had been forced open. Apparently, he said, the R.C.M.P. had spent two months hunting the killer. He had escaped from an institution for the criminally insane in Alberta, cutting a murderous swath eastward, killing five children between Edmonton and Toronto. What drew him to Milton on Halloween night was anybody's guess.

"Milton," the constable said, shaking his head. "Who would have ever expected? I always knew it couldn't have been a local man." He asked me to brace myself, then told me that Patrick was dead. The madman had mutilated Patrick's body almost beyond recognition before he turned his knife on himself. Aunt Etna told me that she'd read in the papers that pieces of Patrick were missing. Apparently he'd had two final child murders on his mind before he committed suicide. And what a suicide. He cut himself to ribbons.

The constable said that the man's body had been covered with dirt, so he must have been hiding over in the meadow up by the caves. It was only through God's good graces that he hadn't done to me the things he'd done to poor Patrick. They released the old man they'd caught in Warner's field, clearly a nutcase, but the wrong man. The other one was obviously the murderer of Audrey Greystone. They'd found bits of her scalp and hair in his rucksack.

Mrs. Winfield had been very upset, but she was away visiting a cousin right now, before she returned home to her own house on Martin Street. She was all right, though.

A few days after I had been found, my mother and Aunt Etna went to visit Mrs. Winfield, to offer her some comfort, poor thing. My mother said that Aunt Etna regretted all the awful things she'd said, and it was only because poor Mrs. Winfield found me in time that I was even alive. Mrs. Winfield had served them tea, and delicate meat pies, in her lovely sitting room. The pies were delicious. Mrs. Winfield must have special spices. Imagine cooking like that at her age? The sitting room was a little dusty, said Aunt Etna, but quite normal for an old lady.

No, the constable explained again, patiently, the basement was an ordinary one, nothing like the one I described in my delirium, No torches, no vaulted ceilings. Nothing like that, just dusty cans of old peaches and preserves. An old lady's basement: lawn furniture, old Mr. Winfield's tools, and a filthy old icebox, stained and covered with cobwebs.

On the night before I was to be discharged, my favorite nurse, Tasia, poked her head through the doorway.

"You have a visitor Randy," Tasia beamed. "A surprise. An old friend of yours." She wagged her finger at me and smiled. "I've told her you can't stay up too late. You're going home tomorrow." I remember smiling as I heard Tasia pad off down the corridor.

And then I heard the click of old-lady lace-up shoes on hospital tile. The darkness swam toward me, and I felt my throat constrict. I couldn't reach for the call button to tell Tasia that if she didn't come back to room 7008 right away, I would never leave the hospital alive.

The footsteps paused outside my door. It swung slowly inward, as I had known it would. Mrs. Winfield walked in slowly, dressed from head to toe in black, her face wreathed in the hungry shadows of my hospital room.

"I'm so glad you're better, little Randy Murphy," she growled, and I saw a flicker of yellow fire in her milky green eyes. "The doctors tell me that in time you'll forget about the awful things that happened in my cellar." She chuckled mirthlessly.

I couldn't speak. Couldn't say a word. Couldn't move at all. Whatever was going to happen would happen.

Mrs. Winfield opened her jaws then, very wide.

Her sharp teeth were dripping with saliva, and she licked them. I wet the bed in a warm gush, part of my mind feeling guilty about the piss, the other part knowing that I was going to die, and she would make it seem like an accident. The fire in her eyes blazed so brightly that I could see the bed's shadow reflected on the wall.

Then, suddenly, she closed her mouth and her eyes. She shivered. When she opened her eyes to smile coldly at me, she was just an old lady again. No one would ever believe me. I knew it, and so did she.

"I'm going away for a little while, Randy," she whispered in a voice like darkest winter. "You and your friends have made it a little crowded for me here." I heard the thwarted fury in her voice, and I was afraid. "I've sealed the tunnel between the hills and my house on Martin Street. No one will ever find it, so never mind your stories.

"I've lived here for a long time," she said, adjusting the flesh of her index finger as though it were a glove. "In one form or another. Longer than you can imagine. I was already old when the English and the French came across the ocean with their religions, and tried to claim this country as their own." She narrowed her eyes. "We've *always* been here. We are *everywhere*. Wherever there are rocks, or caves, we make our homes."

She patted my leg on the bed, and I felt the ice of her fingers through the wool blankets.

"You just get better. Get over your...trauma." Here she gave another clotted laugh. "Don't tell any silly stories," she whispered, "or I'll have to visit you some night and talk some sense into you." She gathered up her black purse and shuffled to the door. She looked fragile, like somebody ought to get the door for her or something.

"Stay away from the caves, boy," she growled. "It's dangerous. Wild things live there." And she hobbled off without turning back. Click. Click. Click.

I stood in front of the window of our apartment for an hour, until the moon went down and the sky began to lighten in the east. Claudia breathed softly. No nightmares for her, just healing sleep. The fog drifting in from English Bay would run down into the smudges at the base of the glass, and in the morning light, they wouldn't look anything like fingerprints. I wrestle with my memories by myself, in my nightmares. I've never told anyone about Mrs. Winfield, not ever.

She'd find out somehow. I've always known that she would.

When the psychiatrists told me that I had suffered a concussion and imagined everything, I told them I believed them. I mourned Patrick's death in a way that I'd never been able to mourn my father's, and I grew closer to my mother because of the shared experience of grief and loss. When I graduated from Milton District Highschool, I moved across the country, and I've never been back to Auburn. I won't go back. I won't. There are more than memories waiting for me there.

And yet, I can't stop thinking about things. Last week, the daughter of a friend found the mutilated body of a racoon in Stanley Park.

"It was awful," she said. "It was all mangled. Other animals must have gotten to it. It's awful what they do to their own kind."

I think about dead squirrels and cats that seem to line the paths of the park more often than they used to. I think about the missing children whose innocent, trusting faces adorn the *Have You Seen This Child?* posters which have lately blossomed along the streets that line the West End. I think about the snowy nights at our cabin in Whistler, when the crack of a frozen branch can be heard for miles, when the winter cold is so cutting that wild things come down from the mountains to feed. I think about tracks in the snow in the mornings, tracks that we can't identify and which Claudia always jokes are made by trolls.

We've always been here, she'd said. *We are everywhere. Wherever there are rocks or caves, we make our homes.*

I think about the old couple beside the seawall yesterday evening, who looked at Claudia and I with their milky blue eyes, and smiled approvingly at our ten-year romance as we strolled past. I looked back and smiled at them. For a minute, the dying sunlight glanced off the old man's glasses and reflected a glitter of yellow fire. Then he turned his head and looked at the ground before shuffling off towards the Sylvia Hotel with his wife. I shivered.

Wild things, I thought as the sun sank behind the mountains, and I hurried home with Claudia through the chilled blue dusk towards Pendrell Street. Wild things live here, too.

The Pines

by Tia V. Travis

Tia V. Travis was born in a farming community in southern Manitoba and spent much of her childhood on farms and in small towns, both in Manitoba and Alberta. These early memories of small town and rural life–particularly of the harsh winters–inspired the setting for this powerful, evocative story.

Recent stories by Tia have been reprinted in the thirteenth and fourteenth annual The Year's Best Fantasy and Horror. *Her first collection,* Down Here in the Garden, *will be published by Subterranean Press in 2002; the title story is a finalist for The International Horror Guild Award as well as The World Fantasy Award. She currently lives in the United States with her husband, writer Norman Partridge, a native Californian who has never experienced the thrill of holding a snow shovel in his hands.*

Hear the wind blow, love, hear the wind blow
Hang your head over, hear the wind blow
Know I love you, dear, know I love you
Angels in heaven know I love you

-Down in the Valley, Old Folk Song

She takes the 2 north from Calgary, driving her brother's '81 Ford with the broken heater and the staticky radio and the permanently frozen windshield wipers. A two-year old husky sleeps on the seat beside her in an old wool blanket. It is twenty-five below zero in the truck. Colder still in the back, but she doesn't like to think about that. Doesn't like to think at all, because thinking doesn't help a damn bit.

On the floor of the truck sits a half-empty thermos of black coffee, two unopened six-packs of beer, and a battered steel pipe.

The pipe has brain matter on it.

Past Red Deer and Lacombe and Bear Hills Lake and all the small towns between, field after field is covered in a thick counterpane of January snow. The snow is topped with a crust of ice so cold it burns, the kind of ice you see only on the prairies in winter under the blue-white shadow of a Canadian moon.

She has tried to keep them warm, Michele and the husky. But it is cold in the front of the truck, cold in the back. Too cold. Her hands are numb and mechanical in their thin mittens, and the condensation of her breath in the sub-zero temperature has frozen the metal of her parka zipper.

In Edmonton she turns off onto the 32. One hundred miles of cold hard earth. Sakwatamau River with stubble frozen banks. Buckbrush and bristle black current capped with an undisturbed blanket of blue-white snow. After that it is the Northern Woods and Water Route that leads to The Land's End, some call it, a place were there are no towns and no people and the pines stand silently close on the hills. The pines....

She closes her eyes a moment and breathes in deep, and she can almost smell cold hard needles and perfume sap in the arctic air.

"We're almost there, Michele," she says out loud. "Almost there." Her teeth chatter.

By ten o'clock the truck makes it into Peace River Country. She and the husky stay the night in a motel outside Chinook Valley. She almost doesn't stop at this town, but after four hundred and fifty miles on the highway no amount of cold thermos coffee can keep her eyes open. She and the husky are huddled in a ball on the bed. The girl's knees are pulled up to her chest. She has not changed her blood-stained clothes. She has not washed her face or combed her hair, and the blood has dried in it like shiny-stiff paint.

Michele lies on the truckbed under a piece of canvas. Snowflakes have settled on the dark fringe of her lashes. Her eyes are open but they do not see.

The girl has read that when a person dies, the eyes turn green. But Michele's eyes have always been green. So have her own.

She thinks about the pipe on the floor of the truck, and as she thinks her mind travels down the pipe's long, cool lines. She thinks about another line, a railroad line. She thinks about the man she has killed and why she has killed him. She thinks about a girl who wanted to kill, but didn't. And it all adds up in the end.

Outside the little room the snow slopes across the fields in hard-packed drifts. Snow is cut away from them by a bitter-cold wind. The wind takes the snow to The Land's End, some call it, where the sky is black and the earth is white and the moon shines cold and empty on open eyes, and the girl in the room with the two-year old husky has never been more alone.

She is laid out flat on a truckbed.

She does not think.

She does not breathe.

She does not move.

But her eyes are as open as the stars.

She had been told to call him "stepfather", but he hadn't been a stepfather at all. He was just some man her mom had been dumb enough to take up with because they had no money and no place to go. But the girl didn't like to think of her mom as dumb. Maybe her mom was just afraid. Afraid like Michele had been, afraid like the girl herself had been. Finally she'd tired of it all. And when she heard what the other man had done to Michele, she had picked up a steel pipe for the first time in fifteen years.

She could see her stepfather's face clear in her mind, even though she had been ten years old when it happened. She could see him in the cotton workshirts he used to wear. She could see how he sweated in those shirts, could see how the sweat made damp circles under his arms. He was home from work in the middle of the day because he did split-shifts at the gas plant. He had one of his headaches again, and she would have to go into the darkened bedroom and rub his forehead for him. Rub the bridge of his nose where his glasses made dark red indentations. And then when she had dutifully rubbed his head he would take her hand and make her rub another place down lower. She didn't know *why* if his head hurt *why* she had to rub *there*, she didn't know, she really didn't know, but his hand was moving her small one faster and faster, and he wouldn't let her go. She tried to pull away from him but he held her there, and that was how it had started. That was how it started a million times.

Late at night he stood in the hall by her bedroom, a still shadow with eyes that were on her always, always.

But now she had a piece of pipe she had picked up in an empty lot. She laid the pipe under her bed and waited for his shadow to come to her. Then when it came, and it always came, she would bite her lip and think about the pipe, think about it and think about it, and she could not breathe for thinking about it, and she could not move for thinking about it, but she could not pick it up, she did not know *why* but she could not pick it up, and then a heavy hand would cover her mouth, and the shadow would tell her *I'll kill you, I'll kill you if you tell*, and then all that remained of her face were her eyes, her round wide eyes that shone white in the moonlight.

And still she would think about the pipe.

Think about what it would be like to pick it up in her hands. Think, as a ten year old thinks, about what it would would be like to kill.

When she called Michele fifteen years later and Michele had picked up the phone in tears, and she'd heard Michele's boyfriend yelling in the background YOU STUPID PIECE OF SHIT, YOU STUPID PIECE OF SHIT, and the phone had dropped on the floor and Michele had let out a half-scream of terror —

When she heard that, she had come to Michele's welfare-rented townhouse with a pipe.

A different pipe, but a pipe all the same.

The door was unlocked. The air was heavy and still. It smelled like dirty clothes and dirty dishes, like dirty thoughts and dirty lives. Michele's boyfriend stood at the door to the basement, hands at his sides. He was breathing hard, and he was sweaty. A slick sheet of it covered his entire body. It made damp circles under his arms.

He looked at the girl in the doorway, surprised to see her.

"Where is she?" was all she said.

But he didn't have to tell her. She had detected the tiniest, involuntary, sideways movement in his eyes.

"Stand back," she said. "Back there where I can see you."

"I didn't touch her," he said.

"I told you to stand back, Russell." The pitch of her voice had escalated but the pipe was dead level and solid in her hands.

He stood back.

She walked over to the basement door and prodded it open with the toe of her running shoe. She looked down. Michele lay at the bottom of the stairs. One arm was snapped back behind her head like a chicken bone. She wasn't breathing. She would never breathe again.

The girl blinked slowly, and in that blink, that half-second of black and white (black like the sky and white like the snow-blanketed earth), she made up her mind.

She removed her eyes from Michele's red-smeared head on the cement floor, removed them from the long straight strands of Michele's blood-soaked hair, removed them from the pool on the floor that was shiny with the reflection from the basement bulb.

Russell stared at her.

She stared back.

In a room down the hall, she heard the prerecorded voice of a telephone operator. It came from the receiver that lay, where it had fallen, face-up on the floor: *The number you have dialled has been disconnected the number you have dialled has been disconnected the number you have dialled has been disconnected...*

It was like something from a bad made-for-TV movie.

The girl held the pipe in both shaking hands and she did not stop herself, did not *think* of stopping herself, because this time it was Michele's life. Michele's life and Michele's dreams seeping out on that bare cement in a deep maroon pool. And this time, *this time*, she would do something about it.

She held the pipe over her head. Then she hammered it down. Hammered it down on his stupid thick skull with all that she had in her, hammered it down and hammered it down and hammered it down until her hands and her face and her wide staring eyes were slippery red, and the blood splashed from the ends of her shaking white fingers.

After it was done she stepped over his body on the kitchen floor as if it were decomposing meat. In the bedroom she put the receiver back on the phone, and pulled a couple of threadbare sheets from the unmade bed. She stood at the basement door a moment, hands on either side of the frame. Then she walked slowly down the basement stairs and carefully, oh so carefully, she straightened Michele's arms and laid them at her sides. The arms were covered in bruises — blue-black and yellow-green and a tan color that was so faint she could hardly see it at all on Michele's pale skin. Marks of ownership.

But she wouldn't think about that. Wouldn't think at all, because thinking didn't help a damn bit.

Instead she parceled Michele up in the sheets, not caring that her thumbs made dark red prints on the white cotton. She did not look at Michele's face. As long as she didn't look at her face she could do what she had to do. It was five o'clock and already pitch black out. She moved Michele's body into the back of her brother's truck. It was hard work, but it had to be done. There was no one who could help her.

She dumped the pipe on the floor of the truck. It landed with a dull thud. Then she whistled for Michele's husky who had taken refuge in the bedroom, and he jumped up beside her on the seat of her brother's truck.

She left the door to the house wide open.

At home she stopped to pick up some blankets, her parka, and her brother's worn-out hiking boots. Then she drove. Drove to the only place she knew Michele had ever wanted to be.

Drove to The Pines.

At six a.m. the next day the girl fills her gas tank and hits the road, eating stale sandwiches from a truckstop on the 32. In the dark she had not been able to see the landscape transform itself but it had. Before it had been aspen parkland and rolling blue foothills to the west; prairies and open spaces to the east. Empty as far as the eye could see, frozen fields and broken barbed wire fences that had stood for decades and would stand for decades more. Lonely stands of dark fir windbreakers that bent like broken old men in the icy wind.

But now it is trees.

Trees like stripped toothpicks, so close to her, so close, and the northern sun slants through them in pale yellow shafts.

Her breath is a cold white cloud in the unheated truck. But she does not stop driving. It is not because she is transporting a dead body in the back of her truck. It is because she is determined to find the place where the pines are cold and dark and let in no light; the place in the song, that cold dark song that is the song of her soul.

In the pines, in the pines
Where the sun never shines
And I shiver when the cold wind blows.

"Almost there, Michele," she says again, and the husky lifts his head and looks at her with imploring brown eyes. She puts her hand under his chin and feels his warm wet breath on her skin. "Almost there..."

She drives on past Mile Zero of the MacKenzie Highway and takes an unpaved road that stretches 626 miles north to Great Slave Lake in the Northwest Territories. Out here it is all sawmills and bulldozed brush, husky lynx and shaggy wolverines, boreal chickadees and northern hawk owls. The trees by the side of the road have been rubbed smooth of bark by bucks trying to scrape the velvet off their antlers.

By nightfall she makes it to High Level, eighty-five miles short of the Alberta/N.W.T. border. She can hear the plaintive yaps of a pack of coyotes, running and running across the frost-stubbled fields with their bushy black-tipped tails between their legs, running and running but never finding anything because there is nothing to find on that frozen earth that is straight and hard and goes on forever.

She hears a train, far off in the distance, its powerful white light illuminating the black pines that close in on both sides of the track. She sees herself and Michele, ten years old, children of summer, racing past the pale yellow wheat fields beside the train tracks, racing past the Indian Red grain elevators, racing and racing like untamed colts. Their hearts pound with excitement as they barrel through the waist-high fields of shimmering, swaying wheat. Steam billows from their quivering nostrils as they take in the hot prairie air.

Take us with you, take us with you...

But the train never stops in their town. It never stops at all. And because the train is made of iron and steel and ten year old girls are made of t-shirts and dreams, they have to stop. Panting, shoulders shaking, heads dropped down to their knees. Thatches of sun-whitened hair falling in their sweaty faces like manes. And the train goes on and on down the line, the puffs of white engine smoke making exclamation marks in the still expanse of the blue sky.

And they watch, she and Michele. Watch as the engineers wave to them and blow the steam whistle. The cars are loaded with fragrant pines. They smell the sap, pungent, heady and sweet. They stand there by the shining tracks and breathe it all in, breathe it all in with their eyes closed but their hearts open.

Take us with you!

The sound of their voices in that empty land makes them terribly lonely, but they don't know why.

Take us with you! Take us with you! But the engineers can't hear them over the whistle.

The girl turns to Michele, who stands beside her on the empty track. She takes Michele's hand in her own, and Michele smiles, a little sad half-smile.

"One day," Michele says, her dark green eyes still intent on the red-painted caboose. "One day we'll catch one."

"How can we do that, Michele?"

Michele shakes her head. She doesn't know. The train disappears into the distance like a dream, and the whistle echoes back on the wind like something you can touch, almost, almost... And then the afternoon sky darkens to deep violet blue and the first glimmer of stars appears high up in the sky.

"One of these days. One of these days it'll stop."

But the train doesn't stop.

It never stops.

And now here they are, fifteen years later, driving north to the place where the train-pulled pines had come. Fifteen years later. Fifteen years too late.

She parks the truck outside a diner in High Level. The temperature has dropped to -40 and the north wind is up. The wind does not lift the snow from the sculpted banks but sends it scudding down the ice-dusted highway. The cold takes her breath away but she breathes in deeply, because she knows that the cold is not so cold if you are not afraid of it.

She walks slowly and stiffly in her brother's hiking boots. Her head is bowed down low, and her hair lashes at her face like a whip. The husky stays close behind her. The diner is a shapeless shadow in the white wind. When she opens the door everyone turns to look at her. There are four people: two Metis men in fur-trimmed, army green parkas who sit at the counter, a blond woman in a thick wool ski sweater, and a sullen, heavy-set man who sits to the right of the two natives. The girl stands in the door for a moment and stares at them, breathless, as beside her the husky's paws make little clicks on the scuffed white floor.

For the first time in hours she thinks about how she looks. Her eyes are red and her nose has started to run and her hair is frozen stiff with ice. She knows they can't see the dried brown stains on her jeans and her shirt, or the dark red rinds under her broken fingernails. But she does not know why they are looking at her like that, looking and looking but not saying anything. She shakes the snow self-consciously from her boots and sits down at the counter.

"Could I have some coffee, please?" she asks. The blond woman in the ski sweater is the waitress. She has blue eyes and a kind smile.

"Comin' up," she says, reaching for the fresh pot. "Sit down there, now, and warm up a little." Then she tells the girl not to take her parka off because it is cold in here, damn gas lines are frozen, and the girl notices two red-hot space heaters behind the counter. The waitress sets a thick white mug of steaming coffee between the girl's mittened hands. She sips the dark brown liquid and listens to the men talk about work and the cold and the pipelines and the cold, and the waitress fills her cup one more time. "Is there a phone I can use?" she asks.

"Pay phone's over there on the wall, hon," the woman says. "Last we heard the lines were still up, but that was an hour ago and anything could have happened since then."

The girl thanks the woman, puts a dollar in quarters in the phone and makes the long distance call. The phone rings four times before the answering machine picks up. The connection is staticky. *You've reached 337-3462. Russell and I can't come to the phone right now, but leave your name and number and we'll call you back.*

There is a long beep.

She holds the cold receiver close to her mouth, takes a short breath. "Hi," she says. "It's me..." She stops. She does not blink because then the tears will spill down her cheeks like little beads of ice. "I just wanted to tell you..."

Tell her what?

She doesn't know. She hangs up the phone and stands there a minute. Then puts another four quarters into the slot.

You've reached 337-3462. Russell and I can't come to the phone right now, but leave your name and number and we'll call you back.

"Michele?" Her voice is a barely a whisper. "If you're listening, pick up...." She waits. There is silence on the other end. Then: "Call me back," she says.

She goes back to her stool and sits down. She stares at herself in the mirror behind the counter.

"You all right, honey?" the blond woman asks.

But the girl does not hear her. She is staring at her face, at the tired eyes and the tired lines etched below them. She is twenty-six but looks like an old woman.

"Honey—you all right?"

The girl meets the waitress's eyes. She smiles a little. "Do you have anything I can feed my dog? A couple of hamburgers or something?"

"I'll put them on now," the waitress says. "You want anything to eat?"

"No. Thank you," she adds.

"Where you headed?" It is one of the parka men.

"North."

"*North?*"

"That's right."

"There's nothin' up there," the other one objects. She says nothing, but they are waiting for her to reply, so she tells them she is on her way to Indian Cabins at the Alberta/Northwest Territories border.

"Indian *Cabins?*" one of them says, dumbfounded.

"You won't make it." It is the sullen, heavy-set man. "Road's closed up past Steen River," he says. "You'll be lucky to get that far."

"I'll take those to go," she says, as the blond woman starts to set a plate of meat patties on the floor in front of Michele's dog.

"Didn't you hear me, little girl?" the sullen man says. "I said the *road* is *closed.*"

"I heard you," the girl says, staring straight at him. Something in her eyes makes him close his mouth. The girl pays her check and picks up the bag of hamburgers. The diner is silent. "Come on, boy," she says to the husky, and she starts for the door. The dog tags along behind her.

"Wait." It is the blond woman. "Here, you take this, it's Elton's old ski jacket. It's not much but he's not usin' it and you can put it around your knees while you drive, okay? It's cold out there."

The girl takes the faded purple jacket the woman holds out for her. There is something in the woman's tired blue eyes that she has seen before, something desperate and sad, something....

She looks past the woman at the dark and sullen man at the counter, at the still and heavy fists at his sides. "Thank you," she says.

"Lynne," the woman says softly. "My name is Lynne."

The girl smiles for the last time. "Thank you, Lynne. My name is Michele." And she turns and steps out into the swirling white.

It is forty-five below now. The snow has blown itself on to Land's End, and the moon is a pale white circle that shines over the dark outline of trees. The truck has stalled on her twice and will not make it more than a couple of miles. Finally she stops at the side of the highway. The pines are there, black shadows on all sides, black shadows on the blacker still backdrop of northern sky. They have always been there, waiting.

She steps out of the truck and breathes in the arctic air. It is so cold that the sides of her nostrils stick together with each breath.

"We're here," she says to the husky, and he looks at her from under Elton's ski jacket with warm brown eyes. "We're here," she says to Michele. She pops the top off a can of beer. It is a half-frozen slush but she drinks it anyhow. When she has finished it she drinks another, and another after that.

She thinks about what it is like to die from exposure. *It is like falling asleep*, she thinks. *It only hurts if you try to think.*

But it is better to die like this, better to die on a bitter night when the soul is solid ice and breaks off piece by piece, falling and falling down into a black river.

She crunches over the top of the packed snow to the back of the truck and sits down beside Michele. Every part of her is covered in canvas. Every part but her face, which shimmers white in the moonlight. There has been a meteor shower tonight, and the girl wanted them both to see it. She thinks about the silver afterglow trailing across Michele's open eyes like shining train tracks.

The husky jumps up into the back of the truck and comes to sit in her lap. He puts his head on her knee. She rubs her hand in his cold fur and stares out into the black. She can see The Pines, tall and dark, and she can smell The Pines, cold and perfumed, and she can hear The Pines, whisper and whisper:

In the pines, in the pines
Where the sun never shines
And I shiver when the cold wind blows

Far away in the dark she hears the train, and its whistle echoes back on the cold wind like something you can touch, almost, almost, and it is loaded with pines, and it is on its way north, always north.

"It almost stopped this time," she whispers. "It almost stopped...."

The Emperor's Old Bones

by Gemma Files

Toronto author Gemma Files' first fiction sale was to Northern Frights 2. *Since then she has sold numerous stories to both small press magazines and mainstream anthologies. In addition, a number of her tales have been adapted for television and produced for* The Hunger, *a half-hour anthology series under the aegis of well-known filmmakers Tony and Ridley Scott.*

In his review of Northern Frights 5, *critic Edward Bryant described "The Emperor's Old Bones" as a "superbly wrought fable of history, immortality, and bad behaviour set consciously against the landscape of J. G. Ballard's* Empire of the Sun." *Following its initial publication here, Gemma's story was reprinted in* The Year's Best Fantasy and Horror 13 *(St. Martin's Press, New York) and* The Mammoth Book of New Horror *(Robinson, London). It was recipient of the prestigious International Horror Guild Award for Best Short Fiction of 1999.*

Oh, buying and selling...you know...life.

— *Tom Stoppard, after J.G. Ballard.*

O ne day in 1941, not long after the fall of Shanghai, my amah (our live-in Chinese maid of all work, who often doubled as my nurse) left me sleeping alone in the abandoned hulk of what had once been my family's home, went out, and never came back...a turn of events which didn't actually surprise me all that much, since my parents had done something rather similar only a few brief weeks before. I woke up without light or food, surrounded by useless luxury — the discarded detritus of Empire and family alike. And fifteen more days of boredom and starvation were to pass before I saw another living soul.

I was ten years old.

After the war was over, I learned that my parents had managed to bribe their way as far as the harbor, where they became separated in the crush while trying to board a ship back "Home". My mother died of dysentery in a camp outside of Hangkow; the ship went down halfway to Hong Kong, taking my father with it. What happened to my amah, I honestly don't know — though I do feel it only fair to mention that I never really tried to find out, either.

The house and I, meanwhile, stayed right where we were — uncared for, unclaimed — until Ellis Iseland broke in, and took everything she could carry.

Including me.

"So what's your handle, *tai pan*?" She asked, back at the dockside garage she'd been squatting in, as she went through the pockets of my school uniform.

(It would be twenty more years before I realized that her own endlessly evocative name was just another bad joke — one some immigration official had played on her family, perhaps.)

"Timothy Darbersmere," I replied, weakly. Over her shoulder, I could see the frying pan still sitting on the table, steaming slightly, clogged with burnt rice. At that moment in time, I would have gladly drunk my own urine in order to be allowed to lick it out, no matter how badly I might hurt my tongue and fingers in doing so.

Her eyes followed mine — a calm flick of a glance, contemptuously knowing, arched eyebrows barely sketched in cinnamon.

"Not yet, kid," she said.

"I'm really very hungry, Ellis."

"I really believe you, Tim. But not yet." She took a pack of cigarettes from her sleeve, tapped one out, lit it. Sat back. Looked a me again, eyes narrowing contemplatively. The plume of smoke she blew was exactly the same non color as her slant, level, heavy-lidded gaze.

"Just to save time, by the way, here's the house rules," she said. "Long as you're with me, I eat first. Always."

"That's not fair."

"Probably not. But that's the way it's gonna be, 'cause I'm thinking for two, and I can't afford to be listening to my stomach instead of my gut." She took another drag. "Besides which, I'm bigger than you."

"My father says adults who threaten children are bullies."

"Yeah, well, that's some pretty impressive moralizing, coming from a mook who dumped his own kid to get out of Shanghai alive."

I couldn't say she wasn't right, and she knew it, so I just stared at her. She was exoticism personified – the first full-blown Yank I'd ever met, the first adult (Caucasian) woman I'd ever seen wearing trousers. Her flat, Midwestern accent lent a certain fascination to everything she said, however repulsive.

"People will do exactly whatever they think they can get away with, Tim," she told me, "for as long as they think they can get away with it. That's human nature. So don't get all high-hat about it, use it. Everything's got its uses – everything, and everybody."

"Even you, Ellis?"

"Especially me, Tim. As you will see."

It was Ellis, my diffident ally – the only person I have ever met who seemed capable of flourishing in any given situation – who taught me the basic rules of commerce: to always first assess things at their true value, then gauge exactly how much extra a person in desperate circumstances would be willing to pay for them. And her lessons have stood me in good stead, during all these intervening years. At the age of 66, I remain not only still alive, but a rather rich man, to boot – import/export, antiques, some minor drug smuggling intermittently punctuated (on the more creative side) by the publication of a string of slim, speculative novels. These last items have apparently garnered me some kind of cult following amongst fans of such fiction, most specifically – ironically enough – in the United States of America.

But time is an onion, as my third wife used to say: The more of it you peel away, searching for the hidden connections between action and reaction, the more it gives you something to cry over.

So now, thanks to the established temporal conventions of literature, we will slip fluidly from 1941 to 1999 – to St. Louis, Missouri, and the middle leg of my first-ever Stateside visit, as part of a tour in support of my recently-published childhood memoirs.

The last book signing was at four. Three hours later, I was already firmly ensconced in my comfortable suite at the downtown Four Seasons Hotel. Huang came by around eight, along with my room service trolley. He had a briefcase full of files and a sly, shy grin, which lit up his usually impassive face from somewhere deep inside.

"Racked up a lotta time on this one, Mr. Darbersmere," he said, in his second-generation Cockney growl. "Spent a lotta your money, too."

"Mmm." I uncapped the tray. "Good thing my publisher gave me that advance, then, isn't it?"

"Yeah, good fing. But it don't matter much now."

He threw the files down on the table between us. I opened the top one and leafed delicately through, between mouthfuls. There were schedules, marriage and citizenship certificates, medical records. Police records, going back to 1953, with charges ranging from fraud to trafficking in stolen goods, and listed under several different aliases. Plus a sheaf of photos, all taken from a safe distance.

I tapped one.

"Is this her?"

Huang shrugged. "You tell me—you're the one 'oo knew 'er."

I took another bite, nodding absently. Thinking: *Did I? Really? Ever?*

As much as anyone, I suppose.

To get us out of Shanghai, Ellis traded a can of petrol for a spot on a farmer's truck coming back from the market—then cut our unlucky savior's throat with her straight razor outside the city limits, and sold his truck for a load of cigarettes, lipstick and nylons. This got us shelter on a floating whore-house off the banks of the Yangtze, where she eventually hooked us up with a pirate trawler full of U.S. deserters and other assorted scum, whose captain proved to be some slippery variety of old friend.

The trawler took us up and down-river, dodging the Japanese and prey-ing on the weak, then trading the resultant loot to anyone else we came in contact with. We sold opium and penicillin to the warlords, maps and pass-ports to the D.P.s, motor oil and dynamite to the Kuomintang, Allied and

Japanese spies to each other. But our most profitable commodity, as ever, remained people — mainly because those we dealt with were always so endlessly eager to help set their own price.

I look at myself in the bathroom mirror now, tall and silver-haired — features still cleanly cut, yet somehow fragile, like Sir Laurence Olivier after the medical bills set in. At this morning's signing, a pale young woman with a bolt through her septum told me: "No offense, Mr. Darbersmere, but you're — like — a real babe. For an old guy."

I smiled, gently. And told her: "You should have seen me when I was twelve, my dear."

That was back in 1943, the year that Ellis sold me for the first time — or rented me out, rather, to the mayor of some tiny port village, who threatened to keep us docked until the next Japanese inspection. Ellis had done her best to convince him that we were just another boatload of Brits fleeing internment, even shucking her habitual male drag to reveal a surprisingly lush female figure and donning one of my mother's old dresses instead, much as it obviously disgusted her to do so. But all to no avail.

"You know I'd do it, Tim," she told me, impatiently pacing the trawler's deck, as a passing group of her crewmates whistled appreciatively from shore. "Christ knows I've tried. But the fact is, he doesn't want me. He wants you."

I frowned. "Wants me?"

"To go with him, Tim. You know — grown-up stuff."

"Like you and Ho Tseng, last week, after the dance at Sister Chin's?"

"Yeah, sorta like that."

She plumped herself down on a tarpaulined crate full of dynamite — clearly labeled, in Cantonese, as "dried fruit" — and kicked off one of her borrowed high-heeled shoes, rubbing her foot morosely. Her cinnamon hair hung loose in the stinking wind, back-lit to a fine fever.

I felt her appraising stare play up and down me like a fine gray mist, and shivered.

"If I do this, will you owe me, Ellis?"

"You bet I will, kid."

"Always take me with you?"

There had been some brief talk of replacing me with Brian Thompson-Greenaway, another refugee, after I had mishandled a particularly choice assignment—protecting Ellis's private stash of American currency from fellow scavengers while she recuperated from a beating inflicted by an irate Japanese officer, into whom she'd accidentally bumped while ashore. Though she wisely put up no resistance—one of Ellis's more admirable skills involved her always knowing when it was in her best interest *not* to defend herself—the damage left her pissing blood for a week, and she had not been happy to discover her money gone once she was recovered enough to look for it.

She lit a new cigarette, shading her eyes against the flame of her Ronson.

"'Course," she said, sucking in smoke.

"Never leave me?"

"Sure, kid. Why not?"

I learned to love duplicity from Ellis, to distrust everyone except those who have no loyalty and play no favorites. Lie to me, however badly, and you are virtually guaranteed my fullest attention.

I don't remember if I really believed her promises, even then. But I did what she asked anyway, without qualm or regret. She must have understood that I would do anything for her, no matter how morally suspect, if she only asked me politely enough.

In this one way, at least, I was still definitively British.

Afterward, I was ill for a long time—some sort of psychosomatic reaction to the visceral shock of my deflowering, I suppose. I lay in a bath of sweat on Ellis's hammock, under the trawler's one intact mosquito net. Sometimes I felt her sponge me with a rag dipped in rice wine, while singing to me—softly, along with the radio:

A faded postcard from exotic places...a cigarette that's marked with lipstick traces...oh, how the ghost of you clings...

And did I merely dream that once, at the very height of my sickness, she held me on her hip and hugged me close? That she actually slipped her jacket open and offered me her breast, so paradoxically soft and firm, its nipple almost as pale as the rest of her night-dweller's flesh?

That sweet swoon of ecstasy. That first hot stab of infantile desire. That unwitting link between recent childish violation and a desperate longing for adult consummation. I was far too young to know what I was doing, but she did. She had to. And since it served her purposes, she simply chose not to care.

Such complete amorality: It fascinates me. Looking back, I see it always has — like everything else about her, fetishized over the years into an inescapable pattern of hopeless attraction and inevitable abandonment.

My first wife's family fled the former Yugoslavia shortly before the end of the war; she had high cheekbones and pale eyes, set at a Baltic slant. My second wife had a wealth of long, slightly coarse hair, the color of unground cloves. My third wife told stories — ineptly, compulsively. All of them were, on average, at least five years my elder.

And sooner or later, all of them left me.

Oh, Ellis, I sometimes wonder whether anyone else alive remembers you as I do — or remembers you at all, given your well-cultivated talent for blending in, for getting by, for rendering yourself unremarkable. And I really don't know what I'll do if this woman Huang has found for me turns out not to be you. There's not much time left in which to start over, after all.

For either of us.

Last night, I called the number Huang's father gave me before I left London. The man on the other end of the line identified himself as the master chef of the Precious Dragon Shrine restaurant.

"Oh yes, *tai pan* Darbersmere," he said, when I mentioned my name. "I was indeed informed, by that respected personage who we both know, that you might honor my unworthiest of businesses with the request for some small service."

"One such as only your estimable self could provide."

"The *tai pan* flatters, as is his right. Which is the dish he wishes to order?"

"The Emperor's Old Bones."

A pause ensued — fairly long, as such things go. I could hear a Cantopop ballad filtering in, perhaps from somewhere in the kitchen, duelling for precedence with the more classical strains of a wailing *erhu*. The Precious Dragon Shrine's master chef drew a single long, low breath.

"*Tai Pan*," he said, finally, "for such a meal...one must provide the meat oneself."

"Believe me, Grandfather, I am well aware of such considerations. You may be assured that the meat will be available, whenever you are ready to begin its cooking."

Another breath—shorter, this time. Calmer.

"Realizing that it has probably been a long time since anyone has requested this dish," I continued, "I am, of course, more than willing to raise the price our mutual friend has already set."

"Oh, no, *tai pan*."

"For your trouble."

"*Tai pan*, please. It is not necessary to insult me."

"I must assure you, Grandfather, that no such insult was intended."

A burst of scolding rose from the kitchen, silencing the ballad in mid-ecstatic lament. The master chef paused again. Then said:

"I will need at least three days' notice to prepare my staff."

I smiled. Replying, with a confidence which—I hoped—at least sounded genuine:

"Three days should be more than sufficient."

The very old woman (89, at least) who may or may not have once called herself Ellis Iseland now lives quietly in a genteelly shabby area of St. Louis, officially registered under the far less interesting name of Mrs. Munro. Huang's pictures show a figure held carefully erect, yet helplessly shrunken in on itself—its once-straight spine softened by the onslaught of osteoporosis. Her face has gone loose around the jawline, skin powdery, hair a short, stiff gray crown of marcelled waves.

She dresses drably. Shapeless feminine weeds, widow-black. Her arthritic feet are wedged into Chinese slippers—a small touch of nostalgic irony? Both her snubbed cat's nose and the half-sneering set of her wrinkled mouth seem familiar, but her slanted eyes—the most important giveaway, their original non-color—are kept hidden beneath a thick-lensed pair of bifocal sunglasses, essential protection for someone whose sight may not last the rest of the year.

And though her medical files indicate that she is in the preliminary stages of lung and throat cancer, her trip a day to the local corner store always includes the purchase of at least one pack of cigarettes, the brand apparently unimportant, as long as it contains a sufficient portion of nicotine. She lights one right outside the front door, and has almost finished it by the time she rounds the corner of her block.

Her neighbors seen to think well of her. Their children wave as she goes by, cane in one hand, cigarette in the other. She nods acknowledgment, but does not wave back.

This familiar arrogance, seeping up unchecked through her last, most perfect disguise: the mask of age, which bestows a kind of retroactive innocence on even its most experienced victims. I have recently begun to take advantage of its charms myself, whenever it suits my fancy to do so.

I look at these pictures, again and again. I study her face, searching in vain for even the ruin of that cool, smooth, inventively untrustworthy operator who once held both my fortune and my heart in the palm of her mannishly large hand.

It was Ellis who first told me about The Emperor's Old Bones—and she is still the only person in the world with whom I would ever care to share that terrible meal, no matter what doing so might cost me.

If, indeed, I ever end up eating it at all.

"Yeah, I saw it done down in Hong Kong," Ellis told us, gesturing with her chopsticks. We sat behind a lacquered screen at the back of Sister Chin's, two nights before our scheduled rendezvous with the warlord Wao Ruyen, from whom Ellis had already accepted some mysteriously unspecified commission. I watched her eat—waiting my turn, as ever—while Brian Thompson-Greenaway (also present, much to my annoyance) sat in the corner and watched us both, openly ravenous.

"They take a carp, right—you know, those big fish some rich Chinks keep in fancy pools, out in the garden? Supposed to live hundreds of years, if you believe all that 'Confucius says' hooey. So they take this carp and they fillet it, all over, so the flesh is hanging off it in strips. But they do it so well, so carefully, they keep the carp alive through the whole thing. It's sittin' there on a plate, twitching, eyes rollin' around. Get close enough, you can look right in through the ribcage and see the heart still beating."

She popped another piece of Mu Shu pork in her mouth, and smiled down at Brian, who gulped—apparently suddenly too queasy to either resent or envy her proximity to the food.

"Then they bring out this big pot full of boiling oil," she continued, "and they run hooks through the fish's gills and tail. so they can pick it up at both ends. And while it's floppin' around, tryin' to get free, they dip all those hangin' pieces of flesh in the oil—one side first, then the other, all nice and neat. Fish is probably in so much pain already it doesn't even notice. So it's still alive when they put it back down...alive, and cooked, and ready to eat."

"And then—they eat it."

"Sure do, Tim."

"*Alive*, I mean."

Brian now looked distinctly green. Ellis shot him another glance, openly amused by his lack of stamina, then turned back to me.

"Well yeah, that's kinda the whole point of the exercise. You keep the carp alive until you've eaten it, and all that long life just sorta transfers over to you."

"Like magic," I said. She nodded.

"Exactly. 'Cause that's exactly what it is."

I considered her statement for a moment.

"My father," I commented, at last, "always told us that magic was a load of bunk."

Ellis snorted. "And why does this not surprise me?" She asked, of nobody in particular. Then: "Fine, I'll bite. What do you think?"

"I think..." I said, slowly, "...that if it works...then who cares?"

She looked at me. Snorted again. And then—she actually laughed, an infectious, unmalicious laugh that seemed to belong to someone far younger, far less complicated. It made me gape to hear it. Using her chopsticks, she plucked the last piece of pork deftly from her plate, and popped it into my open mouth.

"Tim," she said, "for a spoiled Limey brat, sometimes you're okay."

I swallowed the pork, without really tasting it. Before I could stop myself, I had already blurted out:

"I wish we were the same age, Ellis."

This time she stared. I felt a sudden blush turn my whole face crimson. Now it was Brian's turn to gape, amazed by my idiotic effrontery.

"Yeah, well, not me," she said. "I like it just fine with you bein' the kid, and me not."

"Why?"

She looked at me again. I blushed even more deeply, heat prickling at my hairline. Amazingly, however, no explosion followed. Ellis simply took another sip of her tea, and replied:

"'Cause the fact is, Tim, if you were my age — good-lookin' like you are, smart like you're gonna be — I could probably do some pretty stupid things over you."

Magic. Some might say it's become my stock in trade — as a writer, at least. Though the humble craft of buying and selling also involves a kind of legerdemain, as Ellis knew so well; sleight of hand, or price, depending on your product...and your clientele.

But true magic? Here, now, at the end of the twentieth century, in this brave new world of 100-slot CD players and incessant afternoon talk shows?

I have seen so many things in my long life, most of which I would have thought impossible, had they not taken place right in front of me. From the bank of the Yangtze river, I saw the bright white smoke of an atomic bomb go up over Nagasaki, like a tear in the fabric of the horizon. In Chungking harbor, I saw two grown men stab each other to death over the corpse of a dog because one wanted to bury it, while the other wanted to eat it. And just beyond the Shanghai city limits, I saw Ellis cut that farmer's throat with one quick twist of her wrist, so close to me that the spurt of his severed jugular misted my cheek with red.

But as I grow ever closer to my own personal twilight, the thing I remember most vividly is watching — through the window of a Franco-Vietnamese arms-dealer's car, on my way to a cool white house in Saigon, where I would wait out the final days of the war in relative comfort and safety — as a pair of barefoot coolies pulled the denuded skeleton of Brian Thompson-Greenaway from a culvert full of malaria-laden water. I knew it was him, because even after Wao Ruyen's court had consumed the rest of his pathetic little body, they had left his face nearly untouched—there not being quite enough flesh on a child's skull, apparently, to be worth the extra effort of filleting...let alone of cooking.

And I remember, with almost comparable vividness, when—just a year ago—I saw the former warlord Wao, Huang's most respected father, sitting in a Limehouse nightclub with his Number One and Number Two wife at either elbow. Looking half the age he did when I first met him, in that endless last July of 1945, before black science altered our world forever. Before Ellis sold him Brian instead of me, and then fled for the Manchurian border, leaving me to fend for myself in the wake of her departure.

After all this, should the idea of true magic seem so very difficult to swallow? I think not.

No stranger than the empty shell of Hiroshima, cupped around Ground Zero, its citizenry reduced to shadows in the wake of the blast's last terrible glare. And certainly no stranger than the fact that I should think a woman so palpably incapable of loving anyone might nevertheless be capable of loving me, simply because—at the last moment—she suddenly decided not to let a rich criminal regain his youth and prolong his days by eating me alive, in accordance with the ancient and terrible ritual of the Emperor's Old Bones.

This morning, I told my publicist that I was far too ill to sign any books today—a particularly swift and virulent touch of the twenty-four-hour flu, no doubt. She said she understood completely. An hour later, I sat in Huang's car across the street from the corner store, watching "Mrs. Munro" make her slow way down the street to pick up her daily dose of slow, coughing death.

On her way back, I rolled down the car window and yelled: "*Lai gen wo ma, wai guai!*"

(*Come with me, white ghost!* An insulting little Mandarin phrase, occasionally used by passing Kuomintang jeep drivers to alert certain long-nosed Barbarian smugglers to the possibility that their dealings might soon be interrupted by an approaching group of Japanese soldiers.)

Huang glanced up from his copy of *Rolling Stone*'s Hot List, impressed. "Pretty good accent," he commented.

But my eyes were on "Mrs. Munro", who had also heard — and stopped in mid-step, swinging her half-blind gray head toward the sound, more as though scenting than scanning. I saw my own face leering back at me in miniature from the lenses of her prescription sunglasses, doubled and distorted by the distance between us. I saw her raise one palm to shade her eyes even further against the sun, the wrinkles across her nose contracting as she squinted her hidden eyes.

And then I saw her slip her glasses off to reveal those eyes: still slant, still gray. Still empty.

I turned to Huang.

"It's her," I told him.

Huang nodded. "Fought so. When you want me to do it?"

"Tonight?"

"Whatever you say, Mr D."

Very early on the morning before Ellis left me behind, I woke to find her sitting next to me in the red half-darkness of the ship's hold.

"Kid," she said, "I got a little job lined up for you today."

I felt myself go cold. "What kind of job, Ellis?" I asked, faintly — though I already had a fairly good idea. Quietly, she replied:

"The grown-up kind."

"Who?"

"French guy, up from Saigon, with enough jade and rifles to buy us over the border. He's rich, educated; not bad company, either. For a fruit."

"That's reassuring," I muttered, and turned on my side, studying the wall. Behind me, I heard her lighter click open, then catch and spark — felt the faint lick of her breath as she exhaled, transmuting nicotine into smoke and ash. The steady pressure of her attention itched like an insect crawling on my skin: Fiercely concentrated, alien almost to the point of vague disgust, infinitely patient.

"War's on its last legs," she told me. "That's what I keep hearing. You got the Communists comin' up on one side, with maybe the Russians slipping in behind 'em, and the good old U.S. of A. everywhere else. Phillippines are already down for the count, now Tokyo's in bombing range. Pretty soon, our little oufit is gonna be so long gone, we won't even remember what it looked like. My educated opinion? It's sink or swim, and we need all the life-jackets that money can buy." She paused. "You listening to me? Kid?"

I shut my eyes again, marshaling my heart-rate.

"Kid?" Ellis repeated.

Still without answering—or opening my eyes—I pulled the mosquito net aside, and let gravity roll me free of the hammock's sweaty clasp. I was fourteen years old now, white-blonde and deeply tanned from the river-reflected sun; almost her height, even in my permanently bare feet. Looking up, I found I could finally meet her gray gaze head-on.

"'Us'," I said. "'We'. As in you and I?"

"Yeah, sure. You and me."

I nodded at Brian, who lay nearby, deep asleep and snoring. "And what about him?"

Ellis shrugged.

"I don't know, Tim," she said. "What *about* him?"

I looked back down at Brian, who hadn't shifted position, not even when my shadow fell over his face. Idly, I inquired:

"You'll still be there when I get back, won't you, Ellis?"

Outside, through the porthole, I could see that the rising sun had just cracked the horizon; she turned, haloed against it. Blew some more smoke. Asking:

"Why the hell wouldn't I be?"

"I don't know. But you wouldn't use my being away on this job as a good excuse to leave me behind, though—would you?"

She looked at me. Exhaled again. And said, evenly:

"You know, Tim, I'm gettin' pretty goddamn sick of you asking me that question. So gimme one good reason not to, or let it lie."

Lightly, quickly—too quickly even for my own well-honed sense of self-preservation to prevent me—I laid my hands on either side of her face and pulled her to me, hard. Our breath met, mingled, in sudden intimacy; hers tasted of equal parts tobacco and surprise. My daring had brought me just close enough to smell her own personal scent, under the shell of everyday

GEMMA FILES

decay we all stank of: a cool, intoxicating rush of non-fragrance, firm and acrid as an unearthed tuber. It burned my nose.

"We should always stay together," I said, "because I *love* you, Ellis."

I crushed my mouth down on hers, forcing it open. I stuck my tongue inside her mouth as far as it would go and ran it around, just like the mayor of that first tiny port village had once done with me. I fastened my teeth deep into the inner flesh of her lower lip, and bit down until I felt her knees give way with the shock of it. Felt myself rear up, hard and jerking, against her soft underbelly. Felt *her* feel it.

It was the first and only time I ever saw her eyes widen in anything but anger.

With barely a moment's pause, she punched me right in the face, so hard I felt my jaw crack. I fell at her feet, coughing blood.

"Eh—!" I began, amazed. But her eyes froze me in mid-syllable—so gray, so cold.

"Get it straight, *tai pan*," she said, "'cause I'm only gonna say it once. I don't buy. I *sell*."

Then she kicked me in the stomach with one steel-toed army boot, and leant over me as I lay there, gasping and hugging myself tight—my chest contracting, eyes dimming. Her eyes pouring over me like liquid ice. Like sleet. Swelling her voice like some great Arctic river, as she spoke the last words I ever heard her say:

"So don't you even *try* to play me like a trick, and think I'll let you get away with it."

Was Ellis evil? Am I? I've never thought so, though earlier this week I did give one of those legendary American Welfare mothers $25,000 in cash to sell me her least-loved child. He's in the next room right now, playing Nintendo. Huang is watching him. I think he likes Huang. He probably likes me, for that matter, We are the first English people he has ever met, and our accents fascinate him. Last night, we ordered in pizza; he ate until he was sick, then ate more, and fell asleep in front of an HBO basketball game. If I let him stay with me another week, he might become sated enough to convince himself he loves me.

The master chef at the Precious Dragon Shrine tells me that the Emperor's Old Bones bestows upon its consumer as much life-force as its consumee would have eventually gone through, had he or she been permitted to live out the rest of their days unchecked — and since the child I bought claims to be roughly ten years old (a highly significant age, in retrospect), this translates to perhaps an additional sixty years of life for every person who participates, whether the dish is eaten alone or shared. Which only makes sense, really. It's an act of magic, after all.

And this is good news for me, since the relative experiential gap between a man in his upper twenties and a woman in her upper thirties — especially compared to that between a boy of fourteen and a woman of twenty-eight — is almost insignificant.

Looking back, I don't know if I've ever loved anyone but Ellis — if I'm even capable of loving anyone else. But finally, after all these wasted years, I do know what I want. And who.

And how to get them both.

It's a terrible thing I'm doing, and an even worse thing I'm going to do. But when it's done, I'll have what I want, and everything else — all doubts, all fears, all piddling, queasy little notions of goodness, and decency, and basic human kinship — all that useless lot can just go hang, and twist and rot in the wind while they're at it. I've lived much too long with my own unsatisfied desire to simply hold my aching parts — whatever best applies, be it stomach or otherwise — and congratulate myself on my forbearance anymore. I'm not mad, or sick, or even yearning after a long-lost love that I can never regain, and never really had in the first place. I'm just hungry, and I want to *eat*.

And morality...has nothing to do with it.

Because if there's one single thing you taught me, Ellis — one lesson I've retained throughout every twist and turn of this snaky thing I call my life — it's that hunger has no moral structure.

Huang came back late this morning, limping and cursing, after a brief detour to the office of an understanding doctor who his father keeps on international retainer. I am obscurely pleased to discover that Ellis can still defend herself; even after Huang's first roundhouse put her on the pavement, she still somehow managed to slip her razor open without him noticing, then slide it shallowly across the back of his Achilles tendon. More painful than debilitating, but rather well done nevertheless, for a woman who can no longer wear shoes which require her to tie her own laces.

I am almost as pleased, however, to hear that nothing Ellis may have done actually succeeded in preventing Huang from completing his mission — and beating her, with methodical skill, to within an inch of her corrupt and dreadful old life.

I have already told my publicist that witnessed the whole awful scene, and asked her to find out which hospital poor Mrs. Munro has been taken to. I myself, meanwhile, will drive the boy to the kitchen of the Precious Dragon Shrine restaurant, where I am sure the master chef and his staff will do their best to keep him entertained until later tonight. Huang has lent him his pocket Gameboy, which should help.

Ah. That must be the phone now, ringing.

The woman in bed 37 of the Morleigh Memorial Hospital's charity wing, one of the few left operating in St. Louis — in America, possibly — opens her swollen left eye a crack, just far enough to reveal a slit of red-tinged white and a wandering, dilated pupil, barely rimmed in gray.

"Hello, Ellis," I say.

I sit by her bedside, as I have done for the last six hours. The screens enshrouding us from the rest of the ward, with its rustlings and moans, reduce all movement outside this tiny area to a play of flickering shadows — much like the visions one might glimpse in passing through a double haze of fever and mosquito net, after suffering a violent shock to one's fragile sense of physical and moral integrity.

...and oh, how the ghost of you clings...

She clears her throat, wetly. Tells me, without even a flicker of hesitation:

"Nuh...Ellis. Muh num iss...Munro."

She peers up at me, straining to lift her bruise-stung lids. I wait, patiently.

"Tuh—"

"That's a good start."

I see her bare broken teeth at my patronizing tone, perhaps reflexively. Pause. And then, after a long moment:

"Tim."

"Good show, Ellis. Got it in one."

Movement at the bottom of the bed: Huang, stepping through the gap between the screens. Ellis sees him, and stiffens. I nod in his direction, without turning.

"I believe you and Mr. Huang have already met," I say. "Mr. Wao Huang, that is; you'll remember his father, the former warlord Wao Ruyen. He certainly remembers you—and with some gratitude, or so he told me."

Huang takes his customary place at my elbow. Ellis' eyes move with him, helplessly—and I recall how my own eyes used to follow her about in a similarly fascinated manner, breathless and attentive on her briefest word, her smallest motion.

"I see you can still take quite a beating, Ellis," I observe, lightly. "Unfortunately for you, however, it's not going to be quite so easy to recover from this particular melee as it once was, is it? Old age, and all that." To Huang: "Have the doctors reached any conclusion yet, as regards Mrs. Munro's long-term prognosis?"

"Wouldn't say as 'ow there was one, *tai pan*."

"Well, yes. Quite."

I glance back, only to find that Ellis' eyes have turned to me at last. And I can read them so clearly, now—like clean, black text through gray ricepaper, lit from behind by a cold and colorless flame. No distance. No mystery at all.

When her mouth opens again, I know exactly what word she's struggling to shape.

"Duh...deal?"

Oh, yes.

I rise, slowly, as Huang pulls the chair back for me. Some statements, I find, need room in which to be delivered properly—or perhaps I'm simply being facetious. My writer's over-developed sense of the dramatic, working double-time.

I wrote this speech out last night, and rehearsed it several times in front of the bathroom mirror. I wonder if it sounds rehearsed. Does calculated artifice fall into the same general category as outright deception? If so, Ellis ought to be able to hear it in my voice. But I don't suppose she's really apt to be listening for such fine distinctions, given the stress of this mutually culminative moment.

"I won't say you've nothing I want, Ellis, even now. But what I really want—what I've always wanted—is to be the seller, for once, and not the sold. To be the only one who has what you want desperately, and to set my price wherever I think it fair."

Adding, with the arch of a significant brow: "—or know it to be unfair."

I study her battered face. The bruises form a new mask, impenetrable as any of the others she's worn. The irony is palpable: Just as Ellis' nature abhors emotional accessibility, so nature—seemingly—reshapes itself at will to keep her motivations securely hidden.

"I've arranged for a meal," I tell her. "The menu consists of a single dish, one with which I believe we're both equally familiar. The name of that dish is the Emperor's Old Bones, and my staff will begin to cook it whenever I give the word. Now, you and I may share this meal, or we may not. We may regain our youth, and double our lives, and be together for at least as long as we've been apart—or we may not. But I promise you this, Ellis: No matter what I eventually end up doing, the extent of your participation in the matter will be exactly defined by how much you are willing to pay me for the privilege."

I gesture to Huang, who slips a pack of cigarettes from his coat pocket. I tap one out. I light it, take a drag. Savor the sensation.

Ellis just watches.

"So here's the deal, then: If you promise to be very, very nice to me—and never, ever leave me again—for the rest of our extremely long partnership-"

I pause. Blow out the smoke. Wait.

And conclude, finally:

"—then you can eat first."

I offer Ellis the cigarette, slowly. Slowly, she takes it from me, holding it delicately between two splinted fingers. She raises it to her torn and grimacing mouth. Inhales. Exhales those familiar twin plumes of smoke, expertly, through her crushed and broken nose. Is that a tear at the corner of her eye, or just an upwelling of rheum? Or neither?

"Juss like...ahways," she says.

And gives me an awful parody of my own smile. Which I—return.

With interest.

Later, as Huang helps Ellis out of bed and into the hospital's service elevator, I sit in the car, waiting. I take out my cellular phone. The master chef of the Precious Dragon Shrine restaurant answers on the first ring.

"How is...the boy?" I ask him.

"Fine, *tai pan.*"

There is a pause, during which I once more hear music filtering in from the other end of the line—the tinny little song of a video game in progress, intermittently punctuated by the clatter of kitchen implement. Laughter, both adult and child.

"Do you wish to cancel your order, *tai pan* Darbersmere?" The master chef asks me, delicately.

Through the hospital's back doors, I can see the service elevator's lights crawling steadily downward—the floors reeling themselves off, numeral by numeral. Fifth. Fourth. Third.

"*Tai pan?*"

Second. First.

"No. I do not."

The elevator doors are opening. I can see Huang guiding Ellis out, puppeting her deftly along with her own crutches. Those miraculously-trained hands of his, able to open or salve wounds with equal expertise.

"Then I may begin cooking," the master chef says. Not really meaning it as a question.

Huang holds the door open. Ellis steps through. I listen to the Gameboy's idiot song, and know that I have spent every minute of every day of my life preparing to make this decision, ever since that last morning on the Yangtze. That I have made it so many times already, in fact, that nothing I do or say now can ever stop it from being made. Any more than I can bring back the child Brian Thompson-Greenaway was, before he went up the hill to Wao Ruyen's fortress, hand in stupidly trusting hand with Ellis — or the child I was, before Ellis broke into my parents' house and saved me from one particular fate worse than death, only to show me how many, many others there were to choose from.

Or the child that Ellis must have been, once upon a very distant time, before whatever happened to make her as she now is — then set her loose to move at will through an unsuspecting world, preying on other lost children.

...these foolish things...remind me of you.

"Yes," I say. "You may."

Bibliography

Northern Frights
ISBN 0-88962-514-X HB
Mosaic Press, 1992

TEAR DOWN	Garfield Reeves-Stevens
GOING NORTH	Steve Rasnic Tem
UNDERGROUND	Tanya Huff
THE MAN WHO CRIED WOLF	Robert Bloch
WAITING	Galad Elflandsson
COLD	Karen Wehrstein
ASHLAND, KENTUCKY	Terence M. Green
FARM WIFE	Nancy Kilpatrick
DEER SEASON	Lucy Taylor
THE MAP	Andrew Weiner
MARK OF THE BEAST	Edo van Belkom
THE WHITCHES' TREE	Shirley Meier
TORONTO NECROPOLIS (POEM)	Carolyn Clink
COLD SLEEP	Nancy Baker
BOOGIE MAN	Peter Sellers
MANIFESTATIONS	David Nickle
THE SOFT WHISPER OF MIDNIGHT SNOW	Charles de Lint
THE SILVER FACE	Robert Sampson

Northern Frights 2
ISBN 0-88962-564-6 PB
Mosaic Press, 1994

PUNKINS	Nancy Kilpatrick
SOMETIMES, IN THE RAIN	Charles Grant
THESE BROKEN WINGS	Sean Doolittle
THE EDDIES	Garfield Reeves-Stevens
THE POLARGEIST	Mel D. Ames
OBJECTS IN THE MIRROR	Diane L. Walton
MOUTHFUL OF PINS	Gemma Files
OTHER ERRORS, OTHER TIMES	Chet Williamson
THE SLOAN MEN	David Nickle
VANISHING POINT	Hugh B. Cave
THE COLD	Edo van Belkom
THE CODE OF THE POODLES	James Powell
FEAST OF GHOSTS	Mary E. Choo
ICE	Shirley Meier
VALLEY OF THE MOON (POEM)	Carolyn Clink
EMANCIPATION	Cindie Geddes
THE NIGHT SWIMMER	Edward D. Hoch
FOURTH PERSON SINGULAR	Dale L. Sproule

Northern Frights 3
ISBN 0-88962-589-1 PB
Mosaic Press, 1995

WILD THINGS LIVE THERE	Michael Rowe
SILVER RINGS	Rick Hautala
A DEBT UNPAID	Tanya Huff
IMPOSTER	Peter Sellers
EXODUS 22:18	Nancy Baker
THE SUCTION METHOD	Rudy Kremberg
SASQUATCH	Mel D. Ames
GRIST FOR THE MILLS OF CHRISTMAS	James Powell
TAMAR'S LEATHER POUCH	David Shtogryn
SNOW ANGEL	Nancy Kilpatrick
THE PERSEIDS	Robert Charles Wilson
WIDOW'S WALK (POEM)	Carolyn Clink
IF YOU KNOW WHERE TO LOOK	Chris Wiggins
THE BLEEDING TREE	Sean Doolittle
THE DEAD GO SHOPPING	Stephanie Bedwell-Grime
FAMILY TIES	Edo van Belkom
THE PINES	Tia V. Travis
THE SUMMER WORMS	David Nickle

Northern Frights 4
ISBN 0-88962-639-1 PB
Mosaic Press, 1997

VIA INFLUENZA	David Annandale
HELLO, JANE, GOOD-BYE	Sally McBride
THE CHILDREN OF GAEL	Nancy Kilpatrick and Benoit Bisson
ROSES FROM GRANNY	Mary E. Choo
AT FORT ASSUMPTION	Dale L. Sproule
MIRROR MONSTER	Stephen Meade
TRANSFER	Stephanie Bedwell-Grime
NOCTURNE (POEM)	Sandra Kasturi
THE PIT-HEADS	David Nickle
ICE BRIDGE	Edo van Belkom
THE DEEP (POEM)	Carolyn Clink
THE FISHER'S DAUGHTER	Thomas S. Roche
THE INNER INNER CITY	Robert Charles Wilson
RED MISCHIEF	Michael Rowe
SKINNY DIPPING (POEM)	Mici Gold
REASONS UNKNOWN	Scott Mackay
DEAD OF WINTER	Carol Weekes
CONSUMING FEAR	Colleen Anderson
TIN HOUSE	Michael Skeet
HORROR STORY	Robert Boyczuk

Northern Frights 5
ISBN 0-88962-676-6 PB
Mosaic Press, 1999

A VOICE IN THE WILD	Hugh B. Cave
OAK ISLAND	Rebecca Bradley
THE BLESSING	Scott Mackay
TIME FLIES	Gregory Ward
SLOW COLD CHICK	Nalo Hopkinson
PET WORMS	David Shtogryn
THE EMPEROR'S OLD BONES	Gemma Files
CROSSING	Andrew Weiner
FLUSHED	Dale L. Sproule
PITTER PATTER	Carol Weekes
CAVE OF THE WINDS (POEM)	Carolyn Clink
INSPIRITER	Nancy Kilpatrick
OYSTER LOVE	Susan McGregor
THE RAT, PEERING OUT, SEES JUSTICE DONE	Vincent Grant Perkins
JANE'S HEAD	James Powell
DOING DRUGS	Sally McBride
NIGHT OF THE TAR BABY	David Nickle
PLATO'S MIRROR	Robert Charles Wilson

AGMV Marquis

MEMBER OF SCABRINI MEDIA

Quebec, Canada
2001